OMNIS:
Last Man of Earth

Derrick Howard

authorHOUSE

AuthorHouse™
1663 Liberty Drive
Bloomington, IN 47403
www.authorhouse.com
Phone: 833-262-8899

© 2023 Derrick Howard. All rights reserved.

No part of this book may be reproduced, stored in a retrieval system, or transmitted by any means without the written permission of the author.

Published by AuthorHouse 12/12/2023

ISBN: 979-8-8230-1726-8 (sc)
ISBN: 979-8-8230-1725-1 (hc)
ISBN: 979-8-8230-1713-8 (e)

Library of Congress Control Number: 2023921896

Print information available on the last page.

Any people depicted in stock imagery provided by Getty Images are models, and such images are being used for illustrative purposes only.
Certain stock imagery © Getty Images.

This book is printed on acid-free paper.

Because of the dynamic nature of the Internet, any web addresses or links contained in this book may have changed since publication and may no longer be valid. The views expressed in this work are solely those of the author and do not necessarily reflect the views of the publisher, and the publisher hereby disclaims any responsibility for them.

Table of Contents

Dedication ix

Chapter 1 1
    A Gluttony of Treasures 1
    Spectators 3

Chapter 2 25
    Steppingstones 25
    Eyes 27

Chapter 3 49
    Clean Hands 49
    The Harbor 50

Chapter 4 57
    Eclipse 57
    Labors 58

Chapter 5 81
    Free 81
    Aerial 83
    Psalms for Yesterday: The Thrift Store 94

Chapter 6 95
    Pain and Glory 95
    Icarus Complex 97

Chapter 7 122
    Judas Holes 122
    The Passage 123

Chapter 8 138
    Air and Sea 138
    The Badlands 140
    Psalms for Yesterday: Reflections 160

Chapter 9 161
    Stay 161
    Brother's Keeper 162

Chapter 10 185
    Muse 185
    The Great Reaper 186

Chapter 11 201
    Fool's Game 201
    The Doomsday Protocol 202
    Psalms for Yesterday: Labyrinth 215

Chapter 12 217
    Witness of Time 217
    Untethered 219

Chapter 13 238
    Ever Turning 238
    Trigger Happy 239

Chapter 14 246
    King of the Mountain 246
    The War Within 247
    Psalms for Yesterday: Nosferatu's Last Kiss 259

Chapter 15 261
    Beggar's Lot 262
    The Black Spot 263

Chapter 16 276
    Un Tiempo Para Los Vaqueros 276
    Fedda 278

Chapter 17 287
    A Letter Sincerely Written 287
    The Whisper 288

Chapter 18 297
    Deeds and Dreams 297
    Ripple 298
    Psalms for Yesterday: Sweet Words and Promises 306

Chapter 19 309
    Time 309
    I Am A Man 310

Chapter 20 325
    The Glass Warrior 325
    Blood Bowl II 326

Chapter 21 345
    Confession 345
    The All 346
    Psalms for Yesterday: Southern Flight 348

Dedication

This book is dedicated to my ancestors and innumerable loved ones: my parents, Delores and John; my wife, Jessica; my children, DJ, Rachel, Matthew, and Adriana; my seven inspiring siblings; my grandchildren; my blood brothers and sisters; and those who struggle to find reason in this intriguing, stunning world. Peace to all of you in memory, life, and love. D.

Chapter 1

A Gluttony of Treasures

When you are born into the world, the first steps are the hardest,
filled with trepidation but yet a strange familiarity.
Perhaps at that moment, it is best to be blind,
stumbling in the shadow of infancy for fresh footing.

When life ends,
there is a fleeting moment when all that is lost is regained in memory.
After all, from the cradle to the grave,
you are only a fading memory sustained by love or hate.

For all I know of myths and religiosity,
life after death is the zenith,
opening a doorway to immortality.

Derrick Howard

In the bowels of the afterlife,
saints and the wicked believe they join in an exquisite ballet.
For most, there is only death and decay
and the reality that servants are you all.
For a lucky few, the waste and gluttony of life are left behind,
dissension granting a new beginning.

That is the grist of truth.

This, too, is true.
To birth the universe,
The All willed itself to exist in a kaleidoscope,
Time, Matter, Darkness, Light, and Sound.

The birth of Death is the child they fear tolled the end of forever.
Their reign is nigh complete.

Bow ye now in the shadow of The All's majesty,
pray your earthly soul will waft beyond the stars
into a divine river of mystery flowing in the abyss of eternity
to Caellum.

Spectators

Yes, we are watching. We've always been watching.

We've kept an entertained and wistful eye on you above your sky, within and beyond the sleeping stars. We've watched you through the threat of Ice Ages, pandemics, world wars, global warming, *Cancer Cultures*, the attack on rules of law, and for the most part, each other.

All the while, celestials, aliens, and other sentient beings bet trebles and trixies on the day and time you'd cease to exist amongst other children of creation. Aliens—as you like to portray those who are unaccustomed to your social norms—were already aware of your corrupt exploits by conducting clandestine visits to Earth, good old-fashioned probing, and habitually sampling your social media, pervasive pornography, and irrational willingness to allow others to corrupt your truths.

By April 2050, the global population of carbon-based humans—or "Purists"—has been reduced to only two people: a blind, Black, Jamaican American man named Sledge and a buff White American man named Dr. Quinten Hamilton. All other pure humans are buried in the dust or enslaved to remain mindless transhumans or cyborgs in a new caste system.

To pay the wage for countless centuries of human cruelty, on this final day of Intergalactic Independence Day, Sledge and Dr. Hamilton prepare themselves to be thrust into the Blood Bowl Arena, a heavy burden. Sledge and Dr. Hamilton are still figuring out what to feel on this fateful day. However, they know in their gut that their confusion is only a broken compass in troubled minds, misdirected by regret and fear of the unknown.

Hardly anyone in the universe gives either Sledge or Dr. Hamilton a chance to survive the Galactic Council's final solution to rid the galaxy of the creatures deemed the present "scourge of the universe" *Fall 2049 Edition, Cyborgs Today*, Drone Norgon E1 Reporting.

A widely held belief is that the outcome is axiomatic; humans cannot overcome being at their core the slime that slithered from the sea 3.7 billion years ago. Spectators and gamblers know that since you learned how to communicate, your basic instincts have been to suppress, oppress, reproduce, consume, and fornicate. Smart money gets sixty-one odds that you will go the way of Earth's other dodo.

The blind man has little time to consider the evil he participated in to prolong his life and chances at survival by killing other humans trapped in this Blood Bowl elimination tournament. Sledge's six-foot-two frame is usually pumped, hard-edged, and ready to demolish opponents by calling on his prowess as a martial artist. But now his normally statuesque bronzed body gleams from the bright white light shining on him, illuminating the chiseled dips and valleys of his carved muscles and a sickly puke-green patina that portrays an internal struggle that afflicts him.

His usually light, scruffy beard has grown to a woolly bush, matted with sweat and grime collected there from countless battles against Purists, transhumans, aliens, and scavengers roaming what's left of old USA. Sledge's opaque eyes remain transparent, seeing nothing of his turmoil while sensing all that looms on his path.

Behind an impenetrable forcefield, Dr. Hamilton, a curiously buff octogenarian, stares at a scarlet stream of blood and other bodily fluids as they pool in a drain in the center of the arena. By Dr. Hamilton's side, Sledge restrains himself from vomiting on his bare feet. The sick feeling rumbles in Sledge's gut, not from the ratchet, oniony odors emanating from Dr. Hamilton's body that has gone unwashed for weeks but from an unknown ailment that suddenly surfaced.

From a perch light years from Earth, I hear their erratic breathing; I sense their confusion as they struggle to gain footing. I have watched Earthlings' asinine conduct with tepid interest and occasional inspiration. I have read proofs of the Galactic Council's death warrants issued against wayward planets, but your chronicles differ. Earth's annihilation is a parable of the deluded and fearful; psalms for the broken and weak, nepenthe for those seeking redemption.

Besides, today, there is nothing else in the universe, the metaverse Maze, or elsewhere that is as captivating as the human saga: so much potential amid so much loss.

So, I will get a beer and a snack, kick off my shoes, and tune into Gliese Channel 777 now. As a fellow spectator, I suggest you do the same—lest you run out of time. The clock is ticking. Tick ... tock ... tick ... tock ...

For such a monumental event, countless cameras float down the streets and alleys of a massive spacecraft known as Ilem Diwan Godfrey's Floating City. The gigantic metropolis inside the domed vessel houses the prodigy of humans who have nearly become extinct on Earth, where Ilem either converted ten billion carbon-based people to being transhuman or exterminated them for being human.

A camera momentarily lingers in the Floating City's center court, scanning the crowd for animated pedestrians mingling together, the perfect foil for propaganda. The camera pans, then stops in front of a thirty-foot monument of a commanding, sculptured hand jutting through the ground.

Hovering above the open palm of the towering sculpture is a Dyson Sphere, resembling a ball of energy just out of reach. A closer view of the Dyson Sphere reveals a rotating marble sculpture of a naked man in a fetal position. Yellow sparks caress the silent figure like fingers of lightning cuddling a baby's bare skin.

Like a curious child, the cameras pan up to numerous flying vehicles circling in the Floating City's holographic sky. AI traffic controllers actively direct hurried cars through the mid-air intersection and pass the glitzy, 3D advertisements featuring "Black Heart" Kol, a hulking, seven-foot, four-hundred-pound transhuman. The enormous screen bearing Kol's image vertically spans the skyscraper from the ground level to the penthouse.

The cameras gliding through the air capture scenes of life on the Floating City to juxtapose with the end of life soon to occur in the Blood Bowl Arena. A couple of the hovering cameras unintentionally ogle a fantastic scientific feat, renewing life's essence.

From inside a posh condominium, facing the cameras, there is a panoramic view of the festival growing to a frenzy on the streets forty-three stories below. Within the condominium stands an upright life-support tube just beyond the open-air balcony. A white metal orb bearing an infinity symbol levitates inside the life-support tube.

Beyond the cameras' probing eyes, a multi-touch interface computer measuring human carbon life indicates in flashing letters, "Carbon life signs are critically low." The number 180 also flashes on the computer screen.

On a slender desk below the computer are a high-tech hand cannon and a waist holster with several black discs that resemble hockey pucks attached. The hand cannon is a fast break-action laser pistol capable of firing a laser beam using a magnetic repulse. And the innocent-looking "hockey pucks" are packed with Azidoazide azide, the most explosive chemical compound humans have ever created.

Whoever's plans call for these types of party favors may not be someone you want to hang out with on a typical Saturday night. It may be better to stay in the sanctity of your abode, party like it is 2099, and leave challenging the tide of inevitability to the narcissists, the desperate, and the foolhardy.

Inside the condominium's quieter setting, the white infinity orb in the life-support tube generates multi-colored lights that swirl and gradually materialize into a woman's face and naked form. She absorbs light into her ethereal skin through the orb, leaving an infinity tattoo on her lower left abdomen.

Outside the condominium, a Terrafugia TF-X, DeLorean DR-7, and Joby Aviation's Air Taxi collide along the AI-controlled skyways as drivers are inexplicably drawn to glimpsing the woman's miraculous formation before their eyes. *Crash.* Even automated cameras do not seem to know if they should record the infrequent car crash or veer their attention to the genesis of the mysterious figure.

The voice of Pete Bogs, the sports commentator tagged for today's event, booms into the condominium's quiet quarters from a holographic projector as the crowd swells, "Praise, Ilem and the Galactic Council—the universe will be rid of humans today."

Spectators shout, "Yay!"

The woman inside the tube is in her early twenties and is racially fluid. Her name is Sage. Her complexion and facial features do not reveal if she's Black, White, Asian, or Latina, but she is radiant and alluring, whatever her race. Her 5'7" frame is slender but muscular and chiseled. Her face is a pleasant veil, cloaking smoldering intensity and unconstrained purpose.

Sage's breath fogs glass as she stands naked and fully formed in the life support tube. Her full lips are the only thing visible as she whispers a single word, "Omnis." As Sage steps out of the life support tube, clothes materialize with military boots, crimson, low-rise leather pants, a simple charcoal tank top, and a device resembling a wristwatch. A dangling *iSiphon* with a strobing yellow light adorns one ear.

She sees a folded letter on the slender table below the multi-touch interface computer. On the outside of the letter is the initial "Q." Sage unfolds the crumbled letter to read its message. "Sage, Stay you. Fate will take care of the rest." Sage folds the letter and puts it in her pocket to save it. Next, she reads words on the computer that alert her that the "Doomsday Protocol" has been activated. The timer on the computer screen now indicates 175 minutes.

While simultaneously adjusting the coordinates on the wristwatch-like device, Sage stands at the balcony edge, surveying the crowd forty-three stories below on the street. A close-up image of the wrist device shows a grid with a landing spot marked with an X directly through the roof of a VinFast VF 8 SUV idling on the street below. Around Sage's hips, she has already secured the hand cannon in the holster with her cache of explosives.

A strong breeze blows across Sage's upper torso and chest, flapping the fabric of her tank top. She calmly mutters to herself, "450 feet descent. Adjust for wind."

With that momentary pause, Sage leaps from the balcony, adjusting her slender body to sail smoothly as she descends toward the SUV. She continues audibly motivating herself with more instructions, "Readjust for landing." Her landing through the SUV roof is so skillful and cat-like that no one notices her rapid descent.

From a broadcast booth located in the upper levels of the Blood Bowl arena, a Vatrajan broadcaster alerts Pete Bogs, and his partner and sports announcer, Jared Steam, that the show is about to begin. The Vatrajan broadcaster signals to both of them, "Jared, Pete, we will throw it to you in twenty. Be ready to go."

Vatrajan investors funded this exclusive airing of Earth's tragedy from the boiling underground aquifers of Gliese Planet 777. They paid a king's ransom to acquire sole rights to broadcast Earth's final days to all points in the universe. And why not? Even fifty-two light-years from Earth, your exploits have been fodder for aliens to mock as perilous folly or embrace as a *fait accompli.*

The Vatrajan considered the licensing fee of 100,000,000 Tektite gems a drop in the bucket to acquire the thrilling end to the existence of the species deemed the 20th and 21st Centuries' "most rancid pustule on the arse of the galaxy. These creatures must be decimated, removed, and forever banned." *Spring Edition 2049,*

Intergalactic Times, Baxter Robinson Reporting. Metaverse subscribers from the farthest reaches of Orion, the constellation of Cygnus, Vulpecula, and GN-z11 eagerly paid to replenish the Vatrajan's coffers to watch the spectacle unfold.

A male transhuman with the countenance of an overfed, sweaty gambler urgently searches the broadcasting booth in the Blood Bowl Colosseum for some object he appears to have lost. If it were not for the crescent-shaped metal jewelry attached to the helix of both of the slothful transhuman's ears, that is all he would appear to be - a down on his luck, has been sports enthusiast who is color-blind. His wrinkled suit is candy apple red with white stripes like something ostentatious sports reporters wore in decades past to grasp relevancy or camouflage their lack of talent vainly. Meet Jared Steam.

Sitting at the broadcast desk near the discombobulated transhuman is a male drone studiously scrolling through notes on a transparent computer screen to prepare for the looming contest. Please welcome the witty and quick-witted Pete Bogs.

Just over the shoulder of the obese scavenger, Mr. Steam, a clock on the wall ever-so prophetically clicks to high noon. If nothing else, the Vatrajan broadcasters studied Earth's spaghetti westerns thoroughly enough to parallel the mythology of the man in white and the man in black. You know, the gunslinger who faces down a specter personifying his evil past standing just ten paces away.

Today's white knight is the most successful tech entrepreneur in human history who goes by the adopted name, Ilem Diwan Godfrey. Today's black hats are the Purists, Dr. Hamilton, and Sledge, two unlikely contestants in this ultimate game of death.

In utter frustration, Jared, the stout fashionista, slaps some of his notes off the table and into the air. With sweat dripping down his brow, Jared bellows, "Goddamn, Pete, we're on in less than twenty minutes now. I need my pills. You know how important it is for both of us … not just me, but both to look good today." The drone pauses to look up from his notes, exhales, and begins to address ole Sweaty's concerns.

Pete responds to Jared's anxiety by noting, "Jared, you stayed up all night emptying your pocket of Tektite at the dice table. If you lay off the sauce, you'd remember you can calibrate your *iSiphon* to regulate your dopamine highs. If you'd spend your money right, you could buy a modern *iSiphon* model that auto adjusts your PH instead of that old one that consistently needs updates. If you listen to me, you wouldn't need those pills."

Instead of continuing his search of the booth for the pills he has misplaced, Jared begins to fiddle with the metal objects affixed to his ears. Only a moment after, yellow lights blink on Jared's *iSiphon*, his ruddy complexion lightens, and the reek of gin and cheap cigars vanish from his breath. Instead of looking drawn and tired, clarity and vigor brighten his eyes.

The suddenly sober sports announcer and Pete will begin the play-by-play coverage of human extinction in a few more minutes. In the meantime, now that Jared's *iSiphon* has effectively regulated his internal chemical balance, he clears his throat to alliterate toning sounds before the battle begins, "Me, me, me. Mo, mo, mo. My, my, my …"

Simultaneously, Pete touches the pointy tip of his metallic hand against the computer screen, allowing information from the computer to chatter through his circulatory processing system into the *iSiphon* installed in his bot brain. Words on the computer disappear as Pete searches his mind for colorful facts about life on Earth that he can drip out during the contest.

Electricity and equally energizing information flow into Pete's hard drive, "Hey Jared," Pete says, "did you know humans had one and a half million bugs living on their bodies? That's like parasites having parasites! Their bodies are like their own private universe, with peculiar creatures on it that swim through rivers of blood, over peaking innards, and shallow valleys … You get it, right J?"

Annoyed by Pete's interruptions, Jared contentiously responds, "Do you mind? I don't have time for your silly facts. People want action, not bullshit about another race that's soon to be snuffed. We must emphasize today and the future, not relics from the past." Pete needles Jared by sarcastically suggesting, "Now you've got it all together – a real orator, a thespian even! Give me a break!"

The Vatrajan broadcaster's voice screeches through the broadcast booth's sound system like nails on a chalkboard. His sudden outburst startles Jared and Pete back from their brewing dispute. The broadcaster inquires again, "Jared,

Pete, we will throw it to you in fifteen. Are you on your marks?" Pete quickly responds that they're "*ret ta* go."

Jared picks up the sheets of paper scattered around the booth to practice his intro, "1,500 feet above a smoldering D.C ... monuments to past glories and atrocities ... 1,500 feet above ... wait ... below ... Mi, mi, mi. Mo, mo, mo. My, my, my."

Pete mischievously mimics Jared's prep for the broadcast, "Me, me, me. Mo, mo, mo, ladies and gentlemen, here is the pompous star of our show! My, my, my ..." Jared claps back, "Pompous? Know your place! Fans call this show 'Steam and Bogs' for a reason, not 'Bogs and Steam.'"

The girth of his stomach forces Jared to refasten the buttons popping loose on his wrinkly suit as his excitement and irritation balloon, "Listen, Pete, I'm the trans here, and you're a glorified toaster ... So, I suggest you ease up before somebody has you pressed into a shit can! Metal *mf'er!*" Pete snorts like an angry bull, ready to leap at a stylish red flag, "Fuck you back, ya meat suit. If it weren't for your *iSiphon*, you'd be another Purist heading to slaughter today!"

Pete mimes swinging and punching Jared to the moon but restrains himself from doing it or saying too much over the PA system despite Jared's rudeness, doused in liquid courage. Pete warns his partner, "Jared, cool your jets. If you say something wrong where walls have ears and words have consequences, we might find both ourselves stuffed in shit cans! Sober up, and no editorializing!"

To placate his irksome partner, Jared impatiently concedes, "Fine, fine ... Let me show you what I have to whet the fans' appetites."

Jared flips sheet after sheet of his scrawled notes, clears his throat, then launches into his monologue, "Uph ... 1,500 feet above smoldering D.C. monuments to Earth's past glories and atrocities, Lord Ilem's Floating City will be the final resting place for the last two descendants of Earth. Humans who chose to conform to transhumanism did so with the hope that they would survive extermination. Indeed, by surrendering to wearing Ilem's *iSiphon*, many of these new adapts went as far as to denounce their birthright as humans, choosing to become a mechanized cog in Ilem's glorious new metropolis."

Interrupting Jared's impressive repertoire, Pete signals to Jared that he has something to add. "Then I can jump in to say, 'Now that transhumans have found a home on Ilem's Floating City, they and you will take part in the most thrilling spectacle in the history of the universe. A billion years from now, creatures will call it fiction, but you will know it as fact. Before the two remaining Purists are dragged into the Bowl, you should feast on all the Floating City has to offer while we wait for Ilem, our honored Lord.'"

Pete turns to Jared to ask, "What do you think?" Discouragingly, Jared instructs Pete, "Just as long as you remember who's the star of this show, you can spout anything you want. Just keep the festivities going." Pete jokingly chirps, "Mine, mine, mine ..."

Announcements from the Vatrajan broadcaster scurry into the ears and minds of passersby. The stoking words ignite a party for the ages that breaks out among those stuffing inside the Blood Bowl arena. Jared excitedly draws Pete's attention to the throng of Spectators bustling into the building. "Pete, Pete, look at that crowd. We got to be on our 'A' game."

Pete momentarily peaks out of the booth to survey what has caused Jared to be less cantankerous and more buoyant. To tamp Jared's reaction, Pete shrugs again, "I've got enough tidbits to keep those dunders fascinated. Keep your commentary lively, and I'll keep the fans on the edge of their seats. Ah, what say you?"

Pete adjusts the mic volume to ensure his voice climbs above Jared's ramblings and the animated Spectators' buzz as they walk in cadence with every blink of the red, luminous lights displaying the words "Blood Bowl." The eyes of cameras rolling in the air pan by the Spectators gleefully anticipating the decisive battle embroiling Earth's remaining survivors against Ilem's anointed champion and devoted soldier, "Black Heart" Kol.

On the streets below, aliens, transhumans, and humanoid drones continue their rhythmic tramp toward the space-age Blood Bowl Colosseum. They come in all shapes and sizes and from all directions. Transhumans born in Texas still sport cowboy hats, wearing *iSiphons* and the customary breathing device to avoid choking on Earth's putrid air. The green and purple-skinned Wiggles from Proxima Centauri wear intricate sunglasses to protect themselves from extreme ultraviolet radiation. Old drones still leak fluids in the street.

Blood Bowl Earth 2050 has a feel-good atmosphere, like an impromptu block party on a barricaded road. Unfortunately, I am sure humans wanted to be invited to the party as guests by other worlds, not roasted on a spit as the main course.

Like the extraordinary assortment of human life on Earth that once existed, this melting pot of bipetal, flying, brightly colored, and slinking creatures are juxtaposed like a queer sign of prosperity against Earth's tragedies. Today, every intelligent creature occupying Earth has come together as a universal ecosystem united for a common purpose: the extinguishment of humankind.

A projector transmitting 3D holographic scenes of the joyful chaos below displays the arena filling with Spectators and the sound of Jared's and Pete's voices as they continue their pre-fight commentaries. Jared, "So much anticipation in the air! Is it too early to pop corks? Blood Bowl is being streamed live throughout the universe and to Earth's metaverse, the Maze, where the Moji lives, all for the sordid entertainment and gambling pleasure of Spectators wherever there are or at least remnants of intelligent, bestial, or barbaric life."

Pete whispers to Jared, "Hey, how about we dial down to a three, not a ten? Save something for the climax." Jared speaks low, too: "You can't blame a baby for soiling its shorts, can you? We've had so many Blood Bowls that this one should have occurred eons ago. Let's get the crowd a little fired up! I know it's a funeral, but that shouldn't mean we can't have fun."

Angrily, the Vatrajan broadcaster yells into Jared's and Pete's headsets, "Damnit, can you two say something to segue to the crowd!" Pete tries to take the broadcaster's cue instead of answering Jared's controversial statements. Pete, "What a crowd! Let's see who's listening, Jared!"

Meanwhile, the crowd of Spectators on the streets near the Colosseum joyously respond to the news that the main event will start soon. Spectators, "Hooray! Kill humans!" The Vatrajan broadcaster warns Pete and Jared again, "You two had better be glad everyone's more interested in the crowd right now than your uninvited social commentaries."

But only some are interested in becoming a part of the huddled mass. Instead, Sage is more interested in using their festivities as cover. From the vehicle's front seat where she landed, Sage removes the wristwatch-like device to attach it to the dashboard. The timer of the wristwatch reads 165 minutes. Draped over the tail end of a futuristic motorcycle also loaded in the rear of the SUV, Sage finds a hooded cloak in the back of the vehicle. The plate on the bike reads, *"Race the Rain."*

As she begins to exit the vehicle, she stops momentarily to reach for the hooded cloak to obscure her face and physical appearance. Sage whispers, "Hang on, Dad. I will be there soon." Once entirely outside the SUV, Sage is surrounded by transhumans. She thinks but does not dare to exclaim, "They still resemble normal people in most ways. Some have powers and abilities beyond those of Purists. I have to be as unseen as possible."

A transhuman ticket scalper briefly startles Sage when he calls out close to her ear, "Tickets, get your tickets here!" In response to the ticket scalper's clamoring, a crowd of transhumans and aliens from planets light years away - Kubecha, Dau, Apuestas, and Sharad, to name a few - form a line to buy overpriced seats for the day's actions. Undeterred, Sage cautiously moves through the crowd toward the Colosseum.

Within the wolf pack, another alien ticket scalper noisily shouts that he also has tickets for the best seats in the house while protesters on the other side of the road hold signs denouncing "Luddites" and "Purists" as the bane of the galaxy. The protesters and ticket hawks exchange screeches, pitting money against morals, but neither acknowledges the clashing dogmas. The ticket scalper calls out, "Tickets, get your tickets!" Protesters respond, "Down with Purists! Down with humans!"

An eclectic crowd of sentient beings mingle on the streets of the Floating City. Sage evades inspection from a slender, old male transhuman struggling along the road trying to control a leached mechanical bulldog intending to chase a lost automatic cat. The old trans beckons the robotic dog, "Come on, Busta, behave!"

A little boy with robotic arms throws a tantrum to embarrass his mother into buying a VR system that the boy sees displayed in a storefront window. The little boy whines, "I want it, Mom! You promised!" His mother whispers to calm her demanding son, "Jesse, please. You are causing a scene." Sage uses the sudden distractions to stay out of view of prying eyes. While other transhumans and drones absorbed in their worlds pass by, Sage easily remains inconspicuous.

She notices by sound and sight bold figures wading through the crowd. The figures she sees approaching are transhumans and humanoid drone guards in Ilem's militia, whom everyone under Ilem's thumb openly refers to as Ilem's Elite Death Squad. Sage slides to the back of the packed crowd as the militia arrogantly plow straight ahead.

Leading the entourage of Ilem's forces is the transhuman, "Black Heart" Kol. Iridescent, polished metal shining like chrome, with black striations that resemble discolored veins rise to the surface of his galvanized legs. The sturdy armor protecting Kol's torso distinguishes him as the High Guard in Ilem's lethal Death Squad. The crowd loudly chants his name as he passes. Close behind Kol are other transhuman members of the Elite Squadron, fully attired in red and black armor.

Ticket scalpers and protestors retreat to make way for the fighting company. Their swagger and loud stomps show that the Elite Squadron militia dominates the rest of the entourage. Most of the Elite Squadron wear breathing devices to protect them from lingering environmental hazards. After the Elite Squad, the humanoid drones known as the Scout Section or the Sect follow next in the procession. The Sect are all masculine humanoid drones made of black metal with a hint of green veining. Each carries plasma guns on their hips or plasma rifles on their backs as if they anticipate a brawl.

The less revered Trailers are the last pack of soldiers straggling behind everyone else. They are a mishmash of aliens who survived the Galactic Council's destruction of their worlds. The Trailers dress in ragtag apparel and carry old military gear, suggesting they are the fodder forced to garner all the pain on the frontline by sacrificing their lives in servitude to Ilem, but none of the glory.

The Spectators chant, "Kol! Kol! Kol!" With every shout of his name, the metal boots of the military entourage thump in response, thadump, thadump, thadump.

Bringing up the rear of the entourage are four Trailers who struggle to steer an unusual creature to follow with the procession. The animal, known by many as the Alien Beast, is a massive, muscular, reptilian creature shaped like a lion, with the face of a horned dragon, underdeveloped wings, and four eyes. It is a peculiar animal that exudes power and feasts on fear.

The feral monster's place of origin may be unknown to the Spectators and the Death Squad, but the creature comprehends the meaning of the Spectators' sadistic mantra, "Kill, kill, kill!" Simultaneously with the crowd's rising chant for the Alien Beast to provide them with their pound of flesh, the creature loudly growls its approval for delivering the anticipated recompense.

Dressed in everyday clothes like early 21st-century humans, the residents of the Floating City surround the military entourage. The transhuman and drone civilians are plumbers, cops, butlers, cab drivers, couriers, mothers, and fathers, all vestiges of Earth's past "normal" now living in an ultramodern world and a finite future. They have ethnic hairstyles and are multi-cultural in nationality, like a surreal page from a Norman Rockwell painting. The majority who still look human have varying forms of *iSiphons* with blinking yellow lights in their ear canals or attached to the helix of their ear, and the rest have upgraded their bodies with different forms of AI prosthetics.

The Elite Squadron continues cutting through the throng, thadump thadump. Sage peaks coyly around the first gate situated before entering the Colosseum.

Within her view is a female and male transhuman guard. Annoyingly, another ticket scalper peddles his product near Sage's ear, "I got two, front row, center! Whooooooooooo neeeeeeds tickkkkkkkets?"

Sage turns toward the inconsiderate ticket scalper, but she does not appear to be the same young woman she was a moment ago. Instead, she looks like a full-figured, middle-aged female transhuman who spends a copious amount of time in the kitchen. A subtle stream of light is pulled from the ticket scalper's body to Sage's outstretched hand.

She stands within mere inches of the ticket scalper's face. He suddenly stops and begins to stutter when he turns to confront whoever is standing far too close to him, "Ma … mom, what, what are you doing here? I thought you were … ah … too tired to come to the show."

Appearing to be the ticket scalper's mother, Sage scornfully looks up at him and says, "Boy, you better stop yelling at people, or you might get yelled at, too. I am going home to fix your dinner. Make sure you do not get your ass in trouble!" In return, the ticket scalper mutters, "Yes, Mom. Sorry, Mom."

The thirsty crowd pushes and scraps to snag tickets. Sage turns away from the last ticket scalper to wade further into the crowd. She reaches and stands at the Colosseum exterior gate, waiting for attendance by a male guard activating an electronic wand to scan her physical composition, thereby confirming her species. The male guard shouts to other guards supervising his work, "Comp check!" He waves the electronic wand across Sage's body multiple times but does not detect any issues, not even the hand cannon that previously was visible hanging from Sage's waist.

A female guard slaps the male guard on his head with a loud, thudding sound, Slap! She shows Sage on her way with the other Spectators heading toward the final entry gate. The female guard cracks, "Don't be a perv, Harold!" Innocently, the male guard responds, "The comp wand is actin' wacky, not me!"

The throng of gatherers parts enough to allow Sage to continue by the male and female guards and get closer to her ultimate destination. The bickering guards distract themselves from noticing the colored lights flowing into Sage's body from several people close to her.

Sage's face shifts from the appearance of the ticket scalper's mother to that of an older female Latina, transhuman, with a plain version of an *iSiphon* in her ear canal. She is now shorter and broader in the hips, her breasts sag from gravity and age. She intensively scans the Spectators through heavily wrinkled eyes to plot her path to the final entry gate. Unexpectedly, Sage bumps into a gangly, transhuman young male guard as she continues moving through the horde. With perfect Spanish, Sage bashfully pleads, *"Perdóname."*[1]

In the background behind Sage, the young guard heatedly speaks with the male and female guards and points in Sage's direction as she wades through transhumans and aliens. Before she successfully evades detection, the young guard grabs Sage by her shoulder, pulling off her hooded robe. Aggressively, the young guard commends Sage to stay where she is, "Stop, lady, where's your ticket?"

When Sage turns to face the young guard, she is no longer an older Latina woman. Instead, Sage is now a chestnut-haired, thirty-something-year-old woman standing 5'10". A bejeweled version of an *iSiphon* dangles from her ear. Even her outfit has become a plum iridescent mini dress with a dramatically plunging neckline.

Spectators surrounding Sage call out to her as Gianna Fornelli, a famous Italian social media influencer and entrepreneur. Not only is the young guard stunned to be in the presence of such awesomeness, but so are the creatures of all kinds who are close to her.

The paparazzi go crazy, clicking their cameras dizzily, showering Gianna in bright strobes of lights. Autonomous drone cameras hover above everyone to capture Gianna's photo. 1ST paparazzi, "Gianna!" Spectator, "She's so stunning!" 2ND paparazzi, "Gianna, look this way!"

Gianna's presence captivates the young guard. If the diminutive guard could float, he would plank ten feet off the ground before the lovely Fornelli. Gianna gently lifts his chin, bringing his gaze from her curvaceous breast to her captivating hazel eyes. Gianna cozies her lips to the edge of the young guard's ear to whisper a request. Gianna, "I lost my ticket, *bello*.[2] Can you help me find a good seat

---

[1] "Forgive me."
[2] "Handsome."

anyway?" The young guard stammers, "No … no, I'm sorry, ma'am. You got to have a ticket."

Gianna draws a green glow from the young guard's hand to her delicate embrace. Gianna, "Tell me what you feel, handsome. What do you see when you look at me?" The young guard excitedly replies, "You're Gianna Fornelli?" Gianna commands him, "*Guardami negli occhi per quella risposta, bello.*"[3]

Mesmerized, the young guard coos, "Amazing. I just rubbed one ou … sorry, I watched you on my computer only an hour ago." Gianna takes the young guard by the arm for him to lead her into the Colosseum while other envious guards and Spectators look on. Gianna, "Then isn't it fortunate to see me now in the flesh, so to speak." The young guard agrees, "I'm so happy; I'm shaking!"

He glides by his co-workers like his feet have wings. In the background, the male guard who received the slap on the back of his head appears upset that the Elite Guard assigned him to the wrong entryway. The young guard, helpless to escape his trance, answers, "So beautiful." Gianna thanks him, "*Grazie bello.*"[4] Then you will excuse me for not having a ticket?" The young guard surrenders to Gianna's soothing voice, "Oh, yes. VIP seating is right this way. Anything for you!"

While clasping her personal escort's trembling arm, Gianna walks inside the well of the Colosseum and up the stairs to priority seating. The Young guard continues to gaze at Gianna with every clumsy step. If this were a first date, he would gain points for unrestrained attraction to his date but lose a lot more for his gawkiness.

The crowd around them part as Gianna saunters to premium VIP seating reserved for high society transhumans. Even wealthy Spectators attending the event live and from the Maze metaverse are agog as they survey Gianna's beauty from head to toe. Gianna stares deeply into the young guard's spellbound eyes, gaining greater control over his thoughts and emotions. Gianna seductively suggests, "Call me Gianna, *amante.*"[5]

---

[3] "Gaze into my eyes for that answer, handsome."
[4] "Thank you, handsome."
[5] "Lover."

Gianna's kinetic beauty and overpowering allure draw other Spectators deeper into her web while Kol attentively selects a weapon for the ensuing battle. Kol selects a unique khopesh from the array of armaments to use in the subsequent fight. Unlike the traditional khopesh, the blade of Kol's weapon produces a laser along its edge, which Kol studiously activates. Vriiimmmm.

As enchanted as those fans are to see Gianna Fornelli, the more bloodthirsty crowd only has eyes for Black Heart Kol. Those Spectators call out, "Praise our High Guard!"

Kol enters the arena amid the fanfare and praise from those in the Blood Bowl and those watching light years away on Gliese Channel 777. Spectators shout, "Kol, we love you! Bring us Victory!" Behind Kol, the four Trailers corralling the Alien Beast struggle to direct it to the side. Its flame-filled nostrils flare open with every breath, emitting pungent smoke that causes the Trailers to step back. The animal's long, barbed tail whips wildly, coming close to smacking each of the Trailers in their faces.

Worst yet for the besieged Trailers, the Alien Beast's underdeveloped wings allow it to remain aloft before the Trailers wrestle it back to the ground, scraping and skidding their feet. The Trailers finally pull the Alien Beast down to the earth. The creature slowly turns the gaze of its four eyes past each of the Trailers, chilling them to their cores with visions of their flesh and limbs stuck in the Alien Beast's craw. Also, intentionally keeping their distance, the entourage of soldiers separate behind Kol to line the arena's interior wall and away from anything the Alien Beast might consider grub.

The Vatrajan broadcaster jumps back into the fold, "Okay, guys, settle down now! Here we go. Following my intro, it is yours in five, four, three, two, one ... Here we go!"

By ramping up his mic, the Vatrajan broadcaster's voice cuts through all the other noise and excited chatter of those attending the event, "And now, ladies and gentlemen, Gliese Channel 777 presents a grueling battle today, the event for the ages, Blood Bowl Earth 2050. For this once in a finite lifetime event, GC's sports announcer, Jared Steam, and Pete Bogs, our sports commentator, join us from the color booth. Everyone, everywhere, let's welcome Steam and Bogs, who will give you our play-by-play coverage of human extinction."

The cameras frame only Jared and Pete as they high-five and together shout their signature greeting for their fans, "Leeeeeeeeeeeeeeeet's rocket!"

Jared enthusiastically smiles from *iSiphon* to *iSiphon* when the green light flashes that the floor is open, "Ladies and gentlemen, Borgs and Trans, Wiggles and Wags, sentients everywhere, welcome to Bloooooooood Booooooowl Eaaaarth 2050! I am Jared Steam, joined by my giddy friend, Pete Bogs."

Pete eagerly jumps in, "This battle for survival began over four million years ago; 13.8 billion if you count from the origin of the Revered Galactic Council. At high noon, on this hot and hazy day above a smoldering DC skyline, eyes around the universe are fixed on watching the last Purists alive fighting for the right to choose their humiliating fate."

Pete amps up his mic instead of accommodating Jared's attempt to take back over the broadcast. He adjusts his tone to unpack his comments carefully. "Jared, where would we be ... I mean ... none of these glorious events would be possible without Lord Ilem and his company Avant Communication Inc. ... uh, AVI." Pete points toward the arena's edge to direct the crowd to a distant skyscraper lit from penthouse to street with glitchy ads featuring AVI's revolutionary product, the *iSiphon*."

The colossal man centerstage in the *iSiphon* ad is "Black Heart" Kol. His powerful presence is not fully apparent in the ad, but his strength and power are from how easily his transhuman body bursts through a brick wall in the ad. Filling the space above Kol's head is the slogan, "*iSiphon*. Siphon more out of life."

Jared touts the virtues of the *iSiphon*, "I have two of them, one for business and one for play. For those living on other planets, Ilem introduced the '*iSiphon* Ultra-Mesh Earbud' to exclusive, wealthy clientele shortly after the 2018 World Technology Conference in Davos, Switzerland. Although most *iSiphons* are only ½" in diameter and seamlessly fit into or dangled from the ear, its advanced technology streams gigs of information directly into the end-user's brain like a ChatGPT bot spray painting words on a wall. That data appears internally, like words or images on a screen. The *iSiphon* can regulate chemical imbalances too to ward off disease and illness."

Pete chimes in, "Every transhuman, no matter how remote from mainstream society, can now connect and exchange knowledge without wires or restraints. Even the poor can buy slightly cheaper ..." Jared interrupts his partner by holding his chubby, blotted hand in Pete's face, "We will say slightly less advanced model. But at least the financially challenged could join the transhuman revolution and not be euthanized by Ilem like common Purist dogs."

If he had hair, the Vatrajan broadcaster would be pulling it out. "WTF ... enough plugging products! I am sure Ilem appreciates you two selling more *iSiphons* but remember what we're here for ... damnit! Get on with it!"

Jared covers the mic and says to Pete, "I got it." Returning to his scrawled notes, Jared continues his rehearsed soliloquy, "If I am allowed to lure more residents to the Floating City, I have to tell you this fusion-powered palladium is the most impressive craft I have ever seen. This intergalactic metropolis spans one nautical mile in length and twenty decks in height, and every open airspace is ablaze with camera lights for GC 777's broadcast of this competition. And they have a great casino and free drinks. You can stay up all night! Hick ... 'cuse me."

A forcefield restrains Sledge and Dr. Hamilton from escaping as they anxiously await their battle against Kol. They are dressed in bloodied and torn prisoners' clothes. Aside from their weapons of choice, tattered clothes, and skin tone, Sledge is recognizable by his broken, black sunglasses worn to shield his opaque eyes; Dr. Hamilton by his flowing white hair and his long, white goatee that dates him. Despite Dr. Hamilton's advanced age of eighty-one, he is imposing at 6'4" and noticeably buff for a man of any age.

After cracking his knuckles and throwing practice blows, Dr. Hamilton wipes beads of sweat from his head as he contemplates if his daughter, Sage, is anywhere in the arena.

Sledge's dreadlocks obscure his face, just as he hopes they will do. He struggles to control his queasiness and collapses to one knee from the violent storm raging from the back of his neck and the base of his skull. Dr. Hamilton lends Sledge a hand to rise back to his feet, but Sledge brushes him off to instead rely on his staff to find his footing.

Once upright, Sledge continues to massage his forehead, "Fuck, my head hurts, *mon*." Dr. Hamilton assures him, "It will not hurt long. It's a good day to die." Befuddled, Sledge responds, "*Fuck yuh*! I *nuh waan tuh* run out *there an* fall on his damn sword! I thought *yuh* had *ah* plan?"

Vomit uncontrollably bursts from Sledge's gaping mouth against the wall. Violent stomach spasms cripple him to one knee. Dr. Hamilton answers, "Yes and no. Just stay calm no matter what happens." Sledge wipes puke from his mouth with the back of his forearm, "Wah *di* fuck are *yuh* talking *bout*, argh ... I feel like shit."

Dr. Hamilton repeats the wise advice he conveyed to Sage on the crumble letter stuffed in her pants pocket. "Be you. Fate will take care of the rest."

END OF CHAPTER 1

Chapter 2

Steppingstones

Fate is not fickle and quickly changing.
It is an immobile signpost along a long and winding road.

Can you dim it and still walk the path you are on
Or will you stumble in the dark, climbing to higher ground?

How can you set a new stitch in the fabric of time
Without light to help a blundering hand?

Derrick Howard

Are you destined to be
Who you are,
Perfect imperfection,
Groping, searching, reaching
For serendipity to point you
To the certain sun waiting at the end of the beaten road?

Walk with the stable step of knowing
No matter where you go, there you are.

Eyes

On Earth, on a rainless day in April 2050, residents of the Floating City join sentient renegades in hiding on the "Blue Planet," Moji in the metaverse Maze, and other Spectators to watch the looming battle between Earth's last two Purists and the fearsome transhuman, Dominque "Black Heart" Kol.

Light years away, the rogue planet, Caellum, sails through interstellar space without the sway or command of a parent star. Today, creatures gather there to celebrate as humans, the most heinous and feared mortals ever to inhibit the galaxy, prepare to take their last miserable breath in this momentous battle.

On Caellum, a rough and rowdy crowd of sentients huddled to view Blood Bowl at a dank and dusty watering hole called the Harbor Bar. The waterside pub sits at the foot of Mount Idan, a mountain that towers seven miles above sea level. On the other side of the bar is the Port of the Virat Sea, a vast waypoint for merchant ships, travelers, and other lost souls without a home.

The decrepit bartender running the Harbor Bar, Yam, slowly shuffles from one patron to the next, appeasing their drunken desires while pouring out sage advice for other thirsty consumers. His clothes are baggy, dirty, and torn, but that does not deter his cheerful and friendly disposition. With his extraordinarily long arms below his knees, Yam only needs a few steps to reach each end of the bar. Yet, as gay as he appears, he grimaces inwardly as pain daily wracks his body from carrying an enormous bulge between his shoulders.

Despite the riveting agony, Yam does not moan as he pours more drinks. No, the old bartender warmly asks each of his patrons, "Another round of hobo scotch, sir?"

In response to her husband's request, Seraphina brings him more glasses and fresh wine. She walks through a curtain separating the bar area from Sera's garden, where she dutifully works to craft various spirits, elixirs, and brews. While Yam wears tattered, worn, and blah-colored clothes, Sera models a long white wrinkle dress paired with a thin peach-colored hijab and a pastel-colored lace mask adorning her face. In contrast to Yam's odd appearance, Sera's beauty is consuming, even shrouded by cloth.

Etheus, a patron and rival local merchant known for antagonizing others whenever he has the chance, drunk or sober, interrupts Yam's quiet thoughts. Etheus speaks from his booth in an audible whisper, "Talk about Beauty and the Beast; Yam looks like a marriage between a monkey and a donkey gone wrong. So broken, I'm surprised he can still stand straight with that lump of pus on his shoulder."

Etheus turns to the other patrons for support and loudly tells another customer, "Ulabe, check this out. Yam doesn't have a forehead, more like an eight-head. Ha, I've never seen anything as deformed in my life. But wifey, she is a piece of candy I'd like to lick." Ulabe snickers and agrees, "Make a man change his religion."

Sera's continence slowly changes from reserved to being gently assertive. Before she answers Etheus' highly inappropriate comments, Yam signals that he will manage the situation. Sera softly says to her husband, "Yamanu, I no more need a man to tell me what to think or do than I need a man to tell me how to defecate." Yam responds to her, "I know Seraphina. I mean no harm or disrespect. Let me oversee my fine Cancrian friend, and you enjoy your day."

Yam calmly says to Etheus, "I wrestle with making sense out of nonsense. We have seven rules for anyone wanting to step inside here." Yam picks up a heavy chalice made of metal as thick and heavy as galvanized steel and carries it to the booth where Etheus is lounging.

Yam pours four fingers of hobo scotch from a decanter for his patron. He lifts the heavy chalice to his eye to inspect it, then pours a generous amount on the floor for the brothers who ain't here. Before handing the chalice to Etheus, Yam holds it out to him in one hand, then crushes it as if it were a paper cup.

Yam informs Etheus, "I do this not to threaten but to show my restraint. I was a warrior once wielding the strength of many men. I could crush a skull by closing my hand. But just because I can, does not mean I should. Too many sentients have forgotten that and seem to feel every crooked opinion they have should go viral." Continuing to admonish Etheus, Yam suggests, "By devaluing my wife and me, you reveal your inaptness and fear of me."

Etheus stammers as other patrons stare him down, "Why … why would I fear you? I am rich! On my home planet, diamonds rain from the sky into my pocket. You have nothing on me!"

Yam gently walks away from Etheus to place the disfigured mug on the bar top. To command his attention, Yam peers into Etheus' vapid eyes. "Etheus, ugly people know they're ugly when they wake each morning, don't you agree?"

Etheus scoffs, but yet is curious, "Huh, what does that mean?" Yam informs him, "Money does not make you truly rich. Beauty, on the outside, cannot mask internal distress that each of you is aware of when you look into the morning mirror. You fearfully refuse to name it and claim it."

"You note that I am ugly and deformed, but if that is true – and I cannot deny your observations –you question how depressing your life is. You fear me because you have never had such a prize and partner in your life as my Sera, yet my cover is unappealing."

He further comments to Etheus, "The galaxies' lore posits that there was only one perfect person ever born. That myth is fabled in countless worlds for the sanctity of the downtrodden and the dominance of dictators. Show me a perfect person, and I will show you a cross. Perfection was not enough to spare that being from persecution and death by self-righteous judges. Some even go as far as to change the countenance of their messiah to reflect their myopic point of view."

"You look at Sera, and you look at me and must wonder how we even met. In my travels as a peddler of different oddities, I saw Sera from a distance as she painted words on the rock face of Mount Idan. If I recall correctly, her words were, 'A pebble without a ripple, a wind that moves no leaves. You have held your breath so long that you've forgotten how to breathe."

Reminiscing about his chance encounters with his angel, Yam continues, "As I watched those words flow from her delicate hands unto the side of a hard, broken mountainside, I thought it was a private message to me that I should take a chance and risk rejection from someone as breathtaking as Sera. Instead of rejecting me, Sera saw the man I am inside, not the fiend you describe to your friends to roast me constantly. Despite my looks, Sera and I are one soul. She is the yin to my yang."

Ulabe takes a well-timed verbal jab at his pesky friend Etheus, "What the matter is, Etheus? He told you! You too ugly and dumb to come close to sniffing a flower like Sera."

Another alien known as Three-Fingered Bill from Leicath, and his running buddies, Brahski from Monoceros, and Tyson of Balt, interject themselves into the conversation, laughing and gesturing at Etheus. Etheus explodes, "Enough of your yammering, Yam! I would rather listen to Blood Bowl than jab tongues with you."

Other patrons agree by clamoring to Yam, "Yeah, turn that shit up!"

Before the boobs turn back to the tube, Ulabe turns to toss out a few cheesy pick-up lines at a lady Neptunian who has traveled to Caellum to watch the combat in peace, "You've traveled far to watch a contest you could have viewed on Earth." The Neptunian, none too interested in Ulabe, says, "Earth's a shit show. I had to pay thousands of crypts to make it here while not getting close to that calamity. I don't need your bullshit either."

A patron, blocked in the rear of the pub by huddling gamblers, shouts to the Neptunian in a high-pitched voice, "Should I bet on a Purist win?" The Neptunian yells back, "No way, Kol is a fucking machine! He'll fight hand-to-hand with them two to give everyone a show."

The camouflaged gambler stands on his chair, revealing a 4-foot-tall rolling stone and bounty hunter from Farfarout. Aside from his height, like all others from his home planet, this adventurer is tatted from his neck to his heels with ink that tells the tale of every rival he has vanquished. In the center of his intricate, colorful tattoos, this traveler has a grayish-black lightning bolt branded on his chest.

Unfortunately, death or payment is always an option for alien gamblers who fight the drifter from Farfarout upon losing a round of Beggar's Lot. However, misjudging someone because they lack the stature to mount a defense against others who look more physically fit is a grave mistake against the Farfarout. He does not appear twelve years old with an early beard due to a congenital disability or malady. It takes his home planet nearly 1,000 years to complete a single lap around its sun.

Although they lack the strength of apex predators, the Farfarout train for centuries to move blindingly fast and strike at lethal pressure points of their opponents, like a cagey tiger or a bolt of lightning, as in this particular Farfarout case. The Farfarout's combat style emphasizes low solid stances and powerful clawing and clubbing movements that render opponents riveted in place from shock, crippled from internal fractures, or dead from relentless pummeling.

All this Farfarout needs is two minutes without distraction, and he can kill you before your flaccid body hits the ground. He strikes you with rapid, open-palm thrusts that each make you feel like your soul has yanked away a piece at a time until only an empty husk is left. When the carnage concludes, a new tattoo instantly forms on the Farfarout's' bodies that tells the woeful tale of each challenger the Farfarout defeated. Some say that they have seen the image of this Farfarout's victims eerily creep across his body, bulging out like a grim bas relief.

In compliance with Harbor Bar house rules, however, this Farfarout only roughs up his competition instead of permanently putting them to sleep. After slapping cocky gamblers around for the betting pleasure of other patrons of the Harbor Bar, the Farfarout returned his attention to everyone at his table and the wagers to come. "Great, now that that's done, let's start the slaughtering! I'm betting another hundred Tektites on the blind one, Sledge."

Everyone, except the short Farfarout, watches transhumans and humanoid drones fill the Colosseum. The crimson glow from a flashing Blood Bowl sign above the Harbor Bar entrance baptizes each new customer in an unholy rain. The same can be true of the Spectators milling about aboard the Floating City to reach the battle for survival that is about to begin.

The impressive crowd in the Blood Bowl arena who excitedly anticipate the action include Spectators who resemble famous actors, socialites, and politicians. Every one of them has evolved from human to transhuman in the past thirty years, initially to stay ahead of the pack and later to survive the slaughter of Purists. The Neptunian points at the screen to announce the name of each celebrity she met with at Gondwana, Earth's first colony on Mars. She also draws everyone's attention to the well-known Moji, pixelized citizens of the Maze, who are most identifiable by the physical manifestations of their digital footprints.

Even the last President of the United States of the Americas, Adrian Colon, is in attendance. He is notable wherever he goes not just because he is the leader of what remains of North and South America's habitable land but also because he wears a metal exoskeleton from his neck to his feet to support his paraplegic body.

World leaders from the U.S., Brazil, Russia, India, China, and South Africa lounge behind President Colon in the comfort of a private suite, secured by transhuman and drone secret service agents and an impenetrable forcefield. The government diplomats' and leaders' genders and races are mixed, but they all are noticeably transhuman by body implants or through attachment to *iSiphons*.

Jared yells for the benefit of the Spectators spread around the globe and known and unknown universes, "Beings of the Galaxy, without further ado, I give you the Galactic Council's Minister of Light, our Lord Ilem!"

All eyes turn to the majestic figure sitting on a throne descending to the arena floor. Although he is not a combatant, Ilem's dramatic entrance so close to the action demonstrates he is as vital to the Spectators as the fighters, if not more. Despite his decades of international fame as an entrepreneur in communications and space exploration, Ilem only appears to be a 21-year-old White male.

Physically, he has an athletic, six-foot, 185 lbs. body and a flawless, deep tan. Today, he wears his trademark royal blue and gold garments, with a flowing cape bearing a sun symbol. On the edge of the floating throne next to Ilem lays a silver and gold helmet with spiked and bejeweled wings reminiscent of Mercury, the God of Trickery's Helm of Hades. Green lights blink steadily on the wings, illuminating jewels that line its edges.

For those who seek to call Ilem their lord, he is their Messiah, the Holy Grail, the One, the Christ. He appeared from the heavens like a glistening angel, shining his light on the desperate and the brave. His majesty, for them, is a comforting blanket to stay warm in or to veil their heads from blistering winds of truth.

In the middle of the arena, below Ilem's floating throne, Kol raises his arms to exhort the crowd. In the background, a futuristic guillotine with an intimidating executioner standing next to it emerges near the arena's edge. The executioner's fat and slovenly physique reflects the bloated existence humans have adopted by the termination of the planet after several centuries of gluttony, debauchery, vanity, and genocide. Jared loudly clamors, "We also give you the Elite Squadron's High Guard and intergalactic football sensation, Dominique 'Black Heart' Kol!"

A Trailer disengages the forcefield in front of Dr. Hamilton and Sledge, allowing them to cautiously step onto the arena floor to the jeers of live attendees at Blood Bowl. Jared continues his rowdy introduction, "And, last of the Purist, last of the pathetic human race ..." Pete stops Jared to plug the event in a distinctly separate way, "Let's give these Purists a little more credit than that, Jared. I know the odds of a blind man and someone old enough to be a great-grandfather surviving is dreadfully low. Still, they made it through the early rounds against fierce competition. The other thirty-four Purists gave all they had to make it this far but lost."

Jared quickly muffles the mic with his luminescent hand to whisper to Pete, "Fine ... what's their names?" Calling on information transmitted into his central processing unit from his internal *iSiphon*, Pete leans closer to Jared to whisper this answer, "Quinten Hamilton's the old guy; call him something shadowy and provocative like Dr. Q. And the blind guy is ... ah ... Sledge. That is all we have for him. *I*Siphon, provide names of blind gladiators ... Okay, got it. The Romans called them andabata."

Seemingly recharged from Pete's lead on how to stoke the Spectators' anticipation, Jared rises from his chair as he excitedly introduces the human combatants, "The men, the myths, the rebels, the mysterious, Dr. Q and a true andabata, Sledge! Fans on Earth and the surrounding galaxies, I give you the Last Men of Earth!"

Cameras capture an angled, down shot of the entire Colosseum and zoom in on Ilem standing away from his throne, preparing to command Kol, Dr. Hamilton, and Sledge to fight. Dr. Hamilton readies himself to lunge at Kol, seeking an advantage. Sledge composes himself, despite his illness, to rigidly hold the five-foot-long wooden staff in a Wushu defensive fighting stance.

Again, Jared whispers to Pete, "Great intro for the Purists. But who really cares about fodder? It looks like Ilem's ready to start the battle!" On cue, Ilem exhorts everyone when he orders his high guard, "Slay them, Kol!"

Dr. Q charges into the center of the Colosseum, flying in the battle against Kol. Sledge joins Dr. Q by charging at Kol from a different angle. Spectators thirsting for instant gratification scream, "Destroy them, Kol! Rip them apart! Fuck those Purists up!"

While seamlessly launching into his next attack against Kol, Sledge utters a short shout to power his move, "Kiai!" Although Sledge appears to have distracted the High Guard with his call to battle, Kol uses the blunt end of his weapon to knock Dr. Hamilton into Sledge. Bam! The collision forces Sledge to the ground. He drops his staff and returns to clutching his aching forehead again. The excruciating pain causes Sledge to bellow in his native tongue, *"Bumboclaat! Mi a guh dead!"*[6]

Despite his intense pain, Sledge gallantly searches the ground around him to find his staff. Spectators confirm they have no heart or taste for Sledge's survival, "Get him Kol while he's down. Kick the shit out of him!"

After several minutes of the fighters jousting back and forth, Jared notes for the Spectators' edification that "Today's battle caps fifty years of broadcasting the epic we've come to know as life on Earth." Pete replies, "Yes, since intercepting Earth's 'Cosmic Call' launched by the Yevpatoria RT-70 toward Gliese in '99,

---

[6] "Fuck. I'm going to die."

we've been given a front-row seat to human's disturbing but irresistible struggle." Spectators loudly express who they support in this clash, "Get 'em Kol!"

Unimpeded, Pete adds, "Inhabitants of planets in ever-expanding galaxies became even more horrified by the closer view of your misdeeds. Those ensnared by your destructive nature were swayed to replicate your distorted sense of importance as if they had shot the seductive drug called vanity into their veins. Two trillion galaxies, and you think Earth is the only one capable of sustaining life as you know it or one that has creatures with superior intelligence."

Jared, "A blind man and a geriatric against Kol. That is almost unfair." Pete asks, "To whom? The old guy still has skills!" Despite Jared and Pete's suggestion that Dr. Q and Sledge are valiantly fighting for their lives, Spectators, more concerned with their entertainment, chant, "Die! Die! Die!"

The combatants circle each other in the center of the Colosseum to gain an opening. Sledge runs forward with his staff extended in his hands. Pete translates the pending collision between Kol and Sledge if the latter's strike connects, "Fans, I want you not just to feel the excitement here today, but I also want you to visualize their twitching muscles while blood and sweat pour down these brave fighters' faces."

Jared cannot resist giving Kol his props, "You know how the mighty Kol has appeared in countless battles and the IFL football field. His fearful presence looms over this entire arena. Surely, the Galactic Council emissary leaves the Purists stricken with fear, or they are too dumb to realize their chances of survival are nil."

Pete retorts, "What fine specimen Dr. Q and Sledge have turned out to be. Earth symbols of hope and courage decorate Sledge's battered and bruised body. Too bad those are only billboards for squandered hope. Sledge's right wrist is tattooed with an Adinkra icon, *Nyame Ye Ohene*, and a scarred compass is tattooed on his left wrist. He is a specimen, fit, and a more gifted fighter than his handicap would suggest."

Dr. Hamilton circles behind Kol for another bare-knuckled attack.

Pete rhetorically asks, "Has anybody out there forgotten the early 2000s? The *Cancer Culture Wars* nearly destroyed human societies. Everyone tried to corrupt the others' truths, only to run for cover under the shadow of their bloated egos. For a blind man to Shawshank his way through that muck and mire to get this far is astonishing, no matter what distractors say."

While the battle continues, Jared throws in this observation, "Pete, we have a sold-out arena for Earth's Blood Bowl. Pay-per-view Tektite revenues are through the roof! The Vatrajan will double their investment!" Several feet below the excited sports commentators, Dr. Hamilton and Sledge converge on Kol for a tandem attack.

After that exchange ends, Jared briefly turns the crowd's attention to Gianna, watching the battle with laser intensity, ignoring the handful of Spectators around her who still seem enthralled by her presence. Jared, "And sponsors like the gorgeous socialite and entrepreneur Gianna Fornelli have graced us by being here!" Spectators respond, "Yeah!!!"

Pete, "Gianna's Be3D products have not only provided revenues for this event, but they have also captivated the fashion industry from the Floating City to exoplanets in the Sculptor Galaxy." The paparazzi race over to take more pictures of Gianna as if Pete had rung a dinner bell.

Jared adds, "She raked in 300 billion Tektite intergalactically as recently as 2046. She's a transhumanitarian, too. Trailers in the QD have modified her Be3D printers to make clothes, food, even furniture." Autonomous drone cameras zoom in to take more pictures of Gianna. Pete, "Thanks to Ms. Fornelli, Trailers may be the poorest creatures on the Floating City, but the Be3D devices let them live in 22nd-century style!"

Just as Pete's commentary concerning the rich and the poor concludes, cameras roam by a less affluent section of the Floating City with a sign on a wall with "QD" spray painted over the words "Quarantine District." The apartments in the QD are shadowed and made shabby by the second-hand quality of the stacked shipping containers converted into living quarters, compared to the other sections of the Floating City that sparkle with Vegas-style flare.

The condition of the QD is no different than what humans called the barrio, hood, or ghetto in the old world. When someone believes they live in a ghetto, that depressing home may be more than just a place. It also becomes a state of mind. Such is true of Trailers.

Both dubious realities exist in the QD. The Trailers here reside in tiny shipping container houses: 160 square feet. They squat in homes damaged while transporting goods or carrying dangerous chemicals. Modern appliances are difficult to impossible to install, and the structures are made of bent steel.

Just inside the wall that separates the QD from the rest of the citizens of the Floating City is another posting signaling to the Trailers that they are "ghetto" in the worst sense. In letters large enough to dominate a thirty x forty-foot wall, the sign declares, "No animal or Trailers beyond this point without authorization. The Sect will detain, question, and discipline all Trailers on sight."

Raggedy, first-generation models of the Terrafugia TF-X sputter into the QD. One of the viewers watching the battle in his small cube in the QD is a four-armed, middle-aged, bluish-gray-skinned alien called Gabba the Acquilite. Speaking to no one else in the room, Gabba stares out his window, catching sight of the barely functional TX-F, and sullenly mutters, "Old TF-X. Maybe we will get a new one someday."

Gabba stands in front of his holographic TV, holding a remote control that he uses to turn to Blood Bowl. He walks over to a coffee table in the living room to slide it to the side. By moving the table, Gabba reveals a hidden trap door from which his pregnant wife, Zetia, and his daughter, Belle, emerge. Their bodies and bones are all pliable like putty, allowing them to squeeze in and out of tight spaces. Unlike Gabba, Zetia and Belle have three legs and two arms.

The Acquilite reaches into his refrigerator to grab a container of live bugs. With the jar of bugs in his sticky hand, Gabba nestles on the couch between Zetia and Belle to share their planetary delicacy. Dr. Hamilton knocks Kol to the ground on the holographic screen from a barrage of devastating blows. Jared offers more observations about the ensuing fight when he raucously notes, "There's no quit in Q!"

Kol's answer to Dr. Q's attack is a series of uppercuts, lefts, and practiced defensive maneuvers. While Sledge staggers to return to his feet, Gabba remains glued to his screen, watching Kol dominate Dr. Hamilton in battle.

Suddenly, Sledge gathers all his strength to spring high into the air toward Kol and rapidly adjusts his body to attempt a killing blow. Sledge's sustained efforts disappoint Spectators, shouting, "Boo!" Gabba and others in the QD listen to Jared speaking through holographic screens beaming into the homes of transhumans living in skyscrapers that cast shadows on the stacked containers in the QD. Jared, "We have Ilem and the Galactic Council to thank for this gift today."

Jared showers Ilem with more praise, "What a contest. Where would we be if Ilem had not convinced the BRICs to give sanctuary to transhumans after the Garin massacres? For those asleep in another reality, after Garin emerged as the first fully functioning transhuman, the Transhumanism Movement was briefly threatened." Pete interrupts Jared to add, "… and Victor Garin soon after went on a murder spree at the U.N. and Times Square!"

For the first time, Ilem's throne rises from the arena floor and stops parallel to the broadcasting booth. Although Ilem seems only to be engaged in the fight below, he gradually allows his thoughts to reflect on the person he would someday call his son, Victor Garin. Ilem stews to himself as he turns his piercing gaze down on Dr. Hamilton, "Victor should have been in that pit demonstrating his prowess. Q, you will pay in blood what you owe for his loss. You shall pay in full today."

Jared and Pete are startled when Ilem's throne stops hovering directly in sight of them and within listening distance of their every breath. Pete calms his nerves long enough to find words to stroke Ilem's ego while not incurring wrath: "What's Ilem worth now, Jared, a trillion Tektite, an abundance of digital currency, and a cache of natural resources?" Sensing the tide for his independent streams of consciousness has turned, Jared joins Pete in complimenting Ilem in every way.

Jared, "That was a few years ago. He is richer than God now! And wealthy enough to buy transhumans anything we want. It was not just about money for him. Ilem united transhumans worldwide to save us from discrimination and annihilation."

Timely, Pete segues back to the action. "Victor Garin would have made a great High Guard, don't you think, Jared? No disrespect to Kol." To which Jared says, "We'll never know now that Victor was, let's say, prematurely subdued by the NYPD after his last killing spree in Times Square. Anyway, that's a story for another time."

Pete notes, "These noble warriors have waged battle against each other for forty minutes. But I think Kol is toying with Dr. Q and Sledge. Look at him standing in the center of the arena with both arms raised above his head to strike Sledge again. Blood is streaking down his metal legs and arms, which isn't his."

Jared comments, "One more point, Pete ... I gotta say it because it changed my life for the better ... Ilem's leadership freed us from the autocrats who refused our basic human right to live as long as science and medicine allow.[7] And his *iSiphon* freed our minds to dominate our oppressors. It is the smallest and most

---

[7] The physical separation of Luddites and Transhumanists reflected the philosophical demarcation of lucidity and lunacy. At the outset of the 21st Century, Dr. Q, and his cohorts, like Miller, found that "Scientists and their patrons ... do not wish to be seen hanging out with snake-oil vendors. ... A president who announces a war on cancer wins political points, but a president who publicly committed the government's resources to research on extending people's life span would be deemed certifiable." Richard Miller, Extending Life: Scientific Prospects and Political Obstacles, Milbank Q. 2002 Mar; 80(1): 155–174.

advanced supercomputer interface device ever made, and it's had the greatest impact on our lives."

Pete grasps Jared's chain of thought, "Miniature yottaflops at 10k a pop! By 2033, the *iSiphon* became the most coveted item among the wealthiest, most powerful, and most connected figures around the globe. Spectators who watched Earth's soap opera debated if the wealthy would increase their rule over the poor, but Ilem's *iSiphons* answered that question. He reached down from his terrace to offer instant evolution for everyone!"

While Pete and Jared applaud Ilem's efforts to rid the universe of humans back on the rogue planet, Caellum, more bettors fill the Harbor Bar as the slaughter on Earth appears to be near its end. Sledge's and Dr. Q's ability to withstand Kol's ruthless assault wanes every time Kol strikes them.

Accustomed to blood sport, the patrons of the Harbor Bar produce decks of cards as a sign inside the watering hole indicates a "Beggar's Lot Tournament" is afoot. A few suicidal bettors set up seats and tables outside the Harbor Bar to engage in the macabre card game. It is not enough that they have watched Sledge and Dr. Q's struggle for survival. Now they're willing to risk their own lives playing in a card game that knowingly could result in death.

Just when the Beggar's Lot Tournament is about to begin outside, a howling wind strengthens and erupts into a thunderstorm in only a few ticks of the clock. The gamblers who do not retreat inside run to their homes to take shelter. Sera walks down the steps to her home to gather more fruit for the day before the growing storm rattles the bar.

Sera knew, as did other residents of Caellum who had lived on the planet for millennia as she had, that the sudden hazard meant the Galactic Council was near Caellum and, more specifically, Mount Idan. To take all due precautions, Yam battens the window shutters and locks the front door.

A gigantic clay tornado churning and climbing one mile up the mountainside sucks in livid blue-gray clouds while all those inside the bar look on. The throat of the storm melds with the gusting tornado to engulf the tip of Mount Idan's peak. The plundering force strips away rock and hurls boulders and debris in every direction.

From the cataclysmic upheaval of the towering mountain, the residents of Caellum can see and feel the presence of some or all of the Galactic Council returning home. The massive tornado that encompasses the top of Mount Idan grows, booms, and quakes as more of the Galactic Council approaches. Inexplicably, a carpet of lavender clouds gently rests above the mountain despite the rough weather that rings its peak.

An Andromedan shouts to ask Yam a provocative question about Galactic Council lore, "Hear tale, if Diwan Pyron met them there, the whole mountain would crumble into the sea." Yam answers, "Sir, that may be true. But no one's ever told me they have seen them all in one place. They'd cause another bang since the one caused by …" Yam signals air quotes as he finishes his answer, "…no one has ever seen The All other than in the guise of whatever folks consider their god."

A sudden gust of wind blows out of the door to Yam's and Sera's residence inside the Harbor Bar as Sera returns to work. She walks into the barroom conversation as she is always in the middle. The jars of wine she carries clang against each other as she thumps them on the bar top.

Sera queries, "Why do you pester Yam about myths? Ask the Galactic Council to probe the secret of longevity and survival, of living through the jagged moments of a voyage that has taken you through cliffs of sharp emotions." Yam explains to the Andromedan, "Whether they are there or not, we live in fear for those around us. It is like we brought lawn chairs to rest in this valley, safe from uncertainty and despair, but we're only a second from calamity every day."

Sera adds, "Yam and I can offer youthful fancy and aged wisdom here. Caellum is a world of unrequited hope, but it remains untarnished by your realities or myths. Like any place, you must decide to live with the danger while searching for salvation."

Yam inconspicuously displays to his wife the ill effects of chronic lesions he has faced. Sera looks on, "I see more boils have opened. How do you feel?" Sounding miserable and exhausted, Yam tells her, "The innards of my being shift uncomfortably from sitting too long in the wrong position. But isn't that how it is? I have often stumbled about, looking for something useless and forlorn, forgotten until desperate moments like this when we need it the most: wisdom, the last bright bulb in the attic that is seldom realized is sometimes tapped into existence."

Sera gently clasps her soft hands upon Yam's face to say, "I am for Yam, as he is for me. Nothing can ever tear that apart, not even frailty."

A Haumean gambler, Tyson of Balt, staggers out of a booth to reach the bar for another drink. Tyson steadies himself on wobbly feet as he looks around the room for a new lady to annoy. His cyclopes eye scans from side to side, then sets on another unlucky female bettor who has traveled quite a distance to watch Blood Bowl undisturbed.

Tyson's physical appearance is not attractive to all his attempted conquests. His body looks like a swollen, roasted marshmallow, with tentacles for limbs and a single eye in the middle of what can be called his face. Despite his physical disadvantages, Tyson confidently rolls and thrusts his hips to imitate a lustful pumping motion when standing beside the pensive patron, Nabila, of the planet Sedna.

He hoists his fresh drink to his lips, then says to Nabila, "I know a dally I liked to tear into. If you're into more cushion for pushing, I'm your thing."

On Sedna, a Vegrandian Dwarf planet in the Sol Universe, there are only feminine planetarians. Despite her relative lack of experience dealing with masculine beings, Nabila decisively and firmly tells Tyson, "Sit your ass down, puff Daddy. Kol has those dirty, Earth bastards on the ropes."

Sensing that Tyson still has not gotten the point, Nabila slides her hand, tatted with the image of a skull, from her drink to her blade as a non-too-subtle gesture and cautions Tyson, "I recommend you roll your fat butt where it came from lest I snip your tip to show you why Sednians are called the 'Butchers of Oort.'"

The Harbor Bar's gamblers and bawdy customers turn to the viewing screen in near unison to return to the action at Blood Bowl. Ilem cheers with the crowd as Kol lands blow after blow against his opponents. The crowd hushes as Dr. Hamilton sweeps Kol's legs, knocking him off-balance and onto his back. To Ilem's surprise, Dr. Hamilton unexpectedly turns and leaps to attack Ilem on his floating throne instead of trying to slay Kol.

Without hesitation, Ilem travels at the speed of light to move away from his throne and hover above Dr. Q. As though it bathed in a gilded flame, Ilem's golden-colored skin begins to glow brighter and more intensely.

Ilem unleashes a blinding flash of energy at Dr. Q. as the Diwan of Light descends closer to his attacker. Zzzttttt. The flash of energy burns Dr. Q's entire body into a charred shell. Dr. Hamilton wails, "A-aaaa-aa!"

When life ends, there is a fleeting moment when all that was lost is regained in memory. After all, that's what you are: a memory.

Ilem pushes Dr. Q's burning body to the ground, then turns his attack on Sledge, standing in the center of the arena, waiting to defend himself. Sledge focuses intensely on Ilem speeding at him and, miraculously, can swing his staff at just the right second to strike Ilem across his face. Sledge, "Hyah!"

Ilem quickly lands several hard blows against Sledge, who responds with an anguished cry, "Argh …" The Diwan of Light knocks Sledge backwards from the attack, then continues striking Sledge with several blows that do critical damage. Sledge falls to his knees at Ilem's feet, bloodied and dazed. In response, Ilem mockingly looks down and says to Sledge, "Serendipity will have its day. My oath is fulfilled."

Sledge struggles mightily to push up from the ground to continue his valiant fight to live beyond today. He refuses to surrender despite his efforts being in vain. But when he holds up the Vision Staff to guard himself against Ilem's onslaught, Ilem laughs at Sledge's feeble defenses, then slams all his weight into the staff, breaking it in half and away from Sledge's trembling hands.

Kol seizes the weak and disoriented Sledge by his arms from behind and pushes his knee into Sledge's back to restrain him. Once docile, the executioner chops off locks of Sledge's lengthy dreads caked with grime, sweat, and blood.

Moments after the executioner activates a switch, the guillotine he summoned into the arena ignites with crackling energy, drifting closer to him. Like a lamb to slaughter, the executioner straps Sledge on his back on the guillotine as thousands of other Purists experienced to maximize their fear of the inevitable. For once in only a handful of times, Sledge is grateful he was born blind.

Ilem continues taunting Sledge more while strands of electricity wrench Sledge's hands and legs in place. The smirking celestial orchestrating Sledge's death confidently pronounces for the edification of the crowd, "Isn't it a shame he won't see the end of mankind's Anthropocene, the end of Hominis."

Black Heart joins in, exciting the audience as the executioner tightens straps constraining Sledge on the guillotine bed. A pillory of lights distends chaotically around Sledge's neck like nervous spirits rejoicing around flames as the widow takes the hand of another consort.

On the platform under Sledge's head lies a hinged metal and glass container entirely open like a Venus fly trap. The container, emanating a red glow, is positioned where an executioner would place a basket to catch a decapitated head.

Ilem shouts to the Spectators, "We could hang him to maximize your delight, but we have waited far too long for this fateful day. Humans will not pollute our clean air anymore. Fear them not. Shall we remove his head as a trophy?"

The executioner presents Sledge's bound, prostrate body to the masses for a ceremonial fete. All the while, Sledge remains awake, listening to busy vehicles race across a holographic sky that some computer engineer imagined enlivened tranquility. The hapless prisoner struggles to hear beyond Spectators clamoring for his death instead of the comforting sound of planes streaking through warm, quiet summer skies.

In the pit, the Alien Beast breaks loose from the grasp of the Trailers trying to restrain it. Spectators who notice this side action yell, "Pit! Pit! Pit! Pit!" The Alien Beast heads directly toward Dr. Hamilton's charred remains to devour them. Smoke and flames emanate from the Alien Beast's nose as its tail thrashes back and forth while it enjoys its meal. The two eyes above the Alien Beast's ears protect his periphery while his forward eyes focus on Dr. Q's crispy remains. Spectators whose lust feeds on corpses shout, "Crush him, Beast. Eat him whole!"

The crowd goes wild with glee as the Alien Beast devours Dr. Hamilton's remains. Spectators, "Hooray!" Unsatisfied, the Alien Beast lurks for more food.

Unable to constrain her overwhelming sense of loss, Sage exclaims, "Q, no!" The blood-thirsty Spectators hear Sage's anguished scream even above their chatter. They stare at her as they ponder why the fabulous Gianna Fornelli would care about a lowly Purist.

With every ounce of his remaining strength, Sledge struggles to break free of his chains. On Gabba's TV in the QD, the executioner raises the flickering guillotine blade to deliver a fatal blow to the neck of the last man of Earth. Gabba angles a digital pen on a tablet to inscribe a zero into the final column. At the top of the ledger is the number 9.8 billion crossed out with a long red slash.

Basking in the afterglow of his adoring fans and loyal slaves, Ilem continues to crow about his achievement. "Thirty years ago, those who sought to defy mortality became the scourge of society. Bioengineering lifted transhumans to become a meaningful, helpful part of our galaxy instead of a loathsome maggot consuming a gluttony of treasures. We are free of Purists today and for the rest of time."

Spectators encourage Ilem to continue preaching his gospel as they clap, cheer, and stomp in response to his diatribe. "Praise the Galactic Council. Praise Ilem," they chant.

Ilem continues his speech, "There will not be any Purists in the universe to torment your dreams. Today, the most hated and feared predator dies. Hail, transhumans!" The Spectators cheer on Ilem as they toss pink and white oleander flowers into the arena. Spectators call out, "Hail, transhumans! Transhumans rule!"

While pointing at Sledge with disdain, Ilem hovers over what is left of Dr. Q's cooked corpse as the Alien Beast chows down on a meaty thigh bone. Ilem, "Look at him. There are no supermen to save the day. The last man of Earth will yield his life with a whimper, not a bang." With those final words, Ilem signals the executioner to behead Sledge.

In the bowels of the afterlife, saints and the wicked believe they join in an exquisite ballet. For most, there is only death and decay and the reality that servants are you all.

Lord Ilem turns his thumb down! The angled blade of the guillotine propels down fourteen feet swiftly and decisively slices through Sledge's neck in a single, clean pass. As the executioner lobs off Sledge's head, Spectators hush enough for all to hear the sickening "thunk" and shearing sound.

Since the Cosmic Call, every being wanted the death of all humans to be a panacea for the growing cults of personalities contaminating other planets. Sledge's first death was just as Ilem suggested, a meager whisper muffled in the vastness of the universe.

Sledge's severed skull tumbles backward to the glowing container at the base of the guillotine's scaffold. Instead of falling in the vessel, it bounces and rolls feebly on the ground in front of Ilem, to the delight of the Spectators in the Colosseum and beyond. They cackle at the sight, and hardly any look away as they rejoice and taunt Sledge's passing, "Ha ha ha ha!" Ilem kicks Sledge's cleaved head back at the container so hard that Sledge's head might fly beyond the arena seats and out on the Floating City's congested thoroughfare.

Light years away, the gamblers in the Harbor Bar rejoice as well. Unbelievably, the Farfarout, Oba Voss, profited the most from his bet that the last man of Earth would be the blind guy - a fitting end to the existence of civilization too myopic to see the promise they held in their calloused hands. After winning his bet, none of the Spectators challenged Oba's right to the lion's share of the pot once they saw him butcher an alien gambler who foolishly judged the stature of this man sorely by his cover.

END OF CHAPTER 2

Chapter 3

Clean Hands

I pause to ask you this rhetoric.

Do you want to live forever,
trapped between the worlds of frivolity and reality?

Let me paint that canopy; not all dreams are meant to be.

Skin sags on hollow bones: body aches in fits; eyes blind.
Hair turns brittle like straw.

All your family and friends vanished and long gone.

You may someday wink at Dorian,
as you charm yourself in a mirror,
but you will share his curse.

Forever beautiful, eternally forlorn.

So many of you envision forever granting everlasting loveliness,
youth unconquered by Father Time.

Is that why you became susceptible to microwave gratification decades ago,
desperate to drink forever now,
like a prodigal child wanting riches and wine,
pilfered or earned?

The Harbor

At the foot of Mount Idan, Yam and Sera clean the Harbor Bar of the trash littered by disorderly patrons still buoyant from the sadistic entertainment they witnessed moments ago. A traveling astronomer Merlin, or Merle to his friends, ambles to the bar top to order another shot of hobo scotch that Sera mixes with special herbs refined by a local merchant, Raymonté of Caellum.

In their lush, alluring garden, Sera purposefully selected the plants for their color and fragrance, whether they were annuals or perennials, and whether they needed more sun or could survive alone in shadows. Before Sera wedded seeds to soil, she plucked her garden free of weeds and other plants that choke life or spread their roots where they do not belong. She enriched, tilled, and mulched the land to feed and protect her florid brood, not just today but also far into the future.

Sera's garden never rains, yet the flowers grow from water flowing south to north from the Virat Sea. The waters that flow up from the bay have a magical quality that feeds the ground even if it once had a desert set upon it. As hard as Yam works in his pub to hear the patrons' contrition, Sera works no less as diligently to nurture her plants and foliage to their full potential by planting in good soil and watering plants to quench them from wilt.

Sera removes dead, dying, and diseased vegetation from the grass and bans destructive insects, not bees. In the olden days, busy honeybees grouped in Sera's garden for the common cause of survival even in moments of loss or uncertainty, floating from thistle and thorn, gathering sweet nectar to soothe their hunger and unburden their souls.

Even now, a forlorn bee flies through the fertile richness of Sera's lawn, courting welcome pistils to rub down with streams of sticky pollen. The glee the bee leaves behind is a special gift to turn ordinary water into wine, to pour out if not for his lost hive, and then for other flowers to survive.

If only one flower were left struggling to grow strong and rise from the hole in what it knows as home, the single bee would float to the flower's side, waiting in breathless anticipation for a petal to hold out its hand. The bee will freely confess to the flower that he needs her, as she needs him. They will cuddle together, turning windswept seed into a burgeoning burst of life.

If only Earth's people knew of such devotion. If so, they, too, would realize they need each other to reach the sky and shirk off troubles that weigh on mighty wings and weaken crippled minds.

Merle raises the gaze of his orange eyes and stubby indigo-colored finger to attract either Sera's or Yam's attention. Slurring his words, Merle signals that he is not drunk enough to head home, "Bart ... bartender ... hit me with ... one more, one more hobo scotch. Me and my friend going to have a fun time tonight." Yam nods to acknowledge Merle's request, then grabs a glass to mix the Harbor's unique blend of herbs and fluids for another glass of hobo scotch. Yam tells his inebriated patron, "Merle, you know your friends all left. You have been raising your glass to your reflection for an hour."

Yam sits a chalice of foaming hobo scotch in front of Merle. Merle sips from the metal chalice and then stops long enough to engage Yam in more conversation. Merle, "Well, don't let me mutter on by myself, Yam. I'll go home soon. I need just one more drink for my sea legs. That, and a kind word."

Merle gestures to the window, noting, "Bad weather on the mountain, no? It may be too late for me to walk home, anyway. Can I sleep on your floor? Hick. I am just visiting here. I won't stay long. I want to chart more planets near Caellum before I return to my tour of the universe."

The wise bartender stops long enough to inform Merle that the Galactic Council must be there or on their way to Caellum. Yam, "You better stay. I will get you a blanket. Whenever the Galactic Council comes together, there is always a commotion. A few customers say it is surely death for anyone to be on the mountain when the Galactic Council gathers." Inquisitive, Merle asks, "Why's that?"

Before Yam walks over to Brahski to serve him more to drink, he answers Merle's inquiry, "I cannot say it to be true, but rumor says that they all can't be physically together, so they aren't up there. Direct physical contact may cause calamities across the galaxies. Maybe everyone would die."

The antennae dangling from Brahski's forehead crease backwards as he says to Yam, "Well before that happens, can we watch replays of those Earth aliens getting what they deserve? Place … 'Play it again, Sam! I'm thirsty!'" The four slumbering patrons awaken, one limb at a time, until they all rise to the edge of their seats to glue themselves again to view every blow suffered by the last man of Earth, and the enigmatic, Dr. Q.

Back on Earth, while replays play for waning crowds, Jared and Pete begin closing the show with their final comments. Jared speaks first, "Jared Steam and Pete Bogs here for your post-battle recap. There is no denying that this day has been and will always be monumental. What happened here today …"

Pete exclaims, "Oh shit, am I seeing who I think I am seeing? Fucking Negearian horde!" Jared grabs a handful of crumbled notes and screams to Pete while ducking for cover behind the broadcasting table, "Grab your shit, Pete, this show is over and out!"

The remaining crowd scatters as five Negearian assassins unexpectedly leap from the arena seats and charge toward Ilem. They are the last survivors of the planet Negearia in the Lyra Constellation. More than a century ago, Ilem destroyed Negearia and, in recent years, charged Kol with extinguishing all Negearians anywhere they might be hiding.

The Negearians' tell-tale long-twisted braids make them instantly recognizable. Aside from their unique ethnic hairstyles and marble skin, Negearians are best known for being daring and aggressive warriors, and they display the basis for their reputation as they valiantly advance toward Ilem.

Three Negearians open fire at Ilem with their laser rifles and futuristic Magnum handguns. Spectators near the sudden violence shout, "Run! It's the Negearians!" Three Negearians shoot multiple rounds of bullets and laser blasts at Ilem. Bam bam, bzzzzzzt! The other two Negearians courageously continue their charge toward the Master of Light. Ilem discharges light daggers from his golden hands at each of the Negearians to disintegrate the laser beams shot at him. Bzzzzzt!

Ilem points at the dead Negearians as he gets in Kol's face to chastise him for his shabby performance during Blood Bowl and for failing to annihilate all of the rogue Negearians. Ilem shouts, "Damn you, Kol, what was the khopesh for, wagging your shrunken cock? And to top off your insolence, you were supposed to detect intruders like the Negearians to stop them from entering the Colosseum."

Kol lowers his head and sheepishly answers Ilem's tirade, "I'm sorry for my failure, my Lord." Ilem stiffens up and turns to Kol to show him the light energy brewing in his eyes. Testily, Ilem promises, "I will deal with this and you later!"

Lord Ilem retrieves the silver and gold helmet from his throne and orders Kol, "Clear these slugs out! And secure that severed head to halt its somatic death. It will make a fine offering to the Galactic Council."

Kol yells to his troops, "Do what this man, ah ..." Kol mistakenly refers to Ilem in a lesser way than his majesty demands. Ilem's glare is reserved for those he does not see or treat as more than disposable fodder for his schemes. He turns his threatening gaze back at Kol with contempt. Raw energy crackles around Ilem's fist as he contemplates blasting Kol with a light bolt for his insolence. Kol tries not to noticeably gulp as he retreats, "I mean, Lord Ilem."

Ilem walks out of the Colosseum with his helmet under his arm and Kol's entourage trailing behind him. Kol orders Dr. Eli Monroe, a bespeckled transhuman dressed in a lab coat, to preserve Sledge's head for Ilem to present to the Galactic Council as tribute. Kol, "You, doctor! Get your equipment. Preserve that head for Lord Ilem."

The upper portion of Dr. Eli's body looks human, but the lower part is mechanical. Dr. Eli pompously counters Kol's orders by suggesting, "That's Dr. Eli. Uh, in my human life, I was Dr. Eli Monroe." More boldly, Dr. Eli states to Kol, "I still ask for that accommodation to distinguish me from the Luddites who have rejected the benefits of medical technology and, thus, my years of work."

As assertively as Ilem intimidated him, Kol snaps back at Dr. Eli for his insolence and failure to recognize the hierarchy in Ilem's new utopia, "What did you say? Introductions are unnecessary, Dr. Tin Can. I only need your name if you fuck this up!" The Alien Beast lets go of a well-timed "Burp!"

The Trailers who brought the Alien Beast into the Colosseum try to pull the feral monster out of the building and away from what little remains of Dr. Q. The creature snorts flames while swinging its mighty tail from side to side, like a dog that has just filled its belly with crispy bone and buttery marrow.

Dr. Eli bends at the waist to prepare Sledge's head for preservation in the glowing container. Kol reminds Dr. Eli of the consequences of failure, "This strange Alien Beast will still be hungry later on. You better scurry, Doctor." Dr. Eli continues moving as far away from Kol as possible, "Gulp! I understand, High Guard!"

Sage watches Dr. Eli meticulously slide Sledge's head inside the glowing container. The glow from the container turns green when Dr. Eli shuts it.

Two humanoid drones dressed in custodial clothes shovel the rest of Dr. Q's and Sledge's bodies into a large bin marked with a biohazard sign. As the shoveling nears completion, one of the drones carelessly tosses Sledge's staff and broken sunglasses into the container as well. Dr. Eli completes the process to preserve Sledge's head, then calls out to the drones, "Incinerate that waste. No need to contaminate the Floating City with such filth." On command, the humanoid drones wheel the biohazard bin down the exit to the arena.

Still resembling Gianna Fornelli, Sage calls, and waves to Dr. Eli to entice him to join her in the VIP seating area. Gianna, "Doctor!" Gianna waves toward

Eli while trying to use her power over kinetic empathetic energy to connect with whatever human feelings and emotions still reside inside Eli's metal frame and clocklike heart.

Dr. Eli's upper torso whirls around while his feet stay planted on the ground in their opposite direction. Rrrrrrr. With the scrutinizing eyes of a skilled surgeon, Dr. Eli briefly scans Gianna up and down, then expresses his dislike for what he sees, "I don't have time to waste on trans like you, an overripe tart. Find a guard if you need to scratch an itch."

A throng of satisfied Spectators leaving the Colosseum walks far in the background behind Sage. Using their lively celebration as cover, she drifts into the shadows to clandestinely creep in the same direction as Dr. Eli and the custodial drones. Sage needs to catch up on Dr. Eli when the physician enters his office occupied by his assistants. She briefly abandons her pursuit of him to follow the humanoid drones to find out what they are doing with her father's remains.

After passing through a series of hallways and tunnels, the humanoid drones enter a room where transhumans undergo physical enhancements like cars in a ghoulish assembly line. By peeking through the door, Sage notices that there are holding cells containing dozens of aliens she knows are collectively called the Outcasts – creatures from planets that the Galactic Council conquered. Transhumans who revolted against Ilem by chopping off their ears to disconnect from the influence of *iSiphons* also share the small cells with their fellow captives.

A female transhuman medical tech inside the surgical room notices movement in the hallway and calls for a guard to investigate. The transhuman medical tech asks the guard, "Hey, is someone else in the hall?" The Guard responds, "I'll check." Creeeak.

The Guard sticks his head out of the room to look up and down the hallway for what caused the noise that the med tech thought she heard. By the time the guard checks to see who is in the hall, Sage has already vanished.

Unseen by anyone in the assembly room, Sage's essence absorbs back into the infinity orb. Moments before the guard checks for the source of the hallway noise, the globe rises and propels itself down an air vent near the entry to the assembly room. Although Sage's orb easily streaks through the narrow chute, it stops hovering over an incineration room where various foreign and domestic body parts are strewn on blood-drenched gurneys. Sect force captives to shovel the dismembered limbs and other body parts of deceased prisoners and loved ones into the gory melting pot.

The drones who swept up Dr. Q's remains and Sledge's body are already loading everything into an incinerator. Crackle. Sage wills the infinity orb to continue to the next phase in her mission. However, she is devastated that she could not rescue her father before Ilem killed him or even preserve the parts of his body that she needs to advance the Doomsday Protocol.

The infinity orb drops from the air vent, then quietly travels close to the floor to avoid detection. With the metal cover from an open ceiling vent dangling above her head, Sage reforms her body into a tangible, physical presence. Surreptitiously, Sage peers around the hallway corner as Dr. Eli nears the Floating City's infirmary.

Less than one hundred feet from the infirmary, Sage senses the presence of two transhumans. Red and yellow light travel from the guards' bodies into the palm of Sage's outstretched hand. Gradually, Sage morphs her appearance to that of a female transhuman of African descent who is visibly pregnant and struggling to walk toward the guards.

She sets her sights on the two male transhuman guards blocking entry to the infirmary, then contorts her body to mimic the gait of her false persona. She cups her swollen stomach with one hand and frantically waves the other toward the guards to alert them of her maternal distress, "Aww oh! Please help me!" Compassionately, the guards approach her as a larger stream of kinetic energy flows from their bodies to Sage's waiting hand.

The trap is set.

END OF CHAPTER 3

Chapter 4

Eclipse

I searched for the wrong word.
My eyes are new and strain beyond unexpected brightness
like a stargazer peering about constellations.
And there I find you, an eclipse of the past
clearing my vision, blinding my doubts.

A new rapture approaches.
A new kingdom beckons,
and I need only the strength to traverse the sky,
not strain to touch it,
unfettered from reaching for the possibility
that we are new every day
and our world can be an Eden once more.

Labors

Like the labor pains that appear to the guards to be causing Sage to feel unrelenting pain, Yam and Sera comment on the full-blown storm tightening and constricting its grip around Mount Idan. Most Harbor Bar patrons have already left the establishment to seek cover.

Sera tells her husband, "This has been quite a day, right Yam." Yam arches his back to stretch away his aches, then slumps into a chair close to his wife. Yam, "I am getting too old for this, you know. Good thing Blood Bowl does not happen every day."

Yam uses his exceptionally long arms to push himself out of his seat to look out a window at the hurricane brewing into a swirling tornado on top of Mount Idan. Peeking out the bar door, Yam reports to Sera, "They must be incredibly close for the storm to be so bad." Sera responds to Yam, "It is about time for us to settle in any way, Yam. Come back to avoid something hitting you."

Inside the tornado whipping up Yam and Sera's fears, six cosmic chambers separate the awful hurricane from its destructive eye. Unlike the swirling winds that form the cyclone, the inside chambers are quiet and still.

Within one of the cosmic chambers, Ilem sits majestically at the head of a long conference room table in an antechamber to his sleeping quarters. His helmet of silver and gold lies on the table in front of him.

Along the wall of Ilem's conference room are five headless mannequins. One mannequin does not have any clothing or other material on it. The other mannequins display four full-body exoskins, each one different. One is a formidable, steel blue battle armor, sleeker and more form-fitting than the others. An image of a sun is emblazoned in the center chest area of the battle armor. The second exoskin looks like a royal blue business suit with a gold-colored tie. The third exoskin resembles stately clothes a king would wear on his day off. The final exoskin is the fanciest one in the room. It is royal blue and golden yellow, with a long golden yellow cape with another image of a blazing sun on it.

Inside the cosmic chamber reserved for Naihal, the Diwan of Darkness, is visible lounging in the bay window of her Queen Anne mansion in New Orleans. Accompanying the imperial gown that flatters her comely figure, Naihal is wearing long black gloves that cover her Vantablack skin from her hands to her sharp elbows.

Within her cosmic chamber, Onom, the Diwan of Sound, sits alone in an oversized wooden chair that resembles something a land baron would lounge in while enjoying the fealty of her subjects. She appears to be a white, humanoid female whose stunning and comely beauty belies her lethal sway over ethereal echoes and enchanted melodies.

Someone who used a thick cord for the job has crudely sewn her mouth shut. Nonetheless, Onom attempts to drink ale from a decanter, allowing much of the liquid to trickle from her mouth and down her chin. Her feet rest on the limp and bloodied bodies of two aliens she recently slayed by exploiting her command over cryptic vibrations.

Neither Pyron, the Diwan of Death, nor her father, Hyle, the Diwan of Matter, are on the mountaintop in their respective cosmic chambers.

The Diwan of Time, Horol, appears to be a studious, middle-aged Asian monk sitting at a glass desk in his library with rows and rows of books. He waves his mighty hand to reassemble the pocket watch on his desk telekinetically, then calls the meeting to order. Horol, "It is time to gather. We cannot wait any longer for Hyle and Pyron. I can foretell he is on his way, but she is still nowhere to be found."

Together, the members of the Galactic Council chant, "In the presence of The All; the far, wide, and deep; ever-present, and multiplied, we kneel before you, in unity as one."

A few minutes after commenting on the weather and a sundry of other things consuming the Galactic Council's attention, Horol pointedly states to Ilem, "Ilem, it's unprecedented to take so long to subdue such a primitive race," to which Ilem defensively returns, "Please consider there were nearly ten billion of them."

In a coarse tone of voice, Onom strains to omit audible words from her muffled mouth, "Genocide is a necessary cleansing on most planets to control population growth and to divest the universe of undisciplined societies. By my count, however, there are still too many transhumans to consider humans extinct. They would have killed themselves without your *iSiphon* and medical miracles to keep them alive."

Ilem explains, "The soaring urban population posed serious problems for many cities' environment, health, and infrastructure. I birthed transhumans to quicken our depletion of Earth's remaining resources and to increase our fighting forces. You all should be satisfied."

An eye opens on Horol's palm. Naihal stubbornly rejoins the discussion, "At their core, transhumans are parasitic and perfidious creatures because they originated as humans, but Ilem's ability to control their destructive tendencies has made them a zombified legion of killers." Onom contends in her hushed voice, "If you feel that way, Naihal, why coddle your brother's desires?"

The Diwan of Sound stands up and defiantly walks toward the barrier that separates her from the other members of the Galactic Council. She tries to gulp ale from her decanter while she digests the contentious conversation, but due to the cord sewn across her mouth, a good amount of her ale flows down her chin and upper chest. Her comments, nonetheless, stay on the tip of her tongue.

Onom, "How will allowing transhumans to roam the galaxy help anyone but you?" Ilem defensively retorts, "I have secured Earth's remaining resources as a boon to the galaxy, my dear cousin, including human prodigy sired through biomedical engineering."

Ale flops out of Onom's decanter as she walks back to her chair, satisfied that her voice can still wreak havoc even in a wounded state. Ilem fumes to himself as he resists reacting to Onom's accusations. Naihal leans back in her chair, pissed that Onom is always intrusive and argumentative.

To stoke more controversy and division, Onom prods Ilem by asking, "And the woman that turned your head around ... Pu Kwon wasn't it ... what of her fate?" Ilem coyly answers, "You turn an old page. That woman I knew perished decades ago. She was a simple pleasure to satisfy human flesh."

Onom eases back into her chair with her chalice lifted in her cold hand. She closes her eyes, touches her ears with her fingertips, and says, "The steady beat of your precious human heart tells me you're not lying; Pu Kwon is dead and no longer a distraction to you."

Naihal interrupts the discussion to interject her concerns. Naihal, "Enough. My brother completed his mission and commands the minds of millions of transhumans. I am more troubled by Hyle's attempts to force Pyron on this Council than debating the timeliness of Ilem's success." Onom says, responding to Naihal and all the others, "The pages of the story that trouble you concerning Hyle and Pyron are sepia now, as well. Move on."

Naihal's and Onom's contorted, angry faces display that there is an apparent reason they should be in separate cosmic chambers. Naihal, "Pyron shouldn't have a place on this Council, but she and Hyle are so powerful that you all relented to his demands." Onom mockingly states, "I disagree. Death has always had a master. Hyle merely transferred his power to an intermediary that he demands to be called his child."

To interrupt the debate, Horol lets the reassembled timepiece shatter on the table and break into tiny pieces. Horol interjects, "Onom is right. The delicate balance that The All entrusted to us is intact. To sustain that balance, Hyle surrendered his power to manipulate environmental elements - terra, water, fire, air, and space." Naihal answers, "Transhumans are an extension of Ilem's will and an asset to serve this Council. My point is that should not be ignored."

Ilem rises from his chair to grandstand as if he is accepting an award. Naihal intently listens to her brother, say "Thank you, sister. My ... Our army of transhumans has already made our order more powerful. Kol, the High Guard of our deadly and well-trained Elite Squadron, has retained the viciousness that marked his professional football career in the NFL and Intergalactic Football League."

To further list Kol's value, Ilem informs the other members of the Galactic Council, "Kol has taught our forces the effectiveness of his trademark bullrushes. In the IFL, he was well-known for simultaneously taking on two or three offensive linemen, and still, they could not stop him from destroying hapless quarterbacks. In the 2027 IFL Championship, Kol dumped the quarterback on his head thirteen times, a record for such sporting events." Onom sarcastically comes back, "Great, he was good at sports. What makes him the right one to lead an army?"

Ignoring Onom's interruption, Ilem continues praising his High Guard. "Humans subconsciously accepted contemporary football players in the same way Romans and Greeks honored ancient gladiators. A disproportionate number of the male population gathered around their viewing devices every Sunday like clockwork as football was a religious experience and wearing team colors made fans a homogenous tribe."

Ilem continues his sales pitch to convince the rest of the Galactic Council that he has dutifully completed his charge. "I did not invent the performance-enhancing body bots that propelled the expansion of the NFL to the IFL. Before meeting him, those drugs increased Kol's strength tenfold. Since then, AVI has been instrumental in advancing that technology. By transforming the IFL commissioner into the best transhuman businessperson money can buy, the successful outcome of this conquest became clear. AVI took control of the game and all its players. Now, many fill the ranks of our Elite Squadron subject to Kol's training."

The celestial who holds himself out as the third child of The All continues to state his argument to the rest of his brethren, "And the population of transhumans and other sentients aboard the Floating City know his reputation. Kol was famous for his ferocity on the football field. How he inflicted pain on other players reflected his contempt for them."

Horol notes, "But he was an addict, correct? Didn't that nearly kill him?" Onom, opportunistically chimes in, "Didn't his limbs rot from the effects of the performance-enhancing body bots that he abused."

Ilem concedes for Onom's benefit, "To be true, I must admit that Kol was addicted to body bots, BBs on the Black Market. After scores of social media outlets around the globe exposed Kol's doping, the scandal ruined his career. Twenty-two years ago, they wrote him off, declaring him a sham. Although age and pain slowed him, the BBs gave him a short-term edge. The downside of abusing those performance enhancers cost him three limps and his dignity."

"It was around that time that Kol underwent surgery to amputate his legs and an arm. That saved his life but left him an empty shell of himself compared to the punishing bruiser he was in the past. I used Hyle's sentient metal to give Kol new enhancements, making Kol's power ours to control."

Miles from the Harbor Bar and the Virat Sea, an ethereal holographic projection of Hyle suddenly materializes on Caellum. When his specter reaches the edge of Mount Idan, his power is so great that even his shadow can damage the foot of the towering mountain.

Hyle had not returned to this home since the fateful day he tried to knock down the mighty mountain when he heard his daughter's voice echo from inside. Her cries for help faded with each blow he struck until the sound in the mountain silenced, and an echo waved from far away. Thankfully for Caellum's residents, Mount Idan regenerates itself, and Hyle's search led him elsewhere, saving them from a calamitous avalanche.

Unfortunately for the rest of the universe, Hyle's unsuccessful quest for Pyron caused him to punish all those who stood in his way. Thousands fell when Hyle did not get the answers he wanted or the release of his daughter, Pyron.

From Hyle's size compared to the mountain, it is evident that he is a colossal being, measuring at least fifty feet tall and sporting a width greater than ten elephants pressed together. Hyle solidifies from a mere specter into a giant golem made of soil, rocks, and chunks of other materials.

After scaling three miles of the mountain in sheer minutes, Hyle lurches through the mystic barrier separating the cosmic chambers. Even piercing the tornado's eye causes the protective forcefield partitioning the cosmic rooms to buckle and shake. Thunder, lightning, and rippling earthquakes erupt in response to Hyle's movements.

The intimidating Diwan of Matter commands, "Silence, Ilem. I have listened to you crow long enough." Ilem placates Hyle's anger with a warm greeting, "Hyle, I am glad to see you, brother. I was not sure you would be present." Hyle's monstrous body looms in the eye of the storm. Hyle, "We are all connected in spirit, Ilem, even if far apart. I have tracked events on Earth, even while searching for Pyron. Nothing you accomplished would have been possible without my sentient metal."

Ilem concurs, "And I recognize that, Hyle. Much of what I have accomplished is owed to all of you. Our conquest of Earth would have been delayed more without Hyle's infusion of his essence with the vein of sentient metal he found on Virion. That infusion enhanced sentient metal to transform and elevate itself based on the thoughts of whoever controls it. This helmet you gave me, Hyle, allows me to do that, and I am eternally grateful for it."

Ilem gazes at his reflection in the helmet resting on the conference room table. Horol, Onom, and Naihal try to stay out of the conversation brewing between the masters of light and matter. Ilem holds up his hand like a yellow and black yield sign to stay Hyle's reaction and anger.

Ilem offers, "I have a rare conservancy from this quest. The head of the one called the last man of Earth. Please share it with Pyron when you find her. Imagine what you can do with it, Hyle. You can create a better version of humans or a whole new organism."

The Diwan of Matter stomps his foot into the mountaintop, causing a sudden avalanche of boulders and tera to tumble into the valley. Bam. The girth of the tornado continues to expand as it merges with the raging storm, thereby making the impending ruin even more lethal and out of control. Down in the valley, Yam and Sera board up the front of the Harbor Bar to prevent flying objects from battering the doors like an unwanted patron demanding one last beer.

Hyle acknowledges, "That is a valuable prize, which had best be soon." Ilem answers Hyle, "Your gifts are not wasted. Soon, I will shed this frail coil and ascend to the last exoskin you made for me." Momentarily satisfied, Hyle proceeds into the cosmic chamber reserved for him.

Ilem walks to the royal blue and yellow exoskin to admire its quality. The rest of the Galactic Council watch him from their cosmic chambers.

Horol, "Hyle's gifts and loyalty to our order have never waned. Save for Hyle and Pyron, we all wear sentient exoskins now to contain our natural essence. His finest work. Our exoskins permit us to adjust our essence to appear anatomically like any species' form, and you choose humans." Ilem tells Horol, "Wearing this sentient armor and clothing is a simple matter of control. Transhumans adore me as I appear. Upon leaving Earth, I will ascend to Caellum to retake my true form."

Onom picks her nails with the end of her weapon's blade, "Of all the civilizations you've infiltrated, it's surprising that you seem so fond of the human frame." Hyle stomps his foot into the mountain again, causing more sizable portions of it to crumble to the ground. Slam! Hyle shouts, "Enough of this banter. You peck at the carcass of a dead race while my daughter is lost to me."

An AI voice beaming into Ilem's quarters announces that a drone messenger is waiting outside the door to speak with him. The synthesized voice announcing the messenger states, "Message for you, Lord Ilem," which Ilem acknowledges by blessing the drone to "Enter."

The drone messenger enters the room and begins to deliver his message to Lord Ilem. Messenger, "I have a mess …" But cannot finish before Horol stands from his table to cast a freeze-time spell that causes the drone messenger to pause its motion. With the spell's casting, a third eye appears on Horol's forehead.

Horol, "The Declaration of Execution and Warrant against humans was issued not only for their many genocides, but out of caution that they would infect other planets with whatever caused humans to be divisive, self-righteous, and self-destructive. If they came together even as a violent race, at least they would find some commonality in purpose." Onom concludes, "It matters not whether men or females lead them. The outcome would be the same."

Hyle's tense face again fills the eye of the storm as he leans forward to emphasize his impatience with the rest of the Galactic Council and his frustration over not knowing what has happened to his precious daughter. Hyle tells them, "Pyron is my concern now. I shall find out who has taken her. Whoever that is will suffer as fire will rain from the heavens on their heads."

The master of time casts a spell to create a galaxy globe in his left hand as he tries to calm an angry and frustrated Hyle. Horol, "Pyron's fate is a mystery even to someone who can read time like me. It is as if she does not exist anymore, but we know that cannot be true. We each would feel her loss. Let me finish listing Earth's offenses for the warrant before we continue speaking about Pyron. There are many atrocities to confirm. This is the decree that we issued:"

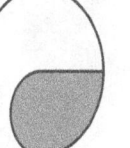

Declaration & Warrant of Extermination
Findings of Facts

Earthlings have become the most vile, self-destructive, heinous, and feared creatures inhabiting the galaxies. Their numerous acts of genocide have been the bane of their existence, albeit the planet's population would have exceeded its capacity eons ago. Samples of their atrocities against one another include,

- The Transatlantic Slave Trade (Sixty million Africans died while enslaved)
- The Trail of Tears (4,000 Cherokee killed, thousands more robbed of their ancestral homes)
- The Holocaust (Six million Jews killed, and millions more of other diverse populations murdered by Axis regimes)
- The Bangladesh Genocide (Three million Bengalis butchered, 200,000 women raped)
- The Darfur Genocide (500,000 ethnic Darfuri killed)
- The Rwandan Genocide (800,000 Tutsi systematically murdered)
- The Armenian Genocide (One million Armenians died)
- The Circassian Genocide (methodical mass murder, ethnic cleansing of One million Circassians)
- The Khmer Rouge "Killing Fields" (Three million Cambodians killed)
- The Holodomor (Seventy million Ukrainians annihilated)
- The Great Leap Forward (Thirty million people, mainly Chinese, were murdered)
- The Mongol Invasions and Conquests (Thirty million Eurasians slaughtered)
- The Collective Inquisitions (Sixty million Non-Catholic Christians wiped from the face of the Earth).

Behold, this is just a sample of humankind's depravity. As Horol, Diwan of Time foretold, the pending use of atomic weapons on August 6, 1945, at 8:05 a.m., is a bridge too far. Another 226,000 Japanese will die, not counting the millions of Allied and Axis forces who will perish or suffer through decades of physical and psychological pain.

Declaration & Warrant of Extermination Proclamation

These creatures have brazenly and foolishly abused their motherland and its fragile ecosystem for centuries. They have destroyed the biodiversity of their planet, ignoring all signs that should have alerted them to the deadly consequences of environmental tragedies. They will achieve limited space travel within the coming decades but will soon endeavor to explore space beyond their solar system. Humans are a disease that must not be allowed to spread.

Their trusted rulers have used psychological, economic, and cultural warfare for centuries to suppress and oppress the weak, infirm, powerless, and poor. The ripple from this conduct has dominated human discourse from the moment they slithered from the sea. The Institution of Slavery, McCarthyism, the 21st Century Cancer Culture Wars, and many "isms" are too voluminous to count. Each mars the promise of human existence.

Thus, and therefore, this Earth year, January 1, 1900, A.D. midnight, the Galactic Council - as wardens of the universe in trust from and stead for The All - issue this Warrant for the extermination of all human inhabitants on and beyond Earth – every man, woman, and child. This Warrant shall be executed by Ilem, Diwan of Light. Said Diwan must reside on Earth until this service is rendered to the Galactic Council for the salvation of all known and unknown galaxies.

Praise The All's Mighty Hands

Interrupting Horol's recitation of human crimes against humanity, Hyle declares, "How do I know it wasn't one of you?" The threatening sound of Hyle's voice whips the storm around Mount Idan into greater fury.

Yam and Sera retreat into the interior rooms of the Harbor Bar for safety as the wind and rain conspire to leave peaceful gardens disrupted by the wind's cruel voice and burning tears.

Ilem, "Brother, we would never ..."

Hyle interrupts Ilem, "Never what? I know you, Ilem. Light seeks light, drawn to its reflection." Onom begins casting a sound spell as Ilem collapses back into his chair. The rest of the Council listens intently. Ilem, "Brother, I am at the cusp of filling my mission here. I ... we have conquered again." Onom snickers, "We? That word sticks in your craw like a fish bone, Ilem. Should I help you pluck it out with the bread called appreciation!"

Horol points at a location on the galaxy globe to draw everyone's attention. Horol, "Stop fighting! Hyle, I stopped searching for Pyron near the KIC 8462852 star. Resume your search there."

Watchful eyes appear on the back of Horol's hands as he releases the drone messenger from the freeze-time spell. The drone messenger continued what it said midsentence before Horol stopped time, "...note for you!" Ilem reads the note, then exclaims, "Damn you, why hasn't Dr. Eli secured the head yet?" The messenger informs him, "He went to the infirmary to prepare it for travel."

Ilem leans menacingly closer to the drone messenger. A ball of energy grows around Ilem's sizzling hand, burning the note. In a tone of intimidation, Ilem commands the messenger, "Make it your life's mission to see that Eli hurries." With that, the drone messenger retreats out of the room in a panic. Hurriedly he says to Ilem, "I'll find Dr. Eli, find him right now!"

The rest of the Galactic Council prepare to leave the meeting as the barrier between them flickers and snaps. Hyle turns away from the top of Mount Idan, looking far into the sky at his next objective. He leaps from the mountain, landing miles away with an intense impact that quakes across Caellum.

Onom wipes the blood off the blade of her kusarigama. The chain of her weapon remains wrapped around the throat of one of her victims. Onom, "Will this take another one hundred years, brother?"

Ilem chokes back his contempt, "Absolutely not. Even Horol can attest that we are each prisoner and master of time. Within mere seconds for us and perhaps months for humans, I and our legion of transhumans will join the Galactic Council's Armata on Caellum."

The Diwan of Sound points at the faint reminder of the scar on Ilem's face from Sledge's last attack, "Clearly, it will not happen soon enough. The frailty of your human existence is visible even on your pretty face." Ilem resigns that the verbal battle might continue without a measure of contrition, "Your compliments drip with contempt, Onom. Nevertheless, I will ascend from this world to continue serving the Council, just as I have done for eons."

Horol moves to a part of his spacecraft that grants a long, panoramic view of revolving worlds. He looks out at the galaxy surveying the birth of stars and moons that occurred eons ago and those yet to come.

Eyes open on the back of his head as he turns through solar maps to finger through past events leading to Pyron's disappearance. Horol paces around a podium near the panoramic window, "Ilem, we will meet on Caellum, but please remember to scrape your heel at the door. We do not need our entryway soiled by the rotting corpses of humans. Then, in the name of The All, we will decide which corrupt civilization we should eliminate next. For now, this meeting is adjourned."

In unison, the members of the Galactic Council, still at the meeting, respond, "Praise The All, ever-present and multiplied." Ilem hesitates but manages to utter the words, too.

Naihal remains seated in her chamber while Horol stands near the edge of his cosmic chamber. Horol crosses his arms, and several eyes appear on his forearms. Naihal tells those still in attendance, "I have more questions for you, brother. Do you mind if I stay, Horol?" Horol replies, "No, but I need your help to find Pyron. His wrath will only grow if Hyle does not locate her soon." After raising those cautious observations, Horol's essence dissipates, and his cosmic chamber closes as he exits the meeting.

Ilem holds his hand rigidly to stop Naihal from speaking until Onom leaves the room. Ilem, "Let us make sure we are alone. You may be the Mistress of Darkness, but deception is a close cousin of the shadows." Naihal concurs, "Yes, stark truths are better left in the dark."

Since they came into existence, Naihal and Ilem have always existed as yin and yang. Albeit darkness is more often associated with weakness and misdeed, white is equally related to ruthless duplicity. Together, they are a formidable force, consuming everything in sight, wreaking havoc wherever they roam, and willingly dividing those around them into rivals.

Naihal asks Ilem, "Do you think they suspect we've kept souvenirs from the Galactic Council's recent conquests?" He responds, "You mean Pu Kwon and your situation in New Orleans?" Naihal replies, "Horol would have detected Pu Kwon in your sleeping quarters without my shroud spell." Ilem acknowledges that measure of deception, "That I know, Naihal. And in exchange, our *quid pro quo* has preserved your throuple and my betrothed."

Naihal removes one glove once inside her mansion to cast a black hole spell that opens a portal between her and Ilem's respective locations. Small horns grow and protrude from the top of Naihal's head as she conjures her magic.

Naihal, "Come closer, brother. We should stay wary of Onom's prying ears. From the shadows, from the deep, reveal the passage that I seek." With that, Naihal's black hole spell opens a portal between her mansion and Ilem's conference room.

Music is already playing inside the room where Naihal is standing when Ilem walks through the portal into Naihal's mansion in New Orleans. Ilem, "Please turn down your music. That incessant sound is deafening." ♫ ♫ ♫ ♫ After turning down the music that slipped into the room, Ilem and Naihal stand together, looking out the window of her Queen Anne mansion, with a forcefield between them, to avoid a calamitous explosion.

Despite the protective barrier, light and dark energy sparks crackle and leap between them. A storm begins to brew over the Mississippi River only a few miles from where these Galactic Council members stand perilously close to one another.

Ilem continues, "Bartering human will for immortality made it easy to divide and conquer their race." 🎵 🎵 🎵 🎵 Naihal comments, "The rich paid to become superhuman transhumans, and the poor mindless slaves." Ilem chuckles, then says, "Harsh sister. Even the cheapest *iSiphon* is the result of apex paradise engineering. As always, they get what they pay for."

Ilem selects a knife to cut a piece of fruit from Naihal's home to chomp. To emphasize each word he speaks, he chops the liberty apple in pieces and tells her, "Now, we only need to keep our end game secret until we gather our army to crush what remains of the Council." Ilem offers Naihal half of the apple along with the knife.

While slicing the apple into smaller pieces, Naihal answers, "Brother, your secrets will remain in darkness." Ilem agrees, telling his dark sister, "As will yours. I'll now return to the Floating City to advance our plan."

He walks back through the portal into his conference room. The sliced apple Ilem left on a table near Naihal has already rotted.

Following the meeting, Ilem returns to his conference room, and he begins to speak cryptic words to deactivate the shroud spell that prevents others from detecting what lies beyond the threshold of his sleeping quarters. Ilem, "By the power of Naihal, Diwan of Darkness. Daughter of The All. Free my mind of shadows. To the light I call."

Ilem walks into his sleeping quarters and stops when he stands over a suspended animation chamber made of metal and glass, which is large enough for two. The murky color of the chamber is black and white, like an undiffused film noir movie. Everything else in the area is full color. Planters containing oleander flowers are in different corners of Ilem's sleeping chamber.

Inside the chamber lies an Asian woman. Ilem stands longingly over her resting place, conveying only to those in love or without sight that whatever beauty she had is captured in Ilem's mind, not from her physical appearance or signs of life. The woman Ilem stands above appears to be nothing more than a lifeless, blackened, brittle husk of flesh. Nonetheless, Ilem greets his love willingly, whether blinded by love or suddenly struck by a malady that robs him of his sight, "*Gajang salanghaneun*, Pu Kwon."⁸

His exoskeleton falls to the floor as Ilem undresses in front of Pu Kwon. The side of the suspension chamber next to him opens. His golden glow is consistent across his body, except for his abdominal core, which is a radiating, red pustule. Ilem lies beside Pu Kwon on the bed, rising on one elbow, with one hand resting gingerly on her abdomen. The rest of the chamber around them still has a lifeless film noir quality.

Ilem joins Pu Kwon in the solitude of her suspension chamber, flesh to flesh. Then he concentrates on releasing a gray glowing force from his radiant hand into Pu Kwon's lifeless body. Pu Kwon's burnt flesh revives, becomes vibrant, and looks normal and healthy again from the energy Ilem has released. Ilem's inflamed abdominal core also shows signs that it is gradually healing.

Pu Kwon wakes from her ill-fated slumber and immediately reaches to touch her lover's face. She softly calls Ilem by the name she knows him by - his earthly name, "Devon." Ilem kisses Pu Kwon, and as he does, he and his lover glow with the gray energy released by Ilem. Their bodies become entwined in lovemaking as Ilem thoroughly enjoys the labors of love and the victories of war. Ilem whispers, "*Dangsin-eun nawa hamkke anjeonhabnida.*"⁹

Would you embrace it if you woke to death lying in your bed? Would you snuggle up tight, close enough to feel its frosty breath on your neck as you curl comfortably in its spoon? Death is such a gentle lover. Its kiss is the last you will ever receive as its clutch roams the curves of your throat, seeks your pulsing veins, and tamps your beating chest.

Would you love death for what its open hands will do for you, or let it go to hook up with someone else in the afterglow of fading twilight? Death, like many faithless lovers, will return at your door, begging for forgiveness, begging for your enduring love. Death wants another chance to dance with you to the prom song in your head, lay by your side, and kiss your pleading mouth to sleep as the sun sets.

---

⁸ "My beloved."
⁹ "You are safe with me."

With a soft voice, Ilem tells his amore, Pu Kwon, "You are safe with me," like death whispers to its forlorn lovers longing to join them in sleepful bliss: nothing to lose, nothing to fear, only the possibilities of tomorrow's silence to contemplate.

While Ilem's attention to conquest turns to fleshly concerns, the two transhumans guarding the infirmary move the harmless, distressed, pregnant woman into an interior examination room. One of the guards gingerly assists the helpless woman in easing onto a cot to comfort her through her intensifying labor pains. All the while, red and yellow kinetic energy flows from the guards to Sage's extended hand. One of the infirmary guards openly defies his orders by seeking immediate attention for a woman who reminds him of his expectant wife. The guard impatiently calls to the other guard, "Fetch Eli, now! This looks like an emergency to me."

Dr. Eli allows the green glow from the somatic container to light his path to the infirmary. He arrives just when the second infirmary guard steps back into the hallway. That guard tells Dr. Eli, "Good timing, Doc. You got a patient inside. Looks like an emergency to us." Dr. Eli snidely responds, "Sergeant, I don't have time for this."

In a gentler tone, the second infirmary guard asks Dr. Eli, "Doc, five minutes. Trust me. It is like I am looking at my wife." Equally desperate, the other guard states, "Me, too. I mean, not his wife, but my baby mama."

Once again, the good doctor feels put upon by those he values as no more than glorified mall cops. Dr. Eli defiantly looks over the top of his glasses as he speaks derisively to the infirmary guards. "Is it your educated opinion that she is having contractions? I am the only doctor here! I will decide what treatment she needs and how long that will take." The second infirmary guard resigns that he must contend with Dr. Eli's overblown ego, "Suit yourself!"

Sensing that Dr. Eli needs more than words to convince him to do the right thing, the other infirmary guard decides to help Dr. Eli change his attitude by gripping him up and pulling him toward Sage. As he pulls back his fist to rap Dr. Eli in his noggin, a drone messenger speaks to the guard through a communication device built into its forearm. Messenger, "Where is he with that head!" Dr. Eli strains to blurt out, "Give me just a moment ... ugh ... I'll be there *tout de suite*."

Ahead of returning to his post, the gruff infirmary guard pushes open the outer door to the infirmary for Dr. Eli to enter the room. Without his knowledge or consent, even before Dr. Eli opens the interior infirmary door, colored energy from his body seep through the door's cracks. By the time he opens the interior infirmary door, Sage has transformed herself to appear as a female humanoid drone laying on the cot seductively and temptingly, with just a sheet covering the "vital" parts of her glistening robotic body.

Dr. Eli questions the infirmary guard about the apparent inconsistency in their report. "Where is the pregnant woman? Not that I am complaining. This is more to my liking." Confounded by the disappearance of the pregnant woman and the presence of a drone, one guard states, "I do not know. I do not know how she could even get out the door."

Erased from Dr. Eli's countenance is the mask of contempt. Instead, his tongue hangs out of his face like an obedient dog panting for water. Dr. Eli shoos the guards away when he sees what lies behind "door number 2." "You can leave guards. Yes, yes, please leave now." Dr. Eli lays the somatic tank with Sledge's head on the floor as he closes the inner door behind him. Click.

He reaches into a medicine cabinet for a syringe and screwdriver to help Sage "relax." He has his back to her, assuring her she is in good and gentle hands. Dr. Eli, "Heh, heh! I may need to sedate you for a full and proper body examination." The slight sound of whirling grows below Dr. Eli's waist as he sprays Rust-Oleum on what is left of his penis.

Sage taunts the overly excited doctor, noting, "I hope you have the right tool for this rendezvous."

Before Dr. Eli can sedate Sage, she picks up the somatic tank and clunks him over his head. Bop! Dr. Eli whimpers as he falls to the floor, "Awww!" In return, Sage sarcastically concludes, "Men are often betrayed by their members. I guess I will never know if that's a corkscrew in your pocket, Doc, or if you were just excited to meet me."

Perhaps in moments like this, it is best to be blind.

Sage steps through the exterior infirmary doors between the two guards, again appearing as the pregnant black transhuman. She softly closes the infirmary door and informs the guards that Dr. Eli is indisposed. Click.

Sage warmly tells them, "Dr. Eli was extremely helpful. I feel so much better. Bless both of you. The doctor should be out soon." Meanwhile, rich tones of reds and blues drift from the guards to Sage's open palm.

Pleased that he has been of service, one of the infirmary guards responds, "Sure, lady. The arena's shutting down. You better go." On cue, Sage cautiously but quickly makes her way down the hallway away from the guards.

A few minutes later, the infirmary guards receive another frantic message from the drone messenger about delivering Sledge's head to Ilem. Messenger, "Where is he? Is he on his way to Ilem!" One of the infirmary guards opens the exterior examination room door to alert the good physician to hustle on his way, but first mutters to himself, "Pushy, everybody's pushy."

Despite the need to support her swollen belly, Sage quickly scampers down the hall. After discovering Dr. Eli unconscious on the floor, the infirmary guards angrily screamed for reinforcements. One of the guards holds the empty suspension animation container that held Sledge's head. Bewildered by the situation, he exclaims, "Oh shit, what the hell is going on!" His doomed partner asks, "Doc, you okay?" We'll all be infamous now!"

Angry drone guards chase a potbellied Sage to a dead end in the Colosseum once they detect her. One angry drone shouts, "Don't let her escape!" In response, Sage tries to hold off her pursuers by pulling out her hand cannon to blast a few away. Then, she places one of the black discs from her holster on an exterior wall next to her and takes off with her hand cannon, ready to blow away anyone who tries to stop her. The explosion blows a hole in the Colosseum wall, removing several guards from the flying debris. Boom!

Using her fledgling powers, Sage generates an invisible barrier around herself as the explosion projects rubble her way. Wreckage strikes several more guards chasing Sage as she sustains minor cuts from the flying objects that pierce her projective shield. To ward off more assailants, she hurls explosive black discs at those chasing her as she runs down the mostly vacant streets from the Colosseum. Baaroom! Boom!

The same SUV she occupied before entering the Colosseum remains idling. The timer in the SUV now indicates fifteen seconds.

When the clock runs out, an explosion blows the back door off the SUV, and the flying motorcycle bursts out of the rear. Boommm. Bam!!! The license plate reading "Race the Rain" flies off the back of the flying motorcycle and sticks in the forehead of one of Sage's pursuers. The unlucky guard bellows, "Ahhh!" For the guards hurrying by him, the smell of manure from the explosion whiffs from the guard's left-over flesh into their noses, followed by the sweet smell of musky almonds.

Sage creates another invisible barrier to protect herself from flying debris and plasma gunfire. Bam bang, bam. The drone guards that survive the blasts scramble to continue the chase as Sect soldiers yell, "Get up, get her!"

Sage runs fast and leaps ahead to grab the flying motorcycle just as it lands with both wheels on the ground, then transforms back into flight mode and on autopilot. Her pursuers continue shooting at her without striking Sage or the motorcycle. She guides the vehicle toward an open bay door on the lower deck of the Floating City, then blows right through it. Several members of Ilem's forces jump on and in an array of military vehicles in pursuit of Sage. Vroom! Another Elite Squadron Officer gives orders, "Get her, don't let her escape!"

To the surprise of the military assembling to catch Sage, after the explosion from the SUV, another blast from Sage's condominium ripped an opening in the skyscraper. Boom! Sect hunting Sage brace themselves for impact as more debris hurdles toward the ground.

Away from all this action, Ilem's peaceful and satisfying tryst with Pu Kwon leaves his body alit from pure white light. He longs to taste Pu Kwon's lips again, but before he can partake, he hears an announcement indicating someone outside his antechamber has requested an audience. A computerized voice announces, "Lord Ilem, entry is requested." Ending his precious time with his love, Ilem's essence seeps into one of the other exoskins.

The drone messenger and Dr. Eli enter Ilem's conference room. Seeing that Dr. Eli has arrived empty-handed, Ilem angrily addresses the doctor and the drone messenger as they inform him that someone has stolen Sledge's head.

To shift blame, the messenger tells his Master, "Lord Ilem, I found Dr. Eli as you commanded." Ilem, displeased by his followers' incompetence, angrily asks, "And where is my tribute for the Galactic Council?"

Stammering and wobbling on his swivel ball joint, Dr. Eli nervously exclaims, "I don't understand why, but a pregnant woman ... that is ... someone that resembled a pregnant woman, or maybe a drone, stole it!" Ilem yells about the head's value as more than just the last piece of organic human flesh, "Do you know what that head symbolizes? Finality, damn it!"

Ilem summons Kol by comm to order him to retrieve Sledge's head, "Computer find Kol. Transmit orders to him to find that goddamn head and bring it to me now."

Ilem turns to look through a window offering a magnificent view of the decks of living quarters and skyscrapers in the Floating City. The top edge of the Dyson Sphere appears so close to Ilem as if he could grip it from its location. For a moment, he holds out his hand as if he plans to do so.

Casually, Ilem turns to walk out of his quarters away from the remains of Dr. Eli and the drone messenger smoldering in a pile of flesh and scorched metal. Kol's face appears in the upper left corner of a panel of transparent computer monitors near the exit of Ilem's room. Kol contritely acknowledges, "Ilem, I received your orders. I'll bring back your payload." Ilem warns Kol, "Do not fail me." Sheepishly, Kol replies, "I won't ... my Lord."

Ilem's demand for Sledge's stolen head immediately stirs every member of the Elite Squad into action so as not to incur Ilem's wrath or discipline from Kol.

The hunt is on.

END OF CHAPTER 4

Chapter 5

Free

Hubris gains life from many trivial things that imperceptibly fill the human spirit
with the temerity to believe that we are all alone,
that might alone makes right, that the loudest squeak should get all the grease,
and even living a life of lies turns fiction into reality.

When this all ends,
The last will praise the crumbs scattered in the dust
and call it a feast.
Like rabid ants, they will crawl over and claw each other for scraps.

The brave fly on the wings of destiny, and the weary
tumble on the weighted wings of despair.
Even in this moment of insanity, stupidity, or whatever
it appears to be to the untrained eye,
glide like a feather on the wind, free and unabashed.

Derrick Howard

One day when we wash upon Caellum's eternal, abiding shore,
We'll have to ask old Daedalus,
Did Icarus sulk in remorse as he fell to his death
or laugh as he embraced the helm of wisdom.

Aerial

Oblivious to the chaos beyond his door and outside the QD, Gabba and his family still sit on their couch when loud banging on their door startles them. Bang, bang, bang, bang. Gabba whispers to his family, "C'mon, hide!"

Several Elite Squadron members are at the QD rounding up Trailers. An Elite Squad member yells at Trailers outside Gabba's door. Like the Trailers who marched in the Blood Bowl procession, those who live in the QD are a ragtag bunch of aliens; you could even call them survivors. "Open your doors, now! Bang, bang, bang ..."

The Trailers hurry out of their homes carrying an assortment of old weapons, including old-school automatic weapons and dated laser guns. An annoying chorus of orders rings out from the Elite Squad members to all the startled Trailers. "Form one line by your rank, high to low. Move it! Get your gear. We have an infiltrator to catch." Bang, bang! "Open your doors!"

Zetia and Belle squeezed their pliable bodies inside the contours of the floor crawl space. Gabba looks through the digital peephole to see who is belligerently thumping on the door. Readings from the peephole's composition checking system indicate the Elite Squad member pummeling Gabba's door is a "Sentient being. Elite Squad. Hunter/Killer." With an understanding of the peril his family and he would face if he failed to comply with the Elite Squad member's commands promptly, Gabba returns, "Eh up, I'm getting dressed!"

When Gabba opens his door, several Elite Squad members crowd into the Acquilite's small apartment. The guards' considerable weight causes the floor to sink within an inch of Zetia's face. One of the Elite Squad members orders Gabba, "Get your gear! Ilem wants everyone out looking for a woman who stole the head of that Black Purist who died at Blood Bowl."

Upon command, Gabba grabs a tattered, mixed-matched, oversized military uniform from a coat hook on the wall. Someone has decorated the old baggy uniform with a Fleur-de-Lys symbol, indicating it belonged to a soldier who fought for the Manchester Regiment during WWI. Gabba closes the door of his quarters as he juggles his gear and guns. Slam! He fiddles with a breathing device attached to his headgear, holding a laser rifle and a sawn-off Winchester Model 97 Riot Gun in his other hands.

Two hours later. Thirty miles from Pittsburgh, PA.

Within hours near old Pittsburgh, PA, the Sect closed in on Sage. She still wears the guise of a pregnant transhuman, deftly maneuvering her flying motorcycle away from laser blasts. Ahead of her is an obliterated, desolate Steel City. The ash and rubble of buildings toppled by an F6 tornado coined by social media as the *2031 Great Reaper* provide Sage with sloping blockades to avoid her pursuers.

One of the Elite Squad members fires its plasma gun to strike the back of Sage's flying motorcycle. Guiding her vessel up and to the left, she dodges the blast and timely fires back. Pew, pew. Bang!

A female Elite Squadron leader hangs out the passenger side of a flying armored car to shoot an electromagnetic bazooka at Sage. The blast connects with the rear of Sage's flying motorcycle, hurling her into the city ruins below. Bzzzzt, bang! Sage wails, "Aww," as she tumbles down on the solid surface. The Elite Squad leader gives orders to everyone to search for Sage. "Spread out, find her!"

Sledge's head rolls near a sewer close to an industrious rat out of the view of the Sect and Trailers searching for her. "Squeak." The sewer lines the street in front of an old, abandoned thrift store. Sage's orb lies in a pile of rubble nearby. The Elite Squad leader barks, "If we have to, we'll take that thief back in pieces. Find her. And when you do … kill her!"

For all I know of myths and religiosity, life after death is the zenith, opening a doorway to immortality. For a lucky few, the waste and gluttony of life are left behind, dissension granting a new beginning. That, too, is the grist of truth.

The air is so polluted and overheated that the Elite Squadron leader directing the search party sports a breathing device to avoid choking on acids sucked into its cold metal throat. When she does remove the breathing mask, she gags on the fetid air, burning her lungs. She struggles to utter the right words to order the search party to fan out to find Sage and Sledge's head. Aggravated, the squad leader aggressively stuffs more electromagnetic pulse cartridges into her bazooka to use against the cunning thief who stole Ilem's tribute for the Galactic Council.

In the distance, Trailers in the search party scamper back and forth in a disorderly fashion to momentarily avoid the ire of their squad leader and the criticism of the Sect. A couple of the more raggedy Trailers piece together their 2020s model handguns and automatic rifles. Unlike the Trailers, who resemble a motley crew of mall cops, the well-trained Sect march in cadence in set directions to find Sage. These more polished and prepared soldiers are armed with superior armaments, laser rifles, plasma pistols, and rail guns.

Gabba leans his Frankensteined Lazareth flying motorcycle against the edge of a building near all the action. He tagged his motorcycle with traffic cop emblems, indicating his day job is merely that of a crossing guard servicing the wealthier section of the expansive Floating City. Like other Trailers, without money to spare, Gabba must rely on old munitions instead of the powerful weapons of destruction available to the Elite Squad. His weapons are his trusty first-gen laser rifle and sawn-off Winchester Model 97 Riot Gun.

To focus the search party's attention, the squad leader continues shouting orders to them to spread out and look for Sage. "She couldn't have gotten far."

In response to the squad leader's commands, Gabba aims his Winchester Riot Gun to mimic the cockiness of the Sect soldiers. Gabba yells at imaginary attackers, "If yer moves, I'll fucking fuck you, yer fucker!" He imitates gunshot noises to enliven his wishful feats of bravery. Gabba, "Schklikt, klikt! Manchester Regiment, unite!" Excitedly, Gabba kicks rocks in random directions as he continues his fictitious display of courage and bravado against make-believe foes. Plonk.

Even without other Trailers around to answer or entertain Gabba in his fantasy land, he realizes his swagger is faux: he has never challenged these rulers and may never. In frustration, Gabba mumbles, "Ah fucking hell! I'm a reet berk," and scatters more rocks by kicking a pile across the ground. One large rock Gabba kicks strikes against a metal orb bearing an infinity symbol. Tink.

Gabba slings his rifle over one of his shoulders and ponders, "What the chuff is this …?" He reaches to pick up the orb, but it rolls away. Gabba tries to pick the sphere up again, but it evades him. He scratches his head with one of his four hands not already occupied holding his Riot Gun, "A master of craft this one."

Just as Gabba tries to pick up the orb again, flapping his arms like a four-winged chicken, two Trailers approach: a Jovian from Jupiter and a Vestan from Mars. The Jovian removes its breathing device to engage Gabba in conversation about his recent find. The Jovian asks Gabba, "What's that?"

Gabba, Jovian, and the Vestan stand over the orb, contemplating what to do next. Gabba speaks up first, asking a critical question, "What the 'eck is this?" The Vestan scoffs at Gabba's actions and warns all of them, "Don't touch it. It could be an IED. Rogues and shell pirates trolling the ruins might have put it there." The more cautious Jovian warns them, "We should be looking for the woman, not picking up trinkets."

The Acquilite extends one of his hands toward the orb and concentrates on opening a hole in his palm that resembles a parasitic mouth with jagged teeth. Gabba emits an orange sticky, blob-like substance from that palm that lands on the orb, causing it to stick in place. Once in his hand, he examines the orb to decide if it is just a toy he can give to his daughter, Belle.

While Gabba and his inquisitive compadres quibble over what to do with the orb, another squad leader approaches and scolds them for wasting time. "What the hell are you three doing?" Gabba snaps to attention, "Now then, Sir, we found here a metal ball. It seemed right out of place here. We thought we might have a gander ..."

The squad leader interrupts Gabba in midsentence and chastises him for dilly-dallying. The two other Trailers also do not escape the squad leader's shrill criticism for their presumption that they have the right or wherewithal to think independently, "Trailers aren't paid to think! Throw it away and move on!"

Gabba reluctantly tosses the infinity orb to the ground and watches it roll away. Clank! Sullenly, he attaches his breathing mask to his helmet, wipes the sweat on his brow, and then slowly carries on with his appointed task.

The whirling lights that signaled Sage's emergence on the Floating City swirl out of the orb again, revolving, fusing, and materializing into the physical appearance that she cast when she first leapt into her mission to save Dr. Q and fulfill the Doomsday Protocol. Gabba carefully hides behind Sage to witness the intriguing sight his commander ordered him to disregard.

Sage picks up the squirming rat that still has its teeth clasped around Sledge's chopped dreadlocks to pull Sledge's head free from the mouth of the sewer rat. "Squeak."

When this ends, the last will praise the crumbs scattered in the dust and call it a feast.

Still spying on Sage, Gabba compresses his body into a gap in the brick to spy on her. She does not notice that he has crept closer.

Carrying Sledge's head by its hair, Sage travels down a deserted alleyway lined by dilapidated, crumbling buildings and paved with colonial cobblestones. She continues down the alleyway, trampling over broken stone and glass, until she reaches a five-story, abandoned building at the end of the road.

She stops before the building to wipe dirt off a sign posted at the front door. By cleaning away the dirt, Sage reveals that the first few letters on the sign are "A.R.I." She finishes wiping off the sign to show all the letters, "A.R.I.E.L. Observatory Project Administration Building."

Sage closes her eyes and tries to recall what each letter in the acronym means and mouths for her benefit, "The Atmospheric Remote-Sensing Infrared Exoplanet Large-Survey Observatory. This is the place."

Sage pries away a loose brick in the wall, revealing a key hidden in a hole. She then grips Sledge's head by the dreadlocks and examines it like she is trying to ensure the blast did not damage his head after her flying motorcycle fell from the air.

To have a rhetorical conversation, Sage steps through the open door while holding up Sledge's inanimate head and talking directly to it. She assuredly states, "I think we should be safe here for now." Sage places Sledge's lifeless head on the floor as she tries the key in different doors along the corridor but continues speaking to Sledge's disembodied head as she does so, "My father set up this safe house right after he went underground."

The next to last key she tries successfully unlocks a door with a sign indicating it is the "Custodian's Closet." Once inside the closet, Sage reaches up to activate a light fixture, then tinkers with it until she finds a hinge to move the light to the side.

She flicks a tiny hidden switch inside the light fixture, opening a concealed door in the closet's back wall. Beyond the wall is a secret laboratory with assorted items, including an examination table and chair in the middle of the room. To the right of the exam table is a long table on which there is a stack of black and green colored metal scraps which someone or something has gathered. On the left side of the room, there is a long table with a computer on. Next to the sleeping computer is an X-ray machine.

However, the most crucial object that catches Sage's attention at the back of the room is a tank-like metal figure sculpted to resemble the head and torso of a human body. The torso is chunky but intricately designed with compartments and air vents. The arms and legs of the humanoid figure are detached, resting on the long table in the room. Sage assures herself, "There's enough metal here for what we need."

While carrying Sledge's head into the hidden room, Sage notes, "My father told me about three men named Mike." Sage pries off the headpiece to the tank-like, humanoid figure she spotted just a moment ago. Sledge's head lies on the top of the computer as Sage continues conversing with it for companionship or to forestall insanity.

Sage notes, "At various times, all the Mikes let others define them and that nearly destroyed them until they found the path to living life on their terms. Whom do you want to be like Sledge?" Chuckling as she does so, Sage activates the computer and comments, "If this works, my dad thinks you can be just like Mike."

An x-ray image of Sledge's head reveals an object with a cone-shaped tip and short stem progressively rotating in Sledge's forehead near his pineal gland. Sage ponders with extreme caution, "Do you get to pick one or none? What will you become, man or machine."

Sage gently places each of the palms of her soft hands onto Sledge's temples, concentrating on connecting with his consciousness as the object visible in the x-ray continues boring through his frontal lobe. She implores the listless skull to do the impossible, "Come on, Omnis, activate." Her frustration increases as the reaction she expected to register does not arrive.

Sage contemplates, "If I can't draw your thoughts out, I'll have to go in." Upon that revelation, Sage begins transmitting a purple glow from her hands into Sledge's skull to reach his Sahasrara chakra.

She cautiously enters Sledge's unconscious mind to find him cowering in a foggy, formless space. With her hands radiating the purple light, she sticks them into a black cloud of light encircling a cowering Sledge. Speaking Jamaican Creole to him as if she were a native of the "Rock," Sage says, "Sledge, *everyting irie. Mi yah tuh help.*[10]"

A ball of light grows from her hands, illuminating the room and cutting through the regenerating darkness. The bright light shines down on Sledge and into his insecurity. Sage kneels before him as he trembles, moving even farther away from her.

For the first time since temporarily entering somatic death, Sledge asks, "Where am I? *Dis doh* feel right. *Dis* isn't possible. I died ..." Sage tells him, "You did die, but I salvaged what I could to revive you."

Sage places her hand delicately on Sledge's leg to comfort him, but he questions her intentions, "Why? Who are *yuh*? *Wah duh yuh* want?[11]" Sage calmly replies, "My name is Sage. I came for Dr. Hamilton, but when the Omnis probe activated, I knew to reclaim you, too."

Sage tries to calm Sledge, who struggles with being in this surreal reality. Sledge, "Salvage me! Hamilton made me believe he would help me survive the Blood Bowl. *Buh nah* like *dis, nah* like *dis!*" Sage informs him, "Death was the only option."

She has both her hands on his shaking legs to calm his concerns. Sledge, "Where am I?" Sage evenly states, "The last place identity goes before you die. The corner in your mind."

Continuing her attempts to inform Sledge about his potential to be more than a docile piece of flesh, Sage states, "This third eye drilling in your brain will allow me to restore your consciousness in the corporeal world, but I have resistance. You don't excrete emotions like a sighted person."

Sledge searches for reason, "*Wah a yuh* talking about?[12] *Wah* is Omnis?" Sage takes Sledge's hand as they continue to talk, "You are Omnis. At least you can be if my father's program is an effective catalyst."

---

[10] "I'm here to help."
[11] "What do you want?"
[12] "What are you talking about?"

"Once Omnis cycles to activate, you can access the full power of your mind. I know this is frightening, disconcerting even, but …" Pushing her away, Sledge interrupts Sage in an accusatory tone, "Your father is … was a madman, and *yuh muss* be insane, *tuh. Laas ting* I recall,[13] Ilem set *di* wheels in motion *tuh chap aff mi ed.*"

Sage again places her patient hand along the sides of Sledge's temples and answers his accusatory outburst, "Sledge, on some level, you must want this. If not, I could never enter your mind. Even someone like me, with the power of kinetic empathy, cannot stop your emotions from being secret. I don't believe I can draw out your chakra because you can't see me to excrete your feelings."

A red haze begins to emit from Sage's body, engulfing her. She asks her stubborn patient, "What do you sense now that I'm here?"

From Sledge's point of view, Sage is silhouetted by unknown light or form of energy. Her features are vague to him, as they have not fully materialized. Sledge slowly conjures words to explain this sensation few have ever experienced, "I … *deh … ah lite …* I sense energy where *yuh* kneel." Sage tries to help Sledge understand what the miraculous sensation of sight allows him to experience, "Red. The color is red. Your chakras are transforming what remains of you from dying flesh to a living consciousness."

Sledge notices that his deep bronze hand is bordered in the red aura, and Sage is close before him. Her features become more apparent to him as he stares in her direction and receives her in his eyes.

Mystified, Sledge informs Sage, "I've *neva* seen *anyting*, let alone colors. *Dis* is incredible." Sage tells the talking head, "And there is much more for you to experience." She holds Sledge's hand blocking his worried face to continue assuring him that he's okay or can be. Sledge, "*Dis* isn't real! It can't be!" Sage assures him she is real despite his disbelief, "I am here, Sledge. Use your senses to know it's true."

Sledge feels Sage's wrist, then slides his probing hands across her shoulders and neck. In the corporeal world, Sage has Sledge's head attached to the limbless, metal figure standing upright in front of her. She continues activating switches on the computer, making lights flash throughout the room.

---

[13] "Last thing I recall, Ilem set the wheels in motion to chop off my head."

Sage, "Let's try this. It works for most men. If you've ever touched a woman ... remember her now. Let your feelings of physical pleasure grow, and I'll draw them into me." Inside the safety of his mind, Sledge hesitates to reach out to Sage but gradually moves to caress her face. For the first time, he sees another person's face, and in this case, a luminous force at his fingertips.

Sage asks Sledge what he sees when he looks at her with his emerging vision. Surprisingly to Sage, Sledge's response is one she has subconsciously longed to hear. In Sledge's mind, Sage is simply the woman she sees when she gazes in a mirror. Miraculously, Sledge sees Sage when she materialized from the life support tube, and as she looks in life, not some other person he has lusted or longed for.

As he glides his finger across her tender lips, Sledge softly whispers to Sage, "*Yuh* lips a full *an sawf*. Familiar."[14]

She begins to stand and help Sledge to his feet, extolling him, "Stand up, walk with me, Sledge." He unquestioningly responds, "I'll try." Slowly, he stands before Sage, erect, shoulders back, chest forward. They walk together through a distant corridor of light that broadens as it leads to a widening portal.

In the corporeal world, most of Sage's physical body is in front of Sledge in the hidden lab, but her left arm remains partially inside his abdomen as she tries to pull out a gentle, fragile thing. From Sage's point of view, she examines Sledge's opaque eyes closely with medical equipment. Sage asks him," Can you see anything now?" Dejectedly, Sledge answers Sage, "No."

Several feet away, Gabba peaks down the hallway through the front door of the A.R.I.E.L. Observatory in search of Sage. The red glow pours out of the room into the hallway, guiding Gabba's eye to his target. He sweats profusely and takes a moment to wipe his forehead again as he speaks with the squad leader who shot Sage's motorcycle out of the sky. Gabba, "Commander, I think I've found the lass." The squad leader orders Gabba, "Stay where you are, slug. I'm sending reinforcements."

Seeking the glory, several Elite Squadron leaders meet Gabba outside the A.R.I.E.L. Observatory, along with several Sect drones and a few Trailers.

---

[14] "Your lips are full and soft. Familiar."

Their commander demands that Gabba, "Get out of our way! We'll take it from here. To the rear!"

Gabba tries to speak up but realizes the futility of doing that, "But ... never mind." Instead of joining the pack, Gabba lingers behind as the Elite Squadron leaders and the rest of their entourage creep forward into the building.

A groggy Sledge and an intrigued Sage continue speaking to each other when they both note a disturbance in their presence. Sledge, speaking low, asks Sage, "Is someone else *'ere*? I feel *someting* coming *dis* way." Sage agrees, "You're right. I do, too."

When Sage peaks around the corner from the custodian's closet, the squad leaders and the rest of their pack besiege her. Bang, bzzzzzttt, bzzzzzttt! Sage swiftly blasts one of the squadron leaders and two of the Sect with her hand cannon. "BAM! BLAM! BAM!"

Her attackers launch several blasts at her, splattering cleaning supplies and other items that line the wall of the Custodian's Closet. Bam! Splash! She casts an invisible barrier protecting herself from the dispelled chemicals, which buckles but holds. Bzzzzzttt! Bam! Crack! Pow! At the last moment of impending doom, Sage skillfully flings sheets of black and green metal at the laser blasts, causing them to ricochet off the walls. Piing pwing. The laser blows a hole through one of the attackers, who cries, "Aaeee!"

Suddenly, Sledge's head tears free from the tank-like metal figure to take a protective position between Sage and her remaining foes. Rrripp. After the coned probe bursts fully through Sledge's forehead, his eyes fill with purple, swirling energy as streaks of dark red blood race across his face, and pale-yellow clots of plasma drop on the floor. Mmmmmmmmmm.

From the wound set in the middle of Sledge's forehead like a third eye, Sledge emits a purple force that blocks the final laser and gunshot blasts discharged at Sage by her assailants—spaaanng spang.

The battle ends when Sledge flashes his fledgling powers again to destroy the drone horde by shooting shards of purple light from the Omnis probe. Sledge shouts, *"Enuf, dis* ends now." The purple blast cuts through the bodies of the remaining attackers like a hot knife does butter.

Sledge's head falls to the ground at Sage's feet, "Thud," with the Omnis probe emanating a sizzling plume of smoke. Sage picks up Sledge's head to examine it. The bodies of those who attacked them lay up and down the corridor of the Observatory.

Sage declares to herself in a satisfied way, "Father, it worked. Omnis lives."

Derrick Howard

Psalms for Yesterday: The Thrift Store

Welcome to the first floor.
Burdened clothes racks
Bear conflicting plaids.
Twenty shoes stand awkwardly on rebuilt cardboard toes.
Like mummers after a New Year's Eve parade
Burnt-out lamps brace intoxicated heads together.

Dry-rotted stairs point to the other antiques upstairs.

Along the walls, a quartet of discarded mirrors sing praises of
Picasso by Paul, and DaVinci by David.

And in the front room, an orange morning collects in the gray palm
Of an ancient goddess.
Her body bows sadly to me as I cross between her
And a grandfather clock.

His pendulum waves for her to perk up, but her eyes

Remain fixed on what is left of her days captured in her hands.

END OF CHAPTER 5

Chapter 6

Pain and Glory

Pain and glory dwarf the moment,
Together be my god tonight.
Take my life in gentle womb

Derrick Howard

Taste whole my hardened might.

Let the madness take the fear away
When our bodies quake for lust.
Let the madness take the moment
Inhibitions turn to dust.

When our flesh turns warm and tender
Hearts combine to grab at pain.
Let our hunger taste the loving height
For the moment it remains.

For the glory burns like thunder
In our loins, feel it melt.
While the language of our bodies
Drinks the power it has dealt.

Cool the wind that licks our bodies,
Laying still – combined as one.
Pain and glory fill the nighttime
'Til the morning has begun.

Icarus Complex

Three months later underground …

For slightly more than three months after Blood Bowl Earth 2050, Ilem's Elite Death Squad rampaged around the world, ruthlessly defeating Ilem's remaining enemies after he began the final stages of his killing campaign. As with dozens of other planets that have suffered a similar fate, the incredible landscapes of the Blue Planet have turned into memories, the many dreams of lost societies overcome by madness.

The Sect and Elite Squadron ordered Trailers, like Gabba, to the frontline to manage what the Death Squad considered their "light work," meaning hand-to-hand battles against those known as the Purified, Lopers, and Outcasts who have emerged from hiding on Earth. Meanwhile, the deck commanders dedicated Warhawks to travel the globe to sow Ilem's harvest of converts still waiting to board the Floating City.

Throughout the months that passed while Sledge's mind regenerated, brutal battle exploded beyond the quiet of his hiding place. All the while, Sledge lay prone and defenseless on the cold examination table secreted inside the Custodian's Closet at the A.R.I.E.L. Observatory.

There are no longer any signs of the purple energy that sizzled from his third eye protruding from his forehead. Instead, remnants of the blood and a blackish-green substance that has steadily streaked his face are still present, reducing him from an incredible power back to the frailties of normalcy. His breathing is labored, his heart races, and his blood pressure has increased. His cloudy eyes rush behind closed lids, and his arms are immobile. Behind those sealed eyelids, Sledge seems distressed by dreams intensifying in his mind. His thoughts loop repeatedly to the day this mortal ordeal began.

Chicago, IL. Two months before Blood Bowl.

On this momentous day, Sledge conceals himself in the shadows of an alley off a deserted street in the old Windy City. A robust, hot wind tosses a street sign that reads "S. Wacker Drive" down an empty road, save for abandoned cars, ransacked stores, and evidence of shattered bones. He adjusts the cloth around his mouth to help him breathe through the extreme temperatures and pollution.

Like most people hindered by blindness, Sledge taps a simple walking stick down the alley to feel his way to the edge of the street. As a vehicle approaches, he quickly steps back to listen in the shadows.

Although nothing hostile jumps out of the corroded Tesla Olympus Max, the sound of the Latin song "Lambada" is intentionally cranked up by whoever is in the car.

"Chorando-se foi quem um dia só me fez chorar …"[15] ♪ ♪ ♪ ♪

After the Tesla stops, a pudgy, 4'11" Latino male wearing black sunglasses on the top of his head and a black, curly wig sings and dances his way out of the car. His T-shirt has a Buddha image between the words, *"Deja ir esa mierda,"* or in English, "Let go of that shit."

Despite the vast distractions and destruction around him, the boisterous Latino, Ignacio Antonio Fuentes II, sings words to "Lambada" like he does not have a care in the world. Iggy, Sledge's life-long friend, is an autistic savant whom Sledge has known since they were toddlers living in the St. Bernadette of Lourdes Home for Infirmed and Orphaned Children in southwest Philadelphia, in a hood most people from that city called "the Bottom."

Plunderers and protesters have reduced the once most prominent and tallest building in the world to a limp obelisk. Graffiti sprayed on the wooden boards along the ground level of Willis Tower denounces the rise of the Transhumanist and the "Rino" political parties: "Down with Trans" and "Rino's Lie."

Iggy sings in front of the building, *"O amor faz perder encontrar …* [16]*"* ♪ ♪ ♪ ♪ Still in the shadows of the street, Sledge shakes his head in disbelief that his friend is being so loud and ostentatious when there is danger everywhere.

Sledge lays down his backpack, then lowers his mouth cover as he sneaks behind Iggy to startle him. The crafty drifter tries to grab Iggy, but when he

---

[15] "The one who made me cry has gone crying one day."
[16] "Love makes us lose and find."

does, Sledge's hands go through Iggy as if he is a ghost. Sledge, "Gotcha ... What di[17] ...?" Oblivious to Sledge's actions, Iggy's image continues to dance and sing. ♫ ♫ ♫ ♫

Unexpectedly, the trunk of the Tesla squeaks open, and out rolls the real Iggy with ghost guns in each hand. When he springs from the car trunk, Iggy's black, bushy wig slips off his dome and onto the ground.

Just as Sledge must do to survive, Iggy covers his mouth with a breathing device and clothes identical to his faux image that is still wildly dancing in the street. Beyond being childlike, diminutive, and bald as a baby, Iggy's physical presence is distinctive because he has four lumps along his skull where the remnants of Ommaya reservoirs have closed.

The only other distinction between Iggy and the doppelganger is that the real Iggy has large metal bands clamped around his wrists. The sunlight flickers off small dials on the bands, intermittently glistening like precious gems. Iggy chuckles, "*Estallido*,[18] I got you, Sledge!" The giddy Bolivian American twirls one ghost gun to punctuate his glee.

---

[17] "The..."
[18] "Bang."

In exchange, Sledge smirks at his clever friend and acknowledges how well Iggy's surprise worked, *"Yah mon, me tienes."*[19] Touching the control on one wristband allows Iggy to deactivate the car as well as the image of himself. Sledge places the wig back on his best friend's head while asking questions about his wellbeing, *"Wah Gwaan?"*[20]

---

[19] "You got me."
[20] "How are you?"

Iggy tries to relieve Sledge of his worries while warning him of the peril that persists across the deserted cities, *"Bueno, but death is everywhere."*[21]

With their familiar and lighthearted greeting, Sledge displays the near-perfect Spanglish he's learned by joining the Spanish Iggy taught him, with a dash of soul that Sledge picked up on the gritty streets of Philadelphia, *"Que pasa, hermano? Dap me."*[22]

Iggy responds with a grin and a stretched hand, *"Sangre."*[23] On cue, the men loudly clasp their hands together and fluidly engage in a choreographed handshake that requires they link thumbs, slide them back to link fingers, then flap, float, fist pump, and pound hug each other in a language that no one else in the world understands.

Their familial clutch allows Sledge to feel the cold metal bands around Iggy's wrists. Although Sledge cannot appreciate the brilliant visual sight of colored, gleaming glass dials, he's confident they have a purpose. Knowing his brilliant friend, the object instantly raises Sledge's curiosity but not a concern.

Iggy lets Sledge inspect the wristbands to garner his approval. Sledge, "I'm glad to see *yuh* found a way *tuh* protect *yuhself.*" Iggy agrees, *tomando nota,* "Si, the projection is a distraction. With tinkering, I'll be able to make a hundred of me *et ínadie sabe cuál es verdadero!*"[24]

To share his trove of new-found survival items with Iggy, Sledge tap, tap, taps his way over to the backpack he left lying near the alley. Several small weapons that Sledge takes out of the full bag include black ninja stars, an ornate dagger, and a leather, hooded jacket that appears to have mesh wings sewn under the armpit to its sleeves. To encourage Iggy to continue preparing for their exit from Earth ahead of Blood Bowl, Sledge heartens his friend by saying, *"Yuh* were always clever. *Respect, mon.* I'm glad *yuh* safe." Iggy replies, *"Gracias, amigo."*[25]

---

[21] "Good, but death is everywhere."
[22] "What's happening, brother?"
[23] "Blood."
[24] "...and no one knows which is the real Iggy!"
[25] "Thank you, friend."

Smiling to show his eager acceptance of Sledge's supportive words, Iggy hands him the sunglasses from the top of his head, rests an augmented walking staff in a back holster against the car, and then says to Sledge, "*Me, halagas. Gracias, hermano mayor.*[26] *Respeto.*"

Iggy accessorized the black sunglasses with an adapter that led to a small earpiece on each end. He describes to Sledge the various improvements he made to the device called the "Vision Staff." The innovative modification of a Zulu *isikhwili* staff carved from African blackwood gave Sledge the means to overcome his life-long physical affliction.

Iggy picks up the Vision Staff and its holster to discuss distinct parts of it as he defines their functions that qualify it as even more than an extraordinary walking stick, instead branding it to be a medical miracle. "Sledge, I enhanced the Vision Staff to work with these glasses. I connected them by a wireless feed." Sledge accepts Iggy's effort with a hearty "*Muy Bueno.*"[27]

He tosses the leather jacket on the top of the Tesla as he takes the sunglasses from Iggy. While removing the entire Vision Staff from the back harness, Iggy suggests that Sledge put on the glasses, too. With Iggy's help, Sledge dons the glasses and inserts earpieces attached to the adapter in his ear canals from behind his ear. Iggy pulls on the bulbous end of the Vision Staff to activate some of its defensive and offensive functions. The Vision Staff reacts to Iggy's tugging by elongating from 2.5 feet to 5 feet in length. Slipt.

Iggy explains his creation to his friend, "I cabbaged vision sensors from a closed Gita plant. That let me enhance the range to about 1000 meters. The sunglasses are your actuator." Sledge drops his ordinary walking stick to take his new weapon from Iggy. Sledge gleefully tells Iggy, "*Big up, respect.* I don't know how *yuh* know *dis* shit, *buh* it sounds tight." Iggy smiles in appreciation and adds, "Uncle Ray, *me enseñó mucho.*[28] The rest I learned messing around his MC shop."

Pleased by what he's been given, Sledge informs his friend, "*Wateva* he taught *yuh, yuh* learned it well." Sledge activates the glasses that allow him to make out

---

[26] "You flatter me. Thank you, big brother. Respect."
[27] "Very good."
[28] "Taught me a lot."

and distinguish objects all around him. The objects are either silhouetted in black or white if they are inanimate or emit red, radiating heat if the thing is living or has a heat source. Although he does not fully appreciate color, he recognizes Iggy's petite body more prominently as a pulsing energy source.

Iggy assists Sledge in securing the back holster over his shoulders, then bends to the ground to pick up three small sticks. He lets the sticks partially poke out of his grip as he details the functions of Sledge's new Vision Staff and the purpose of these very consequential twigs.

Iggy tells Sledge, "With these, you'll see things like a bat and hear like a porpoise. And without becoming a Borg!" While Iggy talks, Sledge twists the bulbous end of the Vision Staff again. In response, the range of what Sledge can sense by using the Vision Staff increases profoundly, thereby expanding Sledge's ability to see the full height of Willis Tower's 110 floors—tick tick tick.

Sledge collapses the hilt of the Vision Staff to its shorter length to slide it into the back harness. Slipt. A moment later, Iggy hands Sledge the leather jacket to put on over the back harness. Sledge, "*Yuh ah* genius, Iggy! This jawn *wuk betta dan* ever." Iggy replies, "I'm autistic, not a genius."

Sledge places his hand on his friend's shoulder for assurance, then tells him, "No, you've always been smart. *Dem* were always *tuh* shallow *tuh* notice. If he were here, Uncle Ray, he would tell you *nobody nuh betta than we.*"[29] Iggy, "They just wanted a guinea pig at the orphanage. I know. *Nadie mejor que nosotros.*"[30]

Iggy tells Sledge that he would rather move on from the disorienting conversation. Instead, Iggy wants to focus on the game of chance he has intended for weeks to play with Sledge since Ilem initiated the clash for survival between his forces against Purists, Moji, and anyone idiotic enough to back their side.

Iggy holds up the three small sticks. He has a mischievous grin as if he knows a secret that Sledge does not share.

Feigning curiosity, Iggy asks Sledge, "You sure you want to draw straws to see who goes in there?" Sledge responds with a laugh, "*Yah mon*, don't volunteer me."

---

[29] "Make room for yourself."
[30] "Nobody better than we."

Sledge tries to adjust the bulbous end of the Vision Staff to activate it without Iggy noticing. Tick. They draw straws from those Iggy has in his hand. Sledge pulls the short straw from Iggy's grip and smirks as he knowingly shows it to Iggy. Sledge, "*Qué lástima.*[31] I guess I win *di* human lottery, not *yuh, amigo.*"

Fast hands are great, but unyielding steel is usually better. Iggy hands a leather belt that Iggy affixed with shuriken to Sledge, informing his friend, "*Estos son diferentes de los otros shuriken que tienes.*[32] You'll need this to *cortar el vidrio*[33]." Sledge gratefully replies, "*Gracias*, I'll put *dis tuh* effective *yuuz*. I ran *outta di* ones from Uncle Ray."

They stand beside each other on an empty street in front of Willis Tower, with howling cold winds circling them. Iggy pulls an open bottle of seizure pills out of his pocket, then shakes it to count its contents audibly.

His friend comprehends the meaning behind the hollow rattling sound without looking Iggy's way. Sledge comments, "After I board the Floating City, I'll find us a way to get off *dis* damn planet before it's too late," to which Iggy replies, "The Rust Belt businesses abandoned their stores years ago after the *Great Reaper*. We need supplies, and I need meds, bad." Sledge responds, "*Si, eso es una prioridad.*[34] They never talk about *dat* shit in *di* movies. *Dis* is real. *Esto es real.*"

From his wristband, Iggy pulls a cylinder that he stretches open to reveal a digital map of the eastern United States of the Americas. Before he surveys the map, Sledge hesitates but thinks it's best to confirm that this is a wise plan. "*We shud* stay *togedda. Yuh* hollow doppelganger not *guh duh* much *'gainst* rogue Trailers and shell pirates."

To alleviate Sledge's vigilant counsel, Iggy assures him, "If that doesn't work, I have this." Iggy pushes another button on the wristbands in response to Sledge's question. Unimpressively, out pops a 12" steel rod with a sharpened tip. Snik. Even after considering if Iggy is right, Sledge, nonetheless, says, "Maybe *yuh* need *tuh* make *dat* a little longer *tuh* give you time *tuh* get away." Iggy, dejected, pushes a button on the wristband again to retract the rod. Slipt.

---

[31] "What a shame."
[32] "These are different from the other shuriken you have."
[33] "Cut the glass."
[34] "Yes, that's a priority."

Together, they look up at the length of the Willis Tower. Iggy recalls how Sledge risked his ass for common thievery or adolescent thrills, "You're worried about me? This building is taller than anything you climbed before."

Sledge takes out of his jacket pocket a sizeable marijuana bud instead of answering Iggy or removing his steady gaze from the skyscraper's height. Following a pregnant pause, Sledge calmly states to Iggy, "*Yah mon*, I noticed," then chuckles and adds, "*Tink's* for building *mi* confidence." Instead of concentrating on Sledge's gallows humor, Iggy suggests to Sledge, "*Cuidado. Si tengo que cruzar, lo haré.*"[35]

Iggy and Sledge continue to share the joint in silence. A detached wing of a dark bird, possibly a sparrow, floats before them in the chilled wind.

After dapping with each other, Iggy pushes a button on the other wristband to replicate a troupe of dancing images of himself, then steps closer to the driver's side door of the rundown Tesla. Sledge promises Iggy, "*Yo no. Lo haré mi amigo. Pero no yo.*"[36] ♪ ♪ ♪ ♪

Preparing to launch himself into an unknown but perilous journey, Sledge pulls the protective cloth back over his mouth, stores the Vision Staff into its harness, buckles the leather belt of shuriken around his waist, and pulls the backpack of supplies onto his back. Simultaneously with Sledge donning his armor, Iggy calls out to remind him of what their Uncle Ray often told them as Eagles fans, "*Este no es momento para vaqueros.*"[37] ♪ ♪ ♪ ♪

Meanwhile, Iggy's doppelgangers continue dancing in the windy, desolate streets as old newspapers drift like confetti. Queen and Mercury's upbeat and tuneful fusion of funk, rock, and disco cause them to bounce and groove around Iggy's Tesla like an impromptu gathering of the first line of a New Orleans funeral. In a typical jazz funeral, parishioners sway to an enthusiastic, uplifting beat to alert mourners that the mood is about to change. They would launch into wilder music with tambourines and drums to celebrate an end and a new beginning. The music and dancing were both a cathartic release for mourners and a celebration of a well-lived life.

---

[35] "Be careful. If I have to cross over, I will."
[36] "Not me. I will, my friend."
[37] "This is no time for Cowboys."

Like those soulful Nawlins tunes, Queen's thumping beat and words of defiance in the face of uneven odds embody Iggy's and Sledge's refusal to concede to Ilem's forces. No, these two agreed long ago and remained steadfast in their rejection of falling into the dirt and dust of dead land or lightly suffering a defeat.

The months before Blood Bowl, Iggy allowed Queen's well-known fight anthem to blare into the street for all to hear and for most to fear. Who other than a crazed person would brazenly court unwanted attention in a dystopian wasteland?

Sledge pulls the Vision Staff out of the back harness and gives Iggy one more piece of advice. Over the raucous music, Sledge speaks loudly to tell his friend that he agrees with the advice he's given, "*Si*, no Hail Marys, I know. We're not desperate yet." ♫ ♫ ♫ ♫ Iggy closes the car door, promising Sledge, "*Aguantaré todo lo que pueda. Las convulsiones son un problema sin medicamentos.*"[38] ♫ ♫ ♫ ♫

Iggy starts the engine and cranks up the lively music that's remained a call to glory and resistance for the downtrodden for seventy years, "Are you ready, hey, are you ready for this? Are you hanging on the edge of your seat?"

Like a pitchy and unrehearsed karaoke singer, Iggy belts the words of the song that he can still remember, then fades out when his singing should give way to Freddy Mercury's deep, throaty rock-growl, or at least for others who don't have to take the funk. "Plenty of ways you can hurt a man … I'm ready … standing on my own two feet. Hey … Shoot out."

If you have ever nurtured a child from a toddler to a young man, it is hard to let them go into a confused, cannibalistic world. You would instead tie them to your side and let them feed from your giving and nurturing table.

Feeling that weight on his back, Sledge constrains himself from calling Iggy back to him. Instead, knowing the urgency of their quest, Sledge reluctantly watches Iggy drift away in the overeager wind as it hustles and huffs Iggy east. Iggy yells final words of support to Sledge, "Farewell, *hermano. Te veo pronto.*[39] Keep it breezy." Sledge nods in agreement, "*Likkle more, Walk good.*"[40] ♫ ♫ ♫ ♫

---

[38] "I'll hold out as long as I can. The seizures are a problem without meds."
[39] "See you soon."
[40] "See you later."

Abandoned cars, smoldering buildings, a fallen passenger plane, and other grisly signs of destruction prove that someone released an electromagnetic bomb in downtown Chicago. Without regard to the evidence of Armageddon, Iggy drives the banged-up, vintage Olympus Max down the uninhabited Chicago streets with his mirror images dancing behind the car caroling, "Another One Bites the Dust."

Turning to his risky task, Sledge activates the Vision Staff to eject a hook and steel cord from its tip to secure it high on the outside wall of Willis Tower. Klink. Given the distance he has to cast the hook to attach to the skyscraper's side, Sledge realizes he is fortunate to be blind.

There is less to fear. There is less to tell you that you cannot succeed, even on a fool's errand. To build his confidence, Sledge reminds himself what he must do to complete another challenge that even ordinary men would not take on, "Focus. Be mindful of the prize."

Once he reaches a window high on the side of the building, Sledge relies on a shuriken that shoots lasers to cut a hole in the glass large enough for him to break and climb inside Willis Tower. From Sledge's point of view, a silhouette of black and white lights the objects, with a sufficient glow distinguishing each object from the other. Suggesting employees used the room to corral people into a waiting area, Sledge senses stanchions partitions scattered in the room. Metal chairs sit around the room, as well.

By increasing the signal of the Vision Staff, Sledge detects five male and one female figure rapidly moving from lower floors up the stairwell. The infrared images of their bodies pulse bright red, a color Sledge cannot embrace, although the strobing glow allows him to appreciate the forms around him. A warning sounds off in Sledge's head as he observes the sextet of marauders approaching him. He briefly entertains the notion that whoever is in the building is up to mischief or worse. Acknowledging who they might be, Sledge mouths that they are *"Thugz!"*

Six people burst through the stairwell door, drinking alcohol and cursing. Shalamar, a huge Black man with menacing scars on his face and disfigured teeth, barks orders to the others to search for loot.

The other thugs with Shalamar are his second in command, Al, a Puerto Rican cage fighter. Al is an imposing woman with a curvaceous physique and chiseled, broad shoulders. Although she does not have the most attractive face, her imposing physique makes up for her lack of stereotypical beauty.

The other four lawbreakers form an unwelcoming quartet of deranged killers: Stank, a Black convicted murderer; Shorty, an Asian mercenary; Benji, a White human trafficker; and Rod, a Latino arsonist.

Shalamar announces to his crew, "I think we've found some good shit. Look around and see what else is here." One of the thugs stops searching for booty when he notices Sledge silently standing off the side of the room. Rod taps Shalamar on his shoulder and points at Sledge to draw everyone's attention to his presence. Pacing forward, the gang of thieves form a semicircle in front of Sledge.

The leader of this unsavory crew of thieves, Shalamar, stops everyone where they stand when he yells, "Hold up! What are you doing here?" Sledge pulls the cloth from his face to reveal who he is to the gang of thieves and extinguish the looming showdown.

Sledge, "*Easy nuh*. I'm just passing through. Go on *yuh* way, and *everyting will be irie*." The confrontation is something Sledge had faced before as he drifted through the USA's rough roads. Now he must square off against the dregs left to scavenge for survival, even to the point that they willingly commit murder, rape, and terrorism to get what they want, and indeed more than what they are entitled to receive.

The crunch of a fifth of grain shattering on the concrete floor echoes in the hollow space. After Shalamar chucks the bottle to the ground, he stokes the flames of contention by rhetorically asking his crew, "Seriously, a blind man thinks he's gonna tell me what to do?" Shorty clamors for the opportunity to shed someone else's blood, "Shalamar, let's cut him up for fun." Slowly, Sledge reaches behind his back to adjust the setting on the Vision Staff—tick tick tick.

In response to Shalamar's approval of Shorty's request to quench his depraved thirst for murder, Shorty brandishes a shimmering machete that he intends to use to relieve Sledge of his limbs, then his life. Shalamar bellows his consent to his henchman to do away with Sledge, a man seemingly limited by his physical handicap, "Go ahead, Shorty. Make it quick."

On command, Shorty lunges at Sledge with angry hands clasped around the hilt of the two-foot-long machete. Sledge strikes a defensive pose and audibly shouts a battle scream that mentally and physically hardens him for this skirmish, "Kiai!"

Surprising to only those who discounted him, Sledge makes quick work of Shorty with a burst of punches that crush Shorty's ribs, causing bones to protrude out of his back and blood to gush from his mouth. Shorty screams in pain, "Aieee," as his bloodied body crumples at Sledge's feet.

Witnessing this unexpected outcome, Shalamar orders the remaining gang members to destroy Sledge. "Motherfucker! Benji, Rod, Stank, finish him!" The three thugs charge Sledge, all exposing Skeleton Hand Claws that they intend to use to cut deep into Sledge's hide.

In response, Sledge pulls out the Vision Staff and swings it like a baseball bat across Benji's and Rod's faces rendering them unconscious. "Bam! Blam!" Cunningly, coolly, Sledge slowly slides the Vision Staff back into its harness.

Sensing his chance to gain an advantage over Sledge, Stank runs behind Sledge to attack him. Unfortunately for Stank, his nickname gives him away. When his reeking odor trails into Sledge's nose, it only takes a second to turn his attack to Stank. Sledge skillfully pulls the Vision Staff out of its harness and over his head in time to block Stank's attempted backstab.

Sledge brings Stank's arm down on his shoulder, breaking it with a loud snap. "Urgh." "Snap." Stank grabs his disabled arm, no longer able to focus on Sledge or answer Shalamar's orders to eliminate their would-be victim.

Sledge drops Stank with a roundhouse kick, causing Stank to reel. Stank, "Ahhh." To ensure this foe is no longer a threat, Sledge grabs Stank by his hair and violently strikes him in his throat, crushing his windpipe. Stank exclaims, "Owf." Next, like a shifting breeze in a growing storm, Sledge fluidly turns to the other assailants, who want to finish him even more now that two of their partners in crime have fallen.

Al places her hand on Shalamar to stop him from attacking Sledge. She confidently assures Shalamar, "Shalamar, I got this." With those ill-fated words, Al leaps into battle. She strikes an impressive boxing stance as she prepares to challenge Sledge and buttresses her resolve by baiting him with more derisions, "Come on baby, I promise not to hurt you … much."

Her fighting skills are undeniable compared to Shorty, Stank, and Rod's pathetic attempts at killing Sledge. Al repeatedly connects with fists and kicks against Sledge's aching body and face. Sledge recoils from the attack, screaming, "Aww!" Still, in control of the fight, Al jumps on top of Sledge as he lies on his back on the floor, then gives him a sloppy kiss while pulling him closer with his leather jacket. Al provokes Sledge by asking, "Is that the best you can do, darling? Smooch."

As on cue, Sledge cuts Al with the laser that shoots out the end of his shuriken, then pounds Al in the head with it. With Al semiconscious, Sledge uses a series of Krav Maga moves to subdue her from behind. Crack!

Rod regains his senses, shaking off cobwebs, and charges at Sledge for one last-ditch attack. Rod, "I'll kill you!" Ahead of Rod, getting within ten feet of his target, Sledge throws five shurikens at him, striking him in his throat and upper body with four, then Sledge spin kicks Rod in the face. "KIA!" The force of Sledge's kick knocks Rod awkwardly backwards into an upright metal chair, snapping his neck like a dry twig. Rod exclaims, "Awwww," after that, Sledge mocks Rod and the rest of his fallen crew as he stands over Rod's lifeless body. Sledge assertively says, "Boy, another lesson in street etiquette."

Between Sledge and Shalamar lay the broken, bloodied, and motionless bodies of Shalamar's crew. Sledge pulls the Vision Staff out of the harness again when he senses that Shalamar's body has tensed up in preparation for a fatal ending. To taunt Shalamar into an impulsive attack, Sledge yells, "Okay, *screw face*[41], it's *yuh* turn!"

Instinctively, like a frenzied bull, Shalamar screams in rage as he charges at Sledge. Shalamar counters Sledge's confrontational words, "Argh! I'm gonna enjoy killing you. You killed my blood, my family. Now it's your turn to die." Without losing focus or calm, Sledge skillfully elongates the Vision Staff to tangle up Shalamar's feet.

---

[41] A contorted/angry face.

He spins behind Shalamar to land a hard, concentrated punch to Shalamar's spine now that Sledge's prey is snared like a trapped animal. Sledge screams out, "Hyah!" Shalamar cannot help but feebly answer with a guttural cry, "Aaaag," as his limp body tumbles out the broken window Sledge climbed through to enter Willis Tower. Crash.

After Sledge confirms that the room is silenced and the coast is clear, he walks to the edge of the broken window and looks down several stories at Shalamar's body splattered on the street below. Sledge, "...*juss* a matter of time."

The exit door slams loudly behind Sledge like the weighted sound of prison bars banging shut. Slam! Undaunted by the fatalistic clatter, Sledge heads up the stairwell to reach the Willis Tower's spires.

He reaches the 100th floor at the front entry to a shuttered Italian restaurant called *Colpo di Fortuna*.[42] Staff gone long ago covered the tables with delicate white lace cloth that had aged sepia brown. The partially eaten meals of patrons sit on tables, uncovered and molded, signifying the last supper in this eatery ended in a hurry.

A Moji holographic Maître D chaotically flickers at a host station near the front of the restaurant. Maître D, "TickTickTickTickTickTick." From the chaotic flickering of her programmed image, it is surmisable that its application became corrupt some time ago, although its program still survives in the Moji Maze. A crooked poster on the wall behind the Maître D refers to Ilem's "2042 Peace Summit."

Undeterred by its worn-out condition, the automated Maître D poses to Sledge the typical greeting that the drone designers programmed it to repeat when welcoming guests to the restaurant, "Evening, sir. My face recognition will find your reservation. Please stand still. Thank you, you, you . . . find . . . you."

Sledge walks through the holographic restaurant host toward the kitchen while addressing the irony of the Maître D's question and purpose, "No reservation, but I *tink* I'll take every seat *yuh* got." The Maître D responds as the typical patron would expect of an automaton, "Wonderful, I believe we have an opening!"

---

[42] "Serendipity."

After rummaging for canned food, Sledge walks through the kitchen and storage rooms until he reaches a posh office. He does not need keys to breach the doors of this room. Once filled with gregarious conversations and liquid laughter, no one remains alive in the restaurant.

Sledge pushes on the wall behind the desk in the office until he discovers a hidden room. Click. Within the concealed space is a small, efficiency apartment with a bed, shower, and a large, broken clock. Conspicuously lying on the bed is a well-dressed male corpse. A knife with caked blood on it remains dangling in the corpse's hand. He is missing an ear, but Sledge spots it beside the dead body. An *iSiphon* remains attached to the severed ear. Someone has written the word "Shell" on the wall in the corpse's blood. Sledge inspects the suicide before him and labels the dead man as a *"Suffera."*

As the sun sets, Sledge climbs out of the top of Willis Tower toward its spire. Relying on the hook and steel cord ejected from his Vision Staff, Sledge scales the last ten stories of the skyscraper from the outside. A cloth to aid his breathing covers his mouth. Sledge cautiously assures himself that his objective is *"Juss ah little further"* away.

He contemplates the perils of what he intends to do as he hangs tethered to the Willis Tower spire 110 stories above the street. Iggy did not exactly program the Vision Staff for distances so great from where Sledge hangs. The fall will be precipitous - success, monumental. While he mulls over his mission, the Floating City breaks through heavy clouds like a majestic hand poised to maul land.

Sledge focuses on his target, assuring himself that if he can drop just below the expansive spacecraft, clasp on its undercarriage with the Vision Staff's hook, and avoid hitting the ground, all from the tallest building in the Western Hemisphere, everything will be *irie*. The steadily amplifying voice of Sensei Ray challenges Sledge to risk the impossible, *"Nuh* sweat. Just *ah lickle* more *dan* landing ah perfect ten."[43] Sledge speaks to the wind, favorably blowing toward the Floating City, *"Sure, na* for *yuh long-seed man."*[44]

Across the Chicago skyline, several strangers to Sledge cling and climb to rooftops of other tall buildings. They also are positioning themselves on those

---

[43] "No sweat. Just a little bit more than landing a perfect 10."
[44] "Sure, not for you old man."

rooftops to infiltrate the Floating City. The other people are equipped with varying types of gliders and sophisticated jet packs, unlike Sledge, who is preparing to freefall. The Sect refer to them as "Lopers" to denounce them as unwanted guests trying to bogart a feast. Sledge cracks a devious smile, thinking silently, "Good, bait."

The Command Deck Captain of the Floating City discusses her pick-up mission with Kol and a few Elite Squadron members. The Deck Captain and Kol review images on a large, transparent computer display showing the dilapidated Soldier Field and the vandalized city in its background. Hundreds of transhumans and Trailers huddled at the conversion camp on the field, waiting to pledge allegiance to Ilem by becoming servants in his Transhumanism Movement. Many wear breathing devices or have the lower part of their faces covered with a protective cloth.

Haziness in the air from the extreme temperatures is also evident throughout the Chicago landscape. The Deck Captain informs Kol of her plans to secure her payload of more transhumans before moving on to the next location, "We'll hover over the stadium while the Sect run comp checks. Kol, after we board the transhumans, we'll leave the Trailers behind to search for Purists. We'll use the interlink system to help Warhawks easily rendezvous with us."

Kol then approvingly says to the Deck Captain, "Good, that's a good plan. But I want you to activate the linking system now. I want all the Warhawks' defense and fusion connection systems operational if Lord Ilem commands us to leave henceforth."

Thousands of sentient beings wait to board the Floating City, or the flock of deadly Warhawks that roam across other countries choked of life. In the Windy City, humanoid drones from the Sect herd new followers of Lord Ilem into separate lines to check their species composition.

Like rabid ants, they will crawl over and claw each other for scraps.

One of the Sect soldiers standing with Kol activates his communication device to converse with the Deck Captain. The Sect Scout provides an update for Kol and the Deck Captain about what others have already witnessed regarding the Lopers, "We have reports of humans lurking on top of buildings near our location."

The Deck Captain aggressively responds to the Scout with excited commands, "Launch sidewinders. That will deter our unwelcome Lopers."

Oblivious to the Deck Captain's predictions, the Lopers launch toward the Floating City. The city's defenses activate from the lower front sides of the vessel to shoot heat-seeking missiles. The Sect Scout asks the Deck Captain how to proceed to complete their mission next, "Should we prepare for artillery attacks?" The Deck Captain reacts confidently, "They would be foolish to attack this spacecraft. Our endothermic shields absorb energy and return the force tenfold. Who wants to experience that devastation, and they don't want confrontation, they want salvation?"

Trying to time his ascent better than the Lopers, who haphazardly propel themselves into the fray, Sledge leaps from the spire when the Floating City comes closest to him.

The brave fly on the wings of destiny and the weary leap on the wings of despair.

He sails through the air by extending his reach to allow air to fill the mesh wings sewn under the arms and side of his hooded jacket. Sledge's Vision Staff allows him to see a horde of missiles screaming toward him as bright orange silhouettes emit streams of fire. Within the reach of his outstretched fingers, another elusive and unabashed feather floats through his grasp.

Skillfully, as this is not his first leap of faith, Sledge evades the bombs by sailing underneath the Floating City. While still close, he fails to cast the hooking device from the shortened Vision Staff to attach to the Floating City's undercarriage.

Instead of lashing the Vision Staff's hook to the bottom of the Floating City, the cord feebly bounces off the underside of the space vessel. Boink. In the foreground and background, missiles released from the Floating City continue to shoot Lopers out of the sky. "Bam! Bam!"

In the distance, Gabba the Acquilite rides his flying motorcycle toward Sledge. Sledge plummets to the ground 1000s of feet below without a chance of redirecting his calamitous descent. Bomb blam! Extending one of his many arms in Sledge's direction, Gabba attempts to grab Sledge before he falls to his death. Despite his valiant try, Gabba's rescue mission is unsuccessful.

As the fortunes of serendipity would have it, Sledge extends the hook and steel cord from the shortened Vision Staff to attach to an old tower crane as he continues to plummet. Once connected, the steel cord from the Vision Staff permits Sledge to swing, twist, and spin his body around the tower crane to regain control of his free fall. Whoosh!

The redirection of his descent propels Sledge with enough force to hurl him around in a semi-circle into Gabba. The defenseless Acquilite plummets off his flying motorcycle while Sledge seizes control of it.

With little hesitation, Sledge steers the flying motorcycle back toward Gabba to rescue him and prevent him from slamming into the ground. Sledge calls out to Gabba, "Grab *mi han!*" Before the two link hands, Gabba's Lazareth flying motorcycle crashes near a toppled Chicago Bean in Millennium Park. Crash. Sledge lands on Gabba's spongy gut as they both tumble to the ground.

Sledge refocuses himself in time to use the Vision Staff to sock Gabba across his face. The blow dislodges Gabba's breathing device, rendering him dazed and struggling to breathe. Bop! Despite Gabba's wobbly condition, Sledge can keep the Acquilite upright long enough to fling him on the back of the flying motorcycle, then head toward the Floating City with Gabba's limb body draped over the tail end.

After they board the Floating City at a landing bay, Sledge ties Gabba up behind a pillar that obscures Gabba from prying eyes. Sledge holds the cloth he used to protect his mouth from the arid, polluted air in front of Gabba's face but stops long enough to convince Gabba that his peril has ended, "I'm *nah* here *tuh* hurt *yuh*. I *juss* need a spacecraft *tuh* get me *an* my *bredren* off *dis* planet."

Still feeling the effects of being flung from a vehicle while in the air, being used like a trampoline, and the additional indignity of being clunked on the head during Sledge's attack, Gabba observes, "Nowt like you much around anymore is there?" Holding the cloth in his hand that he intends on using to gag Gabba, Sledge asks his captive, "What do *yuh* mean, someone who's blind or Black," to which Gabba comes back, "Nah lad, I mean humans."

Continuing the conversation with Gabba, Sledge checks to ensure no one is coming. He then cautiously informs Gabba, "*Nuh, deh* isn't. *Na anless yuh* count *di* Corrupted. *Deh* ransomed their souls for *anedda* man's pipe dream. AVI sold cheaper *iSiphons tuh* those who *hav nuh* resources *tuh* purchase *di bess* model. I just saw one of the Converted in *di* tower, severed ear and *everyting*. He learned *di* hard *weh dat* it was too late to transform back once strands *ah* sentient metal snake *inna* ear."

The faces of his wife, Zetia, and his daughter, Belle, rise behind Gabba's closed eyes long enough for him to progressively worry that his life will end on the cold floor in the belly of the Floating City. Gabba panics, thinking about never seeing his family again, but remembers to disarm his captor through emphatic dialogue. Gabba, "Aye, I'm also the last of my lot. Imagine we have that in common." Sledge concedes, "Sure, *tin* maybe we *hav* more in common *dan* appears."

Despite the distracting words, Sledge still gags Gabba, then creeps through the landing bay toward a staircase leading to the Center Court on the Floating City. Sledge tamps the emergence of overconfidence to ready himself for whatever is ahead, "Go slow. Avoid detection."

He stops his surreptitious creep farther into the Floating City when he sees the sculptured hand reaching for the Dyson Sphere. The infrared image of the Dyson Sphere burns with white-hot intensity. The male humanoid figure inside the Dyson Sphere appears to be facing Sledge but remains silent. Standing so close to the sculpture provides Sledge with a better view of the black metal, with crimson-colored metal parts inside the body where a human's organs would be.

Kol stands near the Center Court of the Floating City, barking orders to his troops to look for human infiltrators, "Search every inch. Capture any Lopers who made it on board!" He uses a hand-held carbon life detector to scan for humans who may be hiding nearby. Kol continues directing his troops to strategically use the tools available to them to end the current threat, "Make sure you comp-check everyone in every home in the QD. Go, go, go!"

Two drone Elite Squadron members discover Gabba bound and gagged in the landing bay. Their imposing shadows hang over Gabba for what he feels is an interminable amount of time. His mind scrolls through myriad emotions: denial, shock, guilt, anger, and helplessness. His worry grows heavier as his thoughts wander to concerns about his family. He wonders, what if he never returns to them like so many other Trailers have suffered when they have been sent by the Death Squad out for a two-hour job and never return?

One of the drones speaks into a communication device to alert Kol about what they found. Squad Member, "Kol, we found a Trailer bound and gagged on the landing bay." Angrily, Kol retorts, "Spread out, all of you. If any humans are onboard, I want them captured and, if necessary, killed!"

Hearing a few guards heading toward him causes Sledge to attempt retreating to the landing bay. He whispers the exclamation, "Damnit," as he strategically assesses the situation.

Elite Squad members confront Sledge as he reenters the landing bay to sneak back to where he left Gabba. They all have their plasma guns aimed at Sledge, locked and loaded. One of the squad members warns Sledge, "Unless you want to get fried, I suggest you stop right there." Sledge reluctantly acknowledges the conclusion of his situation if he resists or surrenders to the guards holding him, "Fuck!"

The throng of squad members berates Gabba for getting captured by Sledge as Kol pushes through the gathering crowd. The squad members on the landing bay floor hold Sledge by his arms. One has taken Sledge's Vision Staff from him and denounces Gabba for his incompetence.

A different squad member taunts Gabba, "Pathetic Acquilite. You couldn't even capture a handicap. Trailers are not fit to clean up after the Elite Squad or the Sect." Another prissy drone bristles as he adds, "Worthless! If you don't return after a mission, who cares? Ha! Precisely why it's important to know your place."

Kol steps in front of the soldiers who have circled Sledge as Sledge struggles in the grasp of the two squad members, still holding his arms. The High Guard asks his troops, "Why are you all wasting time on this blind man?" One of the Elite Squad members suggests, "I think he's itching for a fight." Intrigued, Kol tells them, "Really, let him fight the Acquilite."

With that, Kol grabs Gabba by one of his four arms to pull him toward Sledge. Kol commands Gabba to "Fight him, Trailer. Show us you deserve to serve the Galactic Council." Knowing from experience that refusal is not an option, Gabba resigns to obeying his superior officers' commands.

Gabba involuntarily lunges at Sledge to fight him, but Sledge is amazingly fast, even without the Vision Staff. Gabba's pliable flesh allows him to rebound with Sledge's blows and counterpunches. Still, Sledge can land so many blows against Gabba that the Acquilite is knocked off balance by Sledge's vicious onslaught. Pow. To finish him off without inflicting mortal damage, Sledge kicks Gabba into the militia crowd. Bam! Turning to the rest of his captors, Sledge strikes a martial arts stance, ready to continue the fight. Sledge, "Kiai."

Kol impatiently shouts, "Enough sport! Your lust for death and humor will be more than satisfied at Blood Bowl." Without further warning, Kol charges at Sledge to sucker punch him with a hard hook to Sledge's exposed chin.

Sledge is stunned by Kol's sudden attack. The onslaught sends Sledge reeling as his spirit and sunglasses break. Reactively, Sledge crumbles to the ground. Sledge, "Urgh." He lies on the floor with blood pouring down his face, surrounded by Kol, Gabba, and the raucous drone soldiers. Kol orders Gabba to "Take him to a cell. We'll see how he does at Blood Bowl. And keep track of him. Either he joins us, or he dies." Gabba obediently says, "Aye, sir!"

Gabba helps Sledge to his feet. Gabba carries Sledge's Vision Staff and broken sunglasses in his other hands. Sledge moves along with Gabba but is still dazed by Kol's punch.

After traversing a long corridor, Gabba stops to push Sledge into a prison cell, then tosses in his Vision Staff and broken sunglasses. Sympathetically, Gabba counsels Sledge to remain calm despite his present circumstances, "Easy lad. You'll be reyt in' ere' till Blood Bowl. Thanks for not killing me." Clang clang!

After Gabba activates a forcefield keeping Sledge in the cell, another Elite Squad member grabs Gabba by the throat, demanding an explanation for why he provided Sledge with the Vision Staff. Elite Squad member, "Who told you to give him a weapon?" Gabba winces in pain, straining to answer another superior in rank, "He's fucking blind! Argh!"

The drone relaxes his grip on Gabba's throat but notices that his hand seems to have been stuck to Gabba's flesh. Gabba explains his rash and unauthorized decision to the Elite Squad member.

"Ilem wants cheering up. Thought it'd be funny if he brayed someone." The drone forms a disturbed expression for Gabba, indicating the latter has no redeeming purpose and no right to have independent thought, "So, what? Stop trying to think, you spineless pus." The guard pushes Gabba in his back from behind to hurry him down the hallway, all the while yelling, "Let's go. Kol will hear about this."

Light from a window high in the cell wall shines down to spotlight Dr. Hamilton crouched in a corner, dressed in dirty prisoner's clothes. Dr. Hamilton picks up and inspects the broken Vision Staff lying close to an unconscious Sledge. The end of the Vision Staff pops open enough to reveal that Sledge has stored small pieces of paper inside it. The curious doctor reads the note that says "Forever near" written on one side. He openly marvels at the technology he now holds, stating to himself, "fascinating," as he contemplates a paradox reforming his plans.

Silent, empty, condemned this place I live. Lonely, desperate, bereaved, the price I pay. Prayerful and prostrate, no choice but to believe a new day will break for me.

END OF CHAPTER 6

Chapter 7

Judas Holes

Death for everyone happens in stages, never in a single day.
The affirmed fight against physical death,
seeking nepenthe for their broken spirits sopping with vice, guile, and fear.

The pious drink from a well of promise to reach great heights
only to find the true elixir for internal happiness was always in the veins.

Grab a chalice. Raise it to the sky.
Drink it in, glug it all you want.
The well from which you sip happiness is going dry
in this age of Cancer Cultures.

Pour cheer into the ground for the brothers that ain't here
and wish that your cup is filled enough again to do more
then ladle soup upon doomed souls
or salty tears for the vanished and gone.

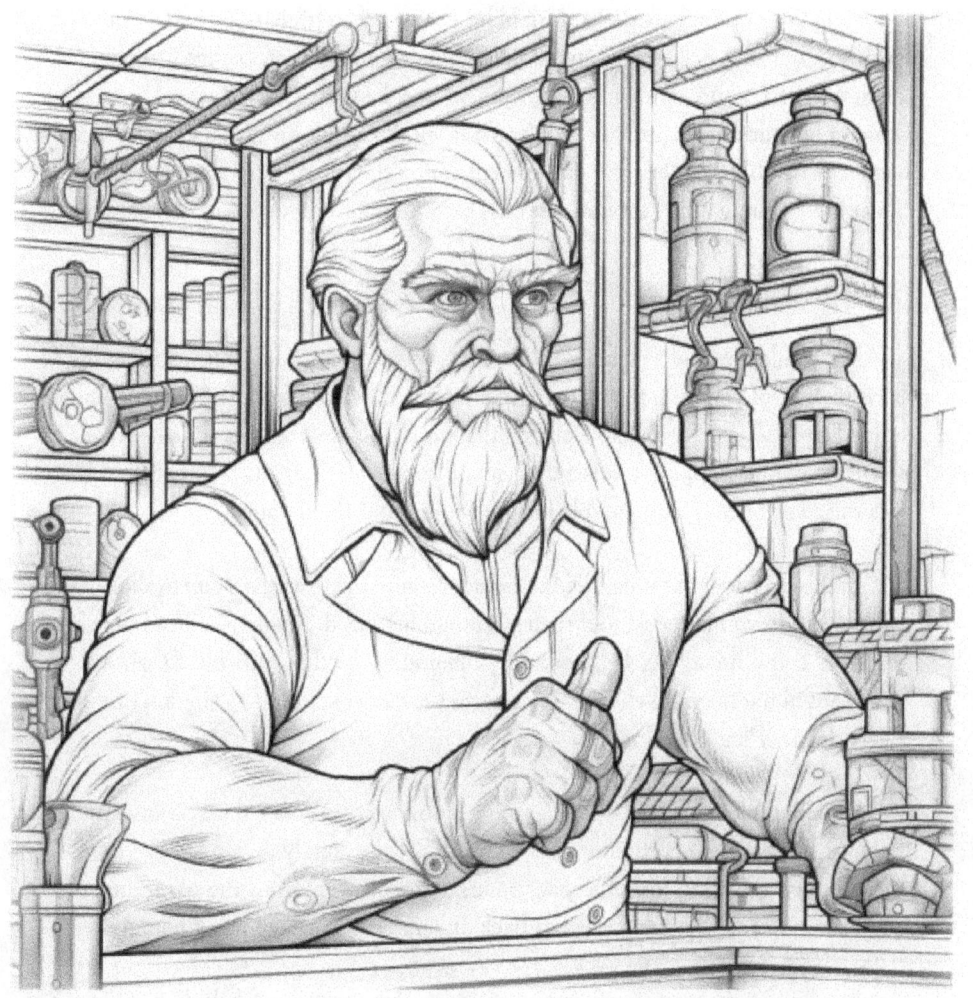

The Passage

What goes on in a man's mind who has lost his head? More than what you imagine. Death for everyone happens in stages, drip by drip, hour by hour: never in a single wave of ocean whisking away the sand. Nor are your burdens laid down at the moment that life streams from your breast, drifting through a familiar tributary to reach a foreign shore. Joy, regret, piety, and decadence pool in your restless, pensive mind for eternity in the depths of memory.

Remnants of Sledge's past thrash in his disembodied head as if it is the cage of a prisoner who has been too often pilloried at the whipping post. Sledge's troubling memories of capture and imprisonment on the Floating City bash along the shore of his mind's eye, radiating outward in all directions away from sanity. His memories sail between his years as an orphan, on the run across USA badlands, down to his humiliating and unwarranted execution for the sins of all humankind.

Sledge's Troubled Waters

He would dive into embracing, cooling waters if he could, but his thoughts burn instead of comfort. In the corporeal world, the heat of molting metal being welded close to his face causes Sledge's thoughts to ignite from worry as he wakes to a frightening, popping and sizzling sound in his ear, a greeting to hell that he was raised to believe was suitable for the wicked and the damned.

In this overwrought state, Sledge cannot contain the tears that fight to slide out of his eyes, down his cheek, and then steep into his sliced dreads. As he anxiously reacts to being immobile, helpless, and vulnerable, Sledge calls out to whoever will grant him a merciful ending, "I can't move. I can't get up. *Dis* shit ain't right. Don't do *dis*. Please, end me!"

To calm Sledge's fear of becoming even more of a freak than he imagines he must be, Sage gingerly murmurs to him, "You're finally awake. *Everyting* is *irie*. I'm just finishing up." Despite Sage's attempt at offering the assurance of comforting words, Sledge screeches back at her, "What in hell is *dat* gonna do!"

Looking away from the operation, Sage pauses to answer Sledge's questions. In a relieving, paced tune of finality, Sage tells him, "There, almost done. I still have to fill your chest cavity with these metal sheets, but your head is safely attached to this HGB body cast." Sledge's response to the involuntary assembly of his head to a machine makes him more frantic.

Without notice, a line of fire streaks out of the end of the welding arm's high-heat torch to seal one portion of the chest compartment—Pzzztt pop. Sage levitates next to the examination table to place more black and green metal sheets into one of the chest compartments. As close as their faces are, so close to touching, Sage feels obligated to converse with her reluctant patient.

Even when tides turn and rough storms dash hope, the journey to safe havens must be endured even when dreams smash upon rock. Sage reacts sharply to Sledge calling her father crazed, but continues to finish the chore of salvaging Sledge, someone who prefers death over life. She tells him, "My father didn't do anything to you. He just used what was left of your body after you died. It's not like you had plans for it." Sledge grows progressively angrier at Sage for her sarcasm, causing him to strain fruitlessly to lift himself off the table.

Although she tries to remain calm, Sage can no longer contain her anger. "My father was never crazy. Before this hell, he was the world's leading biomedical physician and cybernetics engineer." Turning from the exam table, Sage breathes heavily to gather herself and calm her nerves. "He wanted to save as many people as possible, but we had to die for his Doomsday Protocol to succeed."

Recalling the painful path she has walked since her father and Ilem clasped hands causes Sage to momentarily quiver as if the weight on her shoulders buckles her knees. After composing herself, Sage continues explaining to Sledge the path that brings them together in the 25th hour of Earth's death sentence.

Sage continues telling Sledge that her father, Q, pioneered developing Alzheimer's treatments and other regenerative medicines that sustained life well into senior years. She tells Sledge, "My father dedicated his life to advancing biomedical engineering. His work was so advanced that he could form accurate models of every part of the human brain and its 100 billion neurons by 2025."

She concedes, "The downside is Q became so drawn into his successes and followers that he ignored my mother, Fatima, and disregarded me even as an infant."

The pain of childhood memories revisits Sage. When she was seven, her life spun out of control when her father caused Fatima's death in a drunken car wreck, also sending Sage into a coma for two years. Dr. Hamilton was ashamed of what he did to his wife and child. He became obsessed with bringing Sage out of her coma. While Sage was in the coma, Dr. Hamilton was a recluse, working to biohack her mind and create the first printable brain implant to bring Sage out of her coma. While doing so, Dr. Hamilton neglected his company, Quantum Biotech, which lost value and standing in bioengineering.

It took a few years, but eventually, Dr. Hamilton created an imprint of Sage's brain. However, that also allowed Ilem time to reverse engineer many of Quantum's trade secrets which he used to manufacture advanced versions of the *iSiphon*. From there, Ilem produced other products to expand transhumanism, including pharmaceuticals and AI surgical procedures.

Ultimately, in 2029, Ilem contacted Dr. Hamilton to discuss joining businesses in some way to expedite conquering the AI medical field. Ilem told Q that Quantum Biotech's stock became valueless while Dr. Hamilton was gone, so this move would benefit both of them. Dr. Q miscalculated how badly even the decision to partner with Ilem on a more limited basis would lead to the decimation of life on Earth.

Sage recalls for Sledge that it was mid-afternoon on an Autumn Day when her father personally met Ilem for the first time. Outside the entrance to AVI's business complex, the power duo of the world's most famous scientist and the most successful AI entrepreneur exchanged handshakes and joined fates. Sage continues to weave with her words the tattered fabric of the past.

In 2029, Q and Ilem met to seal their deal abroad the Floating City. Ilem designed the spaceship as a business complex to give his workers a positive feeling of trust and cooperation for a shared purpose and values. It had all the modern configurations to infer an accepting microcosm of contemporary lives but in a perfect bubble, vacuous of truth.

Unlike the Floating City cruising above human remains years later, the expansive complex once was a lavish multi-purposed business development. Realtors billed it as a self-contained commercial society, safely maintained by Ilem and his forces in Canada, far from the madness of those outside its boundaries. No resident of Ilem's domain would ever have to put a toe unto the tainted soil of Old Earth. Surrounded by lush foliage and lipid fountains of cool water, the center retained the dreamy air of a modern Pleasantville.

Sage, "By '29, Ilem openly took notice of my father's discoveries." It took a few years, but my father eventually discovered that Ilem was reverse engineering Quantum's trade secrets." Approaching another computer, Sage uses it to attempt to access the Internet. She shares with Sledge, "If I could access the Maze, I could find my father's files; maybe I'll find a message from him to confirm the source of Ilem's power."

She filters through information related to the *iSiphon*. Among the digital files, she finds several of AVI's other product lines for human transformations, pharmaceuticals, AI surgery, and the *iSiphon*. Sage tells Sledge, "Dad told me sentient metal may be present in Ilem's creations, and somehow, he has an unearthly control over everything that contains it." Sledge, "Now we know *wah* it's unearthly, Ilem's an alien prick *fram sumweh* else." Sage finishes welding shutting the final open section of Sledge's robotic body.

Sledge puzzles out Sage's statements, "If he can control sentient metal, can't he control me?" Sage assures him, "The third eye controls your mind, not your body. Unfortunately, we will have to see." Pzzzttt pop.

Sage holds Sledge's quivering hand to comfort him. Frantically, Sledge despairingly responds, "Wait and see! Do *yuh tink* Ilem or his cronies will let me escape if they can control what I'm made of?" Sage, "You are different. If my father's theories are correct, the increased capability of your mind to use one hundred percent of its untapped functionality will be strong enough to resist Ilem's control over your body ..." Sledge interrupts, "*Buh wah*? I never wanted to live forever, *juss* on my terms."

She replies, "Do you think everyone else who walks around with machines attached to their hides wanted to be that way? Americans who could not breathe the polluted air clamored for bioengineering surgery to relieve their burning lungs. Do you blame them when the most primitive and poor citizens only had cloth to drape across their faces to protect them from the air that burned their throats? The rich purchased advanced *iSiphons* that purified the air as it entered their lungs. People waited hours outside the Quantum Biotech headquarters for physical enhancements like they had won the lottery and needed to claim their prize before their tickets expired."

Sledge asks her, "Why didn't your father take a stand sooner if he knew Ilem was up to *someting*?" Sage, convinced that she had turned the tide against Sledge's frustrations, answers, "Ilem had everyone fooled. How could such an altruistic man be so deadly? Ilem convinced the heads of the BRICS into believing his humanoid drones would help end the water wars and outpace the G7 in five hotspots around the world, Colorado, the Nile, Ganges-Brahmaputra, Indus, and Tigris-Euphrates. Every problem we had, Ilem or his minions promised to solve."

"Many observers of the BRICS worried that its growing influence might be accompanied by the normalization of authoritarian forms of 'state capitalism,' and even the unravelling of the liberal order. Others took a more sanguine view, arguing that Eastern forms of state-led development appeared superior in many ways to Anglo-American economic and political structures, and this is reconcilable with – and, indeed, depends on – an open global economy."

"Either way, the concerns of many Western liberals resurfaced following Russia's invasion of Ukraine. Countless Western governments were concerned by the news that other mostly non-democratic states – Egypt, Iran, Saudi Arabia, and Turkey – applied to join the BRICS."

Continuing to enlighten Sledge about other aspects of the tragedy of Earth's greed and shrinking commons, she tells him, "Ilem flew humanoid drones to BRICS countries, accompanied by AVI med-techs. They always traveled with an ample supply of AVI's secret metal used to manufacture various products. He easily commercialized and distributed AI to AVI's customers clamoring for prosperity at a time of widespread need. Humanoid drones worked in several manufacturing and mining industries using sentient metal."

Sage posits, "Ilem gave manufacturers of common AI assistants new models made of sentient metal and sold it practically at cost. AVI even created and controlled simple little dots and other household digital assistants." Sledge summarizes Sage's statements: "So, that's why *dos* little bastards pop on without anyone talking."

While refocusing Sledge on the consequences of failure, Sage notices a multi-colored aura from Sledge's skull. Instead of immediately lashing at the fingers of light to seize control of Sledge's emotions, Sage allows them to seep into her. She realizes in the safety of her silent thoughts that for far too long, she has used her abilities as a shield to protect her, not an open hand, as her father suggested. Suddenly, a rising and unexpected passion begins to quench her thirst from the emotional desert she's wandered through alone.

The refreshing wave of Sledge's bare emotions washed over her, yanking her back to the present, "Countries accepted Ilem's overtures of affluence and what seemed like gifts to compete with each other, even though it meant the Sect spread to every corner of the world. Rich kids wore them publicly first. It made them reckless, driving frantically through sky lanes," Sledge adds, "*Di* knockoffs only cost *ah* few hundred bitcoins, *an di* cheap ones did more damage. *Dem* fucked a lot of people up *wid* headaches, memory loss …"

Sage agrees, noting, "Even worse, people who bought Black Market copies became uncontrollably violent … Many of those who used the faulty devices roamed the streets, wreaking havoc like a pack of zombies." Sledge says, "I had my back against *di* wall a few times warring with *dem* beasts. *Dem* may not have gotten smarter, *buh* they seemed a lot stronger and *ah* lot angrier."

Sledge allows Sage further into his mind by sharing with her, "When Iggy and I was teens, we got into *ah* lot of trouble letting people know we were not happy with the trans movement. We ran around Center City's fire dumps spray-painting *Cáscara* on the wall because we didn't want everybody *tuh* know right away what we were doing. That is why Iggy and I swore we would never use *iSiphons*. The gain is not worth becoming *ah* mindless troll slurping from another man's ladle."

Sage responds, "Like a tightening vice grip, Ilem used the Sect to take control everywhere around the globe. When world leaders realized Ilem's largesse was part of his deception, his drones and transhumans were everywhere. The real fall for human countries was when Ilem held his 2042 Peace Summit to reveal his and AVI's plans for the future of life on Earth. I thought things would change for the better."

He does not mock Sage for her foolhardy conclusion. Instead, he laughs, thinking about the conclave of Purists he fought against at Blood Bowl. They were the final thirty-six Purists rounded up by Ilem's forces to fight in the Blood Bowl arena. Sledge reminds Sage of what she recalled as a tipping point in the struggle for human survival, "Until the last thirty-six Purists were rounded up to fight at Blood Bowl."

Sage, encouraged by her conversation with Sledge, asks him, "Then you'll be okay helping fulfill the Doomsday Protocol, right?" Instead of going with the flow, Sledge tersely responds, "I *neva* went on the Floating City *tuh* become part of Hamilton's twisted plan. I didn't want *dis*."

Although the empath senses that their talk is returning to negativity, Sage assures Sledge that his new existence was not premeditated. Instead, the hands of serendipity cast it, "I do not believe my father planned to bring you into this Sledge. He knew fate was uncertain, but man's destruction was not. He theorized that Ilem wouldn't care about pure carbon-based life if it ceased to exist. But by now, he may know we are still alive." Sledge sarcastically bashes Dr. Hamilton's actions, "I'm glad Q predicted *ah* future where my dead ass was still worth saving."

He cannot help but picture Iggy and him in a small escape vehicle leaving Earth. Sledge tells her with disdain, "He didn't consider *dis* abomination he created might *hav* plans."

They continue to parry regarding Sledge's concern about his current fate. Sledge, "I'm gonna find Iggy *an* get *sumweh* safe, *an* it starts by getting off *dis* goddamn table," to which Sage contends, "Why is escape so important to you? If we stop Ilem, we can save Iggy and what's left of life on Earth."

Iggy: From trickle to wave.

Contentiously, Sledge informs Sage about the crooked, painful path Iggy and he were forced to walk as stolen and abandoned children. "Get real! Who's left to save? And where were *des* mystery people all the years I was alone without a family? Or trying to save my mom?" Sage returns to a calming tone to lower Sledge's aggression, "I didn't mean …"

Like so many other children abandoned by their parents during the World Water War of the 2020s, Sledge's birth mother, Lola Aliko, surrendered him at the entrance to a U.S. military base because he was becoming an unsustainable burden on her. Sledge, "After my father, Bobby, was killed in *di* water wars, my mum left me like trash for *di* military *tuh* find at a Military Base in Carlisle. *Dat* was 2026. *Di* only *ting* she wrote on the note she left with me read, 'Property of the US Government. Sledge.'"

"My Uncle told me *dat* he heard in *di* streets *dat* she went back *tuh* Nigeria in shame. She was *nuh* seen again, but I guess her high-class family in Africa were better off without claiming *ah* handicapped child from an immigrant father."

Sledge continues, "*Tings* were a little rough in *di* orphanage, what *wid* eight orphans, five girls *an* three boys, including Iggy *an* me. *Everyting criss afta* Uncle found me."

Sage feels relieved that Sledge has returned to discussing a subject that calms his aura from an uncontrolled fire to a tempered spark. She expresses to Sledge, "That explains how you got there, but what about Iggy?" Sledge appeases her curiosity by telling her about his friend's tumultuous beginnings.

Sledge tells her Iggy was born in 2027 in Bolivia during the World Water Wars that claimed his father and drove his mother away. Everything was unstable. Refugees populated several pockets of poor and wealthy countries without enough water to survive for a week.

Iggy's parents, Antonio, a typical tin miner, and his mother, Ria, a homemaker, lived in San Ignacio de Velasco, one of Bolivia's largest and most developed mission towns. San Ignacio de Velasco's bustling market center was an extensive frontier hinterland of large cattle ranches and isolated Indigenous Chiquitano communities.

San Ignacio de Velasco was graced by massive swollen-bellied toboroche trees, whose tangled branches blossomed brilliant pink and white in the summer. The town's wide, unpaved streets fanned out from the central plaza, lined with low houses whose tiled roofs extended over the pavement, supported by wooden beams.

Despite the gorgeous canopy of foliage and ethnic homes, Antonio and Ria found themselves in a hell consuming a town increasingly unable to secure clean water. As a result, ruthless gangs began to rampage through and control San Ignacio de Velasco's water flow. Eventually, the gangs started forcing locals to join the gang or be forced to watch their families be victimized and worse if they refused to comply.

Unable to find a way out for Ria, Antonio decided to part with his wife to allow her to escape persecution. Before she departed, Ria met her kind and hardworking husband in the Cathedral de San Ignacio, where they were married.

The collapsed remains of the once magnificent Cathedral retained the painted facade decorated with statues of saints, each accompanied by familiar animals. The interior still housed carved, ghostly Baroque altarpieces and protective statues of saints that abandoned their post decades ago. These mysteries of ancient ruins were accompanied by the ugly modern concrete bell tower squatting in the square.

Miles from the still town, Ria traversed Valle de la Luna. The Moon Valley, as it is often called, was a massive expanse of sandstone monoliths that the dry winds shaped into craggy, space-like mountains. Inconspicuous staircases and trails were carved out so visitors could walk through the site. A pregnant Ria crossed the Moon Valley on her long journey to the U.S. She traveled almost 4,000 miles through dangerous terrain but sustained herself and gave birth to her beautiful boy, Ignacio Antonio Fuentes II, alone in a dusty Laredo field.

Unbeknownst to Ria, this southern border of Texas was a primary drug market in the Texas drug smuggling corridor between the United States and Mexico. Swarms of ICE agents, reinvigorated by Ilem's crackdown on Purists, particularly the poorest crossing the border, snatched immigrants into bondage as quickly as possible.

Ria hurried through the back streets of Laredo, trying to avoid detection by ICE agents while circumventing shady drug deals around her. Although she did all she could to avoid detection, she was snared in the entanglement of the USA's disparate immigration policies. A particularly savage, pumpkin-faced ICE agent ripped Iggy from Ria's arms, and they were never together again. No one wanted to adopt Iggy because he was on the autism spectrum. That is how he and Sledge met.

Uncle Ray the Ocean: Peace, be still.

Still on the exam table, Sledge, for the first time in a while, reflects on the man who rescued him from the horrors and difficulties of surviving in a state-run orphanage system when people are looking for anyone to rob, beat, or cheat. According to Sledge, Uncle Ray looked into what happened to Iggy's mother. Complications from her pregnancy killed Ria while ICE held her. Sledge summarizes Iggy and his plight, "So, *yuh* could say we're *boat* wards of *Babylon*."

"Uncle took me *an* Iggy under his arms *tuh* teach us how *tuh* survive in *ah* world at war, which seemed the more likely outcome of *deh* social discourse bantered about. My father, Bobby, owned a rare collection of weapons *an* trained in various martial arts *wit* Uncle. *Dem* were twin brothers, Raymond, and Robert, *deh* fighting Sledge brothers. *Buh* I *neva* meet my dad. If I had, I'm sure he would *hav* also taught me the martial arts styles best used by *deh* blind."

Sledge recalls fondly a hand-written Jeet Keen Do fighting manual that Uncle said he and Bobby purchased at a gypsy street fare from a flaming-red-haired woman wearing a t-shirt with the words "Hippy Gypsy" on it. Her partner in the dying trade business was an older Asian man who was willing to part with the manual. He handwrote instructions for people who were blind to learn ten specific fighting techniques for offense and defense, which included Wushu, Wing Chun, Brazilian Jui-Jitsu, Judo, Krav Maga, Dambe, Tai Chi, Bushido, Muay Thai, and Escrima.

The twins inspected the manual, marveling at the wealth of instruction contained on each page. The old Asian man proudly pointed out that the manual was one of many he had written over the years to document his martial arts training. Uncle Ray and Bobby did not need long to purchase the manual at a price reasonable for a fare such as this. Before leaving with the treasures they found at the gypsy fare, the older man inscribed LJF inside the book.

Sledge, "Uncle ... Sensei Ray, I mean ... taught me *deh* ways of Jeet Keen Do from *dat* manual."

Sledge remembers the day he first laid eyes on the instrument that would contribute to his salvation. He vividly recalls Uncle Ray carrying the footlocker the military had finally shipped him. Inside were the last possessions of Sledge's father, Bobby. An excited Sledge and anticipatory Iggy impatiently waited for the box to be set on the ground by Uncle Ray like little children on Christmas morning. Sledge, "*Di* weapons inside *dat* box were all *dat* Uncle Ray needed *tuh* train me *tuh* fight at a very early age." Sledge found a cache of bladed, blunt, range weapons and more flexible weapons like nunchaku there.

He informs Sage, "Uncle taught Iggy *an* me how *tuh* survive, using our instincts. Called it our 'glint.' Something he heard in *ah* old Jamaican song. Iggy learned from tinkering with flying motorcycles and out-of-date gadgets at Uncle

Ray's motorcycle shop, the Flying Lancers MC. At the same time, I trained in martial arts that compensated for my blindness."

Sage offers to Sledge, "He sounds like a good man." Sledge remarks, "He was. *An* I swore *tuh* him I would *neva* let anyone exploit Iggy or me because of our ... handicaps."

For a moment, Sledge feels his fists clench as muscle memory reminds him of his training under Uncle Ray. He recalls Uncle Ray would instruct him to remain aggressive even when striking a mere Wing Chun martial arts statue. Under Uncle Ray's tutelage, he once felt his hand had become an axe chopping down the obstacles that blocked his path to a distant road ahead. Uncle Ray would loom behind him and make him repeat the same mantra until Sledge's hands were slightly bleeding and just beyond sore.

Uncle Ray would repeat, "*Again*, Sledge," prompting Sledge to begin pounding on the dummy with hard punches and kicks, repeating the same mantra, "Justice, Courage, Mercy, Politeness, Honesty, Honor, Loyalty, Self-Control ..."[45]

Sledge tells Sage, "When *eva* I *wud* ask Uncle Ray why Iggy didn't have *tuh* do it *tuh*, Uncle Ray would remind me, '*Iggy get im owna glint. Jah gave you one, too.*'"

Uncle Ray was more than a man knowledgeable about how martial arts could train someone to defeat an opponent. The lethal art was also an aid to prevent Sledge's physical limits from being a sign of weakness in a dangerous world.

Uncle Ray taught him, "*When yuh train wid Jeet Kune Do yuh overcome blindness.*"[46] With that knowledge, Sledge continued practicing, increasing the pace of his blows against the fighting dummy with each word. Uncle Ray, "*It goin' tek yuh long to master these fighting styles.*"[47] Undeterred, Sledge continued pounding the dummy into submission, "Justice, Courage, Mercy ..."

"When I last saw Iggy," Sledge shares with Sage, "he gave me a staff *frah* my father's weapons collection *dat* Iggy modified for my use. We called it *di*

---

[45] Bushido's Eight Virtues - Way of the Warrior.
[46] "Training in Jeet Kune Do will overcome your blindness."
[47] "It's going to take a long time to master these fighting styles."

Vision Staff. He started saving parts from Gita *tuh* improve how *di* Vision Staff functioned. *Dar's* no telling what else Iggy could have done if *di* world hadn't gone *tuh* shit."

Sage asks Sledge, "You said you promised not to leave Iggy again." With eyes closed Sledge exhales as a heavy burden has returned to bear down on his shoulders. Sledge, "When I'm peaceful, people take advantage of me. When I'm fierce, they tend *tuh* stay away. Let's say Uncle *gat tiad* of *mi* mischief, and I *gat* full of myself."

Sledge rhetorically asks Sage, "What did I get out of it?" He answers his question while she continues to draw in the infrequent emotions Sledge reveals to her, "*Nutten.*"

So close to understanding Sledge's emotional tipping point, Sage probes further for details of his experiences, asking him, "What were you trying to find? What were you looking for out there …" Sledge interrupts Sage's questions with a self-effacing answer, "Trouble … *dat's* what I am, *an dat's* what I found."

Sledge laments, "Once on the road if I wasn't rummaging *fah* food, I had *tuh* fight gangs who roamed or controlled *di* desecrated heartland of old USA. At its peak, I once had to fight *mi* way through thirty men, *an* in *di* process, I took on *di* challenge of protecting two children *fah di* brutality of people detached from reason." His shifting emotions continue to be emitted from his third eye as he talks about the obstacles he faced on the road.

"There's a block," Sage senses. "Here is where I need to break through."

Turning to Sledge, Sage tells him that she needs to put him to sleep for the next step in the body-casting process, "very painful" is how she describes the experience. Resigned that there is little he can do to stop her, Sledge looks at Sage with sunken eyes of defeat and answers, "Does it *matta?*"

"Pain is what I've known, *an* pain will consume *whateva* is left of my days."

END OF CHAPTER 7

Chapter 8

Air and Sea

She
Is the air
And the sea.

She stretches out to
Engulf me.
If she leaves me,
I suffocate.
When she consumes,
I drown,
But
I can't live
Without each breath
of conflicted air and sea
filling me
for better or worse.

The only thing I want,
I need,
Is for her to be
Near.

Rough surf
And winds,
Please comfort me
Like
Ahab
Going down
With his ship.

I need
Her
To live
And die,
Surrounded by
her
Conflicted
Embrace.

The Badlands

To put Sledge to sleep and calm his Crown Chakra to decrease negative vibes and a less hindered flow of emotions, Sage gently slides her left hand on the back of Sledge's neck, holding her right hand just above the top of his skull. A violet light flows from Sage's curved hand two inches above Sledge's head.

Unlike the other chakras, the Crown Chakra is not on your body. It's located just above your head and radiates infinitely upward and outward. Sage hopes and anticipates that lifting the weight burdening Sledge's psyche will unclog and release his inner self.

On a physical level, the power of the Crown Chakra flows from Sledge's pineal gland, controlling his ability to sleep and his waking bouts of restlessness. The violet glow from Sage's hand intertwines with the darkness troubling Sledge's emotions. Like a cloud, his negative chakra blocks his calm and ability to have lasting peace within. Yet in the quiet of the night, Sage knows that those thoughts that Sledge may be running from often resurface, making it hard for him to see his true path, not just to what he was but also to what he can become.

Sledge falls asleep while talking to Sage. He tells her, "Nothing is what I found …" His last words uttered before closing his eyes carry Sage on his stream of consciousness to one of the recent days instrumental in Sledge's emotional pathology.

It was a day that Sledge's optimism rose with the sun. He knew if he could walk 1100 more miles, he would see Iggy in just a few weeks, and they could take the next step in their plan to abandon Earth.

On that day, lifted by the buoyancy of hope, Sledge needed to buy a few shuriken from the arms dealers who ruled Cannon Air Force Base a few miles from Clovis, New Mexico. This was the day Sledge's circuitous path narrowed straight. I will tell you about his encounter as though you were there because I was, watching, always watching.

Armed with only the items on his utility belt, martial arts skills, and Vision Staff, Sledge fought humans and transhumans bent on committing atrocities wherever they roamed. Having to fight his way to safety daily depleted Sledge's weapons stock, leaving him with only a few more shuriken for long-distance skirmishes or flights to shelter.

Sledge traversed the badlands to Clovis on foot without a vehicle or cover. Months before Blood Bowl, if Sledge did not run into someone desperate enough to abuse a blind man, he collided with rogues, thieves, and shell pirates who wanted more than anything to take his life than all his other property, in no particular order.

Sledge finds himself traveling to the eastern corner of what was left of New Mexico, hoping to negotiate with arms dealers, and, with the hard bargaining concluded, he will be on his way.

Unexpectedly, from a distance, Sledge watches five men wearing Menpo Samurai masks patrolling the Cannon Air Force Base entrance. The masks, designed to strike fear in others, reflect the men's personalities through their familiar spirit animal: if you are a snake, your familiar is a snake; if you are a heel, your familiar is a jackass, and so on.

A large sign emblazoned with a red stone fist bathed in white flames is affixed to the gate. It is the sign of the deceptive and cunning arms dealers Rugga Ton and his cohort, Esteban *El Infame*. They call their posse the Emperors of Death. It may have been a hyperbolic name for their clique, but not many survived a clash with them to dispute the title.

Albeit is not his intent to step inside the barricaded town, Sledge's attention is drawn in a direction he does not want to go. Sledge hears two children that unsavory gangsters are pulling behind the closed gate. From the whispers on the road, the gate has two purposes: to keep travelers from entering the land controlled by the Emperors of Death or to keep transients trafficked into servitude from leaving.

Someone whom Sledge cannot definitively detect throws the children onto the ground. The taller girl grabs the more petite boy to flee from the eleven men wearing the terrifying Menpo guises. Sinister laughter intending to menace the children's efforts to flee the inevitable reveals to Sledge that the vile men intend to harm the children to satisfy their perverse desire to eat their own.

Self-survival is the first strategy for those dumb or brave enough to wander this sterile and perilous world without being under Ilem's protection. Out here, you willingly stay still under control or run from the shadow of Death's reaving hand. Yet, as Uncle Ray taught him, as much as he wants to suppress it, Sledge is compelled to turn his attention to the plight of the hysterical children and away from his quest for food, valuable tools, and a path to his friend Iggy somewhere in Chicago.

As his muscles instinctively flex and tighten, Sledge recalls the mantra, "Justice, Courage, Mercy …." When one of the predators grabs the little girl by the arm, Sledge springs over the gate separating him from an open road away from this chaos, and a one-way street into hell.

He unleashes his last few shuriken to burst open the thick skulls of the deviants chasing after the children. He lands safely on one knee and then listens to confirm which of the children's stalkers is disabled. As he does so, Sledge mutters his training mantra, "…Honor, Loyalty, Self-Control."

Suddenly, shotgun blasts resound near Sledge's head as gang members try to take him down. To avoid the bullets, Sledge rolls his flexible body along the ground, then ducks behind the corpse of a fallen foe. Shots meant for Sledge riddle the dead man's body, proving to be an adequate cover for Sledge and an aid to him to take out another future obstacle.

Following the assailant closest to dragging the little boy away from the girl's grip, Sledge abandons his cover to give the goon a stiff whack in his dick and cocky balls. Aside from his thud onto the ground, the only other sound from the thug echoes the agonizing pain emanating from his busted nuts.

Defeating one, two, and three foes at a time makes the remaining fools think twice about desiring to die today. The cost of violence travels both ways, as Sledge confirms, as more bullets race past his head.

Encouraged that Sledge is pinned down by their snipers, a horde rushes Sledge to take him to the ground. To defend himself from their sudden, relentless punches and kicks, Sledge tucks his body into a ball, cocooning his head to avoid serious harm.

While Sledge continues to flinch in anticipation of blows that have stopped being thrown, one of the thugs hawks a wad of phlegm on the back of Sledge's hand. It is not the saliva that has a stench; it is the smell of bacterium living on the yellow-coated tongue within his mouth, worsened by lingering ashtray breath and cheap wine turned to vinegar.

Even in his apparent helplessness, Sledge knows they will have to kill him before he lets them disrespect him like he was a whipped dog alone and desperate in the streets.

Resorting to his knowledge of Brazilian Jiu-jitsu, Sledge spins his body like a dancer rocking to a sudden beat, bashing the five gangsters across their legs and upper bodies, leaving them off-balanced and defenseless. As each crumble to the dusty road, their bodies slam down with a loud thud, followed by more deafening squeals and wails of agony.

The one thug who can still utter sounds other than howls calls out for reinforcements. He is the same fool who spat on Sledge. To silence his assailant's dog whistle, Sledge snaps his leg above his head as far as his flexibility allows, then smashes the heel of his foot down into and through the assailant's sternum. The human panic alarm silences as he dies from a sharp bone piercing deep into his sternum. Crimson blood paints the disabled thug's lips as dry earth chokes his throat.

Sledge stops to survey the damage he was forced to unleash against the perverts hoping to steal the innocence of frightened children. For only a second, Sledge enjoys the silence of the men he has just killed or seriously wounded. Deep inside a hole in his soul, he longs for the kill, death rattling in his foes' throats. Death's door is a place Sledge has visited; the sound of its bell ringing reminds him of home.

Before Sledge confirms they are all down for the count, he hears the rumbling noise of hostiles charging his way and feels the wind changing as more bullets zip past him. Turning toward the noises, Sledge detects more attackers charging at him, indeed, so many that he does not have enough fingers and toes to count them all.

Abandoning long enough ago the notion that helping two kids could not be too problematic, Sledge takes off to find higher fighting ground using the Vision Staff as a guide. Seeing the pursuing horde, the children call Sledge to run inside the building where they attempt to hide. Without anything else to block the doors from inside, Sledge grabs hold of an old metal chair to push through the door handles, temporarily slowing his antagonists.

The pounding of feet alerts Sledge that he is besieged again. He hides the children in a crawl space under a flight of stairs to have one less worry. With only a few moments to spare, Sledge topples a heavy bookcase in front of the crawl space to conceal the frightened children.

That was a moment Sledge should have spent hiding, too, as the number of attackers grew from five to more than another two dozen cold-blooded bastards bashing at the door. In the heat of the moment, whether foe or prey, his mind must adjust to the ever-changing flow of combat.

Sledge steadies his feet, locking them rigid on the floor, and settles his breath, concentrating on each inhale and exhale of air flowing in and out of his mouth. In this mindful state, Sledge concludes that the Emperors of Death never heard of Sun Tzu. That master strategist's philosophies of war were already engrained in Sledge, who trained at the knee of his wise and skilled sensei, Uncle Ray. Following his Uncle's many instructions, Sledge blocks out the sound of his heartbeat to hear those of the men who want to slay him.

"There you are," Sledge thinks, "I see you now."

He recalls Uncle Ray's voice citing Tzu, "*Der* is no greater danger *dan* underestimating *yuh* opponent." Sledge uses that inspiring lesson to prepare his strategy and lift his energy to defend against the men who want to pin him in a corner and beat him to death. By mentally cycling through all the styles of fighting he learned since childhood, Sledge knows he will need to call upon a martial art that can be used in a standing position because kicks alone will not suffice.

From his years of training and fighting, Sledge realizes that if he is knocked to the ground, his options for victory will be sorely limited. Instead of utilizing one style of all those he knows, Sledge combines his knowledge into his style, drawing on all the techniques most beneficial to someone without sight.

In each their way, Sledge's foes' anxious and hostile ways convince him that they have peered over the edge of oblivion, lost their minds, and returned vultures. Instead of joining the remaining Purists in their quest for survival, they have ruthlessly devoured anyone foolish enough to need or want to cross these badlands. That is unless they came with cash in one hand and a white flag in the other.

One of the attackers forces his way into the building, bending and then cracking the frame of the metal chair. Like many other unwise or undertrained fighters, the first one through the door sees a sightless opponent and assumes it will be easy to dispatch him. He is so wrong, dead wrong.

From his training, Sledge always knows that his lack of sight emboldens his enemies to believe he is an easy mark. To dissuade him of that notion before ignorance boosts their unbridled confidence, Sledge delivers a rapid succession of punches directly into the assailant's core, then quickly strikes him up his body – chest, throat, neck – finishing him with an open palm strike to his forehead. If Sledge were counting his punches, which he has no time to do, he would have counted twenty-eight blows delivered to the victim in less than ten seconds, flying back out the door.

Devastating, deadly, and precise, just as Sensei Ray taught him.

Within the pages of his mind, Sledge flips through the many lessons taught to him by his Uncle. Uncle Ray warned Sledge, who was often hardheaded, "It is difficult enough to fight one person, but two or more could always result in a fatal mistake. Knowing how to defend yourself or when to run can be the difference between life or death."

Of all the styles of fighting he knows best, the one that gives him his best chance in tight quarters against a horde of marauders is Krav Maga. During Israel's existence, Krav Maga was the country's national martial art, similar to Jeet Kune Do and MMA, which meld different techniques to maximize the best skills from multiple disciplines.

From years of training, Sledge knows that Krav Maga will provide him with a solid defense and an immediate offense against more than one attacker. By angling his body to only permit one person down the narrow hallway with the others behind him, Sledge positions himself to take on the next wave of marauders.

Sledge hurries toward the next person through the door, angling to ensure the hood remains before him. His attacker tries to grab Sledge to deliver his finishing blows. Still, in anticipation of the thug's body movements, Sledge grabs his head and neck in a clinch to control his opponent and then kicks the fight out of him several times until he crumbles.

The rest of the horde busts down the door, rushing at Sledge like raging bulls. He hears Uncle Ray again, "Fight or flight, know when and when not." This is a time to run, but before that, Sledge takes hold of the bent metal chair and uses one of its legs as an impromptu spear to jab into the face of the next man, too unwise to let the others go first.

Backing up the stairs puts Sledge in a position to limit his attackers, but the sound of even more of them cascades wildly into the hollow hallway. The following pack of wolves seems even hungrier and determined to kill Sledge. He is only able to use a sidekick against one more assailant. He swiftly lifts his knee to the front, kicking down to strike with his heel, then pulling his stiff leg back. The rest of the gang watches the man fall over the balcony and onto his head.

Their hesitation gives Sledge time to push a steel cabinet over the second-floor balcony on top of another three hoodlums. They are pinned down and subsequently mercilessly trampled by their henchmen trying to get to Sledge. The few seconds Sledge has to reset his defense against the next handful of attackers bustling to the top of the stairs give him enough time to listen for the children. Their infantile cries do not hit his ears, making Sledge briefly pleased to know the children are safe.

Eleven down. Fifteen more to go.

The rest of the horde back Sledge into a large empty training room, save for a few pieces of training equipment. Sledge picks up ten-pound dumbbells in each hand to slam into the haggard face of the next man through the door. The dumbbells smash so hard against both sides of his head that the crook's metal Menpo is crushed, making the brain-dead felon's mouth poke into duck lips.

Backing farther from the room entrance, Sledge lands a flurry of jabs, slashes, and groin attacks against a couple more people after him. Sledge wields his hand like a spear jabbing against two more men, rendering them unconscious. He only wishes he had Karas wrapped around his hands, dipped in glass, like in the old Dambe days.

Today, he will have to rely on the hardness of his bones to bust open his attackers. The last two combatants do just that; lay on the floor clutching their bleeding faces. The faces of the previous five gang members Sledge disabled are not visible through their Samurai masks. However, the audible screams and wails of those still living paint a vivid picture for Sledge of what Uncle Ray described as "suffering the consequences."

10!

The rest of the thugs chase Sledge to the roof. There, he hears the cackling of two men, blood brothers he later learns are named Rugga and Esteban. They casually watched the fun from nearby rooftops like Nero fiddling to oblivion. They are the highest in this poisoned food chain.

Rugga yells at his crew to attack Sledge together, unlike a gang of idiots who know martial arts yet miraculously have never watched a single film to the end to understand the benefits of a blitzkrieg or even the childhood game of "pile on." Indeed, this well-trained pack of wolves comprehend more than moviegoers consuming popcorn. These rabid dogs smell blood on the wind, which instinctively and collectively draws them to attack.

The gang of misbegotten, desert ronin pin Sledge against the wall. One would think they have the advantage, but Sledge repeatedly kicks and punches the mound of flesh away, then moves strategically to a spot where he can regain his footing, fend them off, and protect his back.

Sledge shouts his spirit yell, "Kiai," as he fixes his determined eyes on the Emperors of Death rushing at him again.

Quickly, Sledge draws the Vision Staff over his head and snaps it across the shoulders of the closest man he can hit. Rotating the staff around sideways allows Sledge to smack a few more of his attackers in sensitive spots on their bodies to render them docile. Then, Sledge sidesteps to let two of them race by him again.

Uncle Ray intended to train Sledge in the Escrimador ways to emphasize fighting multiple foes at a distance. Sledge sets his feet to maintain balance against the slew of assailants, forming two triangle points. He steps with one foot to the triangle's third point to quell his attackers and keep a stable position. Most importantly, Sledge focuses on standing low to fight more than a few combatants simultaneously.

With the Vision Staff lifted above his head, Sledge twirls his weapon like a helicopter blade building momentum to launch into flight. Like many Escrimador, Sledge knows several ways to use his Vision Staff to disable his opponents. He continues spinning the Vision Staff in a circular movement to hit one attacker in his left temple from a forward stance, twisting his wrist to an angle as he pulls his attacker's aching head towards his shoulders to deliver a second strike.

Sledge swings the Vision Staff in the opposite direction in a slashing action while slamming the other hand in a diagonal downward swing to the left temple of his foe.

He extends the Vision Staff to strike someone else, with his arm making a backhand slashing swing against the shoulder and hips of the next attacker. For power, Sledge mastered using his body to twist and drop down on his foes to deliver knee strikes, tripping low-line kicks, and stomps. He calls upon those skills to render more attackers gravely wounded or unconscious.

Sledge turns to this offensive tool whenever he sees an opening to take down another enemy. A final strike to those still conscious with the Vision Staff that he spins like a solo bastón smacks and knocks them away. With the last attackers reeling from their tango with Sledge, he stands in the center circle, cautiously scanning the injured men to see who wants to step up next.

But that still left Rugga and Esteban to contend with, both wearing frightening Samurai masks different from those sported by their fallen henchmen. Their masks are attached to *iSiphon*, which flash angry warning lights along their edges.

Tired, beat to hell, bloodied, and bruised, Sledge twists both ends of the Vision Staff, then yanks the whole staff apart, separating it into the three-section nunchaku called the sanjiegun. The elongated staff gives Sledge an added advantage of eight feet of extended metal and chains able to punish opponents, whether close or at a distance.

His thoughts cycle through the perils he has already faced against the small army of deviants. He knows from the whispers that travel on their own across the barrens of the road that instead of relying on steel swords or even automatic weapons, these motherfucking twins are rumored to have some unique abilities from their *iSiphons* that make them the most lethal Emperors of Death.

Esteban nods at his brother, Rugga, then calmly walks downstairs from the roof, where he can view Sledge fighting for his life. As Sledge was warned, Esteban does not need a fabricated weapon to defeat his challengers. Instead, by pounding his fists together, Rugga emits a burning sword in his right hand and a sturdy metal shield on his left forearm. Sledge murmurs, "Holy shit."

Instinctively, he swings the Vision Staff to force Esteban to stay at a distance. Simultaneously with Esteban's attempted attack, Sledge propels the Vision Staff at him to block Esteban's wide slashes of his fiery sword. Esteban responds by shuffling his feet to a more stable position, swaying in response to Sledge's actions, taking them into a sort of fighter's tango.

As Rugga moves, his left hand comes up, and his blade slashes across the gap between the base of Sledge's chest and neck. The sound of the Vision Staff and Esteban's blazing sword clang together like a blazing hammer smashing into an anvil.

Sledge holds the two outer staves of the sanjiegun, one in each hand, to execute a double-stick attack technique. To counter Sledge's attack, Esteban charges directly at Sledge, hollering at the top of his lungs, slicing Sledge twice, cutting his flesh and cauterizing it simultaneously. That sudden damage and branding leaves more time for punishment that stops short of death.

Returning his thoughts to his lessons from Uncle Ray and his quotes from Sun Tzu, Sledge regroups his strategy around the notion that "Strategy without tactics is the slowest route to victory. Tactics without strategy are the noise before defeat." Sledge commits to a strategy, but against these deadly opponents, nothing short of a miracle or a deep search of his training will suffice.

Sledge alternates repeatedly hitting Esteban in his grotesque face and upper body with the opposite ends of the nunchakus. He continues smacking Esteban to the point that Esteban begins to lose consciousness. As Esteban hits the ground, Sledge wraps the middle section of the triple nunchakus against Esteban's throat, then forces his windpipe inward to stop Esteban's breathing.

With his prey down on all fours, Sledge attacks Esteban's legs, whipping the Vision Staff high, then quickly striking Esteban's lower body. When Esteban falls backwards on the ground, Sledge jumps on him, bashing him in his blood-blotted face and upper body as quickly as possible. Esteban is rendered unconscious after this pummeling by Sledge.

Despite successfully defending himself, Sledge turns to Rugga to tell him he wants this over with. As Sledge tries to negotiate an end to the contest, Esteban regains consciousness and uses Sledge's lack of attention to his advantage. Esteban charges at Sledge with his fire sword reared back for a crucial blow. Although Sledge can hear the pounding of Esteban's feet and smell the burning flames, he does not move fast enough to avoid Esteban cutting him for the third time.

Sledge recognizes that the hardship of fending off multiple attackers is not the battle scars you sustain but the anticipation of what is next, and when it will all end. He pushes himself to his feet, using the Vision Staff as an aid. His blood drips on the hot rooftop, slowly baking on the dirty asphalt.

Pointing the weapon at Esteban, Sledge says defiantly, "One more round!" The vulgarities that spew from Esteban's mouth would make a sailor proud, but Sledge is unmoved. He has been pushed too far and pressed too long. No matter how many skulls of foes he must crack to traverse yet another barbaric dystopian hellhole, he now sees as mere steppingstones in a raging river.

Sledge sways from side to side, like a cobra preparing to strike, his fangs, the sharp ends of the sectioned Vision Staff. Esteban leaps toward Sledge with both hands clasped together to maximize the force of his weapon, cutting into Sledge's flesh for the fourth and final time. Swiftly, Sledge raises the sanjiegun and slacks his knee enough to spring into position to block Esteban's attack.

Deftly, Sledge yanks all three sections of the Vision Staff into his clinched hand and then spin-kicks Esteban in his gut. Reeling from the sudden air loss,

Esteban stumbles back and collapses to the rooftop. As he rises, Sledge snaps the Vision Staff away from his body, projecting the farthest tip toward Esteban's face.

The sickening sound of metal busting through the soft yoke of the eye stuns Rugga and tempers his overconfident belief that Sledge would not be too difficult to kill. The flame emanating from Esteban's hand, and his protective shield, gradually turn to smoke and then vanish with the wind. The attackers, who can still witness Esteban's fate, scramble from the roof and down the stairway to their safety. Rugga yells at them, "Come back, you cowards!" His commanding words are greeted by retreating silence.

Rugga is no longer laughing or content to remain a Spectator of this street fight. Infuriated by his brother's death, Rugga jumps down from the higher roof, kicking Sledge away from Esteban. Sledge barely recovers from Rugga's swift attack before Rugga presses his attack again, striking Sledge so hard in his face that it causes Sledge to stumble backwards and drop his Vision Staff. Sledge swings his fist wildly to keep Rugga at bay as he loses his balance.

Rugga smiles contemptibly at Sledge, then begins pounding his hands together, "Come on, drifter. It's payback time, bitch!" Sledge listens as each thud grows increasingly intense. The more Rugga's hands smash together, the more they swell and harden like stone. Rugga picks up the Vision Staff and bends it in the middle as a sign of strength.

Contemptuously, Rugga tosses the broken staff to the ground. He flashes his speed and hits Sledge in the shoulder with a punch so quick and hard that Sledge cannot lift his hand to block it. Rugga again tilts from side to side to confuse Sledge's senses.

Another punch from Rugga to Sledge's solar plexus knocks Sledge back eighteen feet into the roof's brick wall. Trickles of blood drops leave a trail from Rugga's point of contact with Sledge's body to the spot the blind ragdoll now slumps. The anguish radiates down Sledge's legs, rendering them loose and unstable like cooked noodles.

If he is meant to die today, Sledge knows he has fought a good fight and for once the right reasons. With his remaining strength, Sledge sees his way from stumbling in his permanent darkness to regaining his footing. He knows now that all he has to defend himself are the wind, his senses, and his training. Listening intently, Sledge can hear Rugga huffing and shuffling toward him, ready to deliver one more blow against Sledge that will surely end the contest.

Sledge musters his remaining energy to whizz a blow near the space where Rugga's stomach was less than a second ago, but Rugga is too elusive to be hit. Rugga callously bangs his fists together again, then taunts Sledge, "I'm gonna bash your skull in, then have my boys fuck you. You won't leave here alive, nor will that sweetmeat you've hidden away somewhere."

Just as Rugga found a sound strategy to injure Sledge, Sledge advances toward Rugga's voice, snake-like, to confuse Rugga about where Sledge will move or attack from next. Conversely, Rugga knows that if he throws a flurry of punches, Sledge will be pressed into a vulnerable position and eventually receive what Rugga plans to be the *coup de gras*.

The king of the Emperors of Death throws a straight jab, connecting with Sledge's left shoulder. Sledge stumbles backwards, grasping from the escalating pain from all the punishment he has sustained during this relentless street fight. Rugga lands a jab to Sledge's swollen jaw, staggering Sledge back again.

Rugga does not wait for Sledge to revive his senses. Instead, he advances toward Sledge yet again, escalating his speed faster and faster to maximize the collision between his hands of stone and Sledge's jaw of glass.

Rugga leaps at Sledge, ready to crush every bone in his body, starting with Sledge's smug face. Instead of quaking in fear, Sledge flashes a knowing smirk, recognizing his peril would not have existed if he had followed his plan and kept to the road and himself. All this for feral children wandering untamed, he thinks to himself. Sledge knew it was ridiculous, that he should walk away unscathed, but it was too late to barter for a different lot.

Now, Sledge's survival pits instinctive fury and cunning against blind impulsiveness. If Rugga wants a fight to the death, that is what he will get from Sledge, Vision Staff or not.

With a booming yell, Rugga bashes his knee into Sledge's forearms, protecting his head. Luckily, Sledge finds enough space to bob away from Rugga's attack, then steps behind him. With Rugga off balance, Sledge links his ring and middle fingers together to form a pointed weapon to strike Rugga with the first of five moves – five moves only – to deliver the fatal blows known as the five fingers of death.

Sledge concentrates on attacking Rugga's vulnerable acupuncture points to execute this legendary technique. Sledge shouts, "Wataah," as his first jab is from behind into Rugga's neck at the base of the skull. Rugga twists uncomfortably to face Sledge. Sensing his opponent is off-balanced and unprepared to defend himself, Sledge swiftly jabs fingers on both of his hands into the arteries in Rugga's throat. Immediately following Rugga's head falling back from the escalating onslaught, Sledge smashes him in his solar plexus, causing Rugga to crumble to the rooftop.

Without another word, Sledge leaps off the ground behind Rugga to deliver a final crushing elbow to the crown of Rugga's skull. Like a redwood slowly careening to the ground, Rugga first remains rigid on his knees, but shortly after blood begins to leak from his facial orifices, Rugga topples over flat on his face with a loud thud.

Sledge limps down the stairs from the rooftop and helps the children out of their hiding places. He cautiously peaks up and down the road to confirm that there are no more Emperors of Death jumpy for revenge. The streets are empty of any of Esteban's and Rugga's men, just as Sledge hoped he would find. Instead, several needy people waiting outside the gate have run inside the barrier to loot all they can before the guards return.

The children hurry with Sledge to a rusted and disabled camper outside the Emperors of Death's gate, where the children have been in hiding together. They gleefully run to their hiding place inside the rundown, rusty camper. The sounds of joy are soon stifled when a lone guard blasts the trailer with a rocket launcher, instantly killing the children from blowback and shrapnel.

What does burning human flesh smell like? You will know it when you smell it and never forget it. Burning flesh has an awful, acrid odor, like a musky, sweet perfume. The soldiers wounded on battlefields like these fighters experience terror, disorientation, pain, and fear of death as the troubling smell invades their senses and their grisly soup boils in the seething sun. The smell sickens Sledge in his nostril and his emotional core.

Sledge reels back as the explosion engulfs the children. Injured and unable to mount an attack in response to the cruel ending dealt to the defenseless family, Sledge vanishes into the desert as the sun falls below the hills.

As Sledge's image wavers as he walks toward the setting sun on the horizon, Sage's aura untethers from Sledge's memories and fully returns to her body. She continues to assemble Sledge's body cast, armed with a more informed understanding of the source of Sledge's hesitancy to fulfill the Doomsday Protocol.

When Sledge awakens from a restless sleep, he does so to the sound of Sage struggling to pick up one of the arms to reattach to the containment suit. The heavy limb is awkward in Sage's hands, banging against the examination table.

Awakening as though he never ceased speaking when Sage put him to sleep, Sledge picks up where he left off, "...*Nutten ... nutten* is what I found while I hoped *tuh* find *mi* mother. In *di* bottom of *di* weapons trunk from my father *an* Uncle, I found a final note from her saying she *wud* find me, *"Forever near"* in Yoruba, "but *di* closest she ever came *tuh* returning was in my dreams. *Dat* is why I got *tuh* get out of *'ere tuh* find Iggy, don't *yuh* understand. I can't lose him, too." In a sympathetic tone, Sage replies to Sledge's distress by assuring him, "There's still a chance you can."

The clicking sound of Sledge's new arm locking in place wakes a pregnant pause in their conversation. When Sledge does speak, it is only to protest more about what he has become, "Look at me. A talking head. Useless. *Yuh* might as well stick my head in a box *an* leave it *deh*. I can't feel anything. I can't move *an* I'm blind. I'm useless."

Sage struggles to pick up one of the legs to attach to the containment suit. As she does so, she promises Sledge that his cause is preserved despite her hampered efforts to restore his mobility. "You're not useless. If things go according to plan and you willingly activate the Omnis probe, you can telekinetically move your limbs and other objects by the power of thought."

For not even a second does Sledge buy Sage's promises, "How is *dat* even possible? I'm practically *ah* paraplegic."

Sage emphatically answers, "I can help you see and feel." She stops connecting the limbs to rest her tired hands onto Sledge's metal containment suit and inspect her work. Sage explains to him, "Once your mind and body connect, you'll be able to defend yourself again like you could when you were human." Sledge exclaims, "Defend me! How is *dat* even possible."

The last metal leg clicks into place. Panicky, Sledge decries, "I'm less *dan* a man, *an nuh* even *ah* whole transhuman." The back-and-forth leaves Sage uncertain how she can convince Sledge that his fate is not desperate.

In Sledge's mother tongue, Sage assures Sledge, "*Mi can help yuh connect wid unnu mind an body tuh low movement.*"[48] Despite the familiar dialect, he remains skeptical, as proven by his uncontrollable huffing and contentious returns, "I don't believe in miracles." Sage attaches the last arm to the containment suit without responding to Sledge's concerns that she no longer feels she can relieve.

She climbs on top of Sledge at the pelvis area of the containment suit. Although she does not know if she will ever reach Sledge in the ways he needs to free his tortured mind, she feels a tugging of her emotions that she, like Sledge, has learned to protect.

She places her hands along Sledge's temples and coyly says, "Imagine I'm climbing on top of you and wrapping my arms around you." Puzzled, Sledge counters, "I don't know what *yuh tink dis* will do." She seductively whispers to Sledge, "I know you have been with a woman. It would be best if you felt alive. This is life. If you don't need this, I do."

They both feel the physical reality of what is happening; Sage feels it throughout her body, and Sledge, within his mind. She becomes ethereal, and her essence seeps partially into Sledge's containment suit.

In Sledge's mind, there is no resistance as he begins to appreciate how solid and natural Sage's body feels to him. Their limbs become entwined from the passion that rises from despair as Sledge proclaims his astonishment, "I ... I can

---

[48] "I can help you connect with your mind and body to allow movement."

see *yuh* again." Relieved, Sledge caresses Sage's comforting face as he pulls her closer. Parts of her flesh slide through his hands like whiffs of smoke. They climax together from the pleasure of filling unrequited needs.

So many strain to soar to great heights only to find the true elixir for internal happiness was already within.

Miles from Sledge's and Sage's passionate excursion from the despair all around them, Ilem is wearing his gold and silver helmet, which gleams on his head like a beacon calling all the faithful to his throne. The Diwan of Light has Kol at attention in front of a line of Trailers and is holding him by the collar of his armor.

Ilem angrily reprimands Kol for his ineptitude, "How is it possible that you can't find one woman and a fucking head after weeks and weeks of searching?" Ilem gets closer to Kol's nervous face to maximize the intimidation factor. He chides Kol to embarrass him even more as he stands rigidly before his troops, "Kol, the great defensive lineman! You are a joke!" Kol, responding cautiously, pleads with Ilem to understand his failures, "Lord Ilem, capturing the woman was at hand, but an unknown force intervened."

Baring his conceit for all to see, Ilem removes his helmet to admire his reflection. A hint of Sledge's faint image is present in the metal. Ilem, "It is not an unknown force. I can feel its presence."

Ilem dons the helmet again and says, "Whatever it is, it is connected to sentient metal. Living metal that bends to my will. I feel a connection growing even as we speak, a widening of consciousness that I will use to my advantage. Whatever it is, and wherever the woman has gone, my minions will find and destroy them." Ilem grips the helmet of command and concentrates on activating home drones that lay dormant inside barren houses across the old USA.

Kol opens a compartment on his left forearm and huffily slams crossbows into the chamber. The inner, piston-like rod that substitutes for Kol's human bones is visible inside the open compartment. To disrupt Kol's absorption into his own mental safe space, Ilem commands him, "Ready your troops. I have awakened my drone spies to find that woman and whatever creature she has with her."

In distant locations, home AI assistants and humanoid drone servants begin to activate in abandoned houses and commercial buildings as Ilem barks orders to Kol and his troops. Ilem, "Whenever her creature uses its power, I will find and destroy it. This I pledge, and you will deliver."

Ilem crows, "My children are everywhere! Go forth and destroy!"

Derrick Howard

Psalms for Yesterday: Reflections

Reflections of my steps mark the soil
Pressed deep into the ground
Imprints of my plodding soul.

I turn the earth to plant my seed
But it vexes me.

I am an impatient gardener without the temperament
To labor long or dig deep.

More prone to childish toil
Ponderous in the mud
Fixed on the colors of leaves
I've shaken from trees.

In my neighbor's field, she has patiently grown her garden.
I want to be part of her good earth
Rich in possibility.

If only I had more to give
Some flowers I had grown through years of hoeing

But hoes alone are worthless tools.
In the hands of one who fails to do more than
Scratch in vain.

Tomorrow, what will become of the seeds I hold
So gingerly in my hands?
Alms for someone who understands
I need to learn
How to love.

END OF CHAPTER 8

Chapter 9

Stay

Stay With Me

Stay with me, and I'll be
All the dreams you're after
Stay with me, and I'll fill
All your days with laughter

A gold horizon on the sea
A life of joy and ecstasy
Nights of a warm and long embrace
A world of endless, blissful space

All I am and all I own
And never will we be alone
These things I will give to you
The golden sun and pleasant sea
All I am and all I'll be
If only you will stay with me

Derrick Howard

Brother's Keeper

Months after going underground at the A.R.I.E.L. Observatory and relearning the basics of ambulatory motion, Sledge can finally telekinetically put one foot in front of the other to venture back into the precarious dystopia that has consumed human civilization. Sage and Sledge retake their journey at night next to old Road 76, a corridor between the City of Steel and the City of Brotherly Love.

When they come upon an abandoned junkyard, Sledge sees an opportunity to secure a vehicle to hasten their trek to rendezvous with Iggy.

Sledge begins fixing a banged-up 2029 Ford Bronco at the salvage yard. Circling the Bronco are a slew of battered cars, capsized gas tankers, and rusted auto parts. The Bronco is white, but its doors and hood have been replaced with mismatched red and blue components.

As Sledge operates on the vehicle, he says to Sage in a more upbeat tone, "Iggy should be in Philly by now. Once we get *dis* junker running, we can shave days off of *dis* trip."

Using the newfound power of thought, Sledge telekinetically lifts an engine to sit inside the old Bronco by motioning with one hand. Sage peers over his shoulder from behind, inspecting his work.

Sage asks him, "Does it look like it'll run?" Sledge confidently tells her, "*Everyting's irie.*"

She watches Sledge as he tinkers with wires under the hood to connect to the engine while inquiring, "Why don't we find a newer, faster car? This car is being held together with rust and bolts ..." Sledge intuitively completes Sage's thoughts, "... *an* telekinesis. *Deh* may not be gas *fah* miles. *Di* lithium battery on *dis* still has a charge, and the cars off the grid."

Sledge reinstalls the last parts of the car and tells Sage, "Besides, this seems like a child's puzzle *tuh* me. I wasn't good at *dis* before, but rebuilding it feels instinctive." Sledge telekinetically closes the hood of the car, making a creaking sound as clumps of rust break away.

He telekinetically pulls the car forward from the bay door, adding, "Iggy knows *tuh* link up with me in Philly. That was at least six months ago." To further understand Sledge's plan to meet Iggy and seek safety, Sage asks him, "How will you know if he is there? That is still 200 miles from here and days since you both planned to meet."

While she awaits an answer, Sage reloads her hand cannon in anticipation of whatever threatens their ultimate destination.

Sledge answers Sage's question: "If he makes it, Iggy knows *tuh* activate a pulse beam in Center City from up high. The beam should indicate where I can find Iggy using a secret code we made up. Only he and I can read the code or break it."

From Sledge's point of view, Sage's essence is vibrant with multiple colors, illuminating the busted cars that litter the junkyard. Sledge comments, "Without *di* Vision Staff, I *duh* know if I can find Iggy's messages. I can detect silhouettes, but *mi* still blind." Sage inserts the hand cannon into the holster, ready to roll into action, "You can travel faster and see farther by astral traveling."

Sledge holds his robotic hand to his chin as he contemplates the complexity and impossibility of astral travelling, noting, "A few weeks ago, I couldn't find my way without a stick. How do I astral travel without a plane?" Sage takes Sledge's hand from his chin and lifts his gaze to her eyes with her other hand, "Let down your guard, Sledge. Freeing your mind of doubt will unleash more of Omnis' potential."

His eyes are open. The ghostly absence of sight contrasts with the faint shape and colors of Sage's body reflected in his eyes.

She asks him, "Close your eyes. Concentrate on our breath flowing together." Sage reaches towards Sledge's eyes but asks him if she can touch him again before doing so. She guardedly asks Sledge, "May I enter your mind again," to which Sledge answers with an equal degree of timidity, "I guess *suh*, but ..." Before he can finish his disparaging sentence, Sage encourages him, "Do not doubt, Sledge. Sit down in the car and close your eyes." Reluctantly, fearfully, he agrees.

Hand-in-hand, Sledge and Sage walk toward the passenger car side of the dilapidated Bronco. Sage instructs Sledge what to do next to unleash his power to astral travel, "Block out everything else around us. Block out the past. Imagine worries are bubbles that you can push from your mind."

Before Sledge enters the car, Sage places her hands against his temples to transmit a bright orange glow, then tells him, "Nothing else matters except this moment."

As he enters the car, the orange glow fully immerses Sledge in its comforting embrace. Sage suggests to him, "The past is a memory, the future unknown, the present is special because it is all that is real."

She climbs onto Sledge's lap on the car's passenger side. She is slowly wrapped up in the orange glow with Sledge as she instructs him, "Concentrate on our breathing. We will come together as one. Together, we will be all and whole."

Sage straddles Sledge as he reclines the seat, "In your mind, there's a place you've put an extraordinary person ... an exceptional feeling ... hope." Sage concentrates on entering Sledge's mind, this time by touching her palms to Sledge's eyes. Her hands glow yellow while Sledge is still submerged in the orange glow.

She informs him, "To move your consciousness beyond your body, you must touch that moment. With every part of you that has experienced that feeling ..."

Instantly, they stand fully naked in a formless room, surrounded by a yellow glow. Sage still has her palms on Sledge's eyes in the corporeal world as she leads him to "...find your angel captured in time."

Large windows materialize in the ethereal room they are in now. From his sense of smell, Sledge recognizes that this surreal space is the living room he grew up in with Uncle Ray and Iggy. The whistling sound of wind blowing through cracked windows transmits to Sledge that there is no furniture there, only individual pictures on the wall of Iggy, Sledge, Uncle Ray and Sledge's father, Bobby.

A green glow envelops Sledge and Sage as they feed the hungry passion grumbling inside their loins. Unlike the pleasant response she expects, Sledge calls out, "Stop ... stop ... I promised Iggy *dat* I would *neva* leave him *dis* time. I am failing him by trying to deceive my mind."

Having gained a deeper understanding of Sledge's fears, Sage reminds him, "Loss is familiar. The past is an imperfect mirror of the future. Today is the time to be all you were destined to become." Sage removes her hands from Sledge's eyes. A light blue glow now surrounds her hands. Sledge insists, "I can't ..." Sage directs him to, "Open your eyes. Look forward."

She gently places both hands along Sledge's cheek, looks deeply into his opaque eyes, and says, "Open your mind without judgment, Sledge. Sense what you were destined to be without fear. Be here with me."

She moves her lips within inches of Sledge's mouth, speaking faintly, "Breathe with me. Feel my breath entering your body. Feel my skin against your skin." Sage kisses Sledge intensely on his lips, igniting a purple glow that wraps them together like a blanket of quiet, shy rays of light.

Everything around them begins to disappear and transform into the sand, sun, tropical flowers, and moonlight decorating a Jamaican shoreline.

Wanting to taste every drop of the rare fruits on this beach and satisfy a primal need that rises in them, Sledge pulls Sage close to him to share a deep, prolonged kiss. Sage encourages Sledge to reach for her more and feel what is real, "Yes, focus on our bodies touching. You are real. We are real. Remember what life feels like."

They embrace, pressing their warm skin together. Sage whispers to Sledge, "Push away your doubts, Sledge, like waves leaving this shore. Concentrate on being released." They stand intimately close to each other now in the open air on the beach. Sledge repeats Sage's comforting words, "Only *dis* is real ... Only *dis* moment."

Sledge's hands roam the contours of Sage's back and waist as they collapse together on the ground. Surprised and mystified, Sledge gradually begins to see for the first time. What he sees is not some fantasy he gleaned from sorted movies or sight gifted by the desperation of longing. No, it is Sage's face as she appeared before Blood Bowl. At the realization that he, for once, may bathe in such an alluring sight, Sledge exclaims, "I ... I can see *yuh* face. I can see *everyting irie*. *Yuh* are beautiful."

Crystalizing their bodies in the sand, he rolls on top of Sage to gain a closer view of the contours of her beautiful face. A voice rises in Sledge's ears, soothing the concerns that tugged at his faith, "Our movement is now pantomime, as my shy kisses take the breath from her mouth. All the world is a blur, fading out to the distance, as we lay entranced by our desires, mouths parted, ready to begin again."

Sledge touches his face with his wet hands as he sees his reflection for the first time. The purple glow dissipates into the third eye. The atmosphere fills with the natural colors of the objects around them. Sage tells Sledge, "Omnis is taking over, only inside your mind. You must activate its commands in the physical world to unleash the power you feel here."

The crisp water washes over them as they roll into it. Sledge begs Sage, "Stop talking, Sage. I want to enjoy *dis* ... you ... now, nothing else."

Hands glide across wet breasts, and tongues inch closer to touching. Sage pushes Sledge back until he is lying flat in the sand. She reaches down between Sledge's legs to mount him, as the surf partially washes up to splash against their bodies. Sage confesses to Sledge, "I have intercepted other people's emotions as they secrete their feelings. But I have never felt my own. I didn't ... until. Until sharing them with you."

Sage extends her arms behind her on Sledge's legs as she sits cowgirl across his genitals. His right-hand grips one of Sage's wet breasts while his left hand holds the side of her buttocks.

Despite the bleak dystopia around them, Sledge and Sage cling to hope like two cosmic wanderers lost without a ship, their souls entwined in a metaphysical dance transcending desolation threatening to strangle hope. Their encounter is a symphony of defiance against the oppressive, unyielding world, a spark of resilience, and the promise of destiny fulfilled.

In the realm beyond the confines of the material world, Sledge and Sage connect in a dance of energy and desire where the laws of physics no longer apply, but primordial need still prevails. They become ethereal bodies of pure sensation, their connection transcending the physical. Their souls engage in a passionate ballet of light and shadow, where every touch ignites a cosmic fire, and every whispered longing resonates through the cosmos.

It is a union of energies, a merging of spirits, a profound connection that goes beyond the ordinary realms of human experience. In this supernatural embrace, Sledge and Sage explore the uncharted territories of yearning and bliss, an encounter that defies time and space, forever changing them. Their connection is a beacon of hope, a testament to the indomitable human spirit, an incandescent light that pierces the darkest shadows and fulfills their entangled destinies' prophecies.

Sage continues kneeling astride Sledge, pushing off his metallic chest with her hands in the corporeal world and off his bare chest in their interlinked trance. She intensifies the gripping feeling he senses as Sage continues sliding up and down his thighs.

Glory heats their loins when their flesh bakes together and their thoughts tender. A calm wind from the ocean licks their bodies, laying still, combined as one. Rhythmically, Sage lessens her weight on Sledge's pelvis by leaning back and supporting herself on his thighs. When Sledge thinks he cannot take it anymore, all his tension is suddenly released, exhilarating his body. In the corporeal world,

Sledge's essence ascends from his physical body through the front windshield of the Bronco into the ether.

At first, Sledge is stricken by the surreal, unreal feeling of observing himself outside his body. The queasy feeling momentarily leaves Sledge with a sudden and uncomfortable dizziness as repressed memories crush the exhilaration he briefly felt. As whirling water sucked into an open drain, Sledge's conflicting thoughts churned, pulling him down from the air to the ground.

Following his sinking feeling subsiding, Sledge's essence ascends farther into the air again, a wraith lifting higher and higher as his spirit blends and dissolves into the squall. Sledge silently wonders, "I can't believe *dis*."

Initially, as he ascends into the air, Sledge is amazed by how incredible it is to be free from his body and to see things in the real world. He rolls through the air like a newborn bird gliding for the first time without worrying. Sledge is awestruck by his new reality, "I'm whole …"

To his greater delight, in his mind's eye, he sees a beam of light pulsating in the distance. Iggy's signal flashes somewhere in Philadelphia, PA, miles from where they are, but Sledge interprets each flash as a sign of hope. He gleefully tells himself, "Incredible! Iggy! *Booyaka! Boom!*"

But Sledge's feeling of glee is soon lost, as his ramped-up hearing allows him to hear miles away a multitude of AI drones swarming from all around in his direction. The menacing swarm races closer toward them, causing an eerie ehoning sound to vibrate through the air.

After Sledge initially hears the swarm approaching, he sees them up close even though they are far away. They are hundreds of drone assistants that Ilem activated to attack them. They swirl and move through the air like a gigantic, snake-like monster with multiple heads. "Sssssst!"

Sledge mumbles, "Fuck, what is *dat*. Someting's heading *dis* way," which, to his shock, Sage queries, "Sledge … Sledge, what do you see." He is surprised that Sage can hear and speak with him from the passenger side of the Bronco. Nonetheless, he telepathically confirms with Sage, "You can hear me?" Sage informs him that they are speaking through his use of telepathy.

"*Der* are hundreds of drones coming after us from all around," Sledge informs Sage. In an instance, Sledge's astral figure flies quickly toward the car as he yells to Sage, "Start *di* car, Sage. Drive!" In a panic, Sage telepathically shouts at Sledge, "I've never driven a car."

He answers by telekinetically starting the car and the familiar refrain, "*There's a first time for everyting*. Get in the driver's seat and step on the gas!" After Sage slides over to the driver's seat, Sledge uses telekinesis to press her foot down on the gas pedal. It is Sage's first time driving a vintage car, and it does not immediately go well as she tries to avoid old vehicles in the junkyard. Vroom! Crash!

AI assistants attack the car while Sledge astral travels. Ponk, ponk, ponk! Sage drives wild out of the junkyard and onto the highway to evade the drones. Screech! Sledge violently returns to his body from his astral travel as Sage revs the engine.

When Sledge appears physically and consciously back in the vehicle, Sage tries to jostle him awake from his astral slumber, "Wake up, Sledge! I need you!" She steers the car down Route 76 at ninety miles an hour. Sledge fully revives from the experience of astral traveling and ensures Sage, "I'm back. I'm back in my body."

To his dismay, Sledge also recognizes he is blind again. "Dammit, I can't see shit again!" Between attempting to avoid colliding with objects on the road and the pounding of the kamikaze AI drones on the top of the car, Sage has time to tell Sledge, "You can only see here if you activate the passcode to become Omnis fully."

The thought of surrendering to any AI control causes Sledge's panic to return. He refuses to activate the passcode by saying, "I am Omnis," to access his full abilities and give it control over his existence. "No," he protests, "I won't. I cannot. There must be another way!" At that moment, Sledge recalls the words of Uncle Ray, "To never again be a man, measured by his faults, you must be a measured man careful in his walk."

If you have ever flinched when a sizeable bug splattered on your windshield at ninety miles per hour, you understand what Sage watched coming at her, but with much more deadly intent, than a wayward insect.

Sage's erratic driving jostles them in the car. Despite the peril before them, Sledge fears losing his identity if he lets the Omnis probe take over his body and mind. When another drone bangs against the car's exterior, Sledge jerks his body in response: Ponk, ponk, ponk.

While that banging noise rises to a crescendo, Sledge grudgingly utters to Sage, "How do I know I won't become a mindless robot? What will I become?" While taking Sledge's hand, Sage repeats what she said earlier, simultaneously driving to avert danger, "Only this moment is real. The past and the future are illusions."

Remaining extremely concerned about pursuing Sage's course of action, Sledge knocks away Sage's hand. He does not want to give up his name, so he keeps saying he is "Sledge, not Omnis." He is still adamant about fighting and surviving his way, not in an unfamiliar way.

Sledge, "*Nuh*, I'm Sledge, not Omnis. I'm gonna fight my way!" With that declaration, Sledge hangs out the window of the Bronco, shooting Sage's hand cannon at the attacking drones. Bam bam bam! The swarm of drones only increases as Sage drives past more abandoned buildings down old Route 76. "Ssssst ssssst!"

More drones reacting to Ilem's commands activate inside vacant buildings, pouring out of windows like termites boring through rotted wood. "Ssssst ssssst!" Sledge continues to shoot at the drones. Blam, blam, blam! But when he runs out of bullets – click, click – he does not know any action he can take other than fighting his enemies the way his sensei has ingrained in him throughout his life. He opens the passenger side door and climbs on the sunroof of the Bronco as it swerves down the road.

In preparation for a final targeted attack, a collection of drones forms a humanoid-looking figure hurling toward Sledge and Sage. "Hist!" From somewhere within the eerie wavering figure approaching the duo, Sledge hears a mechanical voice command him to "surrender!"

Even in his robotic frame, Sledge moves faster and hits harder than he did as a man. The result of his swinging his hands, which have the permanent appearance of souped-up Medieval gauntlets, is that the AI attackers explode on contact. Nonetheless, the swirling AI drones knock Sledge off balance and overtake him, swarming all over him. Without Sledge acting as the last line of defense, the drones begin invading the Bronco interior, breaking through windows. Crash!

Sage tries to fend them off by swatting them away with one hand. "Ssssstt!" She yells, "Awww," as they slam into her.

The combined drones knock Sledge off the roof of the Bronco and into the highway road at a high rate of speed. "Ooff!" A metal guard rail he rolls into after his body thumps on the ground pierces the DNA diffuser on the side of Sledge's containment suit. Crash!

More drones enter the car to attack Sage, who frantically waves her hands to knock them back, "No! Get Away!" Unable to bat the drones away and keep the car on the road, Sage crashes the Bronco into a mound of earth razed by powerful floods and winds storms. Crash, bang!

The pain, riveting Sledge's feet to his brain, disorients him and sets his mind adrift, like wormwood coursing through his veins. Nevertheless, Sledge pulls himself free from the guard rail by breaking it in half. Crack!

Afterwards, a small piece of the guard rail protruded from the containment suit. Sentient metal oozes from the hole in Sledge's side as a torrent of human blood mixes with the alien liquid. Meanwhile, the swarming AI drones relentlessly pommel Sage in the front seat of the Bronco in the background.

When do you recognize you stand at the crossroads of banality and exceptionality? Do you look at the forks to distinct destinies as the only choices to make, one for the weary and one for the brave?

Sledge powers his thoughts to search for Sage's aura but does not sense her nearby. He realizes this is the decisive moment as he can no longer restrain his growing desperation. He declares, "Only *dis* moment is real ...," then reluctantly says the command words to activate the Omnis probe.

Cautiously projecting into the sky, Sledge says, "I ... am Omnis."

On command, a purple light begins swirling from Sledge's third eye into his human eyes. Swirling purple lights lift Sledge's body into the air. He holds his hand in front of his face as vision returns, and the contours of his face reform to appear more muscular and hardened. Sledge, "I can see. I can see *everyting*."

The audible sound of Sage screaming pulls Sledge in her direction around the bend in the road. He pulls the last piece of the guard rail from his side. R-rip. As the drones surround Sage, dragging her from the burning Bronco, Sledge closes the distance between her and him. "Hsssst ssssst!" As more drones pommel her, Sage moans in pain, "Aaaa …!"

A ball of purple light forms around Sledge's hand. Using the increased power raging inside and around him, Sledge telekinetically flips the burning Bronco at the drones attacking Sage, knocking them away from her. "Zzzzzztttt!" With the distraction of the explosion drawing the drones away, Sledge rescues an unconscious Sage. He swiftly throws her over his shoulder and sprints out to seek safety from the drones.

In the form of a growing hand, Sledge extends the purple glow to grasp an abandoned tanker truck and hurl it at the pursuing drones in the air. The massive explosion destroys the remaining drones. Boom! Sledge holds Sage in his arms as he flies through the woods. Once safely away from the hovering drones, Sledge stops at the edge of the wooded area to check Sage's wounds.

After surmising she needs immediate attention, Sledge checks his wound, which oozes sentient metal. Beyond the metal and the pain, Sledge sees newly formed flesh gradually regenerating inside his body cast.

He implores himself to remain focused on the present peril to "Keep it together, *mon*. Block *deh* pain." Sledge grabs a handful of Earth to help seal and cauterize the hole in the diffuser, then blasts a red laser from his third eye to harden the dirt over his wound. While he burns the injury, his wounds regenerate, sealing his cuts. The earth sets over the gash, leaving a large bump on Sledge's side.

A Dry Schuylkill River, at the edge of the City of Brotherly Love.

Sledge continues carrying Sage until they reach a highway leading to Philadelphia called the Ben Franklin Parkway. The riverbed around the road is mostly dry, but it still has evidence of old wreckage that has laid beneath the water for centuries.

Forging ahead, they discover that, like Chicago, citizens abandoned the streets of Philadelphia. Some time ago, violent clashes narrowed Broad Street to a trail through brutality. Dogma has collided with desperation to destroy the most famous sites.

As Sage and Sledge travel along the old subway lines, they fall through a street section that collapses near the broken Love sculpture. Crash. Sledge uses telekinesis to slow the fall while still holding Sage in one arm but lands on his back several stories below the street level with Sage shielded in his arms. He hollers as the back of his skull thumps against the concrete surface, "Ompf!"

Without shelter, a reprieve from the pain, or salvation from his fears, Sledge gathers himself to continue. He carries Sage onto an old subway train, laying her safely across a row of subway seats to allow her to revive. After easing Sage down to rest, he inspects his containment suit for external damage. In addition to his aching head, he notices dents in the body cast sustained from the fall onto the concrete subway floor and encounters with the AI drone assistants. To steal a moment of reprieve, Sledge slumps next to Sage to allow his aches to heal.

Knowing there is no time to rest, Sledge telekinetically moves the subway car along an abandoned subway line. Creaaakk! The scope of damage throughout the North Philadelphia section of the city is visible along the tracks and above on the empty streets. Relieved to be away from the onslaught he just survived, Sledge telekinetically stops the subway train at a station known as Broad & Onley. Screech.

The Omnis probe begins glowing red as Sledge cautiously exits the subway station and up to the empty street. The decisive third eye signals Sledge that they are not alone. While Sledge approaches a cryogenic bank, a previously camouflaged space vessel reveals itself as it locks its laser cannons on them. Defiantly, Sledge calls out, "Whoever owns *dis ting betta* come out or prepare *tuh* die!"

This is when Sledge encounters two of the craftiest shell pirates he has ever met while wandering the barren lands overrun with crooks, killers, and thieves. The shell pirates that accost him are Jinx, a tall female feline alien, and her cohort, BR12, a short, muscular android, complete with twelve-pack abs and an oversized rocket launcher strapped to his broad back.

When Sledge crosses the road closest to a series of scuttled buildings, he realizes BR12 has the jump on him, and his faulty plans for traversing the damaged city have led to another unwanted encounter. But as the android comes from behind his camouflaged space vessel, Jinx casts a freeze spell at Sledge that goes awry and strikes BR12.

At the sight of her sidekick halting in motion, Jinx screams, "Fudge!" Several digital cartridges BR12 held in his clumsy hands fall to the ground and scatter as gravity takes hold of the android.

Jinx leaps ten stories from the roof of the cryogenic bank, landing with cat-like grace and precision between Sledge and an addled BR12. She kneels beside BR12 to check for damage to her friend from the errant freeze spell.

In the tone of a concerned mother checking on her child, Jinx asks BR12, "You okay, baby?" BR12 holds up a thumb and weakly answers, "Never better." Jinx tries helping BR12 up off the ground but struggles due to the weight of BR12's mechanical body. Sledge stands guarded with an unconscious Sage in his arms, watching cautiously for another unprovoked attack.

Jinx wisecracks, "BR, I told you he's the dude from Blood Bowl!" In a weak and quaky tone, BR12 replies, "You weren't lie … lying, Ji … Jinx. You never forget … a face."

Using a handheld device, Jinx activates the laser cannons on her vessel. Vrimmm! Sledge raises his guard to prepare to fight yet another attacker. Sledge warns Jinx, "Back off! I won't waste time speaking twice." Despite Sledge's protests, he watches the laser cannon's beam aimed at him by the crafty and cunning Jinx.

Sledge extends his re-energized hand toward the vessel, then telekinetically turns its laser cannons toward Jinx and BR12. Cerr! Jinx realizes Sledge has control of her weapons. Breaking off her unplanned restart of their skirmish, Jinx tries to convince Sledge not to renew their fight, "Whoa tin man, we're junkers … I mean, okay … we're shell pirates, not fighters but …"

BR12 begins reviving from the arrant freeze spell as Jinx continues attempting to negotiate a truce with Sledge, "…if you don't test us, we won't test you."

From inside the cryogenic bank, the reflection in its window captures the four figures on the street, blurred by dirt and grime coating the glass. Scavengers raided the cryogenic bank's storage units within the building, searching for anything of value. The word "Shell" is on the wall, spray-painted in large letters.

Jinx assures Sledge there is no need to continue the fight, "We're just passing through salvaging whatever we can find." BR12 echoes her sentiment, "Digital identities have been hot sellers since Blood Bowl. Earth's got great dead celebrities who saved their brain algorithms in ID capsules. We've found shells of politicians, artists … Jagger, Jackson … Shelling is speculative like bitcoin, but what the hell, and we haven't even started to raid the Maze for unsuspecting Moji."

Some thirty years before the last human alive breathed his final breath, humans had created technology that powered wondrous advancements that could have benefited all humans. But human innate self-righteousness and greed spurred division between the rich and the 91 percent who toiled to simulate a meaningful existence. Tensions rose as the swath of have-nots eventually refused to ignore their dwindling share of the Earth's shrinking riches.

After years of dissension fueled by ego-maniacal autocrats, divisive water wars, pandemics, and basic stupidity, humankind unwittingly placed itself on the brink of disaster. That was 2022, the second year in the modern, more treacherous "Roaring Twenties." Now, all around the country, alarming memorials to man's failings pox the land. Sledge takes in all the destruction with the eyes of a child who has never seen a broken toy. He chokes back the hard truth of man's lot as he readies himself for an assault by Jinx and BR12 or whomever else is hiding in the cut.

While assuring Sledge, "We're just passing through, anyway," Jinx helps BR12 get up. Sledge lowers the laser cannon on Jinx's vessel when he hears her concession. The slick cat puts out her furry, copper-colored hand as an act of good faith, "And neither of you looks like you want a fight. So, let us give you a hand instead." Sledge is still suspicious of Jinx and her sudden submission, "*Ah han huh? Fine I will give yuh ah bly.*"[49]

Jinx leans with her forearm on BR12's shoulder and loudly howls about the astonishing truth of Earth's reality show: "Hell yeah, anything for the Last Man of Earth. You look a lot different with your head on, but it's better than when you were carried out of the arena a piece at a time." BR12 preens for invisible cameras as he interjects, "Jinx, you think we're on camera now?"

Jinx carefully considers the implications of BR12's question. Scratching her whiskers into a Fu Manchu, Jinx opines, "I hope not. We've got warrants in four galaxies." Thinking of their many days of pleasure, peril and plunder, Jinx and BR12 chuckle about their wild adventures.

They pick up digital cartridges that fell on the ground when they first encountered Sledge. Jinx picks up the conversation where she left off, probing Sledge for inside information, "It's Sledge, right? We can at least help you two get off the streets and patch you up. Then we'll get on our way. Is that east, by the way?" Suspicious of Jinx's sudden jester of peace, Sledge comes back, "Who knows? *Buh yuh duh* want *anyting* in return. Really?"

On one side of a digital cartridge that Jinx holds in her hand is the DNA image; on the other, the words indicate a series of numbers. Jinx explains to Sledge, "Once we decode the account number, we've found hundreds of valuable shells.

---

[49] "A hand, huh? Fine, I'll give you a chance."

Perfect for the Andromeda Black Market. That's all we want. If you leave here, we'll show you around."

Sledge stumbles along the street, careful not to drop Sage from his arms. He rejects Jinx's offer to pull him into the shell market, a lucrative but risky venture, "*Dat's nuh* likely ... *buh* I'll take *deh* help ... for her." Jinx responds, "Good, we've settled it. We'll help you and then go our separate ways."

In every relationship, passion or platonic, someone wants something and vice versa. That makes a relationship reciprocal: the open exchange of what you got for what I got; I like yours, and you want mine without fuss or diversion. But if only one knows the price, that's not *quid pro quo*. That's deception.

The crafty, clumsy mage, Jinx, flashes secret hand and eye movements to sign to BR12 the next crooked step in their ever-present plan of trickeration. BR12 interprets Jinx's sign language to mean keep Sledge on his feet and from not dropping Sage.

Jinx also signs to BR12, "My spells may go awry, but I always trust my instincts. There is something unique about the woman." The feline gestures toward BR12 to inform him that Jinx intends to distract Sledge while they make their move. To assist in their deceptive plan, BR12 moves into Sledge's peripheral.

Jinx announces, "I'm Jinx, and he's BR12. Just call him BR." Sledge introduces them to Sage, "She's Sage. You already know my name."

With Jinx and BR12 at his side, Sledge walks down the deserted Philadelphia streets, carrying Sage. Sledge, "*Yuh* said *yuh hav* seen me before. Where?" BR12 tells him, "On GC 777, man!"

Sledge shakes his head in disbelief and disgust. Despite the stunning revelation, he does not pause or hesitate in his quest to find help for Sage. Jinx and BR12 need to catch up. Sledge puzzles, "*Yuh* mean *dat* shit was streamed!" Jinx informs him, "Hell yeah, across the universe."

Getting more comfortable with his telekinetic ability, Sledge waves his hand to push open the doors of a three-story abandoned building, then carries Sage up to the second floor. Jinx's sexy cat ass and short tail sway as she trails behind.

At the sight of the first comfortable room to rest, Sledge lays Sage on a couch near an open window. Tramping behind, Jinx and BR12 join Sledge and his ward at the entrance to the silent room. Preparing for phase three of their devious plot, BR12 removes his rocket launcher to lie in the hallway.

To a well-trained nose, you can tell the difference between good weed and cheap grass by the pungent odor forcing its way into the tunnel of your nose. The smoke Jinx rolls is some exotic weed because its fragrance crawls into Sledge's nose like a plump skunk that died two weeks ago. So, it must be the bomb.

The rolling paper has a stamp bearing the classic likeness of the green-skinned, oval-faced alien with bulging eyes. Jinx offers the smoke to Sledge courteously, "Here, this will take the edge off those injuries." Exercising caution, Sledge asks Jinx, "*Wah* is it?"

BR12 works Jinx's and his plan to deceive Sledge, "Tell him, Jinx, it's as natural as Kings Bread." Slowly Sledge reaches across the room to take hold of a bud of the mysterious wildflower. Ever the kind host, Jinx suggests to Sledge, "Keep some. We got plenty." Hoping it will ease his soreness, if not make him want to sleep after eating a bunch of Doritos, Sledge takes a long drag from the ganja.

Jinx offers, "Let's see if we can patch you up." But Sledge suddenly feels queasiness cresting in his body and can only exclaim, *Nuh mon*, I need a *washout*."[50]

BR12 deceptively assures him, "Don't worry, Sledge, Jinx is a certified Borg surgeon. She'll fix you!" Jinx slaps BR12 on his metal rump. BR12 whispers to Sledge to garner humor, "She broke me eleven times!" With the timing of a straight man, Jinx jokily suggests to Sledge, "Just goes to show you all the positions in the Karma Sutra aren't for every sexbot." Jinx and BR12 cackle at their offbeat humor.

The cunning feline has furry hands like paws with short fingers. That may be one reason her spells so often go astray, fingers too inept to grasp things on the fly. In this situation, her fingers are adequate to combine a pinch of biliverdin and a splatter of toad with a sprig of hops to cast a fast-healing spell.

The bump on Sledge's side that he clumsily repaired with dirt begins to decrease in size. Jinx and BR12 examine the effectiveness of the healing spell from afar.

---

[50] A physical cleansing.

Out of curiosity, Sledge probes for more information about people, and aliens, watching him during his entire ordeal at Blood Bowl. "How long have people been watching me?"

Jinx hems and haws until she produces the most accurate response, "Well, not you exactly. We've been watching things on Earth since '99." BR12 adds, "I started tuning in when humans passed the International Anti-Transhumanism Treaty to start the Control Era." Jinx calculates when those events occurred, "32 or 33, somewhere in Earth's history."

Sarcastically, Jinx mimics someone in prayer and chants, "In the beginning, there was The All, and The All was perfect. But The All got bored." BR12 chimes in, "His celestial children became the Galactic Council ruling from GN-z11 and every galaxy beyond." Jinx comments, "Remember, one man's religion is another man's mythology. Whatever, with over two trillion galaxies, this is just rock. That is a lot of unruly puppets for one God to control, no matter what you call it."

Jinx edifies Sledge by describing a universe he never imagined, let alone seen. According to Jinx, of all the Galactic Council members, Onom and Ilem were credited with extinguishing most of the planets that the Galactic Council condemned. Ilem destroyed Gabba's world, and Onom killed the beings on Hunos. The inhabitants of Hunos captured, tortured, and defiled Onom with crude stitches across her mouth. Jinx wisecracks, "The All had much to do, as you can see. The Galactic Council became trustees of the galaxies, directed to snuff out problem planets."

Other members of the Galactic Council were complicit in the bloodletting. Naihal and Hyle destroyed planets throughout the galaxy. On the battlefield, Naihal's horns, already bulging from her cranium, would grow three times in length and project out like sharp spears. Whenever she was in battle, Naihal could remove the black gloves that ran from vantablack hands to her elbow to conjure armies of lost souls to fight for her.

When the Galactic Council chose Hyle to execute a warrant on a planet because of its inhabitants' unbridled treachery, it did not matter how many armies on land, sea or sky challenged him. Ten, twenty, thirty thousand armed forces could war against Hyle, and ten, twenty, thirty thousand would return in caskets, minus one to deliver Hyle's simple but straightforward demand, "Relent."

His power to transmute inanimate objects was unlimited. Even if someone or something attacking Hyle might get within three feet of striking distance, one touch from Hyle allowed him to turn one substance into another, like skin into stone.

Jinx puzzles, "I'm not sure when humans became so gullible, but they forgot the danger of giving too much power away." BR12, "Even now, important decisions like how you identify and live your life are made for you." Sledge adds, "*Den dem* rounded us up for slaughter! Purist, somehow contaminated by *dem* carbon bodies."

Without warning, Sledge begins to experience trouble with his vision. He continues speaking but must stop to acknowledge the sudden sensation of distress, "When they caught me, there were only thirty-six Purists left ... *Raas*, I'm seeing double."

While Sledge struggles with his ailment, Jinx and BR12 pick Sage up by her arms and legs to carry her away. Jinx speaks warmly to Sledge to lure him to a stupor cozy like a pillow, "Shish, lay back, my friend. We helped you. Now let us help Sage by getting her to safety."

The power of the Omnis probe increases Sledge's senses enough to register sounds more than 500 feet away. Relying on his superior sense of hearing, Sledge detects the presence of other beings wandering the streets. They stomp and tramp about like busy vultures hungry for fallen bodies. Still slumped and his vision beginning to blur, Sledge cautions Jinx and BR12 to remain quiet.

Sledge watches three Converted transhumans gather outside the building. All of the Converted have war paint or permanent tattoos meant to hide the mutilated parts of their faces, particularly their missing ears.

Sledge can hear a voice discussing where to search in the distance: "I saw someone go in there. Four of them." A deeper and more menacing second voice warns his party, "There may be more. Tell everyone to spread out and stay on their guard."

A growing army of the Converted surrounds the building. Some wear air filtration masks, other breathing devices, and face coverings.

Sledge extends his hand to telekinetically point Sage's hand cannon at Jinx and BR12, who continue creeping out the door carrying Sage. He warns them, "You two, *doh ramp wid mi.*[51] I've come *tuh* far *tuh* take betrayal lightly."

In Jinx's devious eyes, Sledge can see that the shell pirates are as one plotting their next grift. The ability to control the third eye gradually advances to become second nature for Sledge. A voice in his mind instructs him to "alter them."

Acknowledging the voice inside, Sledge concentrates on transferring his thoughts to Jinx's mind. The expression on Jinx's bemused face suggests she is suddenly in a trance. Sledge tells her, "*Yuh doh wah do dis*, Jinx. The girl has no value." In response to Sledge's directions, Jinx quickly changes her mind about kidnapping Sage. Jinx turns to BR12, "The girl has no value. We don't want to do this, BR. BR, let's trust Sledge's instincts and our own. It's time we take our leave."

Together they release Sage back on the couch, and Jinx decides, "You know, BR, we got better seats offstage anyway. No offense, Sledge."

Sledge still feels the effects of whatever they slipped him, "I'm still seeing double. You did sometin' to me. Heal me, damnit!" BR12 tosses a small potion to Sledge as Jinx tries not to fumble, casting a teleport spell in the hallway. Jinx suggests to Sledge, "If you two survive your journey, we're just a transmission away. Let's rocket, BR!" BR12, ever the happy sidekick, jokes, "Keep your head on, Sledge! Ha, Jinx, you get it! Keep your head on!"

Sledge struggles to get to his feet and then makes it over to a window where he sees that several of the Converted are reacting to orders to surround the building and prepare to attack. Those who answer those orders hurry in different directions on diverse types of airborne hoverboards and augmented, robotic limbs.

Another voice yells, "You four, go around the back. You, you, and you take that side! Surround the building!" Sledge yells back, "Whoever *yuh* are, get away from 'ere. Don't come closer. I warn *yuh*!"

The Converted ignore Sledge's warning and move swiftly on the roof and outside as scores flood the area. Stomp, stomp, stomp!

---

[51] "Don't mess with me."

Sledge drinks the potion BR12 tossed to him to relieve his queasiness. The Converts begin invading the building by knocking down the front door and breaking windows. Bam! Smash! In response, Sledge blasts a massive hole in the side of the building, blowing away an entire side.

He leaps out of the hole in the building wall to the street to exchange attacks with the Converts who have gathered around him. Several of the attackers shoot at Sledge using traditional firearms. Others use rail guns and plasma pistols, but Sledge knocks away their blasts with shots from his third eye. Pow! Pow! Bzzzzt! Kaboom!

Sledge swiftly grabs one of the Converts to put him in a reverse shoulder lock called the Kimura, snapping his attacker's arm. Like a bullet rocketing at the speed of sound, Sledge flies back up to the building floor where Sage is located. He calls out to her, "Sage, I'm here." Desperately shaking her, Sledge shouts, "Sage, wake up! Wake up!"

A short, mysterious male transhuman wearing an *iSiphon* emerges from the crowd. Ornate, leather armor drapes the diminutive foe. The little warrior also wears a t-shirt over the protective gear that reads, "*Generación, Y Carajo No*" or, for the Spanish impaired, "Generation, Y the Fuck Not."

From the gaping hole in the side of the building, Sledge shoots a blast of energy at the little warrior. Bam! Bringing his gauntlets together creates a shield of energy that protects the man of mystery from harm. Even more devastating to his attacker, the shield of energy causes Sledge's blast to backfire on him and Sage. Barang! The rest of the building comes tumbling down on Sledge and Sage with bricks and glass from the ricocheting explosion. Crash.

The resulting rubble buries Sledge up to his chest. Only Sage's face and upper chest stick out of the debris. The powerful, pintsize warrior inches closer to the vulnerable Sledge and dying Sage while the puffing sound under his face mask increases with every step.

The battalion of Converted cheers him on as the incomparable *L'Enigma*.

Derrick Howard

END OF CHAPTER 9

Chapter 10

Muse

Woman is
Light to My soul
Without alone.

Unwoven tapestry. The better half of me.
Untouched canvas, so pure
Like the girl next door.
An unwrapped toy
For pensive boys.

What we need To see
That a man Can never be
A man,
Unless Molded
By her hand.

Woman touch, Woman reach, Woman yearn.
For my hand.

The Great Reaper

Dressed in his royal blue business exoskin with a complimentary gold-colored tie, Ilem strolls along a hallway on the Floating City to proudly inspect his fine work. Tagging close behind is one of his squad leaders chatting with him about picking up more of the Corrupted when the Floating City reaches Las Vegas. Ilem gives him specific and direct orders, "Land at the airport, not the strip. There, we will find fewer buildings for Lopers to hide." Politely and bowing away as a servant often does, the squad leader responds, "Yes, Lord Ilem."

Another of Ilem's underlings patters behind him to report that Sledge miraculously survived execution at Blood Bowl and that Sage escaped capture. The jittery drone, mindful of Ilem's temper, stops five feet away from him with its empty hands cupped and extended as if it begs for alms.

Cautiously, the drone informs Ilem that they have more information about his prey. Drone, "Lord Ilem, the other drones recorded their interaction with the ones you seek." Ilem puts out his hand without even looking in the drone's direction, "Good, show me."

The drone places a small glass cube into Ilem's outspread hand that pulses inside from an oscillating white light. Ilem watches a 3D holographic image of Sledge emerge from the holocube. It replayed when Sledge called on his growing telekinetic powers to destroy the drones attacking him and Sage at the salvage yard.

Ilem watches the 3,300-ton tanker truck spin wildly end over end toward the drones as they try to whiz to safety. A scorching explosion melts the drones that did not avoid colliding with the spinning tank. Boom! Ilem is dismayed when he realizes for the first time that the woman is Sage. He is even more stunned when he sees with his eyes that Sledge, a man who once lost his head, is alive.

I have heard it suggested that sentient machines, drones, and the like do not have feelings. In this instance, the drone in front of Ilem proves it at least knows loss. Ilem testily remarks, "I watched both of them die. How are they alive? Get this recording to Kol. Tell him to deal with them. If he fails me, he better hope he's light years beyond Umbriel!"

Ilem spins the holocube and stops on the image of Gabba escorting Sledge to his prison cell the day Ilem's guards captured Sledge abroad the Floating City. Ilem enquires, "Who is this, Trailer?" The drone identifies Gabba, the Acquilite, as the alien in the recording. "Then," Ilem orders the drone, "Tell him to gather his intel on Sledge and bring it to me."

The drone backs away from Ilem, bowing and repeating, "Yes, Lord Ilem. I will, my lord." Hoping he is far enough from the Lord of Light, the drone cautiously asks how quickly he needs to shuffle his feet and complete this life-or-death mission: "Is there still time before we leave Earth, my Lord."

Scoffing at the panic in the drone's words, Ilem informs it, "We leave this dreadful planet when I say so. I have plenty of time to retrieve Sledge's head and witness Sage quivering on her knees. Victory should be enjoyed slowly like a well-aged wine. I have waited for this conquest for eons."

Violent rays of light spark and snap around Ilem's fists as he enters the antechambers to his quarters and smashes the holocube against the wall. Up and down the hallway outside his chambers, passersby scatter from the sound of Ilem screaming to clear the frustration and rage from his throat, "Still catering to their whims! Still under control!"

The Diwan of Light stands at the entrance to his sleeping quarters, motioning in circular directions as he repeats the words to deactivate the shroud spell that conceals Pu Kwon from prying eyes. "By the power of Naihal, Diwan of Darkness. Daughter of The All. Free my mind of shadows. To the light I call."

Due to her awful, third-degree burns, Pu Kwon lies lifeless and inert. Ilem's lying eyes dismiss the reality of Pu Kwon's singed, leathery, and blistered skin as his golden hand presses down on the lid of Pu Kwon's chamber. His gaze cuts through the charred ridges of uneven skin, which rise and vein out like shadowy dunes. His generous eyes see beyond death to only see her as the alluring oasis that quenches his thirst for compassion and normalcy.

Despite her many trials as a trafficked, comfort woman, Ilem's thoughts drift to a time when Pu Kwon was vibrant and exciting. He remembers their secret nights on Miyajima Island, how he and Pu Kwon made it a shrine to pure love, spending countless nights on the island's ryokan. The evenings were quiet and peaceful, allowing the lovers to grow stronger together, flesh to flesh, heart to heart.

Ilem imagines Pu Kwon has joined him, sitting atop the chamber with a coy, come-hither smirk on her slender face. He reaches for her, then through her to place his hand on the glass cover protecting the suspension chamber from the elements. He muses, "So distant does our love seem. So dark and all alone that once I felt your hand touch mine, So cold, so long ago."

Unable to contain his passion for the woman who still lights the plasma in his heart, Ilem leans closer to Pu Kwon's unsightly face and recites flowery words of affection for his "breathtaking gem." Ilem rhymes, "Wrap your sigh around my lips, taste the tender words love speaks, for this day will never end, for this love will never peak. I see the sun in your eyes, the morning breeze that fills the air, and your touch is like the freshly spun silk that lines a widow's lair."

He ponders how often he spoke those words to Pu Kwon as they lay alone on Miyajima Island. "Every time you whimper, whisper words, or breathe my name, time takes notice of our essence twined together – one, the same."

The past that Ilem sees with his love is a welcome reprieve from his reality. Although he knows Pu Kwon is merely a sepia goddess fading with time, the dream of her is more tangible than the world without her.

To blind truth, Ilem releases a gray glow from his hand that changes Pu Kwon's appearance from unresponsive to how she looked when he first met her, seventeen years old, pure at heart, and vivacious. Color returns to her fair skin, peachy cheeks, and cherry-red lips. Her dry, brittle hair retreats back to its once luscious and long black strands, which Pu Kwon often kept tied back in simple but elegant braids. Her skin begins to smell like an intoxicating and sensual Jasmine flower, a sweet, exotic, and rich floral fragrance that perfumes the air around the lovers.

The complexion of Ilem's hand becomes paler as he revives Pu Kwon. The effects are also visible on his bloodless face, as signs of advanced age increase as the gray glow leaves his body. Ilem tells his love, "For one hundred years, you have been my one indulgence which I eagerly seek, even though keeping you alive has come at a steep price, my love."

Ilem's true essence begins to seep from his exoskin. The exoskin drops to the floor, exposing Ilem's naked, glimmering body to Pu Kwon as a gift. Yet Ilem must acknowledge, "Were it not for Hyle's sentient metal, I wouldn't be able to maintain a form that is pleasing to and pleased by you."

Unexpectedly, Naihal appears from the shadows in Ilem's private sleeping chambers. Chuckling as she enters the room, Naihal finds humor in catching her brother muttering to himself in the nude, "Talking to yourself or your queen, brother?"

Disrupted from his dream, Ilem responds to his dark sister, "Naihal, you should tell me when you intend to invade my privacy. What good is it if someone can easily circumvent a darkness spell?"

Music from inside Naihal's mansion trails behind her into Ilem's chamber. Naihal, "The All connects us, brother, light, and darkness. I sensed your displeasure. You're having trouble securing a dead man's head, am I not right?" ♫ ♫ ♫ ♫ Ilem lifts his hand from Pu Kwon's sleeping chamber, then waves Naihal into his conference room.

Ilem's essence oozes back into the exoskin. He assures Naihal that capturing Sledge is "A mere inconvenience. My transhumans will easily snuff out this abomination. And they are gathering the last transhumans to leave upon my command." Knowingly, Naihal observes, "And what if your army turns on you? What will you do then? Humans are unpredictable and untrustworthy."

The sound of his voice activates computers near Ilem and Naihal. "Computers on. Look, Naihal, the screen proves DNA manipulation is automatic through sentient metal and the *iSiphon*. I control my peoples' every thought and action."

Ilem commands the computer to advance the image, to show transhuman doctors as they implant embryos with AI implants into subdued humans. Ilem informs Naihal, "I created perfect transhuman babies and encoded them with my directives by controlling material, information, and AI."

This was not mere braggadocio by Ilem. He provided free services to human children and their parents' conversion treatment at transhuman clinics in the Floating City. Adoring parents and cute, transhuman children flocked around him whenever he appeared for photo ops. Ilem brags about his accomplishments to his sister, "I have brought the cruel human race to its apex and secured a future for their transformed children among our galaxy's most elite."

On the computer screen, the image of children displayed in the windows of maternity wards is present. Traits and characteristics conveniently labeled each of them. Under Ilem's watchful eye, parents selected their best hereditary traits to give to their offspring or spare them sickness.

Ilem informs Naihal, "Techs designed the characteristics and super intelligence into nanoprobes made of sentient metal. And each carried a code through sentient metal implants that forced them to obey my will like mindless zombies."

The universe of transhumans on the Floating City wade through the bustling Center Court, oblivious of their current disposition or future. But Ilem had a veiled plan for their prospects well before this day, "Humans only wanted their dreams of physical perfection achieved. For the rich, Tektite – the universe's favored form of currency - was no object. For the poor, even their souls were not a sacrifice too great to kneel closer to my light."

The BRICS nation's military accepted AVI's Sect on Ilem's endorsement alone, not common sense. "Nothing is free," Ilem boasts to his sister.

He continues informing her, "Governments around this world purchased drones from me or accepted them as gifts to ease their third-world poverty." Naihal counters, "They wouldn't have been so pliable if they knew how the seeds for their transformations would grow to straggle their worlds like the untamed vines of insidious roots."

Humanoid drones mined sentient metal on Virion, where Hyle discovered the unique metal. Subsequently, he infused the metal with his essence making it mutable on command. He later supplied Ilem with tons of sentient metal that Ilem used to create *iSiphons*. Through Hyle's gift of the gold and silver helmet, Ilem controls all things comprised of this peculiar mineral.

Ilem tells Naihal, "So, they believed my company found sentient metal on Mars? It was better that way to explain where our large shipments came from."

To steer Ilem to the truth, Naihal comments, "You mean until Hyle cut off your supply." Ilem testily responds, "I secured all I needed before that. Only a handful of Purists – thirty-six to be exact – avoided contamination by sentient metal. I would have done it without sentient metal, but I had my reasons."

He points out to Naihal that "Endothermic metal lines the Floating City and soon a new breed of Sect drones who will become unstoppable. My enemies will all quake as my transhuman army crushes them."

Naihal, "Will the helmet of command be enough? Even with it, Hyle wields ultimate control over all things made from sentient metal, not you." Ilem snorts in disagreement, "That is only for now. Soon, very soon, my transhumans will rise to be overpowering, and the Floating City will be unstoppable once enhanced with endothermic shields that absorb the brunt of Hyle's misguided attacks. Until then, we hold Pyron as a chip, if nothing else, as a distraction for Hyle."

A haunting image of Sledge lying in rubble appears from a holocube in Naihal's home. Ilem continues to talk with one eye turned to the replay of Sledge's deeds. Ilem, "Even now, I can feel Sledge struggling against the power of the sentient metal within him. He will fall again."

An AI voice announces to Ilem that Gabba is waiting at his door. Naihal excuses herself to Ilem, informing him, "I'll take my leave."

Ilem scrolls through more of Sledge's bio on the screen next to Sledge's image: DOB, 2026; Place of Birth, Philadelphia, PA, old United States of America. Ilem commands Gabba to "Enter."

Upon entering the room, Gabba drops to one knee to kneel beneath Ilem's gaze that scans him like a searchlight. Ilem demands, "Tell me what you've learned of this man, Sledge." Gabba tries to conceal his fear that quakes and shakes him in his pus-filled core, "He was a wanderer of sorts. Born 2026 in Philadelphia, Pa. Lad was twenty-four when you stiffed him at Blood Bowl."

Electricity begins to crackle and grow around Ilem's hands as he becomes impatient with Gabba's recitation of Sledge's history. Crackle. Ilem, "I can read Acquilite!" Ilem stands over Gabba, now cowering on his hands and knees, staring at glossy reddish-brown blood spots on Ilem's boots.

Ilem taunts Gabba, the servant, "Did you know I can cook an Acquilite inside out by boiling with a finger? *Sous Vide.*" Crackle. Gabba feels his innards bubble as he sinks lower to the floor as if he intends to kiss Ilem's dirty shoes.

Annoyance and anger build up in Ilem, "Try my patience. It would please me to hear that boiling sound again." Crackle. Gabba cautiously reacts to Ilem's demand for information—Gabba, "Second-gen Jamaican American. Born blind in a rough, poor section of Philadelphia called the Bottom. He *wuz* a crim from the offing."

Gabba continues to relay Sledge's background to Ilem with slightly more confidence that he answers as commanded. Gabba's head rises three inches higher from the floor. More assuredly, Gabba offers to Ilem, "Burglary, arson ... Gang affiliations ... Faced manslaughter but dodged it." Contrary to the response Gabba thought he would garner at that moment, Ilem lowers his head again toward Gabba as the crackling sound around Ilem's hand intensifies.

Gabba peaks at Ilem momentarily to prepare himself to take his last breath. From this view of Ilem, Gabba feels like he is melting into a pit of anguish and despair. Nonetheless, Gabba continues to report Sledge's background, "Lad was orphaned by his mum, Nigerian exchange student, named ... ah, named Lola Aliko, after his dad 'popped his clogs' during the last World Water War." Crackle.

The Acquilite continues cowering on the floor before Ilem as the Diwan of Light walks back to his conference table seat. Gabba, "The whippersnapper's father's twin brother, Raymond Sledge, adopted 'im and a lad called Ignacio Antonio Fuentes when they were tikes. His Uncle Ray taught him defensive skills. Sledge may be a master of fisticuffs and more."

Ilem gestures toward the translucent computer screen to pull up a digital file about Ignacio Antonio Fuentes. Gabba, "The other kid, Fuentes, was a savant. No info on his reformation or that someone extinguished his carbon print." Ilem leans back in his conference room chair, intently listening to Gabba and watching the computer-generated image of a teenage Sledge evading cops by jumping from one roof to the next.

Gabba says to Ilem, "Found recordings of Sledge in old databases. I can grab more. I'm reyt' andy me." Ilem, "Yes, tell me everything about his combat training. You'll live to see me blast this human into extinction and not you. And what of his little friend? Intriguing, there is no record of carbon extinguishment like he fell in a hole and disappeared."

Miles away from Ilem's interrogation of Gabba, the lowly Trailer, Iggy removes his breathing device as he steps through the crowd to reveal himself to Sledge as *L'Enigma*, a fully realized transhuman.

Iggy helps dig Sledge and Sage out of the rubble. Surprised to see the man who attacked him is Sledge, Iggy declares, "*¡Dios mío! Oh, mierda!*[52] Sledge is that you!" Iggy grips Sledge's robotic hand to help pull him from the wreckage, then checks Sledge's containment suit and detects other injuries Sledge has sustained.

As Iggy calls them, the Purified continue to dig Sage out of the rubble. Bricks and other falling objects overcame her upper body. She is unconscious and severely injured, as well. Shocked by Iggy's transformation, Sledge asks, "*Wah di hell happened tuh yuh, Iggy!*"

---

[52] "Oh God! Oh, shit!"

Consistent with his light-hearted ways, Iggy replies, "Me, you've looked better." Iggy waves his hand close to Sledge's face to check if he has sight, marveling, "Wait, can you see me? *Increíble!*" Chuckling, if not to lighten the moment, then to evade talking about the hard road he has been on, Sledge summarizes his conversion to his present condition, "*Yah mon*, somehow, I'm able to see because of *dis* ti*ng* sticking out of *ma farid.*"

Sledge telekinetically lifts the rest of the rubble from Sage's legs. The extensiveness of her wounds signals to Iggy that she has not fared well either. Sledge begins to emit from his third eye a purple glow that forms into an ethereal hand and gingerly lifts Sage into the air. Iggy marvels at Sledge's newfound powers and enquires who this unknown woman is, "*Guau! Quien es tu amiga?*"[53] Sledge says to him, "*Su nombre es* Sage."[54]

Iggy kneels next to Sage to examine her condition further. As he does so, Sledge comments to Iggy, "Obviously, *der* more *dat* happen *tuh* me, *buh* what happen *tuh yuh?* The power you unleashed is incredible, *tuh!*" Having surveyed what he can about Sage's condition, Iggy suggests to Sledge, "We'll talk as we go to the safe house. She needs our attention, *ahora.*"

The Omnis probe spontaneously emits a stream of red light from the center of Sledge's forehead—the crimson glow wraps and twirls around Sledge's body. The immediate response by Sledge is to don a look of peacefulness on his face as his chest regenerates and repairs the dents caused by the rubble falling on him.

While Sledge concentrates on healing, the Purified tend to Sage's wounds, as Iggy shares with Sledge other details about what happened since they parted ways in Chicago.

Iggy explains to Sledge that after they separated, he followed their plan and hunted for helpful supplies, like the medicine Iggy needed to cease his seizures and weapons they wanted to fight anyone intent on keeping them on Earth. Iggy tells Sledge that he traveled along old Route 30 that ran from Chicago to Philadelphia but was careful to stay off the broken road itself, instead following it from remote locations to avoid detection by anyone on patrol.

---

[53] "Who's your friend?"
[54] "Her name is Sage."

Forajida[55] destroyed most of the cities and small towns that Iggy traversed. If you entered this part of the badlands, the toll might be your ass or more if someone with evil intent caught you. Iggy did not want that fate, so he would use his doppelgangers whenever necessary to throw people off his track.

He used the trail of the dead bodies that lay like mile markers to guide where not to go. The further he removed himself from signs of recent carnage, the closer he came to areas that war had ruined. It was a grueling and circuitous 1,100-mile trek, doubling in the distance as Iggy tried to evade detection by the outlaws it was best to avoid.

Outside of Middleton, a dusty town southwest of Cincinnati, Iggy located what was left of a looted Big Juicy's Box Store Emporium that still stood despite its proximity to the catastrophic path of the *Great Reaper* F6 tornado that roared through six states before it dissipated close to Middleton.

The small town was poor before the Transhumanism Revolution and even more dilapidated since the *Great Reaper* passed close, carving a swath of destruction through Michigan, Ohio, Illinois, Indiana, Kentucky, and overwhelming western Pennsylvania. The *Great Reaper* was Earth's deadliest and most destructive tornado. After forming in southern Canada and decimating many of that fallen nation's regions, it rampaged at over 450 miles per hour across remnants of the Great Lakes surrounding the Wolverine State. It broadened into a two-mile-wide funnel and increased in strength to an F6 rating, the most powerful possible.

Hapless civilians sought cover wherever it might be found as the skies became hazy from smog and heat and increasingly unsteady and unsure. After a strange quiet crept behind a thunderstorm that lasted for days, the sky turned an eerie dark greenish color, like a traffic light ushering in a reckless, roaring freight train. Thousands died as houses were leveled off foundations and swept away by melted automobiles flung into the air like metal boulders.

Crawling through a busted door once securing the abandoned appliance store gave Iggy access to a few of the supplies he urgently needed. Wanting more light, Iggy tossed a handful of tiny electronic globes the size of fireflies into the air. The shine of the small objects was enough to set a path for Iggy over the broken store items and under toppled shelves.

---

[55] "Outlaws"

As he says to Sledge, "At first, *todo era bueno* ..."[56] The small lights haloed above Iggy's head as he searched the uninhabited box store for what he sought. The few items that remained available, intact, and interesting to Iggy included old game consoles and newer VR devices. Iggy tells Sledge, "I found little *medicamento* and other supplies ..."

Unfortunately, while on his treasure hunt, drone assistants that suddenly woke from hibernation accosted Iggy. Iggy informs Sledge, "But one empty building *no estaba tan vacío*.[57] Drones that were not happy to see me infested it. I ran out of the building to escape to get the hell out of there."

Bullets zooming at Iggy answered his attempt to fight off the drones using his ghost guns and confusing them with his doppelgangers. The drone assistants swarmed and pummeled him until they broke almost every bone in his body. Iggy recalls his excruciating pain: "After they destroyed my doppelganger, it did not take long for them to overtake me. They beat me like a redhead *piñata*."

Luckily for him, the Purified interceded to save Iggy by attacking and destroying the AI drones. A hefty Asian male named Juno, sporting a double-braided beard, led the charge, using a flamethrower to burn the drones out of the sky. Acknowledging his precarious plight, Iggy shares with Sledge, "I would have died that day without their help."

Giving credit where credit is due, Iggy speaks to the aid his crew gave him after that to restore him to health. "The Purified performed surgery on me to heal my wounds."

Iggy pulls the wig off his head to show Sledge the ports along Iggy's skull that the Purified enlarged to fit more extensive electronic parts. Iggy assures Sledge, "They saved me using their best technology. I know you have run into the Corrupted, Ilem's true believers. These guys who saved me said they broke away from Ilem's fold. They are the ones who mutilated their bodies to cease being transhuman, uh, the *Suffera*, as you called them."

Iggy tells Sledge about his rescuers, "They call themselves the Purified. *Purificada*, an offshoot of the Converted. They seek to be Cyborgs that are not

---

[56] "Everything was fine."
[57] "Wasn't so empty."

under Ilem's foot. For most of them, it was a painful process, sometimes resulting in the loss of limbs. They deactivated any AI within their bodies and replaced the sentient metal within or on them with earthly metals."

Sledge responds to all that Iggy has told him by questioning the outcome. "If they wanted to heal you, why did they have to fuck with those ports." Shaking his head from left to right, Iggy conveys to Sledge his disagreement. Iggy, "I needed them to upgrade them for me. I wanted to make a choice, right or wrong. No more *medicamento*. No more seizures. And we are all pure of sentient metal."

Sledge looks on unapprovingly and exclaims, "They turned you into a damn *iSiphon*." Embarrassed by Sledge's suggestion, Iggy puts the wig back on his head to conceal what he has done to himself.

With his veiled gaze directed at the floor, Iggy explains to Sledge, "I use the ports to link to a computer network I built." Using air quotes, Iggy continues, "I 'Frankensteined' the network with the consoles and VR systems to find a way out of here. I'm not fixed on any AI. I can disconnect. But it also helped me figure out how to improve my weapons and chances of survival."

Sledge resigns himself to the conclusion, "*Nida* one *ah* us *hav ah* choice. AVI med-techs forced *yuh tuh* undergo surgeries on your brain and took *yuh* away from Uncle Ray's home." With more determination than Sledge has seen from Iggy in some time, Iggy declares, "I did have choices. *Vive o muere*[58]."

Iggy continues, "As a child, I couldn't sleep one night, and doctors took me to the lab for more experiments. After they probed, plugged me, and left me in my room drugged, I thought I heard my mother's voice, but how could I? I never had the chance to meet her. That night, I dragged myself to the window but stumbled and stopped when I saw the moonlight shining through the window before me, casting an ominous shadow across my face. Then, I heard that comforting voice telling me, 'Ignacio Antonio Fuentes was brave, they say.' I figured it must be the psycho meds fucking with me. I got up the nerve to pull my limp body up to the window to stare out of it for any trace of my parents."

Proudly and without reservation, Iggy contends, "Scientists used me as a lab rat all my life. This was my last chance to control what happens to me." Iggy

---

[58] "Die or live."

cuts Sledge short before Sledge summarizes Iggy's memory, "*Si*. That means we all make the same choice to live or die or fiction versus truth. Only God knows all truth."

The entourage stops for Iggy to check Sage's vital signs. To do so, Iggy waves his gauntlet with strobing lights over her body. Sledge constrains his usual volatile response to these conversations by tempering his anger when he considers who he is talking with and how important it is for them to stay on the same page.

Sledge, "I didn't *hav ah* choice. What happened *tuh* me is an abomination." Disagreeing with Sledge's fatalistic view of their circumstances while pointing out their immediate concerns, Iggy retorts, "No, Sledge, *estas vivo*[59], which is more than I can say for your friend. I don't detect vital signs; somehow, she can still mimic breathing." Refocused on Sage's health, Sledge says, "I know. She is extraordinary. I *hav neva* met anyone like her."

Iggy asks Juno to help carry Sage to the safe house for treatment, "Juno, we need to get there *pronto*[60], or we might lose her." Juno still has his flamethrower strapped on his back as he ambles closer to carry Sage in response to Iggy's request.

Juno, "No problem, *jefe*[61]." Juno and another transhuman pick Sage up as the group travels through the ruins of Philadelphia. They all go into an abandoned subway station, littered with evidence of people bustling in and out of the metropolis and ubiquitous yellow and black signage marking nuclear fallout shelters where humans once hid from each other at the mere whisper of nuclear war.

As Sledge and Iggy discovered, Philadelphia's subway bomb shelters were on a forgotten Broad St. subway concourse branch. Like in underwater hiding spaces, the dwellers below were a melting pot of refugees, transhumans, and aliens. The renegades inhabited the snaking trail of steel rails curling below the surface like blood in the veins of the City of Brotherly Love, cautious to hide from anyone who might do them harm. They only came out when the sun slept.

---

[59] "You are alive."
[60] "Early."
[61] "Boss."

With a whipping tongue of humor, Sledge holds up his hands in Iggy's direction and says, "Whoa, whoa, whoa ... back *dat* up. Iggy, *jefe*?" Iggy assures him, "It's more of a gag. I don't consider myself a boss, just one of the team. Seriously, this is our salvation, not mine alone."

Farther below the street surface, the subway station has turned into an urban waterfall, gushing water into the sunken platforms. A torrent of water ploughing down through buildings and land miles from the east coast shore blots the concrete juggle.

Juno comments on the evidence of sublevel dwellers who have since abandoned their lairs: garbage, crude fire pits, death, and destruction. Juno notes, "Hey, Ig, did you see that old campsite near the water pipes? Must have left in a hurry." Iggy agrees, "*Si*, the water's filled the subway line we must travel through to get to the safe house."

In response to Iggy and Juno's observations, Sledge observes, "*Di stairs inna* subway station leads deep underground, several stories below street level. *Abandoned* for decades by surface dwellers *di* tracks *av bin* forgotten *fer* more *dan* one hundred years. If we can get through the flooded area, we *might* find *di* sublevels *tuh* evade *anyting* else *dung yah dat* we don't want to see." Juno remarks about Sledge's suggested plan, "To reach the safe house as you say, we have to use our reserves of breathable liquid and any rebreathers that still work."

Several of the group, including Iggy, take out rebreathers that hold an additional breath of air to help extend the time they can spend underwater. Those not wearing rebreathers, like Juno, inhale breathable liquid and pass it to others. Sledge attaches a breathing device to Sage's face before carrying her into the water without donning one himself.

The water is murky from sediment, waste and other pollutants mingling together. Sledge needs help navigating the water-logged passageway. To alleviate the group's dilemma, Sledge activates the Omnis probe to cast light in front of his fellow travelers as he swims ahead with Sage in his arms.

The group swims through a maze of obstacles that block a clear path, including a banged-up, abandoned subway train submerged underwater—the bodies of humans who could not exit the wrecked train bob through the subway car like marionettes.

Sledge emerges above ground from the cool water in a grass field before the rest of the entourage finds the same safety. As Sledge stands alone on the quiet street, a cool, passing breeze reminds him of summer days when rains arrived and warm breezes joined in the parade.

Those inconsequential days are gone, like dust in the wind, cast into the distant past.

END OF CHAPTER 10

Chapter 11

Fool's Game

You play it cool. You play it right.
But a fool will always pay a high price.
Playing the fool is a dangerous game,
When something goes wrong, you know who to blame.
Being the entertainer, the media fly,
But deep inside, you stave flooded red eyes.
Just take it easy, play it cool,
And you'll never again be anyone's fool.

Derrick Howard

The Doomsday Protocol

The Purified carry Sage inside a large building at the top of an inclined sidewalk. A sign on the wall indicates this is or, more accurately, was the "St. Bernadette of Lourdes Home for Infirmed and Orphaned Children." More familiar to Iggy and Sledge, this empty building is where Iggy and Sledge called home for the formative years of their lives. They trail behind the rest of the group to reminisce and smoke a doobie, not necessarily in that order.

Inside one of the compartments in his body cast, Sledge has hidden the weed and the cure that Jinx gave him or foisted upon him, depending on one's perspective. Sledge rolls a joint for Iggy and him to share. Eagerly, Iggy takes a drag, "*Qué es esto?*" Sledge, "*Nah*, sure. I got it from *ah* cat named Jinx." Lifting the tiny bottle of antidote in his hands for Iggy to see, Sledge adds, "We might need *dis* chaser, *tuh* keep *di* trip smooth."

Puff, puff, pass: Sledge relights the joint and takes a drag. Iggy holds out his eager hand to accept the blunt from Sledge. Iggy nods and shares an observation he has made about Sage's state of unconsciousness. "Sage's physiology is unusual, Sledge." Sledge puffs and passes the dutchie on the left-hand side to Iggy again.

A slow stream of smoke seeps from Sledge's mouth into the still air, and then he continues detailing for Iggy what he knows about Sage. "Only her father may know what's going on with her." Iggy nonchalantly asks, "Where's he?"

After tossing the roach, Iggy and Sledge walk into the orphanage down a long corridor with old pictures of former residents on the wall. Sledge pictures Dr. Q as the last time he saw him, "Dead, burnt to a crisp, and fed to a wild beast by Ilem for amusement."

A dusty, faded picture of Iggy as a child is still on the hallway wall. There is also a man standing in the picture with him. The man's torso is partially visible, but not his face. Whoever he is, he is wearing a lab coat with the logo "AVI" on the outside pocket. He has a forceful hand on Iggy's shoulder, tightening to a subtle grip. Farther down the hall, Sledge's name is carved into the wall below a space where a picture used to hang.

They stop outside the room where Juno and another of the Purified are laying Sage down on a couch. Iggy warns Sledge that "Without treatment, she may not survive. *Ella morirá.*"[62] The information gleaned from Sage when they argued about her father's lucidity is the only solution Sledge can offer.

Sledge tells Iggy, "Sage said something to me about files on the Internet. I don't know if we can find anything to help her, but I guess we should try."

Iggy gleefully skips down the hallway to turn the lights on in a room that displays his technological advancements. The room contains modified game consoles of various makes, models, sizes, and VR devices. Iggy jumps onto one of two oversized gaming chairs in the room and spins around in a circle, exclaiming to Sledge that they can find any remaining trace of Dr. Hamilton, "By using this!"

The clock on the wall shows it is 2 p.m.

Iggy picks up the headgear that operates his makeshift computer network. Sledge compliments Iggy on his accomplishments since they were together several months ago. He proudly says to his friend, "You've been busy!"

---

[62] "She'll die."

Iggy stops the chair from spinning by stomping his foot on the floor. "Sure have! It's a few dozen full-immersion VR consoles and computers. The Purified bring what they find when they look for supplies." Sledge inspects Iggy's computer network and is impressed by Iggy's ingenuity. Sledge, *"Dis* muss use *nuff* energy. How do *yuh* keep it running?"

Scratching his head, Iggy contemplates explaining his complex computer system, *"Como hago para que entiendas*[63]*?* Advances in procedural generation gave birth to the Maze, a meta-world of breathtaking scale and imagination. Humans may be long gone, but their digital footprints still exist there. Some sentients spend their whole lives digitized as Moji in the Maze. It's almost impossible to tell if digital footprints are from humans or AI."

Iggy flicks several switches that cause electricity to spark the computers into consciousness. He informs Sledge, "Solar panels still work even in vacant buildings like this. Years ago, workers painted the building with photovoltaic paint that powers solar panels on nearby buildings. Fortunately, several still work."

Iggy gives Sledge a better view of the prongs inside the headgear that connect to Iggy's ports. He explains their purpose, "And these ports let me activate the AI systems in this building for power. We'll see if we can find anything about Sage's father in the ether world. *Cual es su nombre?*[64] Strap yourself in Sledge. We are going into the Maze!"

Sledge puts on the VR headset and settles in the chair next to Iggy, and as he does so, he poses a question to his blood brother, "How do *yuh* expect *tuh* find him? He's dead." Iggy knocks his forehead with the palm of his hand, "Duh! I don't expect to find him. We'll have to look for what's left of his digital identity."

A virtual keyboard materializes from Iggy's gauntlets in front of him. Iggy tells Sledge, "We want what's inside the shell." Sledge answers, "There's *dat* word again. How can *yuh* trust *anyting* on the Internet?"

The clock strikes 4:30 p.m. The computer screen suddenly displays a code, QB.QH.BT.2.3.45.

---

[63] "How do I get you to understand?"
[64] "What is his name?"

Iggy excitedly shares his find with Sledge, "*The metaverse es omnipresente. Encontré algo!*[65] It's an encrypted program imbedded in Hamilton's digital footprint." Iggy alerts Sledge, "*Cierra tus ojos,*[66] we're going inside."

Sledge and Iggy strap themselves into the game chairs before their digital images rocket through a cone-shaped tunnel of light that twists and churns as they soar into the virtual Maze. As they sail through the tunnel of light, taking them into the metaverse, Sledge spontaneously responds, "Whoa!" When they come to a stop, Iggy and Sledge are inside the Maze, looking like digitized avatars like all the other Moji citizens in this all-encompassing, virtual galaxy.

Given his lifelong lack of sight, it is understandable that Sledge imagines his avatar to be a Jamaican American without eyes. Even more interesting, Iggy's imagination allows him to form his avatar to look like a six-foot version with the same handsome face.

In front of them is a digitally generated oloid rune that slowly rotates in a circle. They approach the object from the game chairs while the light tunnel slowly closes.

Iggy turns to Sledge to inquire about the next step in their search for helpful information, "Hmm, *una contraseña* …"[67] Sledge responds, "His company was Quantum Biotech. Try *dat*." Outside the computer in the corporeal world, Iggy follows Sledge's suggestion and types on the computer keyboard.

The clock on the wall shows it is 7:35 p.m.

With the stinging sound of frustration, Iggy comments, "*Maldito*,[68] it will take me a few minutes to work around this onion routing." In the corporeal world, Sledge stretches in anticipation of a long night as Iggy continues his diligent work.

The clock shows it is 10:17 p.m.

---

[65] "I found something."
[66] "Close your eyes."
[67] "A password."
[68] "Damn."

Iggy explains to his drowsy friend, Sledge, "The VPN is password protected. I'll have to find a backdoor to unlock the encryption algorithm." Sledge rustles from his near slumber, "Try Sage. Maybe that's the password." Iggy cracks his knuckles before typing the name "Sage" on the keyboard, then patiently waits for a reaction from the computer.

The oloid vanishes, and Iggy exhorts, "That unlocked one node." Sledge gives Iggy dap, *"Booyaka!"*

Before they can form smirks into a smile, another rune appears in front of them, a twirling spiral rune. Iggy steams, *"Maldito!* There's still one more node to clear." Sledge encourages Iggy to be patient and keep searching, "Stay on point. Fatima, try that name. *Dat* was Sage's mother."

Iggy tries "Fatima" as the next password but isn't successful until he reverses the spelling to find continued success. The second rune disappears from the computer screen. Sledge and Iggy high-fived each other. In chorus, they shout, *"Booyaka!* Boom!"

When a third rune appears in front of them, a Metatron cube, the duo's glee turns to quiet despair. To find some humor in their frantic situation, Sledge steals a word of Spanish from Iggy, *"Maldito! Whah* still one more node *tuh* clear." Iggy agrees with Sledge's straightforward reaction by summoning English to bat back at Sledge, "Damn is right!"

After trying a few more passwords, Sledge drops his head as he begrudgingly concedes what the final password may be. Sledge, "Wait ... try Omnis." In the real world, Iggy types in Omnis.

It works. The last rune begins to disappear from the computer screen. It is now 12:03 am. The computer's sterile voice announces, "Access Granted."

After all the runes disappear, Dr. Hamilton's pixelized likeness materializes before them in the Maze. As his face forms, Dr. Hamilton calls out, "Sage, are you there?" When he doesn't hear his daughter's familiar voice or see her comforting face, he asks Sledge and Iggy, "Who are you two? Where's my daughter?" Iggy marvels at this new technological achievement, *"Impresionante."*

Dr. Hamilton turns his questions to Iggy. In his crackling, synthesized voice, the digital image introduces itself, "I am Quinten Hamilton's cerebral transference program, sequence recording 24.3.45. Program expiration in 6 hours, 17 minutes, 48 seconds, and counting."

Calculating that the clock is ticking to get information from this limited program, Iggy suggests to his sightless friend, "We better get what we can, *mientras podamos*[69]."

Still inside the computer, Dr. Hamilton excitedly grabs Sledge by his shoulders. Dr. Hamilton was never jovial and friendly in their cell on the Floating City, so Sledge wonders why he is acting this way now. Dr. Q embraces Sledge, then approvingly proclaims, "Good Omnis, you've been activated, too. We have work to do!"

Iggy pulls Sledge back as Sledge aggressively knocks away Dr. Hamilton's hand. Sledge yells at Hamilton, "Back off! My name is Sledge!"

Astonished by Sledge's reaction, Dr. Hamilton explains why his initial greeting seemed callous. "Sledge, I'm sorry to be dismissive toward you, but I must interface with the Omnis probe to complete the final stage of the Doomsday Protocol."

Iggy tries to maneuver himself between Sledge and Dr. Hamilton. His reward is being smushed in the middle. Sledge points angrily at Dr. Hamilton across Iggy's body, assuring Q, "You'll interface with my fist, old man unless *yuh* give me answers!"

Dr. Hamilton rubs his beard, contemplating the best response to Sledge's aggression. Speaking like an egghead, Dr. Hamilton's computerized presence observes, "I'm surprised you still identify as Sledge. The regenerative technology should have restored your instincts, not your memories."

In the corporeal world, Sledge angrily throws his VR glasses as he reacts to Dr. Hamilton referring to him in the third person. Sledge, "*Wah did yuh do dis tuh me? Wah?*" Dr. Hamilton's avatar unemotionally says, "Q could not consider

---

[69] "While we can."

your feelings. Your death was a statistical certainty the moment Ilem's forces captured you. Your last viable purpose was to finish the Doomsday Protocol."

In the real world, Sledge and Iggy sit in the game chairs while their digital images and Dr. Hamilton's spar on the computer screen. Dr. Hamilton says to Sledge, "I can explain everything later. I must see Sage to advance the protocol!" Iggy informs Q, "Getting you to her maybe *un poco dificil*[70], Dr. Hamilton."

Dr. Hamilton answers Iggy by suggesting, "That's not necessary. Omnis can transfer my code to Sage." Sledge steams, "Stop talking about me like I'm *nuh ere*. Like I'm an object! Fuck Omnis and fuck you!"

In the corporeal world, Iggy tries to convince Sledge to help Dr. Hamilton fulfill his plan, "You carried her here. Uncle Ray taught you why you should fight now. *Justicia, Coraje, Misericordia, Cortés, Honestidad, Honor, Lealtad, Dominio propio, ¿no te acuerdas?* "[71]

Sledge reluctantly places his robotic hand on the computer screen. Dr. Hamilton's digital recording separates again into the three runes previously seen on the computer. His avatar expresses to Sledge, "Thank you. Thank you. This will only take a moment." As the transfer occurs, the oloid, twirling spiral, and Metatron cube runes become visible on the back of Sledge's robotic hand.

His hand vibrates like a generator cranking into action. A white light surrounding Sledge's hand travels up his arm, gradually changing Sledge's hand to Dr. Hamilton's. Steadily, Dr. Hamilton's cerebral recording completes the transfer into Sledge's body, causing Dr. Hamilton's face to retain a combined look of Sledge's hair and a third eye. The third eye ignites with a purple flame.

The words "Expires 5 Hours 28 Minutes" flash on the computer screen as Iggy's and Sledge's avatars disappear.

---

[70] "A bit difficult."
[71] "Justice, Courage, Mercy, Courteous, Honesty, Honor, Loyalty, Self-control, don't you remember?"

Seeing Dr. Hamilton's essence overlayed with Sledge's body overwhelms Iggy with childlike excitement, "*Santísima madre María*.[72] Sledge will be *molesto*[73] if this is permanent." Dr. Hamilton points toward the door leading to the hallway. Dr. Hamilton asks, "Iggy, isn't it? Please take me to Sage straight away. Let's make sure that doesn't happen." Iggy opens the door to the room where Sage is lying on the couch, still unconscious.

Dr. Hamilton places its hand on Sage to transfer the necessary program. The three runes reappear on the back of his hand. Dr. Hamilton's virtual essence materializes separately from Sledge, then sits on the edge of the couch next to Sage.

As evidenced by Iggy's open jaw, the biomedical phenomenon leaves him agog. He inquisitively says, "*Increíble*.[74] How is this possible?" Dr. Hamilton explains to Iggy, who is listening closely, and Sledge, who is facing away from him, "Sage is the key."

Dr. Hamilton takes Sage's hand. Sledge stands next to Iggy rubbing his head, exhausted from his body being used as a conduit by others. Oblivious to his friend's concerns, Iggy asks the good doctor, "How is she connected to you? I mean, is she your daughter?" Dr. Hamilton explains that "Sage is ... was my daughter."

Dr. Hamilton enlightens Iggy that years before Sage's birth, he worked as an intern for Omnis Studios when it designed its rapid application development or RAD tool, which served as a hub between database servers. Dr. Hamilton's extension of that technology created an adaptive failsafe protocol that could salvage the last samples of human DNA.

Continuing to describe Sage's current disposition, Dr. Hamilton tells his audience, "Sage was born thirty years ago to her mother, Fatima, and me. Fatima was breathtaking the first I saw her walking the runway after winning the Miss Universe contest for the US. She was graceful, smart, loyal, and an exotic woman of Persian and Native American heritage. To me and others, she was one of the most beautiful women in the world. Even so, when Sage was an infant in the

---

[72] "Blessed Mother Mary."
[73] "Annoying."
[74] "Incredible!"

hospital held by her mother, I huddled to the side in my world, talking on a cell phone about my next project."

"Sage graduated from MIT at fifteen years of age at the top of her class with a Ph.D. in linguistics, but I still didn't acknowledge her tremendous intelligence and potential. I should have been proud and present for her, but if I was, I did not show it. The most people remember about me being there for her was from coverage on the nightly news and social media of my helicopter blowing over chairs on the lawn during her graduation, with people still sitting in them. I left Sage behind on the lawn, her cap and degree trampled on the ground by frantic people running for cover."

Dr. Hamilton tearfully admits, "I hardly noticed her. My medical practice consumed me." Sledge butts in, unmoved by Dr. Hamilton's emotions, *"An tuh distracted tuh see Ilem coming, I hear."*

Accepting the duplicity that prevented him from making better choices, Dr. Hamilton lowers his eyes' focus from Sage to the floor, "Blunt, Sledge, but true. While ego distracted me, my R&D team confirmed my hypotheses concerning organ development. They printed all seventy-eight major organs in one year. Of course, I was proud of myself if no one else was. Quantum Biotech's R&D personnel broadened my inventions allowing us to use technology to cure illnesses like Alzheimer's."

"Like capitalistic Egyptians, we stored lab-manufactured organs in transparent containers, with my company's molecular logo emblazoned." Sarcastically, Sledge observes more of Q's flaws, *"An Ilem stole yuh secrets an used dem tuh build an army out of sentient metal."* Dr. Hamilton concedes, "All accept how to preserve the human brain."

Memories return to Dr. Hamilton, which he recalls for Iggy and Sledge's edification. Dr. Hamilton continues, "Ilem and I met for the first time in 2029 after he started supplying Sect to BRICS nations as worker drones. The Floating City did not always float. Before Ilem revealed his diabolical plan to rule over Earth and murder Purists, the Floating City was a stationary, expansive business complex. It looked tranquil, ordinary, and inviting, surrounded by maple trees and a fabricated lake. The year I met him was 2029, the same year that computers passed the Turing test."

"I recall it like it happened yesterday because it never stopped haunting me. Over a remote meeting, Ilem and I initially discussed an intriguing business proposal. At first, he offered to buy Quantum and keep me on as a consultant at three times my already considerable income. He planned to expand his drone product lines but claimed first to want to help me build Quantum into the world's leading biomedical corporation for the good of all people."

"I rejected his offer because the knowledge to manipulate humans at the cellular level is malum in the wrong hands. I knew I had to hit the pause button on any mergers. Instead of selling out to Ilem, I agreed to a joint venture that allowed our companies to work together but remain independent."

Dr. Hamilton continued, "I know it is hard to trust me, Sledge. I told you both I would tell you everything. If you will each take my hand, I will activate my instant recall feature, and you can return with me to that day Ilem and I met in person. Please hurry. My program may expire soon."

The trio returns to Iggy's computer room. Reluctantly, Iggy, then Sledge, take hold of Dr. Q's hands to travel them back into the Maze. The light that forms Q's avatar flickers and sparks as images of days gone by materialize around them.

Gradually, the more Dr. Q recalls the environment and surroundings on that day in 2029 when he met Ilem, the more the environment solidifies. The trios' high-quality, three-dimensional digital representations of each other also fill in to look like their actual selves or Moji inhabitants of the Maze. Eventually, they find themselves standing among the crowd begging for entrance to the Floating City on one side of the aisle or denouncing it as a reflection of science gone amok in 2029.

In a low tone, Dr. Q shares with them, "I had a right to be leery. Having arrived at the Floating City complex, scores of protesters outside were railing against Ilem's supply of drones to the BRICS nations for military operations. Once inside AVI's business complex, Ilem greeted me to give me a personal tour on our way to his office. It was one of the most consequential days in my life, Sage's life, and the lives of ten billion humans in every crack and crevasse of Earth. The global catastrophe that arose from Ilem's manipulation was the most momentous day in the universe."

No one can sufficiently underscore Dr. Hamilton's prophetic assessment of that day's importance. He suggests to them, "Let's follow them. No one can see us. If that does happen, they'll think we're figments of their imagination."

They all walk into the Floating City's doors and stand close to Ilem and Dr. Hamilton of the past as they clasp hands. The avatar of Dr. Hamilton explains, "He held out his hand, and I took it. He stroked my ego, and I liked it. He blew up my head more by suggesting he noticed I hadn't been in the public eye much, deeming me 'reclusive.' Despite my reservations, I was pleased to see AVI technicians in hazard suits hustling off in different directions because it looked like they were engaged in important, life-changing medical advancements, like me."

Dr. Hamilton's, Iggy's, and Sledge's avatars glide by a window to a room where AVI's R&D personnel reanimate the extinct Polar bear and Gorilla. As they pass the lab, Dr. Hamilton shares, "Ilem knew some of the most personal details of my life, which again fueled my ego. I was immediately more impressed that he knew me so well than I was cautious about his intentions. And he expressed sympathy for Fatima's unfortunate death and concern for Sage's trauma."

"There was so much to be excited about as a bioengineering scientist. It was easy to fool me. Even the architecture was breathtaking. The most impressive water fountain was under construction as we crossed under the balcony off of Ilem's personal conference room and adjacent sleeping quarters. It was a tribute to humankind's accomplishments, vanity, and insecurities but also projected a feeling of superiority, calm and completion. Often Ilem had to snap me back to our conversation as I was too infatuated with the possibilities for my success in this environment more than anything else."

Dr. Hamilton further informs them, "I mentioned to him that I read the JAM reports and was concerned that his innovative products were controversial. That is when his countenance and demeanor became more dominating and aggressive."

"He conceitedly boasted about the amazing work AVI was doing in areas of science that I longed to pursue. He said, 'By far the greatest impact from global warming has been in the seas and oceans.' He assured me that we could revive them, given time."

"Like many deceitful, self-serving humans, Ilem's observations implied he was one with the environmental movement to end Global Warming, save water, and end starvation. Rising global temperatures created drier conditions for vegetation – producing larger and more frequent wildfires. In North America, the geographic area typically burned by wildfires increased by an average of 50 percent. The worst hit were the forests of the Pacific Northwest and the Rocky Mountains, which experienced a tripling of areas affected. He was sucked into this false vision."

"He knew he was actively accomplishing some of his objectives, so it was not as if it were all fiction or hopeful aspirations. To track and capture remaining water reserves, Ilem offered developed countries access to his satellites to map wind and rain patterns in real-time at phenomenal resolution – from square kilometers in previous decades down to square meters. AVI's climate and sea level predictions offered greater certainty and detail than ever before about the long-term outlook for Earth. Thus, Ilem sped a rapid expansion of desalination technology, profiting in every way."

"Global powers, in blatant disregard to the rights of so-called 'third world' countries, took water without negotiating that right. Eventually, the tension led to the last of Earth's World Water Wars when the leaders of the United States of the Americas and their allies failed to reach an accord with BRIC nations, their allies, and the poor nations that needed fresh, clean water more than anyone else."

Dr. Q reminds them, to the extent they did not already know, by the 2030's, there were an additional two billion people on Earth, most of them in poor countries. The human footprint required the equivalent of two whole Earths for humans to sustain themselves into the future. By that time, prosperity through technology paved the way for future discoveries that promised to finally take humans beyond limited space travel and deep into uncharted galaxies.

Progressively, humans who aligned with Ilem's vision for the future began to extend their presence to mining colonies on Mars feverishly in search of sentient metal. Ilem launched an initiative to have the new USA government approve his importation of the unique, sentient metal from Mars to Earth on Ilem's fleet of space shuttles, commonly referred to as his Warhawks. At Ilem's behest, governments agreed to purchase many of his drones to ship to Mars to assist with mining operations.

"That was what was at stake," Dr. Hamilton tells them. "Ilem slapped me on my back like we were two old college friends discovering independence for the first time while crowing about my accomplishments. Later, when my plans for the future started diverging from Ilem's intentions, I frequently disagreed with him. I told him that breeding green-eyed babies with perfect IQs stroked human vanity, not survival. He looked right through me, gloating and confident in his words that day. 'We'll rule the world,' he said. 'It's at our fingertip. Transhumans have already opened the door to supremacy, and you have provided them with the key. Thank you. I could not have done it without you.' Those words sickened and worried me."

"With that, Ilem held up a glass of champagne in celebration and handed another to me. He said, 'Cheers to the dawn of a new destiny.' Reluctantly, I clinked glasses with him, and took a slow sip of old grapes, stomped, and bottled for the pleasure of the bourgeoisie and the detriment of those who toiled in the field."

"I slurped it up. Vanity filled the abyss of my existence, stupidity fogging my mind. This is where we found ourselves. Desperate for a path forward, burdened by our flaws of the past."

Clink! Cheers to the future of all humankind.

Psalms for Yesterday: Labyrinth

Lies and half-truths
Unmet goals and lost dreams
Set a path on the left before me

Do I stand? Do I go?

To be touched or be known
Should I quietly fade out of view?

Between yin and the yang
Lies an answer for me
In the light and the dark, where I seek
Truth be told sudden fame
Every wealth, every claim
I would trade to be seen
Honestly

Falsity, playing games
Is a phantom I greet in the hall
Or the street when I seek
To go right in my life
Where I hazard to find
Clarity, harmony, the real me

When will you let me be
More than just what you've dreamed
You would have in your life come what may

To be held to be squeezed
All I want, what I need
Is to walk the straight path
And be free

END OF CHAPTER 11

Chapter 12

Witness of Time

Time scratches at my flesh
Digging deep within my core until I come of age
It stays in me, creeps into me
It swims in my blood like a fish in a babbling brook
It twists and turns beneath my flesh
Slowly moving through my body to my mind
Aging all I am

Soon time stops
Reflected on its face, my memories stand still
Transfixed

A laugh, a cry, a smile, a hurt, revolves ... spins ... falls
Feelings stay the same, and change

Derrick Howard

I live and become a part of time
I breathe, I sleep, I learn, I say, I am, and then
I am again

But time ... now creeps through my life and my veins
Searching to find me now
So, I do not look away

Time and I are one, I am a portrait and it is the painter
Someday we'll come together
Blend, melt, touch, and I'll become an eternal Mona Lisa
Painted in the attic of time's mind

A part of a moment, a witness
Gone, gone, gone

Untethered

Deep in the blood, you are family, trillions of species of life, all part of the lost tribe *Hominis*. Somehow, you have forgotten that connection, instead opting for dissent and opposition.

Something happened along the way to building modern megalopolis from caves to castles. You created all manner of monuments from grit, rock, and steel. But your AI clad has the empathy of their programmer, or creator, for those able to distinguish the difference: garbage in, garbage out. Evil in, evil out.

When tomorrow turns from possibility to purpose, where will the children – future stargazers and star walkers – be in dominion with one another? Will AI children speak truth to power, reason to love, or bewail birth to ruin? Will they resemble you – a free mind confined in Meta worlds and fantasy - or a primitive mind too innocent to embrace primal hate?

Such were the questions bantered by Ilem and Dr. Hamilton when they met in 2029 at the AVI business complex to discuss the status of their joint venture. That meeting altered reality for all humankind, even if you were unaware of it at that moment nor had reason to anticipate it.

At one point in the conversation, Dr. Hamilton argued, "Medicine should heal the sick, not allow humans to play God." Characteristically, Ilem responded, "People evolved from simple comb jelly millions of years ago. *Homo sapiens* migrated from Africa eons ago and became mechanized to be nothing like those ancestors. Even humans who have lived on Mars for an extended time are taller and have less hair than their counterparts due to the change in gravitational pull and environment."

Until the end of the people mover, Dr. Hamilton and Ilem continued to debate the medical and moral consequences of advanced bioscience. Unbeknown to Dr. Q, the charismatic Victor Garin approaches them from the rear. Dr. Hamilton does not see Victor in his periphery as he espouses his views to his host.

Ilem gazes back at Victor, pleased to see his "son" approaching. Although they share no blood, they share an innate hunger for conquest. As Ilem pieced together his covert army of followers, he searched the globe for the most depraved in power to bring into the fold.

By manipulating private conversations from home and business, Nest Minis, and other synthesized assistants like that annoying Siri, Ilem infiltrated the personal interactions between individual users and their AI devices. Those pesky, uninvited questions from those voice assistants - "I did not understand what you are requesting. Please repeat your query" were no accident. Even when you have not asked a question, those devices influenced by AVI continuously gathered intel and controlled public discourse.

Ilem's lines of influence and corruption also informed him of Victor Garin's status worldwide, a flamboyant Russian model with a voracious appetite for all things of pleasure, riches, and access. Eventually, Victor wielded influence felt long and wide in business, politics, and among sexual provocateurs.

On a night when Victor's soiree at his plush lakeside estate in St. Petersburg ensued, and everybody was enjoying every body, an unknown transhuman bearing gifts abruptly interrupted Victor's party. Victor was displeased by the possibility that the prying eyes of a stranger spied on his guests' predilections. So, he allowed his goon squad to give the intruder a few lashes before Victor strolled off the dance floor to meet his unplanned captive. It did not matter to Victor who the disrespectful intruder dressed in bloody and tattered military garments was at that point as long as he learned to fear, worship, satisfy, and obey.

Victor's security guards threw the soldier down on his knees in front of him. With the mask of mischief on his face, a guard presented Victor with a crude interrogation kit filled with syringes, scalpels, and other tools designed to cause compliance and debilitating pain. Victor stood scantily clad and smug in front of the transhuman.

The transhuman blurting out his name while choking back a mouthful of blood and frothy saliva, was Grigoriy Semenov, a diplomat delivering a personal invitation from Ilem Diwan Godfrey for him and Victor to meet. Victor spoke under his breath, not allowing anyone else to hear, *"Net, eto lokh. Chto yemu nuzhno ot takoy megery, kak ya?"*[75] Victor changed his tone, in case the uninvited guest was legit, and waved to security to help Grigoriy off his knees and into a comfier perch suitable for Grigoriy's station.

Victor casually answered in his Russian accent, *"Ya zainteresovan.*[76] I am interested. What does the Lord of all things bright want from me?" Grigoriy held up one finger to request a moment to answer Victor's question. Grigoriy quickly adjusted his *iSiphon* to connect to a holocube he held in his unsteady hand to a live feed of Ilem ready to speak with Victor.

First, Ilem's golden skin and engrossing blue eyes drew Victor in. Victor complimented Ilem's allure to himself, "I did not know his tan was so lush and his blue eyes so intense and consuming, like a mixture of flames and cooling blue water tamping my raging storm." While Victor internally gushed about Ilem's gleaming presence, Ilem began speaking to Victor in the latter's native tongue. Commandingly, Ilem told Victor, "Нам есть что обсудить."[77] Victor, without hesitation and for the first time in his life, surrendered to someone instantly, stating, "Lord Ilem, I'm yours, *telo i dusha*, body and soul."

Victor's pledge of his precious body and soul to Ilem soon came to be precisely what Ilem wanted, *sine limitatione*. Victor's transformation from an insatiable sadist to a killing machine loyal only to Ilem started inside out, psychologically then physically.

---

[75] "No, it's a hoax. What does he want from a vixen like me."
[76] "I am interested."
[77] "We have something to discuss."

Before Ilem assessed Victor's compliance and tolerance to enduring the grueling transformation process from human to transhuman, he ingrained Victor in all operations undertaken by AVI to advance its revolutionary bioengineering technology. That is why Ilem viewed an introduction of Dr. Hamilton, his latest target for conquest, to his enforcer and influencer, as vital to pursuing his schemes.

On the day of the first meeting, before he interjected himself into Dr. Hamilton's and Ilem's conversation, Victor listened intently to Hamilton point out to Ilem, "Your theories are as old as Bacon's *Novum Organum*. You would not ask me here if I did not ascribe to science being able to master mortality. But where do we draw the line?"

Ilem contended, "Ancient beliefs and present reality about immortality conflict. The Transhumanism Movement supports every being's right to pursue bioengineering to preserve and extend life." Dr. Hamilton presses Ilem with a question, "Well, Mr. Godfrey, isn't that playing God?"

In response to Q's question, the Diwan of Light posed one of his own, "What if we are living in the dreams of a sleeping celestial? Would you remain still because you feared disturbing its slumber?"

Dr. Hamilton cleverly noted, "So, you ascribe to the Transhumanist Declaration's belief that human's potential is still mostly unrealized."[78] Ilem nodded in agreement, saying, "Of course I do. If humans can change their gender, why not the course of their mortality? AVI first did it with meds, then AI surgery. It's time to revolutionize evolution for every human with a direct brain-to-computer interface technology like the *iSiphon*."

That is about when Victor joined the conversation between Dr. Hamilton and Ilem. Victor had a drone on wheels following behind him, carrying a large, framed painting wrapped in protective paper.

---

[78] Despite Dr. Q's opposition, the comprehensive alteration of the human condition was realized by 2050 through the implementation of iSiphons. This transformation brought about advantages such as the significant reduction of aging, the breakdown of barriers between human and artificial intelligence, the adjustment of involuntary psychological traits, and the elimination of suffering as dictated by Lord Ilem's conditions. As foretold in the Transhumanist Declaration, like bold colonists arriving on a seemingly virgin shore, the United States Transhumanist Party introduced the Constitution of the United States Transhumanist Party to the applauds of the willing and the jeers of those concerned.

Without an open invitation, Victor interposed in the conversation, "Come now, doctor, antiquated Purist views cannot stymie you. Even Franklin was a cryonicist." Ilem paused from sipping from his drink to introduce both men, "Dr. Hamilton, please meet Victor Garin, our R&D Director."

Dr. Hamilton cordially held his hand to welcome Victor into the meeting and the conversation. Victor firmly gripped Dr. Hamilton's hand, stating, "The pleasure is mine, Dr. Hamilton. Ilem can't stop talking about you." Grateful for being the focal point of the conversation, Dr. Hamilton again mildly acknowledged his zeal for being the center of attention, "I appreciate the recognition."

The drone carrying the picture set it on the floor and unwrapped it as the three men watched, then exited the high-stakes meeting. The painting the drone revealed was *The Three Ages of Man*, painted by Titian. Dr. Hamilton and Victor stood close to each other, admiring the artwork. Rhetorically, Dr. Hamilton puzzled, "Is this *The Three Ages of Man*?" Ilem, again to stroke Q's ego, stated, "Good eye, Doctor. Victor not only directs R&D, but he is also a curator of art."

Ilem prepared three drinks while the others studied Titian's artistry. Victor informed Dr. Q of his qualifications, "I am a curator of many things, as Ilem indicated. Are you familiar with Titian's work?" Dr. Hamilton responded, "Vaguely. Unfortunately, I do not spend time on art or finding ways to improve medical advancements for the rich and powerful. I recall reading that Titian was known for his dynamic brushwork and bright, alluring colors. Take this painting, for example. Look at his magnificent use of sharp cobalt and white tones to set moody clouds in the background and winded trees in the foreground."

Victor concurred with Dr. Hamilton's assessment of the classic painting, "I particularly like his use of contrasting shades to accentuate the lovers being drawn to each other." Dr. Hamilton replied, "I agree, Victor. It is an intriguing work, juxtaposing images to stroke contemplation and discussion of the three stages of life: infancy, adulthood, and old age. Victor, there is so much to see here: Cupid's watchful eyes fixed on two infants, the older man's contemplation of death. Truly a master craft."

"But I'm not here to talk art, am I? One question, though: May I ask how you acquired this painting? I thought it was in a private collection." Victor cynically laughed, "Ha. Let us say it was a steal."

Ilem passed double shots of a golden-brown whiskey to the other men as they concluded their discussion. Victor turned to the more important subject, "*Do you want to be the 'ebb of this great flood and even go back to the beasts rather than overcome man'?*" Chuckling openly, Dr. Hamilton replied, "Nietzsche. Your book knowledge is impressive, Mr. Garin." While swirling an ice cube in the glass of whisky, Dr. Hamilton contemplated his response to Victor's astute but controversial statements. Dr. Hamilton added to the intellectual discussion, "Nietzsche advocated personal growth, not a technological transformation of people."

Victor gulped the whiskey, then took Dr. Hamilton by the arm intimately. Victor asked him, "Are you not single doctor? I would love to discuss this over dinner." Ilem gave Victor the side-eye, then tried again to steer the conversation back to business, "Quinten, please excuse Victor. He's an incorrigible provocateur."

Ilem pulled Victor's hand off Dr. Hamilton's arm. Undiscouraged, Victor continued playing with Q's ego and courting controversy for pleasure in front of both men. Victor, "It is 2029, Lord Ilem, not 1929. People should be polyamorous or fall in love with a tin can if they want." Ilem rejected Victor's assertions, "I swear by The All, excuse me – Christ – I swear by the Christ you are contemptible."

Dr. Hamilton walked over to the panoramic window in Ilem's office to take in the construction happening in certain parts of AVI's business complex. In the place where the Dyson Sphere would later stand, a magnificent fountain depicting six featureless riders descending from the heavens was built below the balcony of Ilem's sleeping quarters. Dr. Hamilton remarked, "Social commentaries aside, what does this have to do with me or Quantum Biotech?"

Ilem joined Dr. Q at the window to take in the impressive view of active life bustling in AVI's corporate headquarters, "Yes, to business," Ilem started, "Victor's banter can be distracting. But just as this view suggests, the world of AI merging with miraculous medical advancements is open to us if we only cease vision beyond the walls of the medieval imagination."

Ilem then handed Dr. Hamilton an M&A Venture Agreement and a check for billions of dollars. Dr. Hamilton paced a few steps from Ilem and Victor to read what Ilem passed him. Sensing Q's continued reservations, Ilem said, "I want to buy Quantum. You can stay on as a consultant, but I want your work to benefit

AVI's developments." Victor agreed with Dr. Q that Ilem's offer is legitimate, "Our plans to build a cybernetic implant dynasty will change more than human anatomy. It will alter destiny."

Victor sat on the edge of Ilem's desk as Ilem confidently lounged in his cool, leather office chair. Victor and Ilem tried with more vigor to convince Dr. Hamilton to sign the agreement. Despite their cons and coercion, Dr. Hamilton still declined Ilem's generous offer, "I won't sell out my company to make superhumans." Victor tried to quell Q's fears by stating, "Sell out is such a strong phrase. I am sure Ilem will consider our standard joint venture agreement. I'll even draft it."

Ilem walked closer in front of Dr. Hamilton either to shake hands or intimidate him into submission. Being close in height at 6'0" feet and 6'4", respectively, Ilem could not stare down at Dr. Q as he did with so many others in his circle. Instead, Dr. Hamilton stood his ground and drew the line on how far he would go recklessly tinkering with human evolution for financial gain and power grabs.

Instead of further igniting controversy, Ilem blushingly suggested to Dr. Hamilton, "Although you have rejected my offers, Victor's right. It is more important to advance science. Think it over, Q." Victor also tried to quell Dr. Hamilton's concerns as understandable and legitimate but malleable, "If you need convincing, we can discuss it over dinner." After dropping his salacious invitation, Victor walked to the door of Ilem's office to leave the meeting.

In the tone of an instructive father, Ilem lightly chastised Victor again, "Victor, don't be so forward." Victor, ever confident in his ability to worm into any power struggle, playfully responded to Ilem, "Oh hush, you can even send a chaperon. Someone like your sister Naihal. She is polyamorous, entirely open, and hot."

As the automatic door opened, Victor received a phone call that he answered by tapping on an *iSiphon* air bud inserted in his ear canal. Victor spoke to the person on the other line, "You have Victor." The caller answered him in a thick Russian accent, "Vitya, *ty odinok*."[79] Victor thanked the caller but cautioned him that it was a conversation they should not have within earshot of at least Q, "*Dosvedanya, Q. Net, no dayte mne minutku, chtoby my mogli pogovorit.*"[80]

---

[79] "Are you alone?"
[80] "Goodbye, Q. No, but give me a moment so we can talk."

By 2039 AD, the joint venture Dr. Hamilton eventually entered between AVI and Quantum Biotech was hailed by global industries as sparking revolutionary med-tech improvements. Dr. Hamilton's meta-avatar informs the incorporeal Sledge and Iggy, "By then, I knew how to implant billions of miniaturized computers into a receptor at the subatomic level to restore memories, but I didn't share my findings with anyone outside of Quantum. Soon after making that discovery, Ilem brazenly sent me a new prototype of the *iSiphon*. Albeit an intriguing replica of Biotech's AI products, Ilem made the advanced *iSiphon* from an unusual metal I had never encountered."

"The night that Ilem sent me his prototype, I downloaded as many of Quantum's Top-Secret files to a secure cloud in the Maze as I could fit. I knew I could not reveal my discovery for implanting a brain imprint of a specific individual into sentient beings." Iggy wisely concludes, "If Ilem knew how to do that, he might transfer anyone's identity into an indestructible AI body." Dr. Hamilton concurs with Iggy's hypothesis, "Right, Iggy. It might mean immortality for anyone Ilem seduced to follow him. Imagine if he applied brain imprinting on an exponential scale."

Dr. Hamilton explained to them initially, and without my knowledge, Victor underwent surgery to replace his organs with AI devices made from sentient metal. Ilem was present from the first of Victor's surgery to the last, always sporting a cunning, satisfied look as he watched. Once Victor lost his mind from failed brain augmentations, scores suffered, including Ilem's plans for conquest.

News outlets credited Victor with igniting the first Trans-Purists Conflict of early '40 by launching his unexpected terror attacks against carbon-based humans. He slaughtered many with his M249 light machine gun at the United Nations Secretariat Building entryway. Most of them were innocent people fleeing through the lobby for cover. Victor overwhelmed them with bullets, expressing no mercy for either women or children.

"Even while in hiding, I tracked news coverage of Victor Garin's first murder spree at the United Nations, where he mercilessly butchered sixty-three innocent people. The police captured him with the death penalty, a just outcome. But with the help of someone inside the court, he escaped from the courtroom during the trial. Someone left an Army NGSAR in a car's trunk in the courthouse parking lot because he used that weapon to kill more unassuming people within minutes of his escape."

Instead of derailing the Transhumanism Movement, Ilem convinced the BRICS to protect the growing transhumans from persecution despite Garin's crimes.

After leaving the Maze, Sledge, Iggy, and Dr. Hamilton return to the room where Sage lies. Dr. Hamilton sits on the couch next to his unconscious daughter. He listens with one ear to Sledge talk, and the other ear searches for the beat of Sage's heart.

Sledge observes, "I was *thinkin bout* what would happen if we left control of immortality in wicked hands. Imagine *ah* thousand Hitlers." Iggy agrees, "Or a million power-thirsty dictators like him." Dr. Hamilton chimes in, "Or an army of killers like Victor Garin. Ilem's influence was too far gone to trust anyone. I had to keep my work a secret."

Dr. Hamilton shares with Sledge and Iggy his insight that "The more the imprint transfers, the quicker the implanted mind degraded. I overcame that hurdle by allowing Sage's imprint to gestate for two years. Ilem had yet to make the same discoveries. Because he was slow to catch up to my progress, he formed a plan to deliver the *coup de gras* to my ambitions the next time we met."

Ilem's Supersonic ASR9 JET, 2040.

Eleven years after entering into the joint venture agreement with him, Dr. Hamilton found himself on Ilem's supersonic business jet revealed to the super-rich in 2023 by the aerospace company Aerion. Known as the ASR2, the 2023 model had a top speed of Mach 1.5, 67 percent faster than the top cruise speeds of conventional long-haul subsonic aircraft. Ilem purchased a seventh-generation jet model that exceeded the earlier version's speed and distance capabilities. His ASR9 served as AVI's flagship.

As Dr. Hamilton approached, Ilem stared down toward the tarmac in front of the ASR9. Two of Dr. Hamilton's associates from Quantum Biotech accompanied him to the meeting, or showdown, with Ilem. One carried a briefcase that Dr.

Hamilton handed him before boarding the ASR9. Both of the assistants already had *iSiphons* attached to their ears.

Everyone boarded the plane, Dr. Hamilton, Ilem, and Dr. Hamilton's two assistants. The assistants sat behind a desk while Dr. Hamilton stood near Ilem, seated at a separate table. Dr. Hamilton wanted to stand over Ilem in a way that mirrored a Mexican standoff. On the desk was a rectangular box with a large object concealed inside it. Ilem arrogantly tapped his fingers on the box as he impatiently waited to reveal the white elephant inside.

Dr. Hamilton was very agitated, while Ilem seemed relaxed, stepping away from the table to make drinks. The doctor told Ilem in a wild manner, "The damn doorman at Quantum had to tell me that you bought controlling interest in my company." Inexplicably, Ilem poured five drinks, not just four. Ilem, "I made a solid offer to buy your company. You chose a different path. You had time to negotiate a better deal. That time is up." With contempt twisting in his throat, Dr. Hamilton snapped back, "Better deal? I never agreed to let you steal my inventions."

Dr. Hamilton threw the *iSiphon* toward Ilem and said, "I know you've tried to deconstruct my technology without a license. You won't get away with this, Godfrey!"

From behind a long, cloth curtain, Victor stepped forward to reveal that he was still alive despite the NYPD shooting him back to hell after his second murder spree. He was no longer handsome. Instead, his angelic face was gruesome, scarred by bullets that tore into him, at least one for each of his 109 victims. Abroad the ASR9, Victor's face bore disfiguring injuries and the crudeness of botched surgeries meant to replace his deteriorating body with pearl-white, robotic parts.

Without needing to stroke Dr. Hamilton's ego, Ilem mockingly said, "Apologies, Q, Victor slipped a Poison Pill Clause into the agreement. You die, we take over your company. What could go wrong?" Dr. Hamilton was as shocked by Ilem's and Victor's statements as he was to see Victor alive. The worm turned, leaving Dr. Hamilton without an exit or reply.

Victor threw the liquid to the back of his throat in one gulp. Dr. Hamilton's anger grew more as he and Ilem goaded him. Q rebuked Ilem for his underhanded scheme, "You will not get away with this. You don't have the technology to copy the human mind before it degrades, Victor, repeatedly."

Feeling no shame and to further the insult, Victor informed Dr. Hamilton exactly how he stole Quantum's trade secrets. Victor bragged that at Ilem's suggestion, he held one of his infamous parties with a diverse group of Dr. Hamilton's workers. So many of them wanted to see Victor's playhouse, just like other spectators eager to belong. He could not resist their desires. After he had invited them, he copied any files they had access to labeled "Top-Secret." Victor confessed that he stole Dr. Hamilton's inventions or at least reverse-engineered them. The braggadocious, once baby-faced killer droned on, "I was not as effective deconstructing the secrets that we stole from Quantum. Praise Lord Ilem for replicating your technology."

Victor continued revealing the trap they set and snapped around Dr. Hamilton's achievements, "I discovered the hard way that you are right, Doctor. It felt like everyone could hear my thoughts. I thought my skin was peeling off! I tried to use my machines to transfer my consciousness, but the computers burst into flames, causing me to sustain mental disruptions and increase my destructive impulsiveness. I could not control my rage, and it felt good. That is when I went on my little killing spree."

Ilem supports Victor's recall of events by acknowledging, "After Victor escaped from trial and killing sprees, the authorities tried hard to end his reign of terror. Thankfully, President Colon agreed there was no purpose in jailing Victor in a vegetative state. I convinced him that law enforcement did not need an invalid to care for and that I would deconstruct his brain with nanobots and rebuild his neural network to make him docile."

Dr. Hamilton frantically ripped the briefcase from his assistant's hands after Ilem's tale of Victor's survival and reincarnation as a Borg. Dr. Hamilton revealed an explosive from the briefcase resembling the hockey pucks Sage used to flee the Floating City after Blood Bowl. Dr. Hamilton warned Ilem and Victor, "The human mind cannot be copied multiple times without regression to a primitive state."

Calmly, Ilem held a glass of alcohol out to Dr. Hamilton, who nervously gripped the small explosive. Ilem tried de-escalating the situation by assuring Dr.

Hamilton, "Q, you can stay with Quantum. You cannot imagine what we will accomplish if you only comply." Dr. Hamilton rejected Ilem's submission offer, "There's no damn way I'll do that."

Victor opened the container on the desk to reveal it held Ilem's helmet of command that was gifted to him by the Diwan of Matter. Ilem took the helmet in his confident hands and crowed to Q, "There are so many ways to persuade you. For example, this is the master control for all *iSiphons*." Reminiscent of a royal coronation, Victor lowered the helmet on Ilem's head from behind, igniting Ilem's power to activate the *iSiphon* worn by Dr. Hamilton's two associates.

Dr. Hamilton's employees started to rise from their chairs like string puppets under Ilem's control. Courageously, Dr. Hamilton warned Ilem, "I'll let everyone know about you, Ilem! You're finished!" Laughing contemptuously at Dr. Hamilton's threat, Ilem replied, "No, Q, I have only just begun. I can control them to do whatever I command." Turning to Dr. Hamilton's zombified assistants, Ilem commanded them, "Seize him!"

The brain-idled assistants tried to catch Dr. Hamilton, but before they could, he activated the explosive puck and tossed it at them in time to escape. The miniature explosives boomed loudly inside the plane, rocking it from side to side.

Another burst rang out when a second bomb exploded. The blast dispelled chunks of flesh and bone from the bodies of Hamilton's assistants while Ilem absorbed the deadly discharge that traveled toward him. Although Ilem was able to shield Victor from harm partially, the bomb shredded Victor's arm as he reached for Dr. Hamilton's throat. Victor screamed in pain as the recoil of deadly chemicals melted into his flesh, leaving him bleeding profusely and with one of his limbs involuntarily dangling on one side.

Frigid air rushed into the airplane when the second blast ejected the door. The unexpected odor of sugared almonds with the slightest hint of cherry escorted the powerful discharge out of the airplane's door. Unlike common belief, there was no ground rush sensation when Dr. Hamilton leapt from the plane. Suddenly, he just felt himself plummeting toward the ground at 120 mph.

His adrenaline pumped, and his senses came alive the closer he descended to the ground. The sudden feeling Dr. Hamilton felt of gravity's grip yanking him the first seventy feet was relieved by the next cradling sensation he experienced when the wind slowed his descent toward the camouflage offered by green forests below. Dr. Hamilton briefly enjoyed the breathtaking perspective on the world that was far down, turbulent, and out of control.

Touching down safely on the ground did not give Dr. Hamilton much reprieve because Ilem's Death Squad was still hunting him. The rapid stomping of boots signaled to him that his pursuers were mere breaths away.

Although he was fortunate to escape the first horde searching for him, hiding in plain sight in this environment was a significant task for Dr. Hamilton. Who did not recognize one of the most prolific biomedical engineers in the world? Dressed in camouflage clothing, he was fortunate to avoid detection by creeping around roadblocks and maintaining absolute silence on the highway, leaving only the crickets and birds to serenade his journey on desolate roads.

Although he successfully fled from Ilem's Death Squad by going underground, two years later, Dr. Hamilton watched helplessly from the forest near AVI's business complex as Ilem's guards led an unwilling Sage inside the AVI business complex. He mournfully recalls the turn of events, "Ilem convinced Sage he'd look after her while I was missing. He lied. It was to keep her close while he exploited his Poison Pill clause."

AVI Headquarters, Toronto, Canada – Ilem's 2042 Peace Summit.

Ilem was about to go out on the stage to make his big announcement. Sage grudgingly accompanied him to the event, but they stood together at Ilem's much anticipated Peace Summit. Thousands, indeed, millions around the globe, sit at the edge of their seats and even rustle up from prone positions on their comfortable couches. With their open hands, they all waited anxiously for the gift of peace and prosperity that Ilem promised decades ago.

He tilted his head toward Sage to broach a recurring subject that Sage was halfhearted about: "With control of Quantum Biotech, I'm prepared to move forward with my global plans." Sage clapped back bitterly, "Damn the company, Ilem! I cannot move forward without my father. He has been missing for two years."

The stage director gave Ilem the cue, signaling it was time for him to come on stage. As if Ilem's focus were entirely on his announcement, Ilem straightened his posture and turned his gaze away from Sage. In a faint voice, he said to her, "I understand your sentiment, Sage. After today, my vision for the future is all this world will know or want to embrace." Having walked to the stage podium, Ilem boastfully stood there for a minute, waving to his excited fans. To the side, Sage stood in the crowd praising Ilem. The rabid enthusiasm left Sage with a rising feeling of trepidation.

Nearby, the sculptor of the hand holding the Dyson Sphere was partially built in the Center Court, where the fountain was previously located. The hand jutted dramatically from the ground behind Ilem, creating the illusion that he was an ancient Greek god lifted into the air by a celestial being.

There was an equal blend of humans and transhumans in the crowd attending the Peace Summit live. Most of the attendees in front of the group were reporters. The albino interviewer, Baxter Robinson, was the only transhuman reporter slated to ask Ilem questions. You may recall that Baxter used bioengineering's benefits to improve his sight by donning bulky AI glasses during his '39 interview with the Diwan of Light. One year later, to enhance his reporting abilities, Baxter expanded his use of AI devices to include an elaborate *iSiphon* and a prosthetic covering one side of his face, eyes, and head.

Many people in the audience wore breathing devices and face coverings but could still shout for their respective sides in the growing clash between humans and transhumans. Several patches of humans in the back of the crowd protested against the rise of transhumanism, while those on the other side of the equation protested against moralism.

Baxter Robinson lobbed pre-planned questions to Ilem to set the tone of the "peace summit." Baxter scanned his notes, then asked, "Mr. Ilem, you have suggested your announcement will 'revolutionize evolution.' I've heard nonbelievers say that seems a little grandiose. Please point us in the right direction." Ilem replied, "The most important development for *homo sapiens* has always been communication. Without it, you would have gone extinct millennia ago." Robinson lauds Ilem for his generosity, "And I can say for all of Earth, we are eternally grateful."

To garner all the attention and drown out the murmuring in the room, Ilem pounded down on the podium as he philosophized about government control. The room fell quiet. After that, Ilem continued his proclamation, "Imagine the miracles humans would have performed speaking with one tongue if the Internet existed when Alexander ruled or when the English issued the Magna Carta."

"The *iSiphon* eclipses the limits of human communication through direct human-computer transference. Now humans will take the ultimate step toward intellectual and physical freedom. I invite all transhumans, cyborgs, sentient beings, and advanced sapient life to seek asylum here at AVI's headquarters on my Floating City." Baxter timely chimed in with another question, "How is that possible? Won't the United States of the Americas object? The BRICS nations back you, but won't what's left of NATO oppose you?"

The Diwan of Light stepped behind the podium to respond forcefully to Baxter. "Transhumans who are tired of having their right to self-realization denied may join my new world unfettered by discriminatory laws."

Ilem felt total control of the live audience and the gullible glued to their broadcasting systems and social media platforms. He knew he had them under his control since he pledged his tremendous and growing riches to spread opulence by providing willing governments with contingents of security drones that could tirelessly work to ease hardships in life and improve GDP. Within a year of his promise in '99, Ilem spearheaded the development of ground-breaking technologies in telecommunications, robotics, medicine, energy, biology, and nanotechnology.

His altruism and philanthropy led to national and international recognition on social media sites and magazines like Time to laud Ilem with awards. Eventually, the Norwegian Parliament awarded Ilem the Nobel Peace Prize. Within two years, AVI had already placed security drones in eighty percent of the eligible cities, towns, and villages worldwide or *iSiphons* in the ears of millions around the globe.

Everyone had a reason to trust and follow Ilem. Eventually, the poor and the afflicted bought cheaper *iSiphons*. All those who subscribed to the *iSiphon* were in debt.

Another reporter, tired of Baxter's monopoly of Ilem's attention, cut in with his tricky question, "The U.N. Anti-Transhumanism Treaty forbids performing medical procedures to convert humans to transhumans without complying with strict government regulations. What do you have to say?" Another reporter, sensing chum in the pool, jumped in with her inquiry, "Aren't you concerned nations, or will the church act to stop this bastardization of creation?"

Instead of flashing his fabled anger, Ilem answered the questions with an accusation of his own, "Purists have conspired since the dawn of time to prevent biocultural evolution. Governments foolishly outlawed cloning.[81] They enslaved Blacks, murdered Jews, and forced gays and lesbians into hiding. Haven't humans had their chance to rule? Isn't it time for a final solution?"

Sage watched the U.S.A. President Adrian Colon and his alien and transhuman secret service agents join Ilem from the other side of the stage. Ilem held up his hands in a celebratory manner, waving them about like a frenzied orchestra conductor nearing a crescendo. Ilem, "People of Earth, governments prevented you from becoming *Persona Creatus*. The Earth is dying, and they want you to die with it. It is forced suicide! But with the support of your world leaders, transhumans can come out of the closet."

Kol and the Sect gathered near Sage on the side of the stage, crowding in, almost forcing her from her stiffened position, while Ilem excitedly continued his verbal diatribe. "I assure you, politicians, the rich, the powerful, and those aware won't be left to suffer, only the meek and the weak. Submit to the freeing power of the *iSiphon* ... accept transhumanism, join the creatures of our galaxies that are ready to accept your unique gifts."

Several people in the audience tried to flee to safety, especially the protestors ragging against the spread of transhumanism and other forms of bioengineering, threatening to defy the laws of nature and the province of fabled gods. Sage tried to back through the crowd to escape from the Floating City but was stopped by the immovable soldiers crowded on the stage. Ilem attempted to cajole the audience by warning them, "Archaic beliefs constrain your right to immortality. Purists and

---

[81] Governments, clouded by shortsightedness, imposed global bans on cloning, unwittingly setting the stage for a clandestine era where the rich and powerful secretly wove the threads of their genetic destinies. H. Rept. 108-18 – Human Cloning Prohibition Act of 2003. Despite laws to the contrary, rumors persisted on the Floating City that some gracefully aging celebrities were, in fact, clones.

Luddites are the relics of yesterday. Leave them behind like sand slipping through a broken hourglass."

Ilem pointed at the Floating City's Command Deck and ordered those therein, "Deck commander, release the tethers!"

The deck commander released chains holding the Floating City to the ground near the water surrounding Ilem's business complex. Ilem warned everyone within earshot, "And reporters ... those, like you, who oppose me are too late to realize they are already relics of the past."

Ilem donned the helmet of command to activate mind control over all the *iSiphon* wearers around the world. He pressed his willing and unwilling followers into action, "*iSiphons* activate! Children attack the faithless! Strike them down in the street. No matter the cost, rise transhumans! Rise at the foot of my throne!"

While the Floating City tore from the ground, pipes connected to underground pools of radiated water flooded the area. A green murk submerged people near the rushing contaminated water as chaos ensued. Like mindless zombies, those wearing *iSiphons* flashing glitzy red lights turned to attack those who still held themselves out as "pure" humans. The Purists at the Peace Summit ran for safety, shouting, "Run! We're doomed!"

Ilem and his entourage, including President Colon, Baxter Robinson, and Kol, stood at the entryway to the Floating City as it lifted into the air. The crowd in front of the extraordinary vessel desperately fled in all directions. Dr. Hamilton crouched in the woods, watching the catastrophe unfolding.

But worst yet, swarths of humans attempting to flee suddenly realized they could not remove their *iSiphons* from their ears. One cried, "Oh God, I can't get this off! It's stuck!" As stunned humans searched for sanity, swarms of zombified *iSiphon* wearers overwhelmed them.

The trampling mass pinned Sage against a fence near the Floating City just as she was about to reach an unsecured area that ran parallel to her father's location. The forces pinning her against the fence were so strong they could bend steel and, thus, were undoubtedly stout enough to restrain and overwhelm even a woman as fit and cunning as Sage.

As Sage struggled to save herself, she could feel her energy decreasing while her blood supply to her brain painfully reduced. In thirty seconds, she lost consciousness.

Dr. Hamilton painfully recalls for Sledge and Iggy, "From my vantage point, I was aware Sage was dying, but was powerless to save her from the avalanche of flesh that prevented her from moving. As they rushed into her, her head became locked between their arms and shoulders, and her face racked with fear."

Her father admits to Sledge and Iggy, "I feebly watched her die and couldn't do anything to stop it. I could reach her body as it collapsed amidst throngs of distressed Purists. In six minutes, her brain almost stopped functioning, but I was able to pull her from death."

"I restored Sage's memory to save society by implanting her brain implant in the orb. I constructed the orb to emit her power of kinetic empathy. I planted within her enough genomes to restore 10,000 humans to life on a new home planet as the culmination of the Doomsday Protocol."

"Ilem's conquest relentlessly rolled through one nation after the other. Those who sought salvation by donning *iSiphons* that heightened the functions of their brains and bodies soon came to know Ilem had them trapped. I hid Sage and myself in a secret room in the A.R.I.E.L. Observatory until I could remove her unwanted slumber. I didn't go idle, however. I owed her and the rest of the world a debt. My ego and biohacking were responsible for Earth's peril."

"To reverse the tides, I willingly sacrificed my life."

END OF CHAPTER 12

Chapter 13

Ever Turning

Turning, ever turning like a yoyo on a string,
Monotonous in the way that it never stops. Is it just a dream?

All its many colors never wanting to cease and mix,
Moving in an infinite circle trying to find self-bliss.

The troubles that it faces from shore to mountains high,
Millions are dying daily people are unmoved to cry.

Turning, ever turning, no one knows what the future holds,
It may be the day we all are saved
Or when this yoyo drops, cracks, and implodes.

Trigger Happy

Pentagon Three Months After Ilem's 2042 Peace Summit.

Dr. Hamilton worked tirelessly to honor his pledge on his daughter's life to stop Ilem. After escaping from Ilem's ASR9, Dr. Q went before the US military with overtures of his willingness to help with a scientific solution to the peril Purists faced.

The day the military blowhards finally granted Dr. Hamilton an audience, he pensively waited in a crowded, disorderly room with other scientists seeking a moment to speak with military officials about solutions to quell Ilem's invasion. In the few months that Hamilton hid underground, his once salt-and-pepper hair and beard turned gray as he stressed how to save humankind from Ilem's relentless attacks and save Sage from her unintended slumber. He fidgeted with files in his briefcase, reading them repeatedly as though he was meticulously rehearsing lines for a play.

Dr. Hamilton sat and sat for so long that he felt his legs numb. He watched as military officials granted scant numbers of scientists an audience with the man in charge, General Daniel Keller. He was the commanding officer assigned to plan the USA's penultimate solution to defeating Ilem.

Three hours after entering the room for a meeting, a private escorted Dr. Q into General Keller's office. Joining the General's Office, Dr. Hamilton first thought, "Based on the General's reputation as a fearful presence, this short, rotund man was acting as no more than an annoyed traffic cop."

General Keller took several uncomfortable minutes to adjust his eyes from an active computer display on the wall in the background showing military images to Dr. Hamilton, who politely waited for an invitation to sit down. Dr. Hamilton, "I also thought he would be more professional and astute."

Dr. Hamilton impatiently repeated himself to the dunderheaded, stuffed shirt, "For the fourth time, the Protocol is a resurrection plan. I imprint human minds by simulating the brain at the neuron level." General Keller, incredulous, replied, "And what good will that do? We need final solutions to wipe Ilem and his freaks off the face of this planet, not mind games."

Dr. Hamilton laid in front of General Keller the schematics of the orb he designed to retain Sage's brain implant, then further informed the General, "Gestation takes time. We can duplicate the neural-wiring diagram in temporary storage units until we locate permanent hosts using this device."

General Keller picked up the schematics, scratched his head vigorously, then quietly, unenthusiastically laid the papers back on the table, then slid them back toward Dr. Hamilton. During the pregnant pause, Dr. Hamilton contemplated how one breaks a brick with a tuning fork. It makes a great sound, but it leaves no mark.

Then, Dr. Hamilton pulled from his briefcase a prototype of the orb. General Keller blinked twice, then opened his mouth to mimic an intelligent person, "Doctor, are you suggesting we store memories in a battery of some kind?" Dejected by his inability to explain the Doomsday Protocol to the General, Hamilton summarized his plan, "Even if the units degrade, I believe we can still preserve the integrity of our subjects with a controlled, two-year gestation."

Instead of acknowledging Dr. Hamilton's plan, General Keller picked up the remote control to raise the volume for the scenes of violence on the computer.

The increasing sound started as a polite hum, then Keller adjusted it louder to an ear-piercing blow horn blaring sounds of death and destruction into the General's stuffy office.

Shouting to be heard over chaos, General Keller speculated, "But none of this will work unless Ilem thinks everybody is extinct. Your so-called Doomsday Protocol. Did I get that right, doctor? The images you see are from the real Operation Doomsday of 1945. That's firepower, Quinten." Frustrated and near the end of his rope, Dr. Hamilton replied, "Yes, back to what you were asking. After we're all gone, we may have a chance to bring humans back to life."

Unimpressed, General Keller pointed to the images on his computer, "Look at the screen Dr. Hamilton and open your eyes. China's horde of humanoid soldiers have returned to their high-stepping ways in Tiananmen Square, conspiring with Ilem, and the BRICS are on his side. Last year, China's investment in military AI produced 70 percent of that industry's growth. And they are backing Ilem. We need military solutions, not science babble."

The plump military leader turned his back on Dr. Hamilton, pulled a cigar from a humidor sitting on his credenza, and stubbornly clipped the end. He then responded smugly, "Relying on science led us to this disaster. Our new autonomous war machines will crush Ilem's forces. After that, we will send in the troops and clean out the trannies, boy."

Overwhelmed by General Keller's dismissive tone, Dr. Hamilton irritably rose from his chair, shouting to be heard, "Don't you understand, bombing Ilem's troops into submission won't work. Our last chance to survive is after no one thinks we're a threat!"

Still pleased with himself and oblivious to anyone else's concerns, General Keller aggressively retorted, "We are a threat! We have enough weapons and power to wipe Ilem off the face of the Earth. We do not need your crazy plan."

With that tirade, General Keller took the schematics of the orb Dr. Hamilton slid across the desk and crumpled every page. General Keller concluded his parley with Dr. Q, saying, "Thank you, doctor, but no thank you." After that, men in military uniforms unceremoniously escorted Dr. Hamilton out of the building.

General Keller was right to be cocky about how the United States of the Americas' new weapons of mass destruction would fare in conflicts between one nation against another. By 2046, weapons of war had advanced in staggering ways that permitted vast numbers of nations the means to cripple significantly larger countries.

As General Keller predicted, the USA's and its allies' joint militaries assembled their traditional armies and mass of autonomous war machines to challenge Ilem and quell the Transhumanism Movement that ignited in response to Ilem's sham Peace Summit. The USA and its allies relied on the PL-01, a contemporary stealth tank featuring a thermal camouflage system. Men armed themselves with working railguns to take down Ilem's autonomous soldiers and weaponry.

When Ilem's and Earth's forces clashed, automated jet fighters launched into action. Earth's militaries employed a combination of strong AI, swarming behavior, and hypersonic technology to create near-instantaneous effects to defeat Ilem's Elite Squad throughout the battlespace. With the usual cockiness and overconfidence Earth's first world has shown toward the third world, Earth's governments believed merely rolling out their most advanced weapons would send Ilem cowering to his lair or wherever he originated.

Earth's militaries relied on Joint Multi-Role JMR rotorcraft and the SR-72, a crewless, hypersonic aircraft intended for intelligence gathering, to gain the upper hand against Ilem. A commanding fleet of 2037 bombers was also discharged for battle. As the most advanced aircraft to fly, with its unparalleled stealth capabilities, a range that enabled it to strike targets anywhere in the world, and a payload that included nuclear power, the human military leaders high-fived even before their weapons warmed.

Dr. Hamilton tells Sledge and Iggy, "All of Earth's militaries that weren't compromised attacked Ilem and his troops. Like swinging a fly swatter, Ilem's forces destroyed the mighty JMR rotorcraft, the SR-72, and the PL-01 when they attacked. They tried using the most advanced military weapons they had to destroy Ilem. Those that weren't destroyed on the battlefield were commandeered by Ilem's Elite Squad. Long story short, they got their asses kicked."

"Following those encounters, the Sect rounded humans up for transformation or execution. The mass genocide started with scientists, artists, and the military. Politicians were safe from immediate destruction while they held power as long as they relented to Ilem's control. To maintain the strength of his army of transhumans, Ilem readily annihilated the disabled and humans resistant to vaccines and susceptible to bacterial infection. He had no use for the weak."

His cruelty and brutality did not discriminate. Dr. Hamilton explains to Iggy and Sledge, "After Ilem's forces crushed Earth's militaries, his forces captured and exterminated Purists who refused to join him. Anyone remaining resistant scattered into hiding - underground, underwater, under rocks, into the Maze - or plotted desperate plans to escape Earth."

Sage's moaning in the room where she is recuperating interrupts the men's conversation. In a disappointed tone, Dr. Hamilton observes, "I couldn't save her. So, I hid in a dark web program with my secrets hoping someone would find a solution before masses of people abandoned, or Ilem destroyed Earth."

Dr. Hamilton puts his ethereal hand inside Sage's abdomen. He pulls out the orb to display it for them to see. The technological marvel mesmerizes Sledge and Iggy. Sage's image on the couch disappears. Dr. Hamilton tells them, "Even a yottaflop of storage is not enough to hold the ultimate power of the human mind."

He rolls the orb between his fingers to give them a closer look at the device. He tells them, "After going underground, I perfected this orb to shatter that limitation. Within it, I implanted Sage's brain imprint. But the most important cargo is what she carries in the orb's core. This orb contains the genome to revitalize 10,000 humans to restart our civilization in carbon-based hosts."

He further states, "By 2025, I had sequenced a billion human genomes, about one-eighth of the world's population. By 2030, my company's technology was readily used to create medical nanobots that generate artificial organs. I secretly teleported the first complex organic molecules such as DNA and proteins."

Dr. Hamilton continued uninterrupted, "When I went underground, I activated the orb for the first time to prepare Sage for the world. From this object, my daughter can project a tangible holographic image of herself or any other female she connects with empathically. Her transference is static. No one can remove it from this globe, but it can last forever as long it remains intact."

He adds, "An adaptive failsafe protocol triggered Sage's cerebral programming when carbon life signs became critically low. She is the first variable in the Doomsday Protocol. The Omnis nanoprobe is the second, a combination of planning and chance. There's a third protocol that I'm completing now that stimulates information exchange by touch."

"In the first hour of life, I evaluated Sage using simple frame principles. Within forty-eight hours, she readily consumed information from over five million sources. She started sneaking out without me knowing. She would wander off to walk through a crowd of people and aliens, randomly drawing in auras to read them."

Iggy poses a question to Dr. Hamilton that has intrigued him since Sledge brought them together: "How can she change her appearance?" Dr. Hamilton explains, "She's a kinetic empath. As my friend, Tyson, surmised, her *'intuition comes from life experience and the application of her senses to her environment.'*[82] She draws in the emotions that beings project when they're near her. Even in the infancy of her programming, Sage protected me from capture, sometimes sacrificing parts of herself that I wished she didn't have to do."

"She learned how to turn the tables on the human and transhuman harassers by using their insatiable lust and longings to her advantage. Sometimes, despicable people perceived her as an object to possess. But she's an information sponge. She learned to reach deep into her target's minds to draw the most compelling and controlling image to project back at them."

Despite his silence, Sledge remains antagonistic toward Q. That emotion is substantial in his statement to Q, "If *yuh* Doomsday Protocol was supposed to save humans, *yuh* could tell from how I look it was a failure!"

Dr. Hamilton still tries to come to terms with the notion that Sledge's human consciousness remains, defying science, "That's where you are wrong. The

---

[82] "The Mysteries of the Universe," Jeff Bercovici Interview of Neil deGrasse Tyson, The National, December/January 2017 Edition, p. 53.

Doomsday Protocol is a gambit based on one unassailable premise; one day, humans will end. Most likely by our hand."

Iggy posits Dr. Hamilton's theory's broad-ranging meaning: "If everyone is dead, that pretty much seems irreversible even if you can biohack DNA." Dr. Hamilton agrees with Iggy's deduction, "That is precisely what I wanted Ilem and the rest of the Galactic Council to believe. Once humans are dead, we are no longer a threat. The ultimate symmetry is serendipity."

Dr. Hamilton waves his digital hand to draw a digitized box in the air. Q writes the numbers one, two, and three within the box. Next to the numbers, he inscribes 1: rescue, 2. distract, 3. escape, then informs them what the writing means. "I programmed all my variables to randomize their outcomes to prevent anyone from predicting what would happen. That gave Sage a chance to rescue my remains. If I did not make it, I readied her to salvage the last living carbon-based human in proximity and escape Earth with her payload."

Sledge resists the temptation to dismiss Q's statement but inevitably asks him, "How did you know it would be me?"

Briefly, Dr. Hamilton envisions the moment he is in the prison cell on the Floating City with Sledge after Ilem's soldiers unceremoniously throw him in the cell. He recalls Dr. Hamilton dismantling the bulbous end of the Vision Staff to combine sensors with a nano-device containing the Omnis nanoprobe. The nano-device resembled a tiny, crawling insect. While he envisions the events just alluded to, Dr. Hamilton's palm tingles where the mechanical bug crawled from his grip into Sledge's ear.

With his thoughts in the room instead of sullen storms from the past, Dr. Hamilton confesses to Sledge, "Involving you in triggering a random carbon reanimation did not come to me until you appeared in my cell on the Floating City. Although many might conclude that is not a plan, I'm afraid I have to disagree."

"Randomness is always a plan. Fate rules the rest."

END OF CHAPTER 13

Chapter 14

King of the Mountain

My father taught me to play
King of the Mountain

He paid no mind
To the trail of blood
Streaking my chin
As Malcolm Hunter, high on the mountain
Crushed his heel into my face

The other kids' faces were masked with excitement
As they climbed closer to me
To cast me down from near the top of the mountain
Like a sin-heavy saint

My father licked his butt
lit another cigarette and turned away

On top of the steel pyramid
Sand-littered winds blew the salty flavor of blood
Back to my lips
As Malcolm tumbled, kicked
Like seraph flung from up high

I lost my innocence.
Smiling a toothless smile of accomplishment
Proud of being king

My Father
Snuffed out another cigarette
As the smoke cleared away from our eyes.

Omnis: Last Man of Earth

The War Within

Months ago, on the night that Sledge lay unconscious behind the forcefield that caged him and Dr. Hamilton, he did not realize anyone else was in the cell with him. As he lay immobile, Dr. Hamilton involved Sledge, or at least his corpse, in the Doomsday Protocol. A nano bug crawling into Sledge's ear canal carried the code to ignite Sledge's potential.

For that to happen, Dr. Hamilton dismantled the Vision Staff to extract the necessary sensors to prepare a crude mechanism for the process. He removed sensors from the Vision Staff and combined them with the nanoprobes carrying GDF-11 coding to Sledge's brain. He intended for it to stimulate a random, regenerative sequence in the event of Sledge's death, but that was in theory. Dr. Hamilton did not have time to evaluate his scheme on subjects, living or dead.

Sledge awoke in his cell with his head bandaged and his sunglasses gone. He looked around, and within the sterile room, he only sensed the stench of bodily fluids and the paced breathing of someone else nearby. Without concern or worry regarding anyone else in the cell, Sledge yelled, "Fuck! What *hav* I gotten myself into?"

Within the first minutes of their meeting, Dr. Hamilton sought to test Sledge's mettle. Dr. Hamilton tossed Sledge's Vision Staff back to him without allowing Sledge to adjust to prison life. Dr. Hamilton was surprised by Sledge's reaction, catching the Vision Staff with one hand without moving his body one inch. Sledge assured him, "I can take care of myself." Dr. Hamilton responded, "Good. Same here. My name is Hamilton ... Dr. Quinten Hamilton." Sledge replied that his name was "Sledge, *jus* Sledge."

While he examined Sledge's eyewear from up close, Dr. Hamilton explained to Sledge how the fights would occur at Blood Bowl, "We'll be given our weapon of choice if we make it through the first round of hand-to-hand combat."

Holding his staff in both hands as if he were already prepared for battle, Sledge informed Dr. Hamilton, "*Dis* will *haffi* do." Dr. Hamilton told Sledge, "Yes. I fixed them the best I could, and your head wound. Perfection is beyond my available resources."

Taking the sunglasses from Dr. Hamilton gave Sledge a chance to confirm they were still working. To win a battle at Blood Bowl, Sledge would have to rely on the weapons his captors made available and the fighting skills he had already mastered.

Sledge continued his conversation with Dr. Q, commenting, "This is what's left of my Vision Staff. It's designed to heighten my senses, but it's worthless now." Dr. Hamilton commented, "Whoever made your staff has an intriguing mind. The piconet connection is impressive."

To give Sledge the best understanding possible about defending himself during Blood Bowl, Dr. Hamilton looked as far as he could toward the row of cells holding the last Purists to recall the captors he had seen thus far. Dr. Hamilton reported to Sledge, "There are thirty-six of us. Most of them looked competent to defend themselves. For what it's worth, I'll do what I can to be your eyes. I thank you to do whatever you can to help, too."

Sledge brushes off Dr. Hamilton's offer not so much out of conceit but to draw a line in the sand, "I appreciate *di* offer, but I've been on my own most of my life. Who will I be up '*against*?'" Dr. Q visualizes the faces of the various individuals slated to fight at the Bowl. "The other 'Purists,' as transhumans call us, don't all appear to be ordinary humans."

"Most of them are here because a cryptocurrency entrepreneur named Ivan Levin conned them. From his hideout in a secret part of Saint Anthony Caves in Chernihiv, Ukraine, he orchestrated a dark passage lottery for players to vie for a seat on his rocket, leaving the Earth ahead of hostilities between humans and transhumans accelerated."

"He promised to the twenty-four 'winners' that he would smuggle them off of Earth in exchange for $50 million in digital currency from each person. Once Levin selected the lottery winners in 2045, he gave them two years to pay the fee demanded from each of them for the Bodhi Legion Digital Currency, which Levin intended to sell to transhumans through a second-level adsorption scheme."

"Levin also promised to provide all lottery winners with a three-year supply of a proprietary biological compound that they had to ingest in small, transformative dosages to alter their bio composition. Moreover, he plotted with specific industry insiders and Ilem's followers to join the Bodhi Legion in specific roles that would support escape from Earth on a separate space vessel if necessary."

"The lottery proceeds generated $1,200,000,000.00, of which Levin pledged $200 million to his select insiders. However, before the 'Great Escape' happened, all of the lottery winners were captured by Ilem's forces, purportedly after being betrayed by Bodhi."

"As Sledge and I discovered as combatants in Blood Bowl, the other surviving Purists possessed unique skills to engage in the looming battles. Some were adept in martial arts, while others were experts in special weapons use, including radiation power, chemical power, high tech, and internal body enhancements. Surprisingly, some of the final thirty-four possessed the mystical ability to shapeshift, launch psychotropic defenses, neurotoxins, and cast illusion spells."

"The remaining Purists who did not participate in Bodhi's lottery were a hodge-podge of those in hiding, drifters, and Lopers, captured by Ilem's Death Squadron in various locations worldwide after Bodhi dimed them out. Regardless of who they were, fanciful or real, the final thirty-six shared a common goal: Survival, even if it meant killing one another."

Given his informed knowledge of his future foes, Sledge began concentrating on swinging his Vision Staff to prepare himself for the looming battles. Sledge, "I may be blind, *buh enna* my *han, dis* more *dan ah* stick. *Wah can yuh duh tuh*[83] defend *yuhself*?" Dr. Hamilton confidently questioned Sledge, "Do you detect fear in my voice? I may be eighty-one, but I'm more than prepared for what's to come."

Dr. Hamilton held a strange metal insect between his fingers that appeared inactive. He shares with Sledge, "For the past eight years, I've taken psychoactive pills to enhance my strength, dexterity, and speed. I disguised them to look like bugs. I have a few for whatever Ilem throws at me."

Taking the nano-device from Dr. Q's hand for inspection, Sledge asked, "Where'd *yuh* hide *dem*?" Dr. Hamilton coyly answered Sledge's question, "… you don't want to know."

Remembering that fateful encounter stirs Sledge to anger in the present time. He shakes his fist at Dr. Hamilton as though he is seconds away from punching him. The Omnis probe begins to ignite with purple fire. Sledge, "*Wateva yuh duh tuh mi* Hamilton *tek aweh fi mi* freedom."[84] He turns his back on both of them as he leaves the room. Purple energy crackles around his third eye and begins cycling up and down his body. Sledge, "*Yuh* had *nuh* right to choose me for *yuh* twisted experiments."

Dr. Hamilton admits to Sledge, "I did not. Your head was the last piece of untainted carbon life that Sage could salvage." Sledge snaps back at Q, "So, saving my head was a coincidence, a fluke. Great, for *yuh. Yuh* plan worked. *Yuh* tricked me into *tinking* my life still had a purpose." Iggy goes over to Sledge to pull him back into the room. Dr. Hamilton tries to do the same thing with his words, "The Omnis probe doesn't decide what you will be. You do."

Wearing a gesture glove by a scuttled company called Eru Diagnostics, Iggy operates a computer system with simple movements without wires or Wi-Fi. After Iggy pulls on another glove and holds his hand in the direction of the computer, a code emerges on the palm of the glove: QB. OMEGA.215.

---

[83] "What can you do to…"
[84] "Whatever you did to me Hamilton took away my freedom."

Dr. Hamilton suggests to Iggy, "Iggy use that code to retrieve my notes from the dark web. If anyone can decipher them an intellectual enigma like you can." Iggy imagines the many possibilities for what he can do if he can duplicate, then modify, Dr. Hamilton's enigma code. He agrees with Dr. Hamilton, "I think I can understand some of this already." Dr. Hamilton concludes, "Good, not all great ideas need to come in big packages."

Dr. Hamilton gestures toward the EDG 10 as Iggy looks on and tells Iggy, "If you return after I calibrate Sage's barrier generator, I will show you some wonders I was not able to complete. The third variable requires the perfection of my cerebral transference techniques. That is where Victor Garin went wrong." Iggy excitedly exclaims to Sledge, "*Esto es increíble!*"[85]

Iggy counts to a third finger, "How is your third variable different?" Dr. Hamilton shares schematics with Iggy for another device he wanted to prepare for the Doomsday Protocol. Iggy eagerly consumes Dr. Hamilton's words and schemes, to which Dr. Hamilton comments, "It is more than an enigma code. Consider it a universal remote control but on a larger scale. My theories will be of use to you."

Before Iggy accepts Dr. Hamilton's proposal, Sledge hustles him out of the room, saying, "*Neva* mind *dat*, we need *fi ress* before we blow *dis* rock, Iggy." Iggy assures Dr. Hamilton, "I'll come back, Senor Q. Sledge, *el tiene grandes juguetes!*"[86] Dr. Hamilton turns his attention to working on the open orb but takes the time to say, "And before my program expires, Sage, perhaps I can make a couple of enhancements to protect you better."

Unbeknownst to Sledge and everyone else, Ilem's spies report to him where they are all hiding. A female transhuman delivers the report to Ilem, "Lord Ilem, one spy returned with an important recording." Ilem demands, "Show it to me." He then watches the recording of Sledge defeating the AI drones outside the junkyard.

Ilem orders the messenger to show Kol the recording to have him kill Sledge and bring Sage to Ilem, "Find the High Guard. Deliver this order to him. Bring me the woman alive and the man's head. Nothing has higher priority."

---

[85] "This is incredible!"
[86] "He has great toys!"

Seeking fresh air and space to decompress, Ilem walks out on the balcony outside his quarters, waving to the crowd. A band of revelers play triumphant music in Ilem's honor. ♪ ♪ ♪ ♪ Ilem waves to the masses while speaking to himself. In a low coo, Ilem says, "Victor, hear me."

Ilem continues waving to the crowd, with the Dyson Sphere in the background. A voice with a slow Russian accent responds, "Я слышу тебя, мой Господь.[87] How may I serve you?" Ilem answers, "Kol has failed me too many times. I sent him on a mission to retrieve what may be the answer you and I seek. Kill Kol if he fails to capture Sledge and Q's daughter, Sage. Do so, and you will replace Kol as my High Guard."

The smooth music continues to flow onto the balcony where Ilem stands. ♪ ♪ ♪ ♪

Victor probes the wisdom of Ilem's actions, even though he knows that in the space where he used to have a heart, he will do whatever his Lord commands. Victor, "Even if I do this, will trans accept me? To most, I am a monster …"

Ilem begins walking inside his sleeping quarters. The triumphant music trails close behind. ♪ ♪ ♪ ♪

Victor observes, "It seems highly unorthodox to kill your High Guard when your troops are content with your promises of their roles in your coming kingdom." Ilem replies, "You are the first true child of transhumanism. That makes you the prodigy of my plans. No one will challenge my decision." ♪ ♪ ♪ ♪

Ilem picks up an oleander flower from those tossed on the balcony and shares a tale that spans the century Ilem has resided on Earth with Victor.

He inhales the sweet fragrance of the aromatic, pink, white, funnel-shaped flower to his nose. This flower, which signifies the complicated nature of love and relationships, desire, and destiny, reminds Ilem of the tangled feelings he secrets in his heart. Still, Ilem concedes that destiny touched both with the ability to consume and to kill, Pu Kwon with her beauty, and the oleanders simply by touch.

---

[87] "I hear you, my Lord."

For most of his existence, Ilem has seen himself as the oleander flower: a poison so vile that just touching him would lead to death. Ilem confesses to Victor, "Through millennia, my hands served the Galactic Council as the destroyer of civilizations."

The wobbly sound of the music continues to seethe into the room. ♪ ♪ ♪ ♪ Ilem touches the oleander flower on Pu Kwon's cheek. The flower color overlaps with the film noir color of Pu Kwon's chamber. He speaks the sing-songy words, "So cold, so long ago …" Those words must set his mind adrift as time takes him back to the day he descended to Earth.

WWII Reconnaissance Mission – U.S. Airforce –
Spy Col. Wilhelm D. Godfrey (Deceased).

It was September 3, 1943, Ilem recalls. A Douglas A-20 Havoc aircraft plummeted to the ground with a sole passenger onboard. Thick clouds of billowing smoke rose into the sky, and metal fragments spread for miles, accompanied by a loud crackling noise.

In his natural form of pure light, Ilem was aglow as he descended from the sky above the fallen aircraft. Where wreckage trapped Col. Godfrey inside the pilot's chair, flowing rays of yellow and gold light streamed through the plane's window. Godfrey knew he was dying as the flames and smoke filled the cockpit. But when Ilem appeared, Godfrey briefly thought Ilem's translucent figure was that of a heavenly angel miraculously there to save or escort him to the pearly gates.

Ilem turns his full attention to Pu Kwon, dismissing Victor from the conversation. "My journey to Earth, to you, taught me about sacrifice and loss. Serving the Galactic Council had been too expensive to endure any longer. If the Navy hadn't rescued me, I do not know if I would have found you. Fortune provided a willing host to hide my true form and status to conceal my true intent."

As an agent for the US government, Ilem worked covertly in the shadows of French alleyways to exchange whispers and secrets with soldiers from the Allied forces and the Axis regime. Meanwhile, amid the plots and plans to render humans extinct, Ilem found his flower.

The entrée to Pu Kwon started while actively portraying himself as a Nazi when he first met General Zankoku Takao, a rotund military leader, at the Hiroshima Castle for the first time. As brothers in unity, General Takao gave Ilem a personal tour of Building 1, where the commanders' room and other staff were located. General Takao strolled Ilem by the Air Defense Room to impress him with Japan's advanced war machines.

For Pu Kwon's entertainment, Ilem marvels, "What with my blond hair and blue eyes, it was easy to infiltrate the Third Reich military at a prominent level of espionage. That allowed me to secure information for the Allies."

"To probe for his weaknesses, I allowed General Takao to take me to a local geisha house where your captors forced you to work as a comfort woman. When I first saw you, I felt the expanse between the galaxies suddenly collapse, and we became two moons sharing one sun."

"I started the conversation with you in a stale, bashful way, 'Good evening, young lady. My family calls me Ilem Diwan …' Before I could finish my timid introduction, you tried to repeat my name in an eternally adorable way. "Devon?" I submitted myself to you that day. You were so pure, so organic. I relented to being whatever you wanted to call me. I bowed to your innocence submissively, saying, "Sure, call me Devon. That will do fine …""

Ilem suggests to his speechless audience, "Your peril appalled me. You willingly agreed to sacrifice your freedom for your sister, Miyoshi, to be set free. They told you they would not force her to serve as a comfort woman, but that was a lie. Those evil bastards also kidnapped you, always treating you as less than a girlfriend and more than a wife."

"Your vulnerability and humility, despite your situation, drew me closer to you. It made me wonder if I should spare some humans. I stayed my hand while I pondered that reality. That despicable fate was unjust for you, such a delicate flower."

Back then, Ilem paid the madame of a geisha house money to have Pu Kwon saved only for him. But degenerates still knocked at her door. To protect Pu Kwon, Ilem helped her run away to the Hijiyama Girls High School. He bribed the headmaster, then went back to kill the madame of the geisha house, naturally.

Ilem, "I had to help you run away to stop General Takao and his men from getting their despicable hands on you as he did your sister."

Hiroshima, Japan. August 6, 1945.

On one of the darkest days in human history, General Takao found Pu Kwon and tried to rape her in her room at the Hijiyama School. Ilem angrily states, "But that *Kuso yarō*[88] found you anyway and tried to rape you, too."

Ilem strangled General Takao with his bare hands, flesh upon flesh, eye to eye, a distinctly human thing to do. Ilem unsympathetically concludes, "For that, he paid with his life."

Alas, Pu Kwon was present when Ilem choked the life out of General Takao. At that moment, Ilem revealed his ready ability to slaughter another human being and that he was not human. Who else but a creature from hell could tear open a person's throat to ooze hot, molten plasma down it?

As Pu Kwon saw with her eyes, it was a ruthless death. Takao's head swelled and ruptured as liquid flames burst from his orifices, his eyes boiled and busted like steamed eggs. Pu Kwon was frightened by what she saw, the viciousness and sudden lust to kill shown by her beloved Devon. Even worse, it was the first time she saw him in his true form of pure plasma and light, a spectacle that shocked her into speechlessness.

Following Pu Kwon's flight from Ilem, she reached the T-shaped Aioi Bridge. For a brief moment, Pu Kwon thought of the irony that the bridge's unusual shape reflected her present state of mind: Which way should she go? Beyond the Aioi Bridge stood the Hiroshima Prefectural Industrial Promotion Hall, and behind her, her hellish lover and roads to places unknown.

In addition to displaying and selling prefectural products, the Japanese government used the Promotion Hall for art shows and other expositions. As the war intensified, the Promotion Hall also housed several government agencies. With the possibility of being safe in the presence of slews of people, Pu Kwon hurried ahead on a straight path to the Promotion Hall.

---

[88] "Bastard."

Pu Kwon rushed to the Hall's heavy wooden doors, seeking any haven in reach. Ilem pursued Pu Kwon across the Aioi Bridge, but despite his godly speed, he was a millisecond from getting through the closing door in his human guise.

That day was sunny at 8:00 a.m. in Hiroshima. Citizens passing quietly below peaceful light blue skies milled about riding simple bicycles and tending to their gardens, oblivious of the violent winds of change rapidly approaching. For the Enola Gay, it was optimum that the skies be clear, to maximize visibility and plentiful photo opportunities.

Ilem cried back tears as he reminisced about that fateful day, "I did not mean to scare you by what I am and what you saw me do to Takao. Not then, not when Horol told me what was coming." As the Diwan of Time foretold, five minutes after Pu Kwon ran into the Promotion Hall, the B-29, Enola Gay, dropped Little Boy on Hiroshima from 31,000 feet using the Aioi Bridge as its target.

Forty-three seconds later, a massive explosion lit the morning sky as Little Boy detonated 1,900 feet above the city, directly above the Promotion Hall and near a parade field where soldiers of the Japanese Second Army were performing calisthenics. The Promotion Hall was the only structure left standing in the area where the first atomic bomb exploded despite the many buildings it destroyed and the lives lost nearby.

But why, you ask? Was The All there with mighty hands stretched out to catch the atomic bomb and spare Ilem and Pu Kwon, or was there another intervention?

To save his love, Ilem wrapped her in his arms as they stood in the middle of the building, with the radiation waves furiously washing against their bodies. Using his powers over plasma, light, and their various properties, Ilem absorbed most of the blast from Little Boy that should have decimated the Promotion Hall. Nonetheless, enough radiation doused Pu Kwon that she was nearly cooked alive despite Ilem's considerable abilities.

Outside the Promotion Hall, the 300,000 civilians who called Hiroshima home did not have an entity with liquid plasma flowing through his veins to protect them. They suffered every second of the radiation and flames so intense that they turned people into ashes and set carefree birds afire.

The shock waves – pounding down and across the land – were so tremendous that citizens felt them miles away. The explosion immediately killed eighty thousand people. Behind the fleeing Enola Gay, the horrible, devastating mushroom cloud rose from the Earth. It expanded out, engulfing Hiroshima and the land around it for miles: miles and miles of destruction and evidence of man's inhumanity. Later, tens of thousands more died of radiation exposure and suffered horrendous birth defects.

Ilem paces back and forth in front of Pu Kwon, lying in her suspension chamber as he continues to visualize the events leading to her being in her present state of existence. Ilem laments, "This glass puts us as far away as the ends of Aioi Bridge, but my light keeps us together."

With a wave of his hand, Ilem restores dead oleander flowers to life using gray's radiation that seeps from his pores. Ilem, "I could not tell the Galactic Council that the radiation from the bomb augmented my power. Not after we placed humans on our extermination list." ♫ ♫ ♫ ♫ "They would have wanted you dead with other humans and for me to immediately ascend." ♫ ♫ ♫ ♫

Ilem examines the exoskin he is wearing as he talks. "Sorry, Victor. I cannot say enough how I tire of this life. Now, I need Hyle's exoskins to retain this aging human flesh to remain familiar and acceptable to Pu Kwon without fear or rejection." ♫ ♫ ♫ ♫

"When the warrant was issued, the Galactic Council met on Mount Idan on Caellum to discuss the plight of humans. Thank The All, my siblings were easily convinced that manipulating information and resources on Earth was the right path to domination." The wobbly sound of music continues ♫ ♫ ♫ ♫ but does not distract Ilem from his tirade about his forced servitude.

"The Galactic Council believed weaponizing information would accelerate human extinction. I do not need their minds if I can control their bodies. They will serve me forever." ♫ ♫ ♫ ♫

Victor asks the Diwan of Light, "Master, why didn't you destroy them when they allowed Pyron onto the Council." Ilem notes, "That was a millennium ago. My sights were set on the future, not the past. After WWII, I infiltrated the U.S. government to hide in plain sight. I plotted for the day when I could safely say I had a son who looked so much like me that people would wonder if I pushed him out. That is how I birthed my identity as 'Ilem Devon Godfrey.'"

Looking down at Pu Kwon, Ilem languishes in his reflection resting on top of her, their faces touching lip to lip. Ilem, "Yet none of this would have happened if they had not betrayed their oath to The All by forcing Pyron onto the Galactic Council. They corrupted our order anointed by our High Master out of fear of Hyle's volatile nature. My love for Pu Kwon was secondary." ♫ ♫ ♫ ♫

"I demolished entire planets or their inhabitants as required by the Galactic Council's mandate whether I agreed with the decision. I have been the Council's sword for too long. Within days I will break free of their control to enjoy the riches of my many conquests with Pu Kwon and you by my side."

Ilem walks to the door that leads to the balcony above the Dyson Sphere. Ilem, "Victor, my Death Squad must capture Sage no matter what she is now, trans, human, or something in between. She may be the key to imprinting your consciousness permanently. Is that not what you want?" Victor replies, "More than anything, Master. I will destroy Kol and all your enemies upon your command." ♫ ♫ ♫ ♫

Next, Ilem walks out on the balcony again, waving to his adoring followers. They eagerly toss more oleander flowers up to him. Behind him in the foreground, enough of Onom's eerie face appears from the shadows next to Pu Kwon's suspension chamber to recognize it is her.

Onom's muted whistle hovers over Pu Kwon's sleeping chamber. Onom mumbles for no one else to hear but herself:

"Watch what you're saying when you close your eyes. Where there is deception, silence isn't far behind." ♫ ♫ ♫ ♫

Omnis: Last Man of Earth

Psalms for Yesterday: Nosferatu's Last Kiss

When we live in the darkness
So much untruth is said.

I creep from bed to bed.
Whispering to the eaves
Praying my subtle words
Will draw you into view.

When you invite me in, I scale walls
To slip beside you as you lie
A virgin to my touch
To love me back to life.

After tonight
We'll learn if love is temporal
Like the melting of a candle touched by flame
Or frozen like Petra.

So many lips, swallows' necks, and tender breasts.
I cleave to the inner thigh
High up where your pulse beats
That tender spot that secrets
How you taste like wine.

As if you saw this death in your dreams.
You clutch my flesh to you like a shroud
Pulling me up and unto you.

But I want it to be my last kiss.
I want to know that passion lasts
After the morning comes
After shadows steal away from dawn
Cloaked in naked shame.

Chained to irony (I am)
Humanity dwarfed by legend
Evil enlarged by myth.
All the while scaling walls
To find someone like you, willing
To see me in the light.

END OF CHAPTER 14

Chapter 15

Derrick Howard

Beggar's Lot

Father, you could have been called Tempest.
In your words raged a storm against me,
Readying me to bear the squall of other public eyes.

You escaped from a time.
When men wore their skins like caution signs,
"Niggers yield to white."

You baptized me in spite.
You became a Van Gogh
Warring against your seed
Splattering an unblemished canvas
With a world of jealous greens,
Angry reds, solemn blues,
And other bickering shades.

Your kiss became a smack in the face to me,
But I learned to crave the hatred that you shared.

Omnis: Last Man of Earth
The Black Spot

Gore, a traveling seller of rare minerals, pokes his head into a window at the Harbor Bar to announce that he has ample supplies of exotic minerals for sale. From the planet of Pinid, Gore was less and less available on Caellum, peddling his wares ever since he sold panguite to Ilem's operatives. Gore, the lumbering peddler of precious stones, gems, and alloys, had tepid success selling any of his goods on Caellum. But that may result from his inability to speak beyond grunts and squawks to anyone other than his kind with whom he spoke telepathically.

Native inhabitants of Pinid resemble a truncated ogre or ogress in many ways, particularly their wide girth, unappealing faces, and brutish disposition. Pinids are also distinctive from the spiked quills poking from their skin from their foreheads to their lower back. The males, females, and intersex of their race are legendary for their ability to project their sharp quills in battle.

Gore lowers his face to a bar window to deliver his sales pitch to the bar's owner. Given Yam's command of countless languages, he translated Gore's grunts thusly: "Yam! Yam! I've heard you had good goods, oddities, and sus to purchase. I can make some sales around here if you tell everyone the goods came from you."

Yam listens intently to Gore moan about his recent luck selling panguite to Ilem and his subsequent losses due to poor business practices, occasionally adding his guttural response in Gore's native form of communication. Gore, "I understand that the Diwan of Light needs more panguite for some new things he's trying out."

"Titanium, zirconium, and scandium all in one. Who would have thought? Put it this way, panguite is rare. But I's found a unique way to get a bunc more out of even moving meteorites. Tenfold more. I expect he needs it for some fire shield or sus. It's been an immense help to me with other low sales. If I play my cards right, I might barter for some of the Floating City's disposables, enslaved people, and sus later this week."

Having listened as long as he can to Gore's predicaments, Yam stops to give advice: "Pragmatists know that everything worthwhile takes time; quick success is a fleeting wonder. Have you ever played Beggar's Lot? The originators of the game designed it to underscore that message. Playing a round or two to understand the strategy would be best. If not, you may use it to negotiate with Ilem's people. If nothing else, the game translates well to circumstances where you must play your cards correctly."

Gore pulls his head from the window and discusses the card game with Yam from a distance. Gore, "I never played te game. But I'm willing to learn."

A familiar squeaky voice interjects into the conversation from a booth in a shaded corner of the Harbor Bar. Oba Voss, the Farfarout, offers to play a few hands of Beggar's Lot with the oversized Pinid outside at a table or on a boulder where they both can sit.

In the cascading sound of a sinful church choir, the gamblers call to Yam, "What are the rules of the game?"

Yam tells those traveling gamblers, a Negearian, a Keplerian, and an Orcusijan, Beggar's Lot follows the rules of games you all have played daily in one way or another." He adds, "No need to shuffle cards today with me. I will leave that to other hands. But I can explain the lore behind it. It is a message Gore can use to increase his sales, and gamblers can use when they are caught playing more substantial games on the street."

Gamblers from other quadrants of the universe gathered in the Harbor Bar and listened attentively to Yam's recitation of the myth behind Beggar's Lot. Yam notices how many are watching him and rubs his scruffy beard, contemplating how to relay this story.

Yam starts, "Beggar's Lot is a wagering game created by those who wanted to criticize the rich and powerful for their cruelty surreptitiously." Yam explains, "In this game, however, the poor win, and the rich suffer."

"So as not to alert aristocrats, peasants played the game at night by candlelight, behind closed doors in their huts around cramped tables."

"A standard fifty-two card deck is often used for playing like those on Earth for a round of Five-Card Draw. The aces represent the Realms of Heaven, Purgatory, Hell, and Life. Respectively, the symbols on those cards are the key, the scales of justice, a sacrificial goat, and a Yin Yang tree."

"The Kings represent the time you have to live, morning, noon, sundown, and midnight. The Queens reflect the seasons of life, and each is personified as a woman transitioning through infancy, youth, adulthood, to old age. Usually, the images on the latter cards are the woman as an infant, a girl at play, a woman holding a toddler, and a senior woman praying. The Jacks postulates the tortures of life: a whip, crucifix, iron maiden, and pear of anguish."

"Only the full set of spades, two through King, are needed. The only additional cards required for the game are the seven through ten cards from the heart, diamond, club suits, and, most importantly, the Jokers. None of the other cards in a standard card deck is ever used."

"Two or more players must participate in the game. Once everyone has anted, they receive seven cards from the dealer face down. The dealer places one card into each player's holding spot, which players call the "pit," for eight cards dealt in the first round. Lest sneaky hands prevail, the pit should be in the middle of the table where cards are left for each player to use in the final round of the competition."

"Ordinarily, peasants only played five rounds for want of time for dalliance or sloth. In the first round, all players set one card face down into that player's own "pit." The ultimate goal is to collect seven cards by the final round with either the lowest value or the highest, such as the Jokers representing the Black Spot and the Eye of Providence, the Aces, and twos."

"After each player places their card of choice in the pit, the other five cards still in their hand are played like a round of Five-Card Draw. But, and this is a big but, the power of the numbered and face cards is reversed. In that order, suits of two to nine are more valuable than suits of Jacks, Queens, or Kings. The Aces are all wild cards, useful to substitute for any card other than the two Jokers, the latter being the most powerful cards in the deck."

"A round of betting then occurs. Each player specifies how many cards they wish to discard. The dealer then deals that player new cards, which the player may keep in his hand or use to replace cards already in the pit. Each player exchanges cards with the dealer this way, playing counterclockwise and one at a time."

If Yam's attentive crowd understands even a little from the peasant's version of the game, most astute ones anticipate or surmise that the best cards to discard are the Kings and Queens, not the twos and threes. Although the patrons still have their eyes fixed on the ragged bartender, a few shuffle decks of cards to try out the rules relayed to them by Yam.

Uninterrupted, Yam continues, "Justly, players may stand on the hand they were dealt instead of risking drawing high cards. Another round of betting occurs after this drawing round finishes."

"After the dealer passes out all the cards and the players stash cards in the pit, the players compete against each other using the inverse rules of Five-Card Draw. The winner can take the pot and randomly exchange one of her pit cards with one facing down in any other player's pit after the first round of play concludes. The dealer is the only player allowed to touch the deck during this exchange, lest a player risk losing a hand."

"In the subsequent rounds, the players receive seven cards, with the right to stash one card in their pit and discard the other by returning it to the dealer. Another round of card playing occurs, with the winner again able to select one card from any other player's pit to use in later or the final round, and the right to claim the blinds."

"Play continues until each player has seven cards in their pit. At that point in the game, the remaining players must select one card to leave in their pit, one to discard, and five to play in the game's final round. Most players opt to leave their most valuable card in their pit, and a few players bluff to exchange their worst card with a better card held by someone else."

"The poor man controls the other players' fate, starting by relieving them of the loot in the pot. In the past, commoners bet a pint of ale, or the loser was required to extend an invitation to the winner to share a fire and break bread."

"For the downtrodden, the pit was the daily gamble you and other beings all take to be present and to contribute to the world, instead of sitting bloated ass on the shoulders of others watching the parade go by. The servants who won a round of Beggar's Lot were content to have a morsel of food and a friend to distract them from their laborious lives."

"The peasants who conceived the game could not keep it hidden forever. Eventually, some careless laborers were caught by their master playing the final hand for the night. The "Master" who discovered them was Madame Mayhem, the owner of an underwater gambling hall known as the Sirens & Wails Saloon. A unique characteristic of the structure was that it was an amphibious establishment, built half above ocean and half below to accommodate those who breathed through gills or lungs."

"Madame Mayhem had the distinction on Earth as the 'Queen of the Sea Nomads.' Throughout the millennia she has lived, her home has been underwater. She was not only in harmony with the ocean and creatures that lived therein, but she was also the sea, able to morph into liquid upon command, unless on land."

"On land, she was no more than an ordinary Vatrajan land dweller, confined to living in glass and metal-framed houses like lizards imprisoned in a terrarium. But submerged in her natural element, she wielded dominion over water sources of all kinds. She could drain a body of fluid from her touch or raze the land from earthquakes and massive tidal waves. According to legend, Madame Mayhem demolished the ancient Egyptian city of Thonis-Heracleion in 140 B.C. by creating an earthquake that continuously shook long and powerfully enough to cause water from the Mediterranean to mix with the soil and turn into quicksand."

"She was reptilian in all ways, except she stood upright and resembled a female humanoid, with pointed ears and bulging eyes. Her flesh was scaled but not dry. Madame Mayhem was uniquely attractive, slightly framed, and had two-toned skin of lush merlot and calm, cool lime. Her hands and feet were webbed to maximize swimming capabilities and underwater, hand-to-hand combat. Despite her overall pleasant exterior, like other reptiles, her blood ran cold for everything except the touch of gold."

"Most other Masters would have beaten and berated their servants and enslaved people for the rumored misconduct and disrespect that brewed turmoil amongst the oppressed and their oppressors. Most Masters would have the underlings paraded to the town square for public humiliation and punishment, up to and including public execution."

"Like most premeditated negotiators from Vatra, instead of seeing only another reason to destroy, Madame Mayhem saw an opportunity to exploit. She ordered her servants and enslaved people to expand the Sirens & Wails to cater to the whims and peculiarities of aristocrats daring enough to play lethal rounds of Beggar's Lot. Her minions expanded the gambling hall around a center ring to use whenever profitable blood sport broke out in strict compliance with Madame Mayhem's schemes. They continued drilling deeper toward Earth's core for future amphibious colonies and prepared the Sirens & Wails for flight."

"With a personal understanding of the lengths men will go to measure their members against each other as a sign of superiority, Madame Mayhem fantasized about the booty she would hoard in her watery lair. She knew rich men would pay significant Tektites to vie in a card game like Beggar's Lot, especially if play risked someone else's life or death for a profit."

"In the peasants' version of Beggar's Lot, the winners allowed the losing players to request clemency or the right to 'square up' debts at a more convenient time. Given the wealthy's preference for depravity, it was no wonder Madame Mayhem discarded that rule in favor of instituting a more brutal policy. Under Madame Mayhem's laws, it is best to bargain, but if that fails, some players have found it wise to bet money on their loss to secure a moniker of funds to bequeath to their families."

"For the final rendition of Madame Mayhem's contest, she deemed the Joker would be used as the Black Spot, literally and figuratively symbolizing death. She also announced that the other Joker, the Eye of Providence, would symbolize mercy. To date, these are the most influential cards used for the game."

"In Madame Mayhem's house of gambling and profitable debauchery, instead of the winner only taking a few coins from a meager pot, she, he, or it could mandate the two players with the lowest scores, or their seconds, submit to life-or-death battle, winner take all. Usually, the ultimate winner rallies side bets on who will survive the coerced scrimmage."

"The only card that saved a player from this fate was, and still is, the Eye of Providence. If one of the players with the worst score still has the Eye of Providence, that player may refuse to fight. In that instance, the winning player only receives the ante from the player holding the Eye of Providence. If a gambler has played that card, the two players with the worst scores still must fight if demanded by the winner of the final hand."

"Whenever there are only two players in the game, the players may tussle if they desire the thrill of battle. However, based on a later reinterpretation of the rules, if that player also holds the Black Spot, she, he, or it also has the power to force the players with the highest scores, that is, the losing scores, to fight each other or their respective seconds to the death."

Several groups in earshot of Yam's recitation of Beggar's Lot's history retire stacks of cards to end their hand at the game. As for the others, and as settled by Yam long ago, the wager for the night was a pint of excellent, quenching ale or a night amongst friends sharing tales of days gone by around a cozy, inviting fire, not death on a spit.

At the end of the night, when all their patrons have gone their way, Sera and Yam leave the bar down a long stairway to retire to their tranquil abode and to rest beyond the Harbor Bar under a carpet of twinkling stars and lavender skies. When alone in their home, Yam uses a basin to dab the blistering sores on his body with a wet cotton cloth to remove unpleasant yellow and brown discharge.

Sera emerges barefoot in the room wearing a chartreuse gown with her long brown hair released down her back. She cleans Yam's recurring sores without hesitation or wrenching at the unsightly boils. In a voice that soothes Yam's external and internal aches, Sera asks him if he wants to watch anything on GC 777 or take in the views from her garden. He answers, "Yes, some outside time will do me well."

With Sera's assistance, Yam wanders into their garden to ease into an old wooden chair that creaks as it settles, just like Yam's worn bones. Sera pulls a wool blanket up to his chest and tells him, "You carry the wounds of an old warrior. Too often, you are awash in gloomy rain, falling from distressed tempests instead of wading through the sea of flowers. I understand your ailments. But I wish you were present with me more, not captive to the rambling voices in your head."

Despite the weary, strained gaze that crinkles the lines around Yam's eyes, he cheerfully extends his hands to reach for his wife and answers her question by stating, "Yes, love, I always hear what you say, and know it to be true. I will be better tomorrow. Promise. I want to rest a moment and watch worlds go by."

Sera and Yam embrace and then kiss, but not for long. The old bartender rocks up to the edge of the wooden chair, straining his ear to trace the origin of a distant, whooshing sound. An eyebrow rises, relieving the worry lines on Yam's face, and a sparkle in his tired eyes lifts sleep's curtain.

Yam turns to Sera to pose a rhetorical question. "You hear that, too, right?" Sera reclines on the arm of Yam's chair, leaning on his shoulder for support. While in this position, she lifts her hand above her eyes to block out the blinding rays pulsing from Earth's sun.

She can still make out tiny spots moving across Earth's barren terrains, even light years away. Sera looks away from the bright, yellow flame of Earth's sun to tell Yam, "What you heard was another disturbance on Earth. Soon the sounds of fear and despair will ring in the ears of so many across that planet." Yam pushes himself out of his comfortable chair, saying as he stands, "We should rest. There will be more Spectators tomorrow."

As Yam and Sera retire to sleep, light years away, the Diwan of Sound, Onom herself, runs at the speed of sound, approaching the flooded streets of Atlantic City, NJ. While they fall asleep, Yam and Sera observe the skin of Onom's face pushed back from the wind into a macabre, forced smile. Woooosh.

Onom lands on the orphanage's roof, where the stalwart group of Sledge, Sage, and Iggy slumber. She looks over the edge of the building down toward the Purified who patrol outside, removes her kusarigama from her belt, and begins whipping its chain around faster and faster until it has enough velocity to lift her into the air.

She knows the kusarigama is not the perfect weapon to use in a battle with allies because its long chain endangers them and is ineffective against armor. But in her hands, the kusarigama slices through metal and the flesh underneath with the stinging of a hot knife and the finality of a vorpal sword.

Fearlessly, she leaps off the building, landing behind one of the Purified guarding the building. As she descends to the ground, she increases the twirl of her kusarigama on its chain to maximum velocity. The kusarigama blade cuts through the Purified guard's neck and arteries, causing his head to spurt buckets of blood and tumble to the ground.

Another Purified guard turns the corner of the building just as his cohort's dismembered head flops down. Onom tweets a hard kiss at the shocked guard through the stitches sewn over her lips. Her muffled whistling sound is forceful enough to strike the guard in his forehead, blowing out his brains. He yelps, "Aieeee!"

The Diwan of Sound saunters down the hall in the deserted orphanage toward where Sledge, Iggy, and Sage are sleeping. After encountering her, she steps over the bloodied bodies of a couple of the Purified guards inside the building. Onom opens the door where the trio are sleeping to peek inside. Sledge is asleep in a chair, Iggy on the floor on a pallet, and Sage on the couch.

Onom creeps over to stand over Sledge's shoulder. She grasps her weapon as she prepares to slice Sledge's throat. But she hesitates. Instead, Onom slowly and contemplatively slides her kusarigama back in her belt, then bends down on one knee next to Sledge.

Amused by the endless possibilities to cause chaos, Onom smirks on one side of her mouth and thinks, "Well, aren't you a toss? Ilem so wanted to end you like all the other Purists. Well, it is time to change the tempo."

Instead of brandishing her weapon, Onom pulls out a different object, a pan flute, then whispers into Sledge's ear, "The winds of change are coming. It is time to adjust your sails." Onom blows into the pan flute to channel sound into Sledge's ear. He paws at his ear to fan away an annoyance buzzing around him. ♫ ♫ ♫ ♫

Onom's seductive tune leeches farther and farther into Sledge's mind, causing his essence to step between a world melding the past with the present. Sledge dreams of being a teenager again, walking through an ethnic street festival in Philadelphia called the "*Odunde* Festival" alongside Renzo, a neighborhood hustler. Renzo has once again roped Sledge into burglarizing local houses for petty gains. As they walk together, Uncle Ray intercepts them. The wise mechanic is noticeably pissed that Sledge is hanging around a thug like Renzo.

Uncle Ray calls out to his adopted son, "Sledge, *weh yuh ah guh*"?[89] ♫ ♫ ♫ ♫

Renzo barges into the conversation without invite, "*Espera, mofo, tenemos negocios que manejar.*"[90] He moves to push Uncle Ray back, but the older man

---

[89] "Where are you going?"
[90] "Hold up, mofo, we've got business to handle."

skillfully blocks Renzo's hands away. Uncle Ray warns him, "*Boy, yuh need ah lesson in street etiquette. Estúpido!*"[91] 🎵 🎵 🎵 🎵

Uncle Ray twists Renzo's hand using a Bushido submission hold and tells him, "*Yuh muss recognize wen yuh before yuh master.*"[92] Renzo winces and then runs off while Uncle Ray and Sledge continue talking. 🎵 🎵 🎵 🎵

Puzzled, Uncle Ray asks Sledge, "Why *yuh deh roun a waste man like Renzo? Him in jail more times than mi have fingers.*"[93] Sledge grumpily responds, "He's gonna help me get *enuff* Tektite *tuh* head out on *mi* own, maybe find *mi* mamma or do something with *mi* life." 🎵 🎵 🎵 🎵 The people in the crowd begin to morph into transhumans and other sentient beings, sprouting mechanical limbs, chest plates, and headgear.

Sledge and Uncle Ray continue talking to each other oblivious to the partygoers' transformations—Uncle Ray says, "*Yaah seventeen. Yuh need fi relax and low me fi tek care ah yuh an Iggy.*"[94] Sledge claps back, "Trust *yuh*? I saw Iggy last night. *Yuh was* letting doctors cut on him again. *Yuh waah im tuh* become transhuman." 🎵 🎵 🎵 🎵

Festival revelers dance around Uncle Ray and Sledge. Most are beautiful human women in African garb, but a couple are feminine humanoid drones wearing other ethnic clothing. Uncle Ray tries to convince Sledge that his conclusions are wrong, "*No man, surgery was jus to install ports for future procedures.*" Sledge replies, "It's wrong *dat* it isn't his choice. How can *yuh* betray him like *dis*? He's not a guinea pig." Uncle Ray tries to convince Sledge to the contrary, "*Iggy will be special* and still here.[95] 🎵 🎵 🎵 🎵

They face each other as they continue debating Iggy's situation. Uncle Ray, "*Dem ah connect im brain tuh ah computer. Him nah guh turn inna one.*"[96]

---

[91] "Boy, you need a lesson in street etiquette. Asshole."
[92] "I recommend you recognize when you're in the presence of a master."
[93] "Why are you hanging around a loser like Renzo? He's been in jail more times than I have fingers."
[94] "You're only seventeen. You need to calm down and trust me to take care of you and Iggy."
[95] "Iggy will be special."
[96] "No, the surgery was just to install ports for future procedures. They may connect his brain to a computer, they don't turn him into one."

Sledge testily states, "I don't believe *yuh*. I may be blind, but *mi* other senses *wuk* fine." ♪ ♪ ♪ ♪

Sledge starts to walk away, but Uncle Ray reaches for his shoulder. Uncle Ray reminds Sledge, "*Criss hear wah, man a wah him do. It nuh matter wah him I.*"[97] Rejecting his Uncle's sage words, Sledge retorts, "I've heard that from *yuh* before." ♪ ♪ ♪ ♪ Uncle Ray's hand rests on Sledge's shoulder. Uncle Ray can only assure Sledge that, "*Mi a duh di rite ting by him.*"[98]

Kol and other members of Ilem's Death Squad Cha-cha with revelers in the crowd behind Uncle Ray as he talks. Uncle Ray, "*Di doctors may be able to tap fi him seizures and mek him tek full advantage ah fi him own intelligence.*"[99] ♪ ♪ ♪ ♪

Everyone around Sledge and Uncle Ray is transhuman or a member of the Sect now. Sledge exclaims, "Iggy already is special." Sledge sees Iggy, looking human, wading through the crowd near a protester among the festival revelers holding a sign that says, "I Am a Man."

Iggy is holding a long leash that he attached to the Alien Beast that has already pushed through most of the crowd. Sledge, "There he is! Iggy, wait!" ♪ ♪ ♪ ♪ Despite Sledge's warning, Iggy proceeds through a revolving door as Sledge calls to him. The leash attached to the Alien Beast is the only thing sticking out of the door, as the creature has already gone inside the building.

Sledge chases behind them, shouting, "Iggy, *no es seguro!*"[100] The Elite Squads dancing among the crowd stop their part in the celebration to chase after Sledge, all the while cracking down on revelers as they force their way through the festivities.

Alluding police officers is not foreign to Sledge. On many misspent days, he found himself crouching within thickets of pedestrians, avoiding cops who chased him down weaving streets. He evades them and returns to the festival.

---

[97] "Good, then listen up. A man is what he does, not what he says."
[98] "I'm doing the right thing by him."
[99] "The doctors may be able to stop his seizures and allow him to take full advantage of his unique intelligence."
[100] "It isn't safe."

While Sledge goes through the revolving door, water covers the ground up to his feet. In the distance, Dr. Hamilton is standing in a rowboat with its sail up, and Iggy is fishing from it. Iggy has the Alien Beast chained to the front of the rowboat, propelling it forward.

Dr. Hamilton shouts to Iggy, "Iggy, tight line! Reel it in, boy!" Dr. Hamilton casts his fishing line into the clouds, then warns Iggy, "It's coming in fast, bud! Look sharp!" The fishing line sails through outer space beyond the Sun and its planets, ricochets off an asteroid, and continues toward a giant flaming meteor. The fishing line hook attaches to the surface of the blazing meteor, which, up close, looks like a mixture of rock and muscular flesh engulfed in flames.

As we zoom in on this colossal object, it becomes evident that it is Hyle. His intense eyes ignite with rage and bulge from the side of the round ball of flesh he tucked into. It is clear from Hyle's size next to other objects in orbit that he is massive. Dr. Hamilton points toward the sky to draw Sledge's attention skyward.

Screaming to Iggy, Sledge shouts, "Iggy, we got *tuh* get out of here. We're *deh* bait!" Sledge struggles to reach for the boat as the waters rise over his shoulders. The rowboat sail is torn to shreds. Dr. Hamilton, "*Limitless and immortal, the waters are the beginning and end of all things on earth.*[101] Diwan Hyle approaches. Sledge. Prepare yourself!"

Hyle smashes through one of Jupiter's moons, Europa, sending large boulders of ice and rock careening into space. Bang!!! Doom!!!!

Only Sledge's fleshy hand is above water now. Splash! Iggy leans over the edge of the boat to reach for him. Except for the exaggerated ports running from his forehead to the base of his spine and the unusual gauntlets Iggy wears, his body is suddenly made entirely of an unknown metal but still looks like himself. Iggy reminds Sledge, "*Este no es momento para vaqueros.*"[102]

The Diwan of Matter crash lands on Earth in the Mississippi River next to New Orleans as a gigantic, flaming meteor. Doom!!! When Hyle splashes into the river, the water coats Sledge in a cement-like substance up to his hand. Splash!!!

---

[101] Heinrich Zimmer, https://www.azquotes.com/quote/579932.
[102] "This is no time for Cowboys."

Eventually, the cement coats Sledge's entire body. As he struggles to survive this unwanted transformation, Sledge's face contorts in pain and anguish as his body remains in a running stance. The rowboat capsizes, and rough winds rip its sail away. Iggy and Dr. Hamilton lay unconscious on the ground.

As if residents of Caellum can feel Hyle's power and presence from Earth, in the morning, Yam and Sera walk together, wearing protective cloaks, through a nearby marketplace, looking for needed supplies. They comment to each other about an approaching storm as store owners work quickly to board up their shops to protect their goods from damaging winds and whipping rains.

At a herb shop that remains open, they stop to speak with the store's owner, an alien named Raymonté. He is the only local merchant with the ingredients to make the Harbor's trademark, hobo scotch. Raymonté is a Caellumites by birth, one of the few to claim that distinction.

Yam and Sera politely haggle with Raymonté about his selection of fruits and mixers they want to purchase. Yam explains to Raymonté, "These goods would not cost us so much if we grew them in our garden. I may not be a good gardener, I know. I leave that to Sera. She is good at nurturing plants, while I am better at dealing with problems like this. Shave your price by 15, 12 percent, and you have a deal."

Yam raises one of his long arms to reach out to Raymonté to signify they have a deal. Hesitating, Raymonté knows they haggle all the time, more often than not settling on Yam's price.

As the couple walks away, hand-in-hand, back to their establishment, Yam gazes at the mirage reflected in a store window that captures the revelers from Sledge's dreams dancing to the Harbor Bar.

Instead of commenting on the mirage, Yam calmly asks his Sera, "What about that weather?"

END OF CHAPTER 15

Chapter 16

Un Tiempo Para Los Vaqueros

Everglades cada vez más pequeños
(un ecosistema frágil que brinda refugio a especies raras y en peligro de extinción)
entre los mundos de las hidras
(un mal múltiple que no se puede vencer con un solo esfuerzo).

Convirtiéndome en rostros que una vez en vida conocí
(parecidos a los muertos).
Y cada vuelta de revolución parecen encogerse y morir de nuevo
(todos los días vuelven los muertos).

*Y formar costra y agruparse en arenas de lo que el mundo fue
planeado en un principio (combinarse para volver a la pureza).
Encogiéndose más pequeño que el ojo de un enano,
un mundo de hidra se derrumba
(el mal terminará si nos unimos a tiempo).*[103]

---

[103] "Shrinking Everglades (a fragile ecosystem that provides sanctuary to rare and endangered species) among the hydra worlds (a multifarious evil not to be overcome by a single effort). Turning over into faces that once in life I knew (resemble the dead). And every revolution's spin they seem to shrink and die again (every day the dead return). And crust and cluster into sands of what the world was firstly planned (combine to return to purity). Shrinking smaller than a midget's eye, a hydra world comes tumbling down (evil will end if we unite in time)."

Fedda

Yam flips the sign on the front door to his pub from open to closed for the night hours after toiling through another tiring day at the Harbor Bar—the sign swings for a few seconds, waving goodbye to the bar's many patrons.

Sera returns to nurturing her ailing husband, "Yam, go … kick off your shoes. I will get you a beer and a snack." Yam disappears down a steep staircase so far down you cannot see the bottom. Once he reaches the last step of his decline, Yam travels up the stairs to his wife's home garden, where he tips his toes, careful not to disrupt the flowers and fruits that Sera has carefully cultivated.

When Yam goes to bed, Sera is there to greet him. He tells her that strangers insulted him about the hump on his back again, "just as yesterday, the day before, and so on." Sera observes, "Ugly people know they are ugly when they wake in the morning. True beauty is invisible but for the actions one displays." Yam echoes Sera's comments, "Like a retched bile bursting from their veins, they're barely able to restrain their secret disdain for others, if not themselves."

Sera reaches over to help Yam remove his shirt stained with spots of burst pustules. She tries to uplift Yam's unhappy mood, "Same as yesterday, and the day before, and so on. Yam, it is too late to worry about anyone outside our door. My comfort is you, as I am yours."

The ever-young bride kisses her betrothed on his lips, offering to him, "Your secret beauty is blinding like I am staring into the sun. I know it will consume me, but I cannot help but risk all I have to look upon your face and do nothing else until I expire, aflame in your love." Yam blushes from hearing his stunning wife take favor in his unusual appearance. Yam, "You are ever the poet and a light in my darkness."

She leans close to Yam to kiss him on his forehead, then on his lips. The loud sound of a clattering noise inside the pub interrupts their solitude and moment of affection. Sera tells Yam, "Rest, rest. I will see what's going on. Finish your drink."

Yam cannot erase from his weary face the concern for his wife's safety, "Please be careful, Sera. At my age, I have a right to be old-fashioned. A lady should not be alone at night. It would be a hard stone to lay on if anything happened to you." Sera smirks at Yam with a familiar look that tells him she can care for herself.

Haval, a male Negearian, and Lanae, a female Orcusijan, have broken into the bar. When Sera returns there, a weary Haval and Lanae explain that the Galactic Council has hunted them to complete Haval's extermination and Lanae's containment in the QD or confinement with the Outsiders. Breathlessly, Lanae pleads to Sera to let them stay. Graciously, Sera relents to their pleas.

After Lanae and Haval settle into a booth at Sera's insistence, Lanae engages Sera in conversation. Lanae, "Thank you for letting us stay. We will sleep on the floor, but it would be nice to get back to where you call home."

Inquisitively, Lane asks Sera what is beyond the door where she and her husband retire at night. Sera answers, "The steps are old. You can go down them if you want to. There is no reason to resist. If it is your fate to know about the world behind that door, so be it. But be careful. The first step can be dreadful, and the landing grim."

Sera continues speaking with the aliens to understand their pain and why they hurt others for survival. Haval explains that the Galactic Council oppressed his people by allowing them to die or become slaves, just like on Earth. He shares with Sera that he and his companion hide on Caellum because they believe it is the last place anyone would look for them.

Sera laments, "Sadly, persecution like that has happened too often throughout the galaxy. There are known stories, and there are unknown or barely known stories. Some stories will never end, only become legends of hope or despair."

The trios' conversation ends abruptly when a gusty wind blows open the Harbor Bar's front door. Calmly, Sera steps outside the entrance to the pub and begins listening closely for sounds that have stirred in the distance.

In her mind, Sera watches Sledge wake from his dream, mouthing the words "hope and despair." He starts coughing the greenish sentient metal from his mouth, and a small bubble pops from his nose.

Sledge coughs uncontrollably as he looks around the room to see if Iggy is still there. Only the pallet Iggy slept on, with a ruffled blanket, is still in place. Sledge kneels beside Sage, still recuperating on the couch, touching her cheek as she sleeps.

In another room, Sledge finds Iggy already up working. Sledge watches Iggy connect wires from the ports on his head to an active computer. Although Iggy can tell Sledge is not pleased with what he sees, Iggy greets him by saying, "*Hola. Cómo estás?*" Deadpan, Sledge responds, "*De mierda.*"[104]

Putting aside his work for the moment, Iggy stops to talk with a visibly shaken and fidgety Sledge. Iggy, "*Que pasa?*" Sledge dejectedly tells Iggy, "I'm losing my mind, Iggy. Since activating *dis* thing in my head, I've felt like my mind is rejecting my body. I can't sleep. I keep having visions ..."

Iggy stops Sledge from talking to share what Dr. Hamilton's notes have revealed, "Based on what Q wrote, the sentient metal and the Omnis probe conflict. The Purified can extract the metal from you and replace it with another substance, but it'll hurt a lot." Sledge wipes his mouth and nose to remove the sentient metal from his face, then cautions, "I don't know if that'll be enough, but I'll risk the pain."

A continuous alarm rings from the computer, indicating the whereabouts of the Floating City. Checking the images on the computer, Iggy sees the mighty vessel flying away from the City of Sin. By tracking the radiation trails emitted by the Floating City as it travels across the old USA, Iggy can track where it has been and its likely destinations.

Iggy shows Sledge the radiation trail and suggests that it is heading in their direction, "This might make you feel better. I tracked a radiation trail from the Floating City. We can plot a course away from its path to make our escape." Iggy gestures at the map on the computer, "It's stopped at major cities from the east coast to the west, and now it's traveling back through the south."

A careful observation that Iggy points out for Sledge is that "Smaller Warhawks are returning to the Floating City with more of the Corrupted passenger

---

[104] "Shitty."

onboard. It may not be long when they leave the planet, but a millisecond for Ilem is a century for us."

Sledge crosses his arms, contemplating what strategy they will pursue to take every advantage to fool Ilem of their plans. He says, "Where the Floating City moves, the Warhawks trail, 'cause they're interconnected. I prefer we get out of 'ere by *den*. Who knows *whah dem* will leave in their wake prior *tuh* Warhawks berthing with *di* Floating City?"

In the middle of his statement, Sledge suddenly stops in response to a subtle noise that creeps into the room. Sledge, "Iggy, did *yuh* hear *dat. Whah di* …!"

A low skittering sound taps in Sledge's ear. He scans the room and, hiding in the crack of the adjoining walls, sees one of Ilem's tiny drone spies camouflaged and attached to the ceiling.

Iggy jumps into action, "I'll get it." Instinctively, he launches one of his gauntlets at the drone to destroy it and smashes it against the wall. Two other drone spies become uncamouflaged and skitter in different directions. Skitskitskitskitskit.

He launches his other gauntlet at one of the drones to destroy it. Fisst! Surprising to Iggy, Sledge telekinetically stops the other drone in midair, then shouts, "No, wait!" Sage appears in the room just as Sledge and Iggy bicker over whether to destroy or save the drone spies. She must still brace herself against the doorframe, appearing weak from her injuries. Sage, "What happened? I heard a loud crash?"

Sledge telekinetically pulls the drone into his hand and observes, "I am glad *yuh* are up. Ilem's drone spies infiltrated the safe house." Iggy displeasingly informs Sage, "And he wants to save them for some dumb reason. Sledge, he'll know our plans now!"

They heatedly continue discussing their options. Sage is gathering her strength in the background, unable to engage in verbal warfare. Iggy, "You wouldn't run from anyone else. *Porqué ahora?*"[105] Sledge places his hand on Iggy's shoulder. Sledge, "*Estoy pensando.*[106] War is won over time, not in a day. *Di* only plan

---

[105] "Why now?"
[106] "I'm thinking."

should be *tuh* save our asses. Otherwise, we are going *tuh* die like in my dream. Sage, *dis* is Iggy. Iggy, Sage."

Sledge spins Iggy with one hand and grabs him by the shoulder, admonishing him to listen. Sledge still holds the AI drone in his other hand when he asserts, "I've already been a pawn in *dis* game with Ilem and Hamilton."

Sage reaches for Sledge as he relaxes his grip on Iggy's shoulders and says, "Are you still talking about leaving? Stay! We are connected. I know you feel it!" Sensing only the slow burn of fury rising in his gut, Sledge yells, "*An* I'm *di* only one 'ere connected to Ilem, right! *Nuh, yuh*, Iggy or *di* Purified."

Sledge aggressively spins to face Sage, who recoils from Sledge's sudden aggression. Sledge shrieks at Sage, "Do *yuh* think I *wuld* help *yuh* just because *yuh* fucked my mind? I'm just a desperate, sacrificial lamb *tuh yuh*. Bullshit!" Iggy looks on with disgust.

Sledge pushes by Sage to exit the room, then informs Iggy, "I'll bring back an escape vehicle large enough for all of us if I can, and I'll do it for the Purified, but I'm done playing Beggar's Lot with the Black Spot held *'gainst* me."

Sage and Iggy listen to the stomp of Sledge's feet as he plods down the stairs, determined to seek his path, unconcerned about the feelings of others. Sledge stops to stand in the doorway leading outside. Iggy runs up behind him, demanding, "Apologize for being so crude, Sledge," to which Sledge dismissively snaps, "Fuck *dis*! *An* her! If she wants *tuh* go with us, she better catch *dis* ride now."

Sage reaches the front entrance at the wrong time to engage Sledge in conversation. She hears Sledge's last statement and feels her temperature rise, fuming at Sledge's callous responses to Iggy's pleas. Yet, Sledge stands silently at the doorway as though he has been unmoved by Sage's emotions.

When Sledge releases the drone spy outside, Iggy looks incredulous about his blood brother's actions. Fed up and spent from trying to convince Sledge to change his plans, Iggy asks him, "*Que carajo*, Sledge?"[107] Sledge tells Iggy, "We cannot be Spectators here. Remember, those who tell don't know." Iggy finishes

---

[107] "What the fuck?"

Sledge's thought, "*Los que saben, no digan.*"[108] Finally feeling he has made his point, Sledge adds, "Yes. This gives us distance from *wah* Ilem knows *an* what he thinks."

The two friends walk down the hill from the orphanage entrance. Sledge shares with Iggy, "*Deh* may be more spies listening. Please explain it to her later. We want Ilem *tuh tink* we're fractured." Iggy and Sledge begin packing the supplies they believe they will need for a space voyage that could last months to complete.

As they diligently work to prepare for their escape, three hours later, the drone spy that Sledge released streaks through the air closer and closer toward the Floating City. Whoosh! A dust cloud follows behind Kol and the 20-some members of the Sect Squad that he has brought with him to attack Sledge, Sage, and Iggy. The "thadump thadump" of their boots pound into the ground around the Sect Squad as they march toward their prey.

Kol raises his metal hand above his eyes to see the small object flying at his entourage. He intercepts the drone spy, listens to the recording, "*War is won over time ...,*" and then orders one of the Sect drones to transmit the recordings to the Floating City for Ilem. Kol, "Ilem will be pleased to know we are near our target. Quickly communicate the recording to the Command Deck."

Meanwhile, at the safe house, Sledge has detached his head from the containment suit, and his head floats above it. The containment suit is upright with its legs crossed as it remains in meditation. Iggy has returned to the computer to study the path of the Floating City with Sage by his side.

Bitterly, Sage observes, "I see Sledge is still leaving." Iggy despondently tells her, "*Sé.*[109] Anyway, look at the screen. The strongest radiation signals come from the Floating City center and an area that may be living quarters." Sage moves behind Iggy to join him in studying the movements of the Floating City. Sage, "That's the energy source for the Floating City. Hard to tell where the other signal originates."

---

[108] "Those who know, don't tell."
[109] "I know."

Iggy adjusts the settings on the computer to zoom in on the Floating City and the location of the radiation spikes. He concludes, "Based on the signals' calibrations, the second radiation trail follows Ilem. Look, these surges were on the final day of Blood Bowl." Sage scrolls through Iggy's findings, then concludes, "Ilem emitted a powerful surge of energy when he killed my father and the Negearians."

Several hundred miles away, the Floating City dips further south over Dallas to destroy the Dallas Cowboys' stadium. Sage says, "Great, it looks like they're crossing Texas and headed this way."

Iggy notices and shares with Sage, "There is one more thing. Ilem's radiation varies. A few energy fluxes were harmful, but there's a stream of gray's radiation every night." Sage recalls, "Q taught me that gray's radiation heals." Iggy makes notes, then says to Sage, "Do you think Ilem needs that for himself? The duration of the signal has not changed since I started tracking it, but its intensity has weakened."

Sledge returns to the threshold of the door to the room where Iggy and Sage are working. He interrupts their discussion to inform them, "Miles back, I saw stranded cargo ships in *di* river. I'll see if I can find *anyting* useful *deh*. Can Juno find a 3D printer *tuh* replicate my shuriken?" Iggy responds, "Fine, he'll upgrade them, too … Sledge, I don't think it's right to leave her alone."

Still unwilling to relent to his friend's comments, Sledge disagrees with Iggy's position. Sledge, "*Yuh* all in *di* clear. *Yuh* don't *hav* poison inside *yuh*. Ilem can make me his bitch anytime he wants. Cough!" Sledge coughs up sentient metal with droplets that splatter on the floor. Unlike the green and black substance Sledge previously regurgitated, this fluid comes out with a purplish-red color.

Sledge folds his arms defiantly and suggests to Iggy, "*You travel lite*, remember? You learned too much about being a bleeding heart from Uncle." Iggy suggests, "*Quizás deberías haber aprendido más.*"[110]

Shocked by Iggy's dismissive tone, Sledge says back, "Really? So, I could end up shot in *di* street defending strangers, *tuh*? No justice, no peace, remember. All *di* promises of a modern utopia because we *hav* super tech were a lie. We're

---

[110] "Maybe you should have learned more."

still stepped on *an* snuffed out like Uncle. I *cyaan* go through this anymore. I, we, need balance. We gotta eject what we don't need *an* move on, now!"

Iggy looks disheartened as he raises his gaze from his friend into the sky, looking for inspiration in the overhead ethereal clouds. Unable to gather all the words in his adoptive English or the Spanglish Sledge has gone to comprehend, Iggy resorts to his roots to express how he feels.

"You want balance? *¿Balance? Eso es lo que pasa con el equilibrio, nunca es perfecto. Sufres la locura de la perfección. Todo se reduce a esto; siempre eres el común denominador. Eres el único destroyer or architect de tu propia existencia. En algún momento, tienes que aprender a dejar atrás el pasado, tus transgresiones y las de tu contra para segu atron ente. Move forward, atronrón a la vez y esfuérzate por hacerlo mejor. Esto también es cierto. Y no grano para forraje.*"[111]

Sage approaches Sledge at the door. Instead of acknowledging her presence, he tries to ignore her to conclude his discussion with Iggy, "Be ready to go when I get back."

Sage tries to convince Sledge not to run by suggesting, "Ilem will not stop hunting us. We both have something he wants. You are the last of your kind, and I am the first of mine." With every step Sledge takes away, she begins to glow assorted colors that emit from the orb.

Sledge turns back toward Sage and telekinetically begins to close the door. He calmly tells her, "Our best advantage is time and distance." The door closes between them as Sledge walks away, speaking to himself, "Some things you don't put in the air."

As the door closes, Sage kicks it back open. She yells to Sledge's back that she is done asking him for help and declares she will challenge Ilem alone. Sage, "Sledge, fuck you back!" Iggy walks to her side, trying to console her.

---

[111] "Balance? That's the thing about balance; it's never perfect. You suffer the madness of perfection. Perfection is far too hard to sustain. The whole thing boils down to this: You're always the common denominator. You are the only destroyer or architect of your existence. At some point in time, you have to learn to let go of the past, your transgressions, and those against you to move forward. Move forward, one patter at a time, and strive to improve. This, too, is true. And not grist for fodder."

Continuing to yell at Sledge at the top of her lungs, Sage shouts, "I am a goddamn empath, Sledge, you stupid ass. I know you're pushing me away. I don't need you to do this if you have not noticed. I've been alone, and I can do it alone!" Sledge replies, without a hint of emotion, *"Den* prove it."

Then, Sledge gets into an armored pickup truck carrying in his hand all the equipment he thinks he will need to complete his polarizing mission.

It is dawn when he leaves behind his friend and the woman who opened his eyes to possibility. In his rear-view mirror, Sledge watches a cloud of dust rising around Sage, leaving her shrouded from their past and his future.

The road is forlorn, and the curves deceptive.

END OF CHAPTER 16

Chapter 17

A Letter Sincerely Written

Not to fold your hands in my life
Or oppress your eyes to look no other way
Undo your right to sprout wings or tears
I don't want anything
You won't feed me freely
Not words, smiles, or kisses
Or tastes of Opium on your neck
I don't want anything
That sits in my mouth, bitter like a lemon
Love isn't worth needless hell
Or the caged passion
Of one, forced touch

The Whisper

Within a few hours of Sledge's hasty departure, Sage rattles cartridges the size and shape of old-school D batteries in her hands. One by one, she fills the chambers of her red, black, and gray hand cannon with the shells. Given the considerable size and weight of the weapon, one would conclude it would be too heavy for Sage to hold and manage, or the kickback might be so much, but she twirls it with one finger with ease, then swiftly flips it into its holster.

Her newfound friend, Iggy, approaches her, concerned that the look of determination on her face is a tell-tell sign of reconciliation with a contentious challenge. "*Qué pasa*," Iggy asks Sage. She responds, "I am going after Ilem. Alone if I have to." Iggy grabs Sage's hand as she is about to unholster her hand cannon, then begs of her, "*Senorita, por favor*, wait for Sledge to return. If not, the Purified will go with you."

Iggy follows Sage outside the safe house, continuing to probe the rationality of her intentions, "*Además*, why is it so important to defeat Ilem alone? Why can't we do what Sledge has said and flee?" Relying on her linguistic skills, Sage explains why she is so determined to challenge Ilem, *"¿Dónde podemos ir para escapar del Consejo Galáctico? Ilem nos localizará."*[112]

Thunderstorms rise in the distance as swift updrafts capture warm, moist air layers. The crackle of lightning and boom of thunder echoes in Sage and Iggy's direction.

Sage, "I was on my own for some time. I fought off men who wanted to use me, not because I drew them to me, but because they were vile. No matter what language I spoke, to ask them to leave me alone, those who wanted to exploit me were persistent with their attacks. No, please! *Ne molim! Maya, fadlan! Não por favor!* –To stay true to myself, no matter how alone I felt, I remembered my mother suffering to receive love. She once said, 'It's okay to want a man, but never get so lost in love to need one.' I don't, and I won't."

Sage digs into her pocket to retrieve the damp letter her father left for her before Blood Bowl, then reads his wise suggestion, "Stay you. Fate will take care of the rest." She takes a moment to contemplate what her father was trying to convey, then acknowledges what she must do to bring life to those words.

In Iggy's ancestral tongue, Sage signals that it is time for her to go, *"Que estes bien*[113]*, mi amigo."* She heads off in the opposite direction that Sledge traveled, a road sign indicating she is heading toward 30 West.

To no avail, Iggy pleads to Sage, "Sage, don't go!" When she travels away anyway on an old flying motorcycle, she leaves Iggy standing outside, watching her advance toward the unseen road that awaits her. Iggy turns to Juno, who stands patiently by his side, to say, "Gather everyone to go after Sage. I'll follow once I finish with Q's research."

Sledge drives to the Philadelphia waterfront a few miles away, where the Delaware River has gone dry. A capsized cargo ship is still present. Some shipping containers have fallen onto the dry riverbed and are in various states of rust and decay.

---

[112] "Where can we go to escape the Galactic Council? Ilem will track us down."
[113] "Be well."

Sledge kneels on the dry riverbed, contemplating his next move. He declares to himself, "I don't owe any of *dem anyting*." He lets the dry soil he picked up from the riverbed slip through his robotic fingers. He thinks to himself, "I was dust. But somehow, I am still alive."

Sledge angrily throws several shuriken at the old, busted containers. The container doors barely move, although each strike of his shuriken makes an explosive sound.

He uses telekinesis to unbury a long tree limb that has similar dimensions to Sledge's Vision Staff. The roots dig into the soil like a frantic hand scraping to hide underground. He tries to pull the tree limb from the ground with his bare hands, but its roots are too deep. Sledge exclaims in frustration, "Shhit!"

He calls out for help from the god on high that's worshipped by many but called different names, "Jah! *Wah, mek!*"[114]

A familiar voice tugs on Sledge's ear, calling him back from his fret and despair. Sledge tosses into the air a question he expects will be true, "Uncle Ray … is *dat yuh?*" The vaporous voice answers, "*Yah mi bwoy. Mi wid yuh.*"[115] After considering what to say to the hazy voice, Sledge implores, "Help *mi. O cyaan mi* survive?"[116]

The visible spirit of Uncle Ray materializes in a kneeling position next to Sledge. Uncle Ray questions Sledge about his troubled mind, "*Wah mek dat important? Why are you calling on Jah when you've said gods are fiction to justify a moral compass?*"

Sledge replies, "*Yuh* made me see that I could measure more *dan* flesh and bone, *buh* I failed *yuh.*" As a wise soul, living or dead, Uncle Ray offers to Sledge, "*Truss Jah. Im areddi eena yuh. Unnu faith eena even di unseen will guide yuh.*"[117]

They stare ahead in profile as Sledge recalls the incident that led to Uncle Ray warning him about the Vision Staff one day becoming a crutch. Sledge

---

[114] "Why"
[115] "Yes, my boy. I'm with you."
[116] "Help me. How can I survive?"
[117] "Trust Jai. He's already in you, your faith in even the unseen will guide you."

pleads, *"Mi cum dis faar."*[118] As if to snap Sledge back into reality, Uncle Ray breaks the tree limb with a well-placed karate chop, then examines it as he talks with Sledge. A black feather is stuck in the top of the tree limb that Uncle Ray plucks and sets free. Uncle Ray, *"Jus likkle a di dust slipping tru yuh hand. Di wind kno which way tuh carry yuh."*[119]

Uncle Ray throws the tree limb in front of Sledge. Sledge looks up at him while still kneeling. Uncle Ray, *"Yuh can tun dis whole tree limb inna Vision Staff. It would be best if you juss tried but don't lean on it too much. A crutch will slow your stride."*

But Sledge and Iggy never intended the Vision Staff to be a crutch. Only in time did this luxury become a burden. On the day Iggy and Sledge excitedly searched through the trunk that once belonged to Sledge's father, they chanced upon a Zulu *isikhwili* staff in two pieces that needed attention or trashing.

After they removed all the pieces of the Zulu *isikhwili* from the trunk and thoroughly inspected it, Iggy tinkered with a rectangular device to calibrate settings on a bulky and less refined version of the sunglasses Sledge later wore while fighting at Blood Bowl. Given that Iggy had never created a device as complex as he described to Sledge, it was understandable that Sledge asked, *"Yuh* sure you can do it? It's just a broken stick to me." Iggy confidently answered Sledge's well-timed question, "I just need to figure out the calibration between these sensors."

On the day that the Vision Staff was born, Uncle Ray crept up behind them and continued examining the staff with them. Uncle Ray asked his adopted sons, *"Why unu nuh go outside an leave Bobby truck alone,"*[120] to which Sledge begged, "But *yuh* said it'd be mine one day." Uncle Ray waved Sledge on, but not away from the trunk of weapons, *"It will be, but you need to be responsible wid dem."*[121]

Iggy grabbed a football to go outside to play while Sledge carried the Vision Staff with them. The Vision Staff had a flashing, metal device stuck on its end that seemed to beep in tandem with the lights on the sunglasses Iggy gave Sledge

---

[118] "I've come this far."
[119] "Just like the dust slipping through yuh hand. The wind knows which way to carry you."
[120] "Why don't you two go outside and leave Bobby's truck alone."
[121] "It will be, but you need to be responsible with them."

to wear. Uncle Ray told them, *"Tek wateva yuh waan but stay right yah suh.*[122] Dinner almost ready."

Once outside, Iggy threw the football in Sledge's direction repeatedly. Iggy had the rectangular device strapped to his hand, with the Vision Staff stuck in the ground between them. Sledge came close to catching the football, but it fell feebly in front of him. Iggy told Sledge, "You'll hear a click to time your steps, then cut to your left. Keep your hands out." While tossing the football back to Iggy, Sledge confidently stated, *"Yah, mon,* I almost had it!"

Considering the distance and speed of Sledge's strides, Iggy tinkered with the Vision Staff to calibrate its settings. Iggy assured Sledge, "Just a little more adjustment …"

Seeing that Sledge was ready to try again, Iggy threw the football in Sledge's direction. Sledge failed to catch the ball try after try.

To help him reach his goal, Iggy instructed Sledge, "The clicking should tell you when to turn …" With the additional instruction, Sledge ran as far as he could, all the while counting off the number of steps he needed to take as he reached for the football, "31, 32, turn … ooofff!" Iggy shouted more instructions to Sledge, *"No lo dudes.*[123]

Although they were almost done practicing for the day, the football rolled down a hill. To retrieve the ball, Iggy trotted off to find it. Iggy, *"entiendo."*[124] As quick as he ran in the direction where the football went, the faster he ran back up. A group of rough and disrespectful teens led by Renzo, a neighborhood thug, chase Iggy back up the hill.

Iggy slipped on broken glass on the blacktop, badly cutting his knees. He screamed in pain, "Awww," while the hoodlums laughed at his misery. "Ha, ha, ha, ha, ha!" In response to Iggy's call for help, *"Ayuda*[125], Sledge came to his aid without delay.

---

[122] "Take whatever you want but stay close."
[123] "Don't hesitate."
[124] "Got it."
[125] "Help."

As Sledge went over to help get Iggy inside their house, Renzo yelled at Sledge and Iggy to taunt them. Renzo, "Hey, nutball! Hey, Stevie Wonder, you ain't gonna do shit. We could come at you, and your guide dog, and you wouldn't know it 'til it's too late."

One of Renzo's boys yelled, "Dumb ass, whackadoo." Another one squawked, "Kookalu! Piece of shit, motherfucking freaks!" Uncle Ray was at the window but remained silent and unmoved.

Sledge helped Iggy stand and pluck glass from his wounded leg, and then he pulled the Vision Staff out of the ground. Uncle Ray closed the kitchen window with a sudden slam.

Sledge handed the Vision Staff to Iggy for the necessary adjustments, then turned to face the bully and his boys—tick, tick, tick. Iggy handed the Vision Staff back to Sledge. Sledge's confidence was emboldened with the Vision Staff in his hands, "If we run, it wouldn't be from *yuh*. Go ahead and try."

The bully whistled between his fingers, and, on cue, one of his boys threw a stone at Sledge. Renzo, "Fweeeet!!! Wheewwww."

In response to Iggy warning Sledge from which direction the stones were coming, Sledge hit rocks back at the bully who threw them at him. Swinging the staff like a baseball bat allowed Sledge to smack the stone right back in the face of the kid who threw it. Tap tink! Sledge could tell his strike was true even without sight as he heard the kid cry, "Ouch!"

Renzo signaled to another kid to throw a stone at Sledge. Renzo, "Fweeeet!!!" Iggy clicked the device again to warn Sledge. Click click. Sledge again hit the rock back off a street sign, ricocheting it back at the kid who threw it. The boy yelped, "Ugh!!!"

"Let's play catch," Sledge hollered, picking up a handful of stones, tossing them in the air, and then hitting the rocks with the Vision Staff. Tink tink tink tink! The stones screamed into the air, as did the boys whom Sledge struck with the hard objects, "Argh! Awww!"

The next bully to pay the price for their insolence was Renzo. Sledge pointed the Vision Staff at him, cautioning him, "Unless *yuh* want more pain, I suggest *yuh* back off."

Sledge and Iggy walked back inside the house as Renzo and his boys ran in the opposite direction. Uncle Ray stopped them at the door, saying, *"Nice device yuh got der. Iggy do a decent job.*[126] *Yuh know wah dis reminds me of? Ah crutch. Nuh get too used to it, son."*

Years from that crucial day, as Sledge kneeled on the Delaware riverbed, he recalls that the first day he handled the Vision Staff, it comforted him that the future held promise. He now finds himself shadowed between tomorrow's undrawn shade and the tattered curtain of yesteryear. After they have returned their focus to the present, the spirit of Uncle Ray still stands on the riverbed beside him, advising Sledge on how to address his concerns. Suddenly, the howling and chaotic wind twirling disturbs the parched soil around Sledge's feet.

The specter of Uncle Ray begins to fade next to Sledge while rotating the tree limb to demonstrate how Sledge might use it as a weapon. Uncle Ray advises, *"When yuh get chrang using a crutch mek yuh weak."*[127] Dejected by his present reality, Sledge sheepishly replies, "I'll always need a crutch to get around, Uncle. I'll *neva* see."

Uncle Ray swings his body to a position to perform an Abanico Corto martial arts move. While ascending from a standing position, Uncle Ray completes the athletic move he started by quickly snapping the Vision Staff within inches of Sledge's face. Whoosh! Uncle Ray tells him, *"Yuh memba wah mi tell yuh?"*[128] As Sledge nods yes, he remembers what Uncle Ray taught him, "Everyone knows fear. Fear baptizes us in it just as our sense of sight welcomes us into the *werl.*"

Uncle Ray lifts Sledge's gaze using the edge of the tree limb against Sledge's chin. Sledge concedes to his Uncle, "If I can't overcome the blindness that greeted me into *dis* werl, how can I beat Ilem?" Uncle Ray unapprovingly asks him, *"Nuh tell me seh a tuff man like you fraid a di unknown?"*[129]

---

[126] "Nifty device you got there. Good work, Iggy."
[127] "When you get strong using a crutch makes you weak."
[128] "Do you remember what I told you then?"
[129] "Don't tell me a tough man like you are afraid of the unknown."

He leans forward toward Sledge while holding the tree limb with both hands. Their faces are fairly close. Uncle Ray, *"Nuh care wah yuh do—life rough. Rainfall pon di just and unjust."*[130] Uncle Ray's reflection is visible in Sledge's translucent, green eyes. Uncle Ray, *"Haffi learn fi smile at the storm."*[131]

Sledge shakes his head in confusion, *"Yuh* make it sound easy." Sensing Sledge's continued turmoil, Uncle Ray wisely counters, *"Yuh* can live today as if *yuh* can calm the seas, *buh di* storms will blow while *di* trials of life test *wah yuh* know. If *yuh* feel beaten down, believe *dat yuh* get up."

Uncle Ray blows the feather stuck in the top of the tree limb out of his hand. The feather rises in the wind near him as Uncle Ray instructs Sledge, *"Be like a fedda. Life hit yuh, just gwaan float pon di wind."*[132] Uncle Ray jumps toward the feather, swinging the tree limb in its direction. Uncle Ray tells Sledge, *"Di fedda know di powa of sacrifice, di vastness of nuttin, di singularity of innocence."* Whoosh.

The otherworldly sensei continues fading from view as the feather lands in his hand. Uncle Ray passes the tree limb to Sledge, and Sledge grips it tightly in response. While Uncle Ray disappears from view, he blows the feather toward the containers. Uncle Ray, *"Yuh feet goin get tiyad, but the shoes fit you just fine."*[133]

Several feet from Sledge are the capsized cargo ships. Sledge twirls the tree limb telekinetically, keeping it at the edge of his fingers, testing the mastery of his staff and the power gifted to him by the Omnis probe. Whirl. Powered by Sledge's will, the feather floats above in front of the containers.

Sledge rips more limbs from the tree, twirling them together like buzzsaws. He telekinetically hurls them toward the elusive fedda, then launches other limbs at a pile of cargo containers lying awkwardly on the side of the capsized cargo ship. Two cargo containers fall to the dry Delaware Riverbed, and their doors crack open. A cargo container falls on top of the other. Crash bang. Sledge notices that the one on top has a flying motorcycle wheel sticking out.

---

[130] "No matter what you do, life is rough. You can't escape the consequences of your life. Not even God can do that."
[131] "Float through bad winds unafraid of the outcome."
[132] "Be a feather on the wind."
[133] "Your feet may get tired, but the shoes will fit just fine."

He telekinetically tears the dangling doors from the cargo containers. Rip. Several Indian flying motorcycles fall from inside the container with a loud "bang, clang, bang" as each machine tumbles on top of the other. Sledge smirks at his discovery and utters words marking his feeling of accomplishment against great odds, "*Booyaka!*"

The feather glides effortlessly into Sledge's open palm as the dust settles.

END OF CHAPTER 17

Chapter 18

Deeds and Dreams

Let me hide away from sorrow
Resting from things that were
Let me hide from love's last visions
While they slowly turn a blur

For a shadow wakes inside me
While in mourning, tears I bleed
Still, this night shall have no morning
From my lost love born of dreams

Let me run from what abounds me
Let me rest what I have lost
Let the lonely seal their dreaming
That hide secrets in their hearts

Derrick Howard

Ripple

Dear Zetia and Belle,

I wish I had time to maintain the façade that has kept us alive for decades by making *summat and noffin*, but *I c'unt do it*. Straight away, I love you both and always will.

On the battlefield, we've been at war in service to Ilem for several grueling weeks, bleeding into months. I shalt say more, but death does not discriminate. Everyone will find the same *ginnel* on this road to hell. All around me, hills and valleys are sloped with uneven slabs of decaying bodies, bloated from gas reeking of excrement and bile.

Trailers are forced to sleep on the jagged, unforgiving ground each night without cover or a scrap of bread. Our chilled breath wafts out of us as if we're slowly surrendering our souls to the ether. I pray that wherever the Floating City has you, you can see the shooting star tonight and know my eyes are upon you like that great, eccentric orb.

Tearfully, I must say, I don't know if I'll ever see you again, my love or my darling *bairn*, Belle. So, I'll let this message blow away from my hand, joyfully lifting farther into the sky aloft your love and endless possibilities of being with you again.

Ta'ra today, love you always, Gabba.

The battlefield reeks of a pungent metallic smell. The shadow of cloud storms waves approvingly above the graveyards scattered below.

Bridges burn, and hopes are lost by scores of warriors fighting for survival. The sheer scale of the battleground exceeds those ever fought on Earth. Its battle areas encompass a front six hundred miles wide in the United States of the Americas and several hundred more miles across the barren regions of Europe, Africa, and what remains of Asia. This final world war clash bleeds into weeks and months, resulting in over a million battle deaths.

The battlefield on which Gabba still finds himself through innumerable days fearing for his life is within a few miles of the rendezvous point with the Floating City. Soon, if he survives sudden clashes with unwanted foes, he may return to his wife and daughter and whatever life they can eke out as a lowly Trailer and his family of illegal aliens.

High above a pending battlefield in New Orleans, Hyle sets his sights on his landing spot as he hurls toward the Big Easy. The velocity of his colossal body skimming the Gulf of Mexico raises its deep waters into a tsunami.

Naihal lies between her lovers, Gorman, a Negearian, and Tirzah, a buxom Eridian from Epsilon Eridani C. Like most Negearians, Gorman's skin has an obsidian marble pattern that gleams in the light dangling over the bed. In this instance, his skin has a black-and-white pattern. He also has an Afrocentric mohawk hairstyle. Eridians are humanoid beings with hair made of multi-colored writhing snakes. Tirzah keeps her snaky hair at bay by wrapping her locks in an open-ended turban.

Naihal rests her head on Gorman's chest and slides her gloved hand toward his lower abdomen. Gorman asks her, "How long can we lay here knowing your brother is coming?" Naihal, tells him, "Gorman, you have nothing to fear. You are under my protection." Gorman rises from his laying position, surprising Naihal and Tirzah. Gorman pleads to Naihal, "Mistress, please listen to me."

He slowly slides to the edge of the bed to fetch his boots. Naihal reaches for him; Tirzah clings to Naihal. Gorman continues imploring Naihal to get her to understand his fears, "Your brother turned light beams into shards to kill everyone on Negearia. Children playing in the sun ... women working their fields ... everyone!" Despite his cries, Tirzah begs, "Listen to her, Gorm."

The Diwan of Darkness gets out of bed to reach for Gorman as he stands beyond her reach. A tearful Tirzah remains curled on the bed. Naihal, "We will be leaving soon. Wait until the Floating City arrives. Until then, I will shroud you." Gorman reacts decisively, "I cannot wait for what happens next. Ilem would have slaughtered those who escaped if we did not hide inside Messier 57."

Gorman walks to the top of the winding staircase in Naihal's Queen Anne mansion. He walks down the stairs toward the front door as Tirzah kneels on the bed, clinging to Naihal. Gorman tells his lover, "I know you could easily stop me, Naihal. But I must go to stand with my people." As Gorman pulls the front door to close behind him, a gush of wind forces it from his grip, slamming the door back inside the wall in the entryway. He reaches back inside Naihal's home and, for the last time, wades into the pool of her consuming blue eyes.

The storm whipping above New Orleans is so tremendous; its rippling clouds of ebony and muted grays trouble the air miles away above Iggy's safehouse and the air above thousands of miles worldwide. Like the furious storm that foretold the Great Babylonian Flood of 1,700 BC, the sky releases a plague of rain that threatens to drown Earth just as the flood sent by Sumerian gods did to destroy human life. Mindful of how quickly the storm has moved in, Iggy works more diligently to complete the project he has taken on based on Dr. Hamilton's research.

He reconnects to his makeshift computer network and flicks a switch that causes electricity to run into the gauntlets before him. Lights streaming through the windows reveal the tremendous use of power. Rrrrrrrrrrr!

As the sound cranks up, Kol appears outside the orphanage to fight Sledge. Electricity continues to beam out the windows from Iggy's work on his gauntlets and shoots toward the sky like its power streams from the supernatural.

Without fear of what he brushes off as a few raindrops, Kol commands whoever is inside the safe house, "Come out and face me, fools!" Rrrrrrrrrrr! Iggy looks at everyone assembled outside, *"Mierda, es uno grande."*[134] In preparation for whatever happens next, Iggy pulls the cover off the concealed object in the room.

When the cover hits the floor, it reveals a new body armor that Iggy built. It is an impressive body armor that matches Iggy's improved gauntlets. Suddenly the electricity stops inside the building, and everything gets quiet, even Kol's drenched troops assembled outside.

Iggy appears outside the building wearing his upgraded body armor *sans* his wig. Now, the ports on his head are visible, and he is holding an upgraded ornate helmet. While slipping on his helmet, Iggy calls to those outside, "You'll find no fools here, *mi grande amigo.*" Kol demands, "Tell me where they are now!"

Without delay, Kol charges toward Iggy to attack but cannot catch him, as Kol's feet slip on soaked dirt. Kol slams a hole into the wall, barely missing Iggy. Iggy's image dissipates just as quickly as it appeared. The real Iggy is behind Kol, taunting him. The specter of Iggy sizes Kol up with an evident and sobering observation, *"Más rápido,* big man!"

Iggy presses a button on his gauntlets to produce more images of himself. Click. Unlike the jovial doppelgangers who danced in the deserted streets of

---

[134] "Shit, he's a big one."

Chicago at Iggy's command, these mirror images stand protectively around him, appearing more like digitized Moji than physical bodies.

Kol's followers attack the images but cannot avoid hitting each other as their blows go through the mirages and smash against each other's faces. "Awww!" "Oooof! Watch out!" Kol's forearm opens to reveal the compartment that shoots short crossbow arrows at his opponents. He shouts, "I'll get you maggot!" Iggy uses his shockwave shield to block the crossbow arrows by reverberating displaced energy back at Kol. The burst knocks Kol back from one of his charging attacks. Boing.

Tired of this game of tag, Kol extends his arms to hold everyone back from attacking Iggy. "All of you, stay back! I'll handle him." Iggy answers back, "I am L'Enigma." Kol aggressively comes back, "Mr. 'Nigma, it's time to die."

As though his determination has peaked, Kol whiffs on his next attack as Iggy skillfully ducks under Kol's arms. Discouragingly, Kol's troops laugh at his feeble attempts to catch Iggy, "Ha, ha, ha, ha, ha!" Ignoring their mocking laughter, Kol and Iggy continue to fight, with Kol doing devastating damage to the building and other objects in the area. Blam. Iggy continues to scamper out of harm's way until he slides into the mud and loses footing.

Seeing an opening to attack, Kol leaps in the air to come crashing down on Iggy with both coal-black, large hands clasped around the hilt of the khopesh. Iggy screams as he tries to avoid the enormous mass of man descending on him. "Aaaa!" Before Kol can crush him with his weight, Iggy activates his gauntlets to discharge needles at Kol. Iggy declares, *"Estaré en todas partes. ¡Toma eso!"*[135]

Kol lands with all his weight on Iggy and pushes the khopesh through Iggy's body. Responsively, Iggy screams in pain, "Argh!" Kol stands up and picks up Iggy's limp body by one leg, declaring, "He's done."

Ilem's High Guard directs his followers, "Let's head back." Unceremoniously, Kol and the rest of the Squadron begin their trek to the Floating City away from the orphanage. The damage from the battle between Kol and Iggy is prominent when assessing the damaged building. The loss of Iggy's life is evidenced by his dilated eyes and blood seeping into the ground to feed thirsty weeds.

---

[135] "I will be everywhere. Take that!"

Kol brings up the rear behind the entourage as they walk through the deserted streets of Philadelphia. He tosses the ornate, upgraded helmet that Iggy was wearing to the ground. Kol directs his troops, "We will watch for Sledge and the woman. We find them, and we finish them, too!" As his forces trail behind him, Kol plucks the tiny needles in his metal armor's chest plate.

On the Floating City, Ilem awaits word from his armies that they have accomplished their mission. Ilem stands in his proper form instead of being dressed in his exoskeleton. His steady golden glow shines against his room's mirrors, casting light back at him like he is about to step onto a Broadway stage.

Gloating, Ilem stops before his fanciest exoskin, "This will do nicely for my coronation. My ascension to supremacy." He transfers his essence to the exoskin and puts on his gold and silver helmet. Strutting like a peacock, Ilem goes to the balcony adjoining his quarters.

Only the top of the Dyson Sphere is visible off the side of Ilem's balcony. Ilem begins speaking to seemingly no one but himself. "Victor, it is time ..." Unexpectedly interrupting Ilem's sentence, Dr. Hamilton appears on the balcony wearing a hooded cloak. He sarcastically asks Ilem, "Talking to the dead? I'm the only one here, Godfrey. It is time to face me!"

Ilem fumes as he reacts to Dr. Hamilton's sudden appearance and taunting words, "You will not trick me with mind games, Sage. I know your father is dead!" Ilem shoots a blast of light energy at Dr. Hamilton's specter. The light energy cuts through him but does no damage. Dr. Hamilton heckles Ilem more by saying, "You have no control over me now, Godfrey."

With his anger increasing, Ilem screams while lunging at Dr. Hamilton, "Damn you!" Although Ilem attacks Dr. Hamilton with all his fury, his efforts are in vain, as his hands pass through the annoying phantom of his nemesis. Ilem brags, "It does not matter, anyway. I control Sledge. The sentient metal coursing through him is connected to me."

Ilem conjures light to mold into a replica of Sledge's decapitated head. He holds the skull before Dr. Hamilton and boisterously declares, "This will be my trophy again by the end of today. I will have it cast in sentient metal to use whenever

I want to hear him squawk." Ilem bellows, "Wherever he goes, I will find and destroy him. No, wait, I will make him part of the Sect."

On cue, Ilem's Sect charged to his aid. Dr. Hamilton braces himself for the collision but keeps his cautious eyes on Ilem. The physician retorts, "Sledge may be a coward, but others will rise against the Galactic Council." The Sect pile on top of each other, thinking they have captured Dr. Hamilton. Surreptitiously, the infinity orb flies from under the pile of confused Sect undamaged. Abruptly, the image of Dr. Hamilton rematerializes off to the side and away from the Sect attackers.

The disruption did its job, just as Sage hoped. Sage leaps over the balcony toward the Sect assembled in the Center Court in her guise of Dr. Hamilton. Ilem directs the Sect to pursue her, "Sect, seize her!" For a moment, the Sect look for the woman Ilem wants them to capture instead of the man they saw on the balcony.

Ilem looks down from his balcony into the Center Court to see Dr. Hamilton captured by the Sect. However, they need clarification because Dr. Hamilton has disappeared again.

The Diwan of Light returns to his sleeping quarters and stops to stand close to Pu Kwon's sleeping chamber. While speaking to Pu Kwon, Ilem removes the accoutrements that adorn his armor. Ilem tells her, "My darling, I will complete this mission for us. We will travel far away to a galaxy we command, eternally side by side."

Ilem reaches for his most impressive battle exoskin, then activates a comm device to tell his Elite force, "Rally my troops! We will annihilate all who oppose me!" As Ilem leaves his chambers, Sage's orb flies from behind a curtain in the room near the balcony doorway.

Sage lowers the cloak's hood revealing she has changed her appearance to her usual self. She walks over to Pu Kwon to examine the source of Ilem's weakness. Pu Kwon is lifeless under the glass covering the sleeping chamber as Sage reaches through the glass to draw the gray film noir color from Pu Kwon's body into her own. The glare of her eyes intensifies as she reads the kinetic energy that has flowed between Ilem and Pu Kwon for more than one hundred years.

Kol has already arrived for the brawl with the Purified on the battlefield. He swings his khopesh like a bat, knocking away and dazing multiple attackers. Boom blam. All around Kol, the opposing factions rage against each other like medieval warriors. The battle is bloody and gory. Organs, guts, and mutilated robotic and fleshy limbs clutter the battlefield. The wounded scream for help, crippled by debilitating pain, overcome by sorrow.

Feverishly, more of Ilem's troops join the brawl, running up the mount of a raised hill with their poles sticking out. Unimpressed, scores of Purified pushes forward to engage with their enemies. There will be no prisoners.

Sledge returns to the safe house where he left Iggy and Sage, driving the flatbed truck with two futuristic motorcycles in the truck bed. A large cloud of dust is behind him as Sledge gets out of the truck to find Iggy dead and everyone else gone.

Sledge chokes back tears and anguish rising from and in him, "*Compadre. Este no es momento para vaqueros.*"[136] He touches Iggy's unresponsive body to read his armor as an object present to see what transpired when Iggy died. Rhetorically, Sledge pleads to Iggy's corpse, "*Wey yah guh?*"[137]

Carefully, he picks up Iggy's limp body using telekinesis to bring him into his arms, then carries him into their safe house. Creaakk. He delicately lays his friend on the couch and covers his body with a blanket.

Sledge shakes his head and sadly tells his blood brother, "*Siempre, amigo.*"[138] Sledge checks the computer monitor for the Floating City's radiation trail, but, as he pledged, he zooms away on the vintage motorcycle opposite where Sage and the Purified went, a large cloud trailing behind him.

Varooomm.

---

[136] "Buddy. This is no time for cowboys."
[137] "Where are you going?"
[138] "Always, friend."

Derrick Howard

Psalms for Yesterday: Sweet Words and Promises

Exhausted by his perpetual shadow-boxing
The Negro is still running,
Tripping in the entanglement of chains
He can no longer see

When he swings
The maker of his oppression fades away.

He frets,
I am afraid
Of an image that greets me in my sleep
A mask of macabre complexion
Pale, with small, blood-red lips that part
To cast out words of hatred
And confusion. I wrench in pain,
Vomit sweet words and promises.

Omnis: Last Man of Earth

In their artful code, they label me
A useless porch monkey,
I strike at them with shackled hands
Blue eyes sparkle with delight

Again, I am their animal.

I find hope in that
Christ too was an animal.
Daily I plead my case to him
Just as my mother told me to do
But he is deaf to my woe
Too busy lusting after
The affections of his father.

I seek shelter
Among the vanquished American Indian
Wherever I try to fit in with my half brothers
I fall victim to self-incrimination,
My hair is not straight enough.
My lips too large.
My nose too flat.
My manhood monstrous and misshapen.
My Cherokee kin call me Shadow Dancer.
Because I chase an image
That will never be a part of me.

On every television, newspaper, and airway
There are advertisements
Telling me I should be proud to be an American,
Freedom is my pillow,
Liberty, the diva
That will guide me through my fits of anguish.

At night, the diva loves me.
Her diaphanous gown is soaked
Around the nipples with nectar
Her smooth, hard hands guide my lips

To feed me, but before I do
She squashes my bones and marrow
Into digestible juices,
Her fangs suck my life
Until there is nothing left

I become a statistical error,
Another X, churning in the bowels
Of her system.

I wake to the sound of my voice
SHOUTING
again, and again
Sweet words and promises.

END OF CHAPTER 18

Chapter 19

Time

Going through the tunnel in the corner of my mind
I see all that has happened
In the world of endless time.

Going through the tunnel in the cracks and all their holes
I see inside my body
I see inside my soul.

I Am A Man

Having penetrated the underground level of the Floating City, Sage becomes invisible to sneak closer to the treasure she has come to find. Slowly, she creeps into the area where prison cells are filled with aliens whom Ilem is holding captive in the Floating City. They are even lower than Trailers in the eyes of Ilem's Elite Squad.

The Galactic Council has held these opponents for the execution of disciplinary warrants for decades, confined to living in 8' x 9' sweat boxes with no light, mattress, or running water. All they had was shit to keep them warm once they became desperate enough to smear it on their skin. Urine eventually made for a fragrant and superb beverage.

Every society has them: the lowest of the low, the dregs, the Outcasts, aka Ilem's prisoners. All they had to do was bow to the Galactic Council when the powerful celestials served warrants. Instead of complying with the Galactic Council's mandates, these prisoners sought to overturn their rule.

Their price? Now, and forever more, they pay for their opposition to the Galactic Council by being compelled to endure never-ending torture, toil, and castigation. It is fair to say they are fodder for universal slavery, sold into unfamiliar worlds, in some places to be beaten by their captors, some areas eaten, but in all places first to be driven mad. This panoply of sufferers' many faces bears the scars of centuries of torture at the hands of the Galactic Council.

The female transhuman medical tech working in the operating room after Sage invaded the Blood Bowl arena is still in the lab, working feverishly to meet her quota of conversions for the day. Limbs of creatures formerly alive dangle from pinchers connected to operating tables above her head. Other med techs shift gears and activate various devices to program more transhumans to serve at the will of their Lord Ilem.

A more locked-in cell guard quickly detects Sage when she tries to sneak outside the lab, unlike her first foray into the Floating City when she went undetected.

When the cell guard sees Sage, he immediately yells for her to surrender. But she does not. Instead, Sage crouches and then rolls forward toward the charging guard. Stopping within two feet of the cell guard, Sage pulls out her hand cannon and shoots him center mass. Sage slams the pistol into the jaw of the next cell guard running up the hallway, then pulls the trigger as he falls to the ground at her feet. Blam!

The medical tech whom Sage has watched more than once mercilessly and shamefully slice and dice creatures for their parts like Mengele tries to escape the room. Sage shoots at the medical tech but misses. She fires again, and the pesky tech ducks underneath the bullets. Bam.

The medical tech fires a laser pistol at Sage to keep her at bay. Bffzzzzttt. Summoning upon her skill of converting the auras around her into an impregnable shield, Sage creates a forcefield that causes the laser blast to ricochet and strikes the medical tech. Ping. Bang! When the fatal encounter ends, Sage returns to the Outcasts, keys in hand, to relieve their suffering.

More than 1200 miles from the battlefield and the other scrimmages that suddenly drag the Floating City into chaos, Naihal and her female lover are alone. Only a few hours have passed since their lover, Gorman, left to join the fight against Ilem's Elite Squadron.

Instead of warning Ilem about Gorman's plan, Naihal dismisses Gorman's contribution to the brawl as minimal, no more worthy of Ilem's attention than a bug whining in his ear. She is more content to meld with her remaining lover, Tirzah, and listen to the eclectic melody of vintage jazz as it teasingly sways around the room.

The embrace of the music holds Naihal in her seat in an oversized chair, resting in front of a bay window in her mansion. Lovingly, Naihal strokes and kisses Tirzah's snaky hair.

Tirzah, kneeling at Naihal's feet, asks her, "Should we go after Gorman?" Before she can respond, Naihal excitedly pounces from the chair and nervously yells to Tirzah, "Oh shit, by The All, Gorman was right. Something is coming this way, and I sense who it is."

The windows of Naihal's house begin shaking. Confused by Naihal's sudden alarm, Tirzah asks, "What is that noise?" With a stern look in her eyes, Naihal warns Tirzah, "We're too late! It's Hyle!"

Hyle crash lands as a massive, flaming meteor on Earth in the Mississippi River next to New Orleans. Starting merely as a ripple from Hyle's splash into the water causes a nineteen-foot storm surge to rise and break through New Orleans' flood walls. The rising wall of liquid smashes through levees and rips apart homes. The water from Hyle's violent splash engulfs Naihal's house. Boom.

The Diwan of Matter rises from the river, reshaping his fifty-foot body into the concrete his hand touches as he climbs out from the River. Hyle calls out to Naihal, "I am here now, Naihal. No one will protect you from me!"

Naihal's shortened horns grow out of and lengthen from her head. The absolute blackness covered by her gloves creeps up her arms to her shoulders. Storm clouds begin to amass and grow in size and intensity, mirroring the angry shadows forming around the Diwan of Darkness.

Naihal casts a darkness spell inside her house to keep Hyle at bay. Naihal chants the words, "Wave of darkness, surge of force," and after she finishes uttering those words, a burst of black light blows a hole in the wall in the basement of her home, which allows Tirzah and Naihal to reach an escape vessel.

In less time than the two hours it used to take passenger jets to fly 1200 miles, the disruptive ripple and tremor from Hyle's impact with the ground triggers landslides and avalanches across the land within seconds. The Earth cracks hundreds of miles away to the battlefield, leaving deep trenches segregating the elite from the poor—rumble roar. Several dozen on the battlefield stumble into the ditch as if it is a grave spontaneously opening its trap to consume them, marrow, and bone.

The fight between Ilem, Kol and the Purified continues. Kol effortlessly flings one of the Purified out of his way while impaling one of the Purified with a broadsword. Ilem hovers on his throne above the fray, blasting his enemies and laughing, pleased by all the destruction he ignited by his lust for power, "Ha, ha, ha … you are no match for me."

Scores of bodies pile below him, including many of his troops. Instead of efficiently extinguishing the small rebellion, Ilem only watches from on high to bask in this phase of his conquest. Occasionally, for his amusement, Ilem casts jagged shards of light like daggers at the Purified, leaving a disjointed line of death wavering across the frontline.

The clashing armies of Purified and Lopers against the Elite Squadron zombified Corrupted, and AI drones produce more casualties on the side of those who refuse to surrender to Ilem's rule. His trained forces overrun the disorganized rebels and the daring who risk their lives to challenge him.

Close to where Ilem is majestically hovering above the melee, Sage appears on the top of a hill wearing the amiable mask of a healthy Pu Kwon Lee. While listening to the conquering glory of conquest, Ilem's ears halt when he hears a familiar voice shout, "Devon!"

He is captivated by the brightest light he almost let slip through his fingers. Stunned, he declares, "By The All," as he stands up on his throne to look upon his dear, Pu Kwon. His thoughts fix on her, the sounds of battle bowing lower in his ears.

Pu Kwon holds out an oleander flower toward Ilem until the flower transforms into tarnished metal in her hand. A platinum, silvery-white and shiny trail slowly glides from the flower into Pu Kwon's waiting hand and continues up her arm to her shoulders, neck, and down to her chest, thighs, and legs. Eventually, Sage transforms her image into a metallic sculpted statue of Pu Kwon posed like an avenging angel amid a gory battlefield.

Shock overwhelms Ilem at the sight of his love transforming into a transhuman. He shouts, "No! Please, no!" His cry is answered by the growing rumble of the Outcasts as they emerge from behind Pu Kwon and begin flooding the battlefield. Pu Kwon drops the oleander flower from her hand. Reacting to the falling flower like a flag waved to spark a drag race, the Outcasts rush toward Ilem with aerial weapons loaded, screaming, "Get him!"

Several of the Purified leap up to grab Ilem by his heels to yank him from his throne. While he seems vulnerable, Juno shoots flames from his flamethrower in Ilem's direction. Even more surprising, the Moji, friends only to themselves, stream out of the ground, fully materializing into a deadly force attacking Ilem's army. Ilem screams, "No, betrayal? Pu Kwon, no!"

While this battle rages, Hyle rises above New Orleans, looking like a mass of concrete, metal, and decades of debris brought up from the bottom of the Mississippi River. Explosions resound from Naihal's mansion as her escape vessel bursts out of the basement of her mansion. Boom. Hyle attacks Naihal by manipulating gravity to push the ground up and at Naihal's escape vehicle as she tries to flee. He then warns her, "Try to run, Mistress of Darkness! I will find you even in your beloved shadows!"

Naihal's escape vehicle collides with the street. Crash! While trying to escape with Naihal, flying slivers of glass impale Tirzah in the back. She cries out in agony to Naihal, "Ahhhh, save me," but Naihal is too late.

Naihal, with horns extended, is silhouetted in all black as she walks out of the flames, carrying Tirzah's listless body in her arms. The celestial wails and screams to release the bulging knot of anguish that wants to close her throat, "Why, Hyle! Tirzah was innocent!"

The Diwan of Darkness removes one glove to touch the asphalt. Shadowy figures begin to rise from the ground as an army of darkness spawns at Naihal's command. Naihal's army of darkness members carry Tirzah away from the burning spacecraft. Naihal's horns have grown to their most extended length as she defiantly yells back at Hyle, "You'll pay for this!"

In response, Hyle throws a large chunk of brick from a fallen building at Naihal's army of darkness. Boom! Undaunted, Naihal's shadowy minions swarm Hyle like an army of agitated black ants. To shake them off, Hyle burrows into the ground and disappears, leaving a massive hole in the center of Bourbon Street. Rumble roar! The large hole Hyle has ripped in the street collapses as he burrows away from the landscape of destruction he has left in his wake.

The concrete collapses along a stretch of Bourbon Street as Hyle burrows underground away from New Orleans, leaving behind fire and destruction. Kadam! The almost rhythmic sound of glass clattering against brick and steel strikes the ground behind Hyle like a joyful jazz procession through the otherwise mournful Big Easy.

Naihal falls to her knees, grieving over losing her lover, Tirzah.

Back where Ilem's forces clash with rebels who challenge his dominance, Ilem descends into the battlefield to find Pu Kwon. Most of the fighters scatter from the area, frantically pushing and fighting anyone in their way to find safety from the Diwan of Light's ire. The sloshing sound of entrails under metal boots causes some retreating from Ilem into mounds of dead bodies to stumble over each other.

Landing on the ground, Ilem projects a circle of blazing light around him that incinerates all those brave enough to charge toward him. On the edge of the forcefield of light, Kol takes on a Purified and an Outsider trying to attack Ilem.

The Jovian, whom Kol eyeballs, lowers his rail gun to correct his sightline to strike the Diwan of Light. The Jovian squints his right eye, staring down the sight, while keeping the other eye closed to allow the Jovian a straight shot at Ilem.

A big bang, bang sound booms from the rail gun at Mach 7, creating a rippling supersonic shock wave that combatants near Ilem hear and feel screaming past them. The loud sound of gunfire swallows the cries and wails of thousands wounded in this clash. As the Jovian reloads his weapon to launch another shot at Ilem, Kol slams his khopesh into the Jovian's back, knocking him to the ground and leaving him bloodied but not fatally wounded.

Another brave warrior, a greenish-gray-skinned Martian, kneels within sixty feet of Ilem to steady his hands and nerves as he concentrates on firing a ground-to-ground rocket-propelled grenade to destroy Ilem. Ahead of the Martian firing another shot, Kol hurls a round metal shield at the Martian, striking him in his left arm. The blow is powerful enough to knock the Martian off balance and cause him to lose his grasp on his weapon.

Ilem opens the forcefield of light that protects him, allowing Kol to step closer. Ilem, for once, turns to Kol to offer his hand to the High Guard in gratitude for his timely service. He refers to Kol as "My shield." A resolute Kol extends his hand to Ilem, offering a firm clutch to his master. Ilem is again stunned that one of his trusted loyalists has turned like a worm when Kol directs his offense to Ilem and shouts, "I am … no longer … your shield or your slave."

After declaring freedom and defiance, Kol bashes Ilem across his chest with his khopesh, laser humming, causing an opening to appear diagonally across Ilem's flesh. Instead of blood, the cut releases a ray of light that is so intense that it momentarily blinds Kol. The light shines between Ilem's fingers as he touches his wound, exclaiming to Kol, "Traitors! All humans are traitors!"

To reinforce his troops, Ilem touches his gold and silver helmet to command Victor to break free of the Dyson Sphere. Ilem says, "Victor, my child! Rise against my enemies!" The Dyson Sphere instantly explodes, and Victor Garin, the first fully functional transhuman, emerges. His reputation as "Ruka Smertik", or "Death's Hand", precedes him, as does the flying shrapnel jettisoned when the Dyson Sphere explodes. Boom!!!

After several years incubating in the Dyson Sphere, Victor's appearance has drastically changed again. Although no longer the handsome rake, Victor has been reborn as an android made of pearl-white metal. As he descends onto the battlefield, Victor confidently crows, "Who shall I kill first?" He aims his angry eye at Kol, the first victim of his attack.

Two Purified shoot Victor with rail guns built into their bodies. BANG, BANG! Defiantly, Victor spreads out his arm as if to take in an advancing lover. When the laser blasts slam into Victor's metallic body, he absorbs the energy into it and then ejects it from his hands. Zzzztttt! Both of the Purified burst open from the spray of fire. Victor brushes the smoke from his chest, then boasts, "Panguite endothermic metals, like the Floating City itself."

Victor shoots another blast at a large Purified group, yelling, "Feel my power!" Zzzzttttt! Victor's blast immediately slays most of the group. Bada boom!!!

Kol runs as Victor pursues, bowling others out of his way. Below Victor's deltoids, four-foot wings expand and jut out along his shoulders, lifting him above the fray and closer to swooping down on Kol to finish their tussle. The sharp-edged wings disembowel a retreating Trailer.

Sage, still appearing to be an automated Pu Kwon, fires her hand cannon at a group of the Elite Squadron and the Sect. Despite her valor, Ilem's Death Squad, who band together, outgun her when they combine to launch a concentrated attack. Bam bam! Sage covers behind a mound of dead bodies smothered by a blanket of flies. Bam bam!!!!

The Elite Squadron and Sect fire back at Sage, shooting through the corpses that flank her rear. Bam, zzzttt. Organs spurt and splatter on Sage's back as gunshots cut through them. She fires at them to fan them back, striking two attackers. Bam, bam.

Her black explosive disks also provide ample defense against her attackers. The three bombs that Sage tosses indiscriminately over her shoulder explode near them, blowing most of them to pieces. Kaboom.

Ilem hears an explosion and a commotion behind him, then spins to lock eyes on the area where the noise came. Various human and alien factions that hid from Ilem have come to attack. Boom!!! The Negearians join the fight, including Naihal's male servant, Gorman, who rallies his people by encouraging them, "Kill Ilem! For Negearia!" His Negearians brothers respond in their native tongue, "Ot Ilem det," or "Death to Ilem!"

Ilem flies up in the air to prepare for the Negearians attack. As he climbs higher in the air, his command of all things made of sentient metal allows him to sense Sledge flying away from Earth, away from the battlefield, and finally to safety. Ilem laughs sarcastically, "The Negearians have more heart than that coward. Run, boy, run! Wherever you go, you will still be mine!" Confident that victory is firmly in hand, Ilem flies down to the battlefield, swinging a sword of pure light to impale attackers.

Far away in the opening sky, Sledge appears on the horizon riding a flying motorcycle as an immense cloud of dust trails behind him. Vroom! Soldiers and rebels on the battlefield can faintly hear the thumping of music, as well. The radio blares, *"Preacher man ... Heaven is under the earth ... the story has never been told."* ♪ ♪ ♪ ♪

As he revs the motorcycle's engine, Sledge hears the faint lure of a child's voice, turning his vision toward the ground. The familiar voice climbs into Sledge's ears, brain, and emotions. Igniting the Omnis probe, the memories of who is calling to him create an image in Sledge's mind's eye of the little girl brutally killed by the Emperors of Death. The little girl calls out to Sledge, "Please help me! Please don't go!"

Her desperate plea for help causes Sledge to hesitate from ascending through Earth's stratosphere. His eyes narrow as he focuses on a distant star to guide him away from the hell Earth has become. He knows this is the moment he has fought for, longed for, and now has in reach: freedom from oppression, freedom from humiliation, freedom from the loss of loved ones.

With this "victory" in sight, Sledge sets his eyes on the bright compass before him, turning the vehicle's handlebars back to a course to safety into outer space. Although he struggles against the tugging on his heart, Sledge is determined to escape Earth's turmoil.

Still crouching behind dead bodies riveted by gunfire, Sage concentrates on projecting one more voice into Sledge's head, her own. In a calm voice that belies the situation on the field, Sage whispers to Sledge from afar, "Only this moment counts. Nothing else matters." Sage allows the sound of gunfire and groaning to cut through her desperate words to unlock Sledge's closed mind.

Sledge cannot resist wanting to be more than a Spectator in this decisive moment. Instead of sailing through the strata to safety, he telekinetically straps his wrist and hands to the flying motorcycle's handlebars. The radio screams, "Get up!" ♪ ♪ ♪ ♪ As if swaying in time with Marley's uplifting song, Sledge pilots the cycle down from space to a collision course with the Earth, with at least one hundred other flying motorcycles he telekinetically pulls behind him—vroom vroom vroom.

Mentally scrolling through his choices, Sledge deliberates on how to end his kamikaze mission, "Sentient metal needs a host to connect to Ilem. No matter the cost, I gotta cut it loose …" Sledge accelerates the flying motorcycle's descent into Earth's lower atmosphere. As he does, he astral projects his true essence into the sky.

Ilem shields his eyes to see what is falling through the air. All around him, plummeting motorcycles come into view. The radio continues to blare Marley's song, "…Stand Up." Boom! ♪ ♪ ♪ ♪ Cycles explode as they hit the ground. Sage and Kol jump out of the way to avoid injury, unlike many fighters on the field who are too slow to avoid harm. Kaboom. ♪ ♪ ♪ ♪

Sledge rejoins his body cast just as it gets close to striking the ground near Ilem. He assures himself that his plummet into the fray is worth the risk, "…to be free!" The voice from the radio assures him, "Life is your right." Boom! ♪ ♪ ♪ ♪ Sledge's astral presence rejoins his corporeal body moments before it strikes the ground strapped to the flying motorcycle. After it does, Sledge rolls to his feet and exclaims, *"Booyaka!"* Kaboom!

Ilem rises above everyone and begins to radiate raw energy. He blasts flying motorcycles out of the sky, casting shrapnel into the crowds, killing several of those fighting on all sides. Thippp boom!

He flies into the fight at the speed of light and begins indiscriminately blasting the Purified and the Corrupted. Zzzzztttt. Behind him, a swarm of AI drones follow Ilem into battle.

Sledge fights his way to Ilem. A kick to the head of one attacker and a knee to the skull of another mark Sledge's path. His aggressive pursuit causes several more of those attacking Sledge to suffer broken bones, collapsed metal limbs, and injuries that will gradually lead to death, if not from sepsis from long-term injuries, then immediately from perfuse blood loss.

As Sledge gallantly approaches Ilem, the Diwan of Light touches his hand to his helmet again. Suddenly, Sledge's robotic body begins breaking at its seams, falling apart from recent battle wounds. One of the compartments on his chest uncontrollably starts leaking sentient metal. Sledge's audible response to the sudden loss of control is, "Urgh."

Ilem concentrates on increasing his control of Sledge's body movements. Ilem declares, "I have suffered enough fools, wasted enough years with humans!" He controls Sledge's body movements to force him to attack Juno from behind.

Juno is unaware of the pending attack, facing the other direction with his blowtorch. Sledge lands the first four steps in the Five Fingers of Death technique against Juno's back and neck. Crack. Sledge unwillingly finishes Juno off by landing the last move against the back of Juno's neck. Juno screams in agony, "Argh!" As he collapses, Juno shoots a last flame from his flamethrower, setting several combatants on fire. His dead body crumples to the ground at Sledge's feet.

Ilem warns Sledge, "We're not done yet, boy!" Under Ilem's control, Sledge crosslines a Negearian. "Ahhh!" Ilem forces Sledge to seize the Negearian by the neck. Although he tries to resist Ilem's power, Sledge is not the master of his body's actions. Sledge screams in anguish as he snaps the Negearian's neck, "No!" Ilem laughs at Sledge as he struggles for control, "Ha, ha!"

Ilem's forces continue to amass, blocking Sledge's path to their leader. The Diwan of Light senses the tide turn in his favor when a horde of his minions converge on Sledge. Ilem commands his troops, "Destroy them, my children! Every one of them!" Sledge fights the Sect using his martial arts skills while calling out to Ilem, "Rainfall *pon di* just and unjust, Ilem!" The Diwan scoffs at Sledge's frail determination as he hovers above the fray, safe from real danger.

As troops fight Victor on a distant part of the battlefield, Sledge braces himself for Ilem to attack again. Ilem vainly suggests to Sledge, "I have the power here, boy! I have been present from the beginning of time. You are less than an infant to me."

Ilem continues to use his command over sentient metal to control Sledge's every move. Sledge tries to resist Ilem's control but is still powerless. Ilem declares, "You are nothing but a puppet to me." While defending himself against Ilem's attacks, Sledge focuses some of his attention on another part of the battlefield to shoot Kol with a red, laser-like beam from the Omnis probe. Kol yells, "Aah," as Sledge's beam strikes him from behind.

Energized by his accurate attack against Kol, Sledge regains his footing to deliver a killing blow. Ilem swiftly overtakes Sledge to assault and pummel Sledge with a combination of left, right and left fists. Bam bam, pow! Ilem heckles Sledge, "You want more," as Sledge collapses to the ground coughing sentient metal that has changed from black and green in color to a deep red and purple. Sledge, "Aaaa ... ugh!"

Ilem swoops down on Sledge, landing a series of more punches. Boom! When Ilem lands a devastating uppercut to Sledge's chin, Sledge is severely injured and nearly knocked unconscious. The intense blow knocks Sledge into a throng of transhumans fighting for Ilem. Blam! Sledge shouts in return, "Eeeehh ..." Ilem's attack renders Sledge unconscious, entirely vulnerable to whatever fate the Diwan of Light has in store for him: Sledge's extermination or enslavement readily at hand.

A distance across the battlefield, Ilem's Death Squad has Sage pinned down and running short of bullets for her hand cannon. Her plight worsens as more attackers join those already firing at her. She strategizes to herself, "No time for long-range battle. Even with new weaponry, many fatal fights are up close, hand-to-hand encounters. I may have no choice but to rise from this pit."

An unfired hand grenade catches her eye as she scans the pit for anything she can use to deter Ilem's forces. She strains to grab the explosive without exposing herself to attacks, then lithely flips the grenade into the circle of soldiers attacking her. The resounding boom is just enough distraction to allow Sage to turn invisible and slip around the raging battle undetected.

Dead Outcasts and Purified wallow in patches of excrement and blood around Sage and other parts of the expansive battlefield. As more combatants fall, warriors rush in to continue fighting for their respective sides. On both sides of the equation, war takes countless lives.

An Elite Squadron Member orders Gabba and the other Trailers to join Ilem's forces to finish off the Purified. The Elite Scout yells, "Trailers finish them off. Attack!" Instead of marching lockstep to those orders, Gabba yells, "Fellahs, are you radged? Why are you fucking fighting for the Galactic Council of clowns?" Int' past, we were hard-working dads and mams. We had our dreams. Before they fucking fucked our worlds, the fuckers!"

Gabba continues exhorting the Trailers to fight against Ilem. The Elite Scout takes a plasma pistol to silence Gabba's insolent tirade. Gabba, "If we sell out t'Galactic Council or run, eckers, we'll be slaves forever …" Forcefully, the Elite Scout orders Gabba, "You shut your mouth!"

To reinforce his directives to the usually submissive Acquilite, the Elite Scout pistol whips Gabba across the face, then taunts him to rub salt in the wounds, "You know your rank, you piece of dog shit."

Gabba's repeated huffing carries the sound of someone ensnared in a crippling panic attack. The rapid breathing causes Gabba's chest to expand and contract like an old accordion, accompanied by gurgling and wailing. His arms stiffen as if rigor has struck his body before destiny drags him into a waiting grave.

After his stomach stops churning and twisting, Gabba's once baggy soldier uniform gradually tightens around his biceps and his belly bloats and hardens like a beer keg. The ghastly, parasitic mouths on his palms protrude from gaping holes, and the orange sticky, blob-like substance foams from his hands.

When the Elite Scout storms over to Gabba to kick him while he is down, his feet suddenly stop when he looks closer at the footstool risen to a fearsome foot soldier. Gabba's puny arms are solid like hardened steel, while his stomach is engorged like a 20-gallon beer barrel. In a deep, thundering voice, Gabba demands of the Elite Scout, "Don't try to run now!" Before the Elite Scout can get away, Gabba propels a massive clump of orange slime at the Elite Scout's feet, gluing him in place.

Gabba easily swats the Elite Scout more than thirty feet away with the back of his hand and throws a sticky, bluish ball of slime against the Elite Scout's mouth to shut him the fuck up. Bloop. The Elite Scout drops his weapon, trying in vain to pull away the goo that is suffocating him. Gabba whips his sawn-off Winchester Riot Gun out to unload the entire clip into the Elite Squadron Member's sternum. Blam!

Gabba turns to all the other Trailers near him and exclaims, "You daft 'apeth will never be free running with our missus and nippers. We can be Spectators in our self-destruction or participants in our survival. It's owt or nowt! We gotta bray Ilem!"

Gabba raises his rock-hard fists, the sawn-off Riot Gun in one hand, his trusty laser rifle in another, and broadswords in the other hands. A clumping orange substance fastens all the weapons in place, locking them in his hands as determination locks in his eyes. Gabba shouts, "Freedom, lads!"

Trailers respond as one, "Freedom!"

END OF CHAPTER 19

Chapter 20

The Glass Warrior

I am the warrior.
I have fought the world in search of triumph
I have flown the air on battered wings
And see the world through flowing eyes.

I am man.

Please do not confuse me with the strong and valiant lords
Of glory who have walked before me.

I am not strong.

I am like crystal glass
So wanting to be held
So fragile to be touched.

In all, I am
What life has made me
No more and struggling to be no less.

Like the world, I am a dream
Dreaming that life is more than what it seems
More than an endless battle.

Like the light of the morning dawn
My heart burns bright.

For I am the warrior
I am every man.

Blood Bowl II

Like the besieged Purified, Ilem has Sledge beaten and bloodied on the ground and is ready to strike a final blow. Without warning, Kol intervenes by knocking Ilem away with a bullrush, interrupting Ilem's climactic ending of his fight with Sledge.

Ilem's avenging angel, Victor, dives down in hot pursuit of Kol and forestalls the anticipated showdown between Kol and Ilem. Ilem shoots Kol with a massive burst of fire, taking advantage of Victor's rapid decline and momentarily distracting Kol. Ilem, "I will have no more of your treachery! Victor, finish him."

A surge of energy from Victor strikes Kol in his side. Victor grabs Kol from behind and flings him away from Ilem. Kol responds as he violently sails away, "Aaaa ..." He lands into a crowd fighting in the combat zone as he stumbles back. He opens one of the compartments built into his forearm. Out pops a laser gun that springs directly into Kol's hand. Kol grips the laser gun in his right hand and fires three shots at Victor. Zzzttt.

Effortlessly, Victor swats the laser shots away like flies. Victor taunts Kol by stating, "Pitiful! You don't deserve to be my Lord's High Guard."

Victor stomps over bodies to attack Kol, still lying on the ground. Kol screams in pain as Victor rips off his right arm. Kol howls, "ARGH!" Blood squirts from the gaping wound on the side of his shoulder. Barely able to raise his arm, Kol manages to fire one more crossbow from his left forearm against Victor. Stitstitstitstit. Brazenly, Kol tells Victor, "You talk too much!"

Victor grabs his throat with both hands like he is choking when tiny needles wedge into his mouth. Victor involuntarily chirps, "Gawk!" With only a moment to intervene, Sledge uses his psionic abilities to slow Victor down and then tosses him in the air away from the prone Kol. A pool of blood soaks the ground around the former football star's body. Sledge hits Victor with a spin kick and palm strike, followed by a straight kick to the belly and a clinched fist to Victor's chin.

In concert with yelling his battle cry, "Hyah," Sledge socks Victor with a bolo punch combining the wind-up and wide circular motion of that blow with a stern and stiff uppercut. Weakened, Victor crumpled to the ground.

Feet away, Kol calls Sledge his brother in Spanish. "*Sangre*, dap me up." Kol mimics the handshake Iggy and Sledge have done hundreds of times, requiring them to link thumbs, slide them back to link fingers, then flap, float, and fist pump.

Sledge runs to aid Kol after realizing this mortally wounded soldier is none other than Iggy. Iggy greets Sledge with a labored, "*Hermano, no lo haga. I migliori eroi sono invisibili.*" *I am L'Enigma.*"[139] Sage shifts her body back to her normal appearance as she fights to Sledge's side. Arriving unscathed, Sage reassures Sledge, "I'm here. I'll take care of him. Go!"

As Sledge heads off in the distance to find Ilem, a fearsome-looking Sect challenges Sage, and a small battalion of Sect androids guard the Sect's back. The Sect member shouts, "It's you and me, bitch!" Sage picks up a wasp injection short sword from the body of a fallen combatant to defend herself, then answers, "I ain't your mother or any other kind of bitch. Let's dance!"

The Sect soldier swings a massive, glowing short sword with both hands at Sage so close he nearly cuts her in half. But the Sect member narrowly misses connecting with the infinity orb as Sage disappears, leaving only the orb levitating.

---

[139] "Brother don't hurt him. The best heroes are invisible."

Confused, the Sect soldier yells, "What …?" Its blade connects with Sage's wasp-injection short sword falling freely after Sage turns into the orb. Clang!

Her solid hand rematerializes below the Sect's guard chin just in time to catch the wasp injection short sword before it hits the ground. Seamlessly, she raises the blade of her weapon to and through the Sect's tender throat. The Sect soldier emits an audible "Gurgle."

A pulsing flash of energy charges through Sage's body to the wasp injection short sword and out of the Sect's head, causing a devastating and loud explosion of metal, flesh, and bones. Kablamm. Sage pulls the wasp injection short sword out of what is left of the Sect guard's head while sarcastically remarking, "Fuck yeah! It's a keeper."

While she battles the Sect soldier, its troops fan out to encompass her and launch sneak attacks. Before they can do so, Gabba charges to her aid. He splatters the eight Sect who sought to overwhelm Sage with goo that fastens them to the ground and leaves some stuck together. Gabba wades through most of the incapacitated Sect, quickly dispatching five with slashes and strikes from his broadsword. Sage subdues the rest with her nifty toy and handy hand cannon.

She nods to Gabba, expressing appreciation and acceptance of a comrade in arms, multiple arms, to be exact.

After fighting through other hordes of Ilem's forces, Sage makes her way to Kol, whose face is masked by pain, then says, *"Está bien, lo entiendo."*[140] Sage closes Kol's anguished eyes as he dies on the battlefield. In search of help, she scrolls the battlefield and stops her gaze sharp when she sees Sledge steaming forward to strike Victor down. Sage casts an invisible barrier between them to prevent Sledge from bashing Victor into the next world, shouting, "No! It's Iggy!"

Gabba comes over to help Sage and Victor safely, telling Sledge, "Sledge, I'll look after them. I'll see'um safe. I have a ride ready!" Quickly, Gabba helps Victor to his feet.

The more robust, heroic Gabba picks up Victor to help him get to the Ilem's ASR9 flagship vessel that the Acquilite stole from the Floating City's docking

---

[140] "Okay, I understand."

bay. Sage runs with Gabba, passing the clanging swords and rattling throats to safety. No one gets in Gabba's way after seeing the meek Acquilite at least twice his normal size tearing the limbs off transhumans who mistakenly challenged him.

Away from that fray, Ilem punches Sledge in the back of his head and thinks he has the andabata beaten for good. Standing over Sledge, Ilem brags, "You never had a chance to defeat me! I am a true child of The All!" Ilem begins to generate energy for a massive, final blast to kill Sledge. "Now I'll cure you of your wretched manhood for good!"

Combatants across the battlefield feel the ground quake and hear a loud rumbling sound rapidly advancing. Rumble roar! The clouds that hover above the battlefield churn into a strong storm. Just as Ilem has gathered a massive globe of radiation, fire, and light three times the size of the Dyson Sphere, Hyle's powerful hand bursts through the ground to clobber Ilem from behind. Boom!!!

The radiation surge from Ilem roars into the sky as the Diwan of Light recoils from Hyle's vicious attack, "Oof." The ground makes room for Hyle's emergence as he climbs out of the hole that has expanded to accommodate his girth. Ilem lies staggered in front of Hyle.

The storm intensifies as Hyle's booming voice drowns out the moans and cries of fallen soldiers. Hyle, "I know you have my child, Ilem! Tell me where she is, or I will pound you into atoms!"

Hyle scoops Ilem's entire body up in one hand. With the other free hand, he pounds Ilem in the face repeatedly until he knocks the helmet off of Ilem's head. Bam!

This mighty helmet of command rolls within inches of Sledge as he lies on the ground bleeding. Ilem squirms and struggles to free himself from Hyle's powerful grasp, but he cannot. Hyle bellows, "You took my Pyron from me. Now, I'll take what you love." Between Sledge and Hyle lies Ilem's helmet, the key to the salvation of Sledge's mind from Ilem's control, and the transformation of Sledge's physical body. Sledge knows it, but he has trepidations.

Hyle orders Sledge, "Pick it up, human. Seize power over the sentient!" Sledge shields his eyes from the sun's glare poking through the roaring storm over

Hyle's broad shoulders. Sledge, "*Respect,* Hyle. What if I do?" Hyle lowers his marauding face closer to Sledge lying on the ground as Ilem squirms in Hyle's grasp. Hyle asks Sledge, "Do you know who I am?" Sledge calmly and coolly answers, "A leader of the Galactic Council."

Ilem tries to push out of Hyles's grip. Ignoring the squirming, mortal flesh in his hand, Hyle tells Sledge, "Only The All and Time have existed longer than me."

The helmet lies in front of Sledge. Sledge rises to one knee near it. Hyle says to him, "Touching that helmet will give you power over all things made of sentient metal. Total control." Sledge kneels in front of the helmet, contemplating what to do. Hyle warns him, "You can do whatever you want with it except betray The All or me." Calculating his options, Sledge asks, "*Anyting*?" Stepping two steps closer, Hyle towers over Sledge. Hyle, "Yes, anything."

Sledge reaches for the helmet with renewed confidence that his next action will not result in Hyle squishing him like a soda can. He begins to stand with the helmet in his hands as Hyle continues admonishing him about this decision. Hyle, "Remember, obey The All and answer when I summon. The rest of your existence is for you to choose." Sledge pledges to Hyle, "*As a god!*"[141]

He places the helmet on his head. Agitation of the Omnis probe causes his body to twitch and gyrate uncontrollably. Sentient metal projects from his mouth and nose like the blood of a pugilist who has taken one too many head blows. Sledge's heart pounds and contracts irregularly from high voltages of electricity that seethe through him. An overwrought expression on Sledge's face reveals the riveting agony coursing through his body.

Suddenly, the power and energy generated from the helmet ignite through Sledge's containment suit. Violently, his unclothed body finally bursts out of his body cast with a loud boom. Inch by inch, his body transitions from sentient metal and earth's hardest minerals to the flesh of a fully formed, naked, and vulnerable human. Now, with confidence and a sense of dominion, Sledge acknowledges the words he has hesitated to let leave his lips.

---

[141] "Swear to the truth of this."

After staring at his bare feet, he yells at the top of his lungs, "I am more than man; I am Omnis!" With those final words of acceptance, Sledge's third eye erupts, and the colors of the chakras engulf his naked body. The contours of his face change as it becomes more muscular, hardened, and intense.

Thunderous squalls furiously roar at one another while lighting the sky with fireworks. Through all the commotion, Sledge hears wavering voices proclaim, "Behold, a bottomless vessel of consciousness filled to the brink and overflowing."

The storms become more violent as Sledge lifts his hands to the sky, allowing rain to wash blood down his fingers. Stinging bands of lightning grab hold of Sledge's outstretched hand, leaving a streaming bolt of lightning in it.

Sledge grips the bolt and hurls it at his stunned enemies. Those not immediately killed when Sledge strikes them with the jolting lightning experience excruciating pain. The crackling beam of lightning slams into the "lucky" survivors, leaving them moaning on the ground from burst arteries in their brains, heart attacks, and broken bones. Other warriors lay paralyzed on the ground, staring up into Barabbas-black skies.

As lightning trails off Sledge's hands, the raised wounds that have scarred his tattooed compass for years heal.

Hyle throws Ilem to the ground in front of Sledge. He then turns to Sledge to tell him, "He's all yours. But your debt is not fully paid yet, Ilem." Hyle charges toward the Floating City. Shaken by the hurdling mass of flesh and stone, the Deck Commander orders weapons fired at Hyle, "Ready weapons! Raise the endothermic shields. Unload all weapons! Unload them, goddammit!"

The endothermic shields rise along the sides and top of the Floating City to shield its glass dome. Like the expansive wings of a condor, four hyperspeed boosters expand from the undercarriage of the Floating City. Defensive weapons extend out along the sides and front of the space city. Whirl rrrrippp! As the vessel accelerates and diverts from the battlefield, Hyle leaps over 2,000 feet into the Floating City, causing a violent fusion chain reaction that booms across the sky.

The residents of the Floating City run from the destruction away from the Central Court, including Baxter Robinson, the Judas reporter. Several are injured and struggle to survive the fires that rampage out of control.

On the field, Ilem blasts away sentients near him with his bright energy daggers, then rubs his throat to release it from the painful throbbing he feels. Ilem mocks Sledge, "You insolent human. I am more man than you will ever be."

Inexplicably, Sledge responds to Ilem, "*Quiza. Buh,* I do *nuh* want *tuh* find out." Raw energy begins to crackle around Ilem's hands. His throne lifts from the ground and slowly glides near him, waiting for him to ascend. Ilem cackles at

Sledge's sudden submission, "I knew you would yield. Wise decision. Perhaps you are worthy of becoming my new High Guard."

Sledge swears, "By Jah, I will be loyal *tuh dis* calling from now until *di* end of time." Sledge entreats Ilem, "I can fight until *yuh* overrun me, or I can barter *tuh* escape *dis* goddamn planet. I only ask one *ting*, Lord Ilem. Please spare *mi* friends. For *dat*, Lord Ilem, I'm your body *an* soul."

Ilem cannot contain his gleeful laughter at Sledge's pitiful attempt to beg for mercy, "*Sine die, sine limitatione.* Finally, you bend the knee and beg me to spare sheep I prefer to slaughter. Spare them, you ask. Fine, fine! They will be welcome additions to my collection of Outcasts. And, Sage, I will make a special present of her to my army to straddle on a well-laid bed."

Resigned to his fate, Sledge raises his hands above his head to convey to Ilem in the least threatening way that he surrenders to the Diwan of Light's superior, godly celestial powers. After removing the helmet from his head, Sledge dropkicks it just in front of Ilem's feet.

Ilem takes the helmet into his hands. Heartlessly, Ilem taunts Sledge for his surrender and sudden contrition, "This is my helmet, my power, my world. Soon the universe will kneel before me just like you." With that, Ilem proudly lowers the helmet on his golden locks, then slides it in place to adorn his cranium in silver and gold.

Ilem knows he can destroy not just Earth but, combined with his military, the Galactic Council. To demonstrate for all the universe to see, Ilem proclaims, "And now, feel my godly power over light, fused with the mighty power of this helmet of command. Behold, I am greater than The All! Children, we will rule forever!"

Once more, the heavens explode in response to Ilem's activation of the power in his hands. The clouds roll, the thunder ... wait, the thunder cracks a little ... What Ilem feels is a lot of nothing. The storm tears up with laughter that rains down on the mud and Ilem's head.

Sledge backs away from Ilem with his hands raised while keeping his steamy gaze in line with Ilem's sapphire eyes. This man, whom some have called the Last Man of Earth and others already call a legend, chuckles for a moment, then turns deadly serious. Sledge enlightens Ilem, "Hyle told *mi di* power is mine, weren't *yuh* listening or does cockiness wax *yuh* ears?" Sledge screams in Ilem's face, "*Mi* oath *tuh* Hyle I'll keep. But for anyone like *yuh*, I will be *di* scourge of *di* galaxy."

Ilem tries to use the helmet again, but nothing happens. No one moves, no one cowers. In turn, Sledge uses his new power over sentient matter to telekinetically pull the worthless helmet off of Ilem's head. Sledge proclaims, "*Der* is no power *der*. I am *di* power *yuh* sought. It is in me, not of me. I will be *di* damnation of all who oppose my survival *an di* rebirth of all my *bredren*."

His voice resonates in the air like thunder heaved from the heavens as he warns all to hear, "Serendipity may *hav* its day, *an* fate be fickle, *buh* legacy is not. If humans are damned, *dat's* a rock I can lay my head upon. Today I fight for humanity, not humans."

Purposefully placing both his palms around the helmet, Sledge presses the metal into the length of the Vision Staff. Sledge, "*Mi* vision is clear, Ilem. I will destroy *yuh Babylon dis* day."

Sledge sticks the Vision Staff into the ground and challenges Ilem, "Fight me like *di* man *yuh* wish *yuh* could be!" Sledge stretches his hands as far as they will go above his head, with his palms facing the sky and his third eye rapidly shifting through the conflicting thoughts and emotions that have cascaded in his mind all his life.

Disregarding the doubt that clouds his third eye, the fear that zaps his strength, Sledge opens the long, tall door in his mind that instantly empowers him to seize control over the mental processes and bodily functions of all creatures on Earth comprised of sentient metal. By pushing aside his many conflicting desires and concerns rivaling to dominate his mind, Sledge latches on accomplishing this one goal to halt the aggression of one race or culture against another. Rippling from Sledge's third eye to those on the battlefield and out to all others around the globe, a steady carpet of calming, light blue energy rolls across macabre meadows.

Like an expert puppeteer has commanded them to form a mortal arena wall, the motionless fighters come shoulder to shoulder to stand in a circle around Sledge and Ilem. Combatants on and around Warhawks from the West and East hemispheres momentarily cease their clash, silence pressing down on war's chaotic laughter as Sledge's power grows. The Floating City drifts slowly above the fray as if no one is piloting it.

Only the sound of crickets playing violins and the crescendo of crows cawing accompanies Sledge's reengagement with Ilem. Sledge quickly advances at Ilem to land a swift, left-right punching combination. Unsurprisingly, Ilem's light speed allows him to block the blows. Ilem jabs at Sledge's bobbing head from a southpaw stance then clocks him with a left hook. Down goes Sledge! Down goes Sledge!

Without further warning, bright circular lights burst into the air around Sledge and Ilem as if the stars had fallen from the sky to get a closer view of the action. And these are stars of a kind. The bobbleheads of Bogs and Steam genuflect up and down inside the levitating cameras spotlighting the immobile soldiers.

Our erstwhile Blood Bowl Earth 2050 sports reporters have returned to close out the show. Their Vatrajan host for the evening is no other than the shrewd businesswoman Madame Mayhem. Her Sirens & Wails Saloon is filled with aliens, transhumans, drunks, Wiggles, and Wags. A sign that indicates an invigorating "Beggar's Lot Tournament" is underway, hanging from the rafters.

Peter excitedly shouts into his mic, "This is the showdown for the ages. *Mano a Mano!* Will Sledge get up? Is this the end of his valiant struggle for survival? We do not know, but viewers, you better stay glued to your screens. This ain't a time to turn to Bambi!"

Jared throws in, "Ilem strolls toward Sledge, that's right, sentients. Through all the chaos and destruction on the battlefield, Ilem confidently walks to his fallen foe, giving Sledge a lasting lesson in hand-to-hand combat. I don't think anyone can stop him. Really folks, if our Vatrajan broadcasters can manage it, let us get a close-up of Ilem's face. Look, Peter, not a drop of sweat on his brow, but plenty of blood on his hands."

Peter, "That's the fifth time Ilem has knocked Sledge down during this unexpected clash of Titans. I'm not sure Sledge will get up this time."

Jared remarks, "We gotta give that fighting machine credit. Sledge continues to find the strength to rise to the sound of that personal bell tingling in his head. Watch Peter! I think he's positioning for a counterattack. He sways from side to side like a cobra, with occasional feints, just enough to keep Ilem guessing when Sledge will strike him with his fangs."

Pete counters, "From the start of this scrimmage, Ilem has knocked Sledge back to his reality of being just a piece of dead flesh sustained by science's magic. Sorry folks, it is true. That is what makes this fight for existence compelling. Humans have historically treated the handicapped as part of the herd to thin."

Jared warns Pete, "Ilem may have knocked Sledge down repeatedly, but the light in Sledge's attic still flickers. Based on his determination to get up when knocked down, Sledge's light gradually returns." Pete challenges Jared's observation by asking, "How do you beat someone who can travel and swing his buzzsaws at the speed of light?"

To counter Jared's color commentary with his shrewd views, Pete states, "Sounds like he better be ready to get out of the way. Sledge cannot charge recklessly. If you will, I think he is trying to measure his speed to whack Ilem across his face like he did during Blood Bowl I. The first scrimmage was a shock for Sledge. He had to fight against thirty-four other Purists, only to have the Galactic Council thrust him back into the ring against Black Heart Kol, an Alien Beast, and finally, the cherry on the cream, he tangles against Ilem."

"I'm amazed by this kid. Sorry, Jared. He's fought long enough to declare he is a man without equivocation if nothing else. Despite having to keep up his dukes against all kinds of foes, he floats like a feather and sways like a tree. I know that's odd phrasing, but it is a work in progress ... So, natural in his movements, you would have to conclude his roots in this fight for survival are organic – ferocity born in the tamped soil of desperation."

Jared comments, "Like the pugilists of old, Ilem and Sledge have fought each other while reacting to attacks from their respective enemies for countless rounds, not twelve or fifteen rounds, but innumerable, like the gloved champions of yesteryear, the Boston Strong Boy, and the Galveston Giant. Sullivan and Jackson don't have anything on these two warriors. Ali would be a step too slow. Fire against fire. Ilem's stinging lefts against Sledge's hammering rights that travel at the speed of thought."

Pete interrupts Jared to draw the Spectators' attention to the action on the ground, "Left hook for Ilem. A big low kick from Sledge to Ilem's thigh punctuates that encounter. Ilem's combo catches Sledge off guard again. Look at his head flopping back like it's a fast bag. It's a miracle that Sledge handles some of Ilem's hand-to-hand attacks. If he had a corner man, they might consider reaching for a towel."

Swopping his observations for those of his partner, Jared shouts, "Dog ear that comment, Pete! It may be too late to expect a miracle that lifts Sledge's hand in victory. Down goes Sledge on Ilem's straight left hand. Perfect shot by Ilem." Pete agrees with Jared about Sledge losing steam and soon his life, "It is a good thing that the three-knockdown rule is not in effect. Jared, we have seen that this guy can survive death. So, we know he has no quit in him. Still, Ilem is trying to seek and destroy. Sledge's counterpunching is getting weaker and slower."

Far out of earshot of Pete and Jared's revigorated broadcast, Sage finds herself safe on a space vessel with Iggy, who has used Dr. Q's enigma code to transfer his consciousness into Victor. Their fortunate pilot, Gabba, and his wife, Zetia and daughter, Belle, are safe aboard ASR9 traveling away from the violent scrimmage.

Although Gabba has sunken to his normal size, his courage has not diminished. He skillfully focuses on piloting the craft away from the action below and closer to safety while mowing down a line of Ilem's Death Squad with his ship's rocket blasters. Sage calls Zetia to tend to Iggy. Sage, "Please, look after his wound." Sage pulls the tiny needles from the crossbow lodged in Iggy's chest. Zetia answers, "I'll be right there."

Ilem uses his light speed to swiftly overtake Sledge, who can only recoil in pain from the mighty blows, "Argh." Thud! Sledge falls to the ground for the sixth time while Ilem tries to seize the Vision Staff to regain control of the transhumans, precisely what he does.

When the Diwan of Light wrests control of the Vision Staff from Sledge to reactivate his command over his transhuman army, Ilem commands them, "Reactivate," but nothing happens. Sledge looks up from the ground, then levitates into the air, raising his hand to activate all combatants worldwide. The sentient beings come to life and fall back into battle.

Sledge, "*Yuh can't* hide behind pawns!" Focusing his thoughts on physically seizing the Vision Staff from Ilem, Sledge rips the staff from Ilem's hands. With the Vision Staff back in his possession, Sledge continues his verbal assault by declaring, "My mind is the strongest part of who I am. You were foolish to let the most precious part of me remain."

In response to that challenge, Ilem blasts a hole in the head of one of the Purified, who rushes to attack him. Then, he bitterly replies, "That is a mistake I will rectify!"

He draws in all the energy stored in his core to blast Sledge back into extinction. So much devastating energy accumulates in Ilem's hands that the battlefield becomes ablaze in the burning light. Sweat streams down Ilem's face for the first time as the ball of light mixes with the searing radiation.

Suddenly, Ilem redirects the mighty force of energy at Sledge. The intense, molten plasma, radiation, and light that rockets at Sledge from Ilem's hands saturates Sledge's entire body in a stream of devastation. The discharge of destructive energy overwhelms Sledge enough that he immediately recoils in agony, losing control of the Vision Staff and his chance to survive this grueling fight.

Even with the enhanced power bestowed by the Omnis probe, Sledge is no match for one born when The All architected the universe. The overwhelming heat that has poisoned Ilem for more than one hundred years, and the scorching, intense plasma that was his right at birth, turn Sledge's skin from black to white and charred black again in a flash.

The skin on the front of Sledge's body bakes on his bones responsively to the extreme temperatures. Sledge's dreads and bones burst into flames as he screams, "Aaaaa!"

Despite tremendous pain, Sledge gathers his remaining resources to cast a telekinetic shield before him, forcing the blast to travel around and away from his body. Expectedly, fighters battling each other close to Sledge are suddenly disintegrated and turned to ash by the overwhelming energy Ilem released.

Sledge persuades himself that he "Must turn ... sentient metal ... *tuh* flesh." Upon command, he spontaneously regenerates the flesh on his face and the rest of his natural body. As Sledge reforms his human frame, Ilem regenerates another ball of radiation more destructive than Fat Man and Little Boy combined.

Swiftly, Sage drops down from the horizon. With her enhanced ability to control forcefields, she surrounds Ilem inside a translucent dome that compresses the radiation blast over the Diwan of Light.

Sage shouts out to Sledge, "I can't hold it long. Get away!"

In response to Sage's distressed voice, Gabba opens a wormhole to move the vessel out of the range of calamity. Whirl. Sledge begins to fly away in the same direction as Gabba, but something more substantial than fight or flight compels him to turn back to confirm that Sage is safe.

Like fireflies desperate to flee a toppled jar, the burning inhabitants of the Floating City are tossed about within the vessel. As they are flung in the air, the bodies that smack into the vessel's dome splatter on contact.

The rapidly falling Floating City plummets awkwardly toward the ground, slicing through ominous clouds shaped like menacing clawed paws. Sage's forcefield, momentarily trapping Ilem's concentrated power around him, cracks and disintegrates as the Floating City pierces it.

The convergence of the Floating City's flaming fusion reactors into the expanding radiation and destructive light force spewed from Ilem's body causes violent energies to detonate around the Diwan of Light. The subsequent wave releases a firestorm more devastating than a fifty-megaton explosion. The blast incinerates every part of Ilem's exoskin and flesh.

Sledge retreats away from the loud, encompassing mushroom cloud that threatens to set even air ablaze and rend all within reach to ether. He tries to redirect his body in Sage's direction to rescue her from the catastrophe that has befallen all others on Earth. He is close to pulling Sage away from the blast, so close he feels the tips of his fingers clip hers when a sudden shockwave propels him off course.

The expansive shockwave slams into Sage. Her head flops back, and her physical image violently flickers. Rapidly, a sucking force pulls her aura into the white orb, now badly singed from jolts of radiation. The raging gravitational and electric forces that flow into the wormhole opened by Gabba absorb the damaged orb inside.

Hyle stands in the breach of the raging explosion, awash in all the destruction. Even this blast is too great for the Diwan of Matter to withstand at one time. Eventually, Hyle's physical body is devastated by the explosion and scattered everywhere. Flashes of lightning reverberate across the globe as the remnants of Hyle's body rain down from on high like hot ash surging from an active volcano. Kadam!

A second explosion erupts when Ilem's radioactive essence stretches to engulf Earth. The sky lights up in every direction as if an entire continent were set ablaze. The brooding storms that stalked the battlefield are sucked into the core of the blast, only magnifying the massive size of the noxious mushroom scorching every inch of land and boiling what was left of the seas that once sustained life on Earth.

The mighty explosions expel an incapacitated, unclothed, Sledge beyond Earth's stratosphere like a rag doll. Kadam!

Bogs and Steam pick up their commentary far from the mass destruction as the Sirens & Wails Saloon is jettisoned into the air.

Jared shouts, "Holey Moley!" Pete yells back, "People of the galaxy, we have witnessed history! The end of life on Earth and a serious blow to the Galactic Council." Jared pulls out his hair excitedly, adding to Pete's revelations, "For the first time in universal history, Diwans Ilem and Hyle have been destroyed."

Spectators from around the galaxy - in bars and sporting venues and sunken couches - roar with excitement as the promise of Earth's saga comes to a climatic end and new beginning. Spectators scream, "Yahoo! Outstanding fight!"

The Diwan of Time's omnipresent gaze breaks away from what he has seen. Although he knows the fate to come, Horol is still shocked as he confronts the stark reality that two of his brethren have fallen at the hands of a sightless man. Horol stews to himself, "Sledge triumphs, but others from the Galactic Council have observed this battle."

Horol contacts the remaining Diwan to meet again on Mount Idan. Stepping into their cosmic chambers, they find Horol standing in front of the panoramic window on his vessel. Instead of the stars and planets appearing in space before him, the last moments of the fight between Ilem and Sledge are continuously looped.

Horol comments to the rest of the Galactic Council, saying, "Council, we need to gather now!" Horol stands at the podium, writing a warrant for Sledge's capture or execution. He has multiple piercing eyes on his head that pop open as he concedes, "I cannot intercede. But I will issue this warrant throughout the galaxy for this human's demise, be he called Sledge or Omnis, I care not."

Naihal appears in her cosmic chamber holding Tirzah near the burning escape craft and a pile of rubble. Naihal, "Look at what your brother has done! Hyle killed my lover. My brother is gone!" Onom appears in her cosmic chamber, cackling in a shadowy stone tower. Without mixed emotions, Onom mocks Naihal's ails by saying, "Heh, heh, heh! Poor, Ilem! All his plans and schemes have gone awry!"

Somewhere else in the universe, the Diwan of Death, Pyron, twists and squirms in the clutches of a mystic prison cast around her by the Diwan of Darkness and sealed by the Diwan of Light. Pyron screams inside her cage that mockingly reverberates and regenerates around her as she casts her spells to fracture the magical bounds that restrain her.

Her metallic body is red hot from being too near the scorching heat cast off by the walls of the mystical cell. Her once-porcelain skin, now resembling alabaster sculpted by the relentless flames of a scorching oven for a century, bore the cruel imprints of time's fiery touch. As she has done daily while she remains Ilem's and Naihal's captive, Pyron calls her father to save her, "Hyle, help me!"

Omnis: Last Man of Earth

On Mount Idan, Horol pontificates to the Galactic Council like an irate priest dictating from the pulpit. Horol, "This man may have survived his battle with Ilem. Its unique earthly properties and sentient enhancements make its structure nigh indestructible."

Onom's and Naihal's ethereal images stand in front of Horol at the podium as he raises his hands, exulting the heavens above, "Whenever he activates his powers, we will sense his presence." Naihal demands, "Sledge must be killed anywhere he is found to avenge our family."

Onom cackles through her muffled lips, projecting her wicked sound into the cold expanse of space. She poignantly notes, "It is ironic. Ilem was right about Hyle building his order of demigods in violation of The All's trust."

In that bleak sea called outer space, worlds turn, suns are born, and meteors roam for home. Amongst the stars, and with garbage of Earth cocooning around him, Sledge's limp, naked body floats deeper into space toward an asteroid storm. He knows not where he will travel, only that he is Omnis, the Last Man of Earth, "a bottomless vessel of consciousness filled to the brink and overflowing."

END OF CHAPTER 20

Chapter 21

Confession

Silent, empty, condemned
This place I live
Lonely, desperate, bereaved
The price I pay

Prayerful, prostrate, no choice but to believe
A new day will break for me.

Ask The All to forgive me when you know I am gone
Think of me as a whole again
Want me despite my faults
A new day will break for me.

A new dawn will wash over me
When I know my memory is safe
In your heart and know this debris of life
Can yet remain.

Remember me as I was
A new day will break for me.
When I rest upon the coast of Caellum
And you see me as I was molded to be.

Derrick Howard

The All

At a merchant's fare near the Virat Sea, patrons and peddlers exchange words, Tektites, and goods before the shops close and the streets fall quiet. Jinx and BR12, fresh off their mischief on Earth, set up a booth to pander their digital shells and other Black-Market wares to gullible customers.

Down the road from the street fare, the sound of Yam hammering a sign on the outside wall of the Harbor Bar knocks against the silence. The sign Yam has hung is a wanted poster bearing Sledge's face. The poster declares above Sledge's image that the Galactic Council will reward one million Tektites for Sledge's capture, dead or alive. As Yam walks away from the wanted poster, bounty hunters from various parts of the universe crowd before it for intel on their pending prey.

On the side of the Harbor Bar, Yam has also erected a cage that holds an unusual being from parts unknown. This feral creature is known throughout the galaxy simply as the Alien Beast. It lies on the cage floor, eagerly devouring a large bone and burps from the food it is still digesting. Alien Beast, "Burp!" The Alien Beast wipes fatty liquid from a little white goatee that has sprung to life on its chin with its wet paw.

With all the patrons expelled into the night, Yam and Sera walk down the stairs to reach the top of Mount Idan. The wooden chairs they sink into in Sera's garden curve to cradle them, including the bulge of Yam's hunched back. There they rest after another long day of parsing words and pouring drinks at the Harbor Bar.

Yam points out to Sera the twilight action he sees mingling near the bar. He sees Jinx and BR12 attempting to lure the Alien Beast to the Black Market to barter and run away with their goods. Sera tells Yam, "You should not pay them mind, husband. The Beast is a handful. If they want to play with fire, let them. Why don't you come over here to help me in the garden? You are too close to the edge, anyway. What will happen if you fall again."

Yam laughs, "I haven't been that drunk in a long time, my love."

Sera brushes off her husband's humor by changing the subject, "That's fine. What of the singularity?" Yam asks his lovely wife, "See, you say stay out of what is happening near the Harbor, but you ask about something light years away. Whenever have we interceded, Sera?"

It is too late in the evening for Sera to quibble, so she tells her mate, "Yam, I know you see the similarity between interfering in the Harbor and meddling worlds beyond. You stay your hand when you could weld it to parse lies from truth. Your reserve is why you are my all." Lovingly, Yam answers his wife, "As you are mine."

Sera and Yam tenderly embrace. Forever together as one.

Light years away, Sledge's body floats through space, accompanied by a faint voice whispering, "Remember whence you came. Debris of life is life continued."

Derrick Howard

Psalms for Yesterday: Southern Flight

I live in a small town now
In the Mountains of the Appalachians
The Southwestern small toe of Virginia
Hours from my usual comforts
Far from the trodden road.

Grundy pings with a country twang.
The old folk perch
On wrap-around porches
Watching fancy dams built
To detour the next flood of Slate Creek.

She is so dry now that she chokes for water
Just as the barons choke the earth
For the last tins of coal.

They are an uneasy, old couple.
Married for generations
Barren of terms of endearment
Yoked by common disdain.

Their youth worry about being stuck in the mines
Like a canary
Guarding the shaft between yesterday and tomorrow,
Rocked out on meth,
And an uneasy refrain
That their children's voices
Will echo in empty hollers forever.

My ego is big enough to dream
That God intends more of me
Than this divot in the road.
My bones are weary enough for me to hope
That I can stop
And call this fork
Home.

END OF CHAPTER 21

Printed in the USA
CPSIA information can be obtained
at www.ICGtesting.com
LVHW090322061124
795841LV00001B/62